Disclaimer

The stories in this book are based on my cousin Tony Vega. Tony joined the U.S. Army in 1940 and was assigned to the Logistics Command. In 1941 Tony was assigned to a unit that was assisting in the shipment of small arms and communications equipment to England. After Japan and Germany declared war on the U.S. in 1941-42, Tony was transferred to the OSS. Based on his expertise on logistics and fluent in several languages, Tony assisted the English Special Operations Executive (SOE) in the transport of men and equipment to the French Resistance. The actions by Tony in France remain classified, thus I have used a fictitious name, Francisco Vargas, as a substitute for Tony.

All other names, characters, places, and incidents in this book are from the author's imagination and are purely fictional. Any resemblance to actual events or persons, living or dead, is entirely coincidental. Where an actual name of a person or an event has been used or occurred, reference footnotes have been provided within the text. The stories in this book use the factual background of the world events leading and occurring during WW-II. Where appropriate, the author has provided footnotes for the source material of world events.

Armand Publishing
LLC PO Box 11815
Alexandria, Virginia 22312-0815
ISBN: 978-0-578-24478-5
Version 3.2

Acknowledgements

I would like to acknowledge several friends who were instrumental in the publication of this book: Special thanks to Scott Moore, who did a great job designing the cover and providing advice on the overall theme of the story.

In completing this book, I had four beta readers who read the final manuscript, provided excellent comments on the continuity of the story, and made sure that what was said in the closing chapters was consistent with the opening chapters.

Jason Elwell reviewed the action scenes and recommended that I included more details on the surroundings. Jason also corrected my "naval terminology." Chris Gorman reviewed the manual script and provided recommendations on character dialogue. Frank Nigro, who provided excellent advice on the technical areas and the geography of the stories. Becky Soltrero added a woman's touch and gave me major encouragement when she said that she really liked the stories. She could not put the book down.

Dedication

This novel is dedicated to all those who fought in WW-2 and 1. With a special dedication to my relatives and neighbors who were part of the greatest generation.

Jay T. Walker	Father-In-Law	WW-2, Europe
Antonio Vega	Cousin	WW-2. Europe
Ramon Arvizu	Uncle	WW-2, Pacific
Israel Armendariz	Uncle	WW-2, Pacific
Hector Pena	Neighbor	WW-2, Pacific
John Utterback	Neighbor	WW-1, Europe

Note from the Author

The idea of writing "Forgotten Heroes of WW-II, the French *Résistance*, occurred to me in late 2019. While researching for my book "Generations of Faith," which is a historical documentary of my family, I found that a number of my family members had played significant roles in wars that totally shaped the current state of the world. I also found that women had played a major role in these wars.

I decided to write the story of these brave men and women who played a vital role in the defeat of Japan and Nazi Germany. Uncle Ramon and Israel fought in the Pacific. My father-in-law, Jay T. Walker, and Cousin Tony Vega, fought in Europe.

The character Francisco (Chico) Vargas is based on the military historical records and discussions with Cousin Tony while we were both stationed in Berlin, Germany, in the 1970s. Tony was a counterespionage agent and served in France in 1943 and 1944. He entered the Army as a private in 1940 and received battlefield commissions in 1943 (Lieutenant) and 1945 (Captain). In 1978, Tony retired as a full Colonel.

After researching the records of my cousin Tony and having read more than twenty books (fictional and documentary) and research on the internet about the period of 1935 to 1945, I was amazed by the many men and women who fought and sacrificed so much to ensure that democracy would prevail. In the late 1930s, Americans entered Canada illegally to enlist in the Canadian Armed Forces to join the fight against Germany. I was surprised that a great number of U.S. citizens favored German Fascism or pacifism. The United States had a good chance of entering the war on the side of Germany.

From September of 1939 to summer 1941, Great Britain and Free France were alone in fighting Nazi Germany. Great Britain, through the BBC, pleaded for experienced aircraft pilots. Hundreds of pilots from Poland, France, Canada, Australia, other Commonwealth nations, and Americans answered the call. Through these pilots who answered the call plus the thousands of young English pilots, Great Britain was able to prevent the German invasion. The British also gave sanctuary to Charles de Gaulle, who used the BBC to broadcast to the French to resist the Germans. In the 1939 to 1940 time period, President Roosevelt had to walk a tight rope. In the late 1930s, the U.S. had a strong German influence. German sympathizers existed in Congress, and influential Americans such as Charles Lindbergh favored Germany. Roosevelt had to first win the election in November of 1 9 4 0 . In the spring of 1941, Roosevelt, with continuing opposition from Congress, passed the Lend-Lease Act, which allowed much-needed aid to the nations at war with Germany and Japan.

Table of Contents

Forgotten Heroes of WW-II
the
French resistance

Luis G Armendariz

Prologue

In the 1930s, the German Bund (Federation), stages rallies in several cities in the U.S. During the 1930s, the Germans had powerful sympathizers in Congress and highly respected U.S. citizens. Examples are Senator David Walsh from Massachusetts, who opposed the U.S. supplying arms to Britain and Charles Lindbergh, the American aviator. Lindbergh was enamored with German technology and was a devoted follower of Hitler. At the 1936 Olympics, Hitler had provided Lindbergh several seats near his observation platform. Henry Ford also favored the Germans. In the 1930s, he was benefitting from the German war production. He had major contracts with the German industrial complex and was a good friend of Albert Speer.

After the Germans attacked Poland in September of 1939, Britain and France declared war on Germany. By late spring and early summer of 1940, the Germans had conquered Norway, Denmark, Holland, Belgium, and France. The Battle of Britain was now taking place. Before Germany could begin their invasion of the British Isles, the Luftwaffe had to have control of the skies over England. The British Royal Air Force (RAF) had the planes (Hurricanes and Spitfires) but did not have sufficient trained pilots. Through the BBC, the British broadcast to the world for help. They needed pilots. A number of U.S. citizens with pilot experience answered the call. However, U.S. Congress passed the Neutrality Law, which outlawed U.S. citizens from joining any of the nations at war. The penalty for breaking this law was five years in prison and up to a five thousand dollar fine. To circumvent these restrictions, U.S. citizens illegally crossed the border into Canada and joined the Canadian Armed Forces.

In the summer of 1941, the war in Europe was going well for the Axis powers. Germany and Japan were confident of an eventual victory that would be theirs. Germany and Japan met in Berlin and agreed on how the world would be divided amongst themselves. To accomplish this conquest, the agreement stipulated that Germany would first drive through Africa. Germany would then invade South America and invade the United States through the Carolinas and Virginia Beach. The Japanese would invade through Alaska and down the Canadian Pacific coast. Germany would control the eastern and Japan the western parts of the United States.

Following the Berlin conference, the Germans launched Operation Barbarossa, which was the conquest of Russia. By the late fall of 1941, the German Army was well within the Russian borders and was on the outskirts of Moscow. Only the Russian winter prevented the capture of Moscow.

Based on the success of Germany, the Japanese then moved forward with their agreement. On December 7, 1941, the Japanese attacked Pearl Harbor. At the time of the attack, Hitler believed that it was to Germany's advantage. The U.S. could not sustain a two-front war. Thus, Germany now had free rein in Europe.

By the summer of 1942, the entire world was at war. The British had several advantages, and they used them for maximum effect. In the 1939-1940 period, the code breakers at Bletchley Park, England, had broken the German secret Enigma encryption system. Second, the British had a superior intelligence structure. For the last fifty years, they had a robust signals inter-cept capability. It was the British that intercepted the communications be-tween the Germans and the Mexican Government in World War-I. The British informed the United States of Germany's attempts to convince the Mexicans to attack the United States on its southern border.

In 1940, when the Germans invaded France, many independent re-sistance cells were formed in France. Initially, these resistance cells provided only minimum opposition to the Germans. The opposition was in the form of strikes, bureaucratic delays, and occasional vandalism. What the French re-sistance needed was coordination, weapons, and training. To provide all groups that were resisting the Germans, the British formed the office of the Special Operations Executive (SOE). The SOE started training agents who were either flown or parachuted into the occupied territories. Through the 1940-1942 period, the resistance cells were provided short wave radios, weapons, and SOE covert agents, which provided training. Beginning in 1942, the Allies were engaged in bombing the Germans in the occupied territories. The bombing runs resulted in Allied planes being shot down. This, in turn, resulted in Allied fliers parachuting behind enemy lines. The French re-sistance would find some of the downed fliers before the Germans. The re-sistance formed a series of safe houses to move the downed fliers through France and into Spain. From Spain, the fliers were taken to the British consu-lates. From the consulates, the fliers were transported back to England via sea transport. The resistance was credited with saving hundreds of fliers through this underground network.

Another advantage that the Allies enjoyed was the British expertise in Special Warfare. The British had a long tradition with small elements of their Armed Forces conducting special operations behind enemy lines. In 1941 the Special Air Service (SAS) was formed. The unit consisted of a Brigade with two British, one French, and one Belgium regiment. These SAS units operated behind enemy lines and were credited with many successful raids on German installations. Examples are, Operation Narcissus, July 1943, capture of a lighthouse in Sicily, Operation Avalanche, Allied invasion of Italy, Begonia Jonquil 1943, rescue of POWs in Italy, Operation Freshman, raid on Norwegian Heavy water plant, 1942. Before the Allied Normandy invasion of June 6, 1944, smaller teams consisting of four to six soldiers were parachuted into France. Members of these specialized units were known as the Jedburgh's. Their motto was, "surprise, kill, and vanish." To increase the chances of success, the Jedburgh's were integrated with members of the resistance. The combined teams of Jedburgh's and resistance greatly aided the Allies during and after the Normandy invasion. Both General Eisenhower and Winston Churchill said after the war, that the French resistance had shorten the war by six months and saved thousands of lives.

Chapter One
Britain Under Siege, 1940
The Battle of Britain

Squadron 204 of the Royal Air Force (RAF) pilots are based at Air Base Langtoft, situated in a sector responsible for protecting the city of London. So far, the German Luftwaffe has primarily targeted English coastal air bases and communication towers. Unbeknownst to the RAF, the German High Command had changed its tactics in response to a bombing raid by the British RAF on Berlin, causing significant damage to the Kurfurstendamn area. This area, known as the Ku-damn to the Germans, is akin to the Champs Elysée in Paris or Pennsylvania Avenue in Washington D.C. Hitler, angered by the RAF's attack, directed his fury at German Air Marshal Hermann Göring, who had promised to protect Berlin from bombings. In retaliation, Göring ordered a reprisal attack on London, which occurred on September 7, 1940, with a large formation of Luftwaffe bombers escorting Messerschmitt's crossing the English Channel to bomb the city.

Herman Hutchinson, an American flying with the Polish Air Squadron, is relaxing in lawn chairs with Captain Alfons Kowalski, a Polish pilot, while admiring the sunset in the western sky. Ski remarks, "It will be a perfect night for a German bombing raid, given the full moon."

Herman responds, "Yes, but it's also perfect for our fighters. The moonlight will illuminate the German bombers."

As Herman explains the origin of the name "Orogrande Mountains" in his home state of New Mexico to Ski, a phone in the Quonset hut begins to ring off the hook. The fliers know the drill. The call is from Air Command, indicating that German planes have been spotted and will receive their orders once they are airborne. Twenty-five pilots quickly gather their flight gear, including goggles, warm fur-lined jackets, gloves, 45-caliber handguns, and leather caps, and as they rush to their Spitfires, they pull up their air overalls. Upon reaching their planes, parked behind sandbags, maintenance crews assist the pilots in climbing onto the wings and into the cockpits. Two additional ground crew members help the fliers with their primary and backup reserve parachutes. The final item is the Mae West life jacket in case they crash or parachute into the sea.

Herman climbs into the cockpit and starts the engine, ensuring his instrument panel is in order and confirming a full fuel tank. He gives the ground crew technician a 'Thumbs-Up' and the Spitfire begins to roll forward with the wheel chocks removed. The airfield's design allows for quick takeoffs. Herman opens the throttle and drives another thirty yards straight before turning left. After

Spitfire Pilots Answer a Call, Battle of Britain

another thirty yards, the plane is on the runway. Five Spitfires rev up their engines, release the brakes, and gradually gain speed. Once they reach the required airspeed, all five Spitfires smoothly ascend into the sky and bank to the left. Within one minute, all twenty-five planes are airborne. All pilots have practiced this maneuver extensively. They switch their radios to the command channel.

Air Command instructs, "Vector to 180 degrees due south, altitude twenty-two thousand feet."

Squadron Leader (Ski) acknowledges, "Roger."

"Hold at the given direction and altitude until further notice."

"Roger."

The radio has two channels: Air Command and plane-to-plane communications, known as the operational channel. All pilots have dual headsets, using the left ear for command and the right ear for the operational channel. Strict radio protocols must be observed. The radio channels use push-to-talk (PTT) and operate on a first-come, first-served basis, so the command and operational channels must remain accessible for the squadron leader. Once the battle begins, the operational frequency will be used by all pilots. The pilots have short call names; Kowalski goes by Ski, and Hutchinson is known as Aquila due to a minor pronounced aquiline feature on his nose. Shortening the names is essential for immediate communication and security. The plane-to-plane operational channel is encoded but not encrypted so the Germans may decrypt the recording after the battle ends.

After flying at 22,000 feet for twenty minutes, they are well into the English Channel. Air Command orders, "Vector to one hundred forty degrees, reduce altitude to 15,000 feet. You will encounter a formation of over 300 Heinkel-He 111s and Dornier German Aircraft, escorted by Bf-109s. Fire at will, happy hunting."

Ski responds, "Roger will engage upon visual."

All twenty-five pilots of Squadron 204 are tense, and their anticipation of battle heightens. Ski positions the fighter formation tightly to attack from the West, utilizing the west-to-east wind to maximize the range of their .303 machine gun bullets compared to the German bomber planes' cannons.

As the 204th squadron's pilots look downward, they spot an unusual formation of German bombers, unlike anything they have encountered before. Moonlight reflects off the bomber surfaces, and the thunderous roar of the 300 propellers creates a deafening drone, resembling a swarm of bees, only much louder. Initially, the Spitfire pilots think it will be easy, but they soon realize that these "fish" can fight back. When Ski gets a visual on the German formation, he issues the order, "Dive in formation, follow my lead."

All twenty-four pilots acknowledge the command with a double-click on their radios, signaling, "Received." Ski leads the first dive, and the twenty-four Spitfires descend at a forty-five-degree angle, exceeding speeds of 350 mph. This diving maneuver has been practiced and exe-

Spitfires in Tight Formation

cuted countless times, and the attack unfolds with precision, catching the unsuspecting bombers off guard. The initial assault brings down twenty-five German bombers, but chaos ensues as the escorting Bf-109s retaliate. The Spitfires become the prey, and the pilots of Squadron 204 employ all their skills to turn the tables. Unfortunately, four Spitfires fall victim to the German pilots.

As Herman downs a Heinkel-He 111 and pursues another German aircraft, he receives a radio transmission: "Aquila. Aquila, bogie on your tail."

Without hesitation, Herman pushed his plane into a daring dive, angling it down at a sharp forty-five degrees, hurtling towards the earth at an incredible speed of 400 mph. His keen eyes remained fixated on the altitude meter, which whirled counterclockwise in a frenzied manner. When the gauge hit the 2,000-foot mark, he increased the dive angle to an even more daring fifty-five degrees. In the midst of the intense aerial battle, conscious thought was a luxury he couldn't afford. This maneuver had always served him well; this situation was no exception. The pursuing Bf-109 mirrored Herman's dive angle, holding at a perilous 55 degrees. As they descended to just 500 feet above the sea, Herman made subtle adjustments to his right-wing flaps, deftly pulling up on the stick, and skillfully manipulating the wing and tail flaps with his feet, all executed within a fraction of a second. The masterful maneuver prevented his aircraft from plummeting into the channel waters below. His plane, affectionately named "El Bambino," narrowly missed the ocean's surface by a mere ten yards. Glancing back over his left shoulder, he witnessed the Messerschmitt of his pursuer spiraling uncontrollably, crashing into the unforgiving waters.

With swift composure, Herman regained both his focus and altitude. He checked his fuel gauge, which displayed a mere ten minutes of flight time before he'd have to return to base. Fortunately, his knowledge of several grass fields near Plymouth extended his combat time to a more reassuring twenty minutes. Climbing back to 10,000 feet, he seamlessly rejoined the squadron formation, ready for another engagement with the bomber formation.

Herman transmitted a message on the Air Command Channel, "This is plane 3014; guide me to the Luftwaffe bomber formation. "The Air Command quickly identified plane 3014 through its transponder and directed him, "3014, head fifteen degrees north. ETA to bogies at 4,000 feet altitude: five minutes at current speed. Happy Hunting."

"Roger, thanks," Herman acknowledged.

Herman proceeded directly towards the enemy formation, ascending to ten thousand feet, and preparing for another dive. As he descended towards a selected Heinkel-He 111 this time, he noticed glimmers from the tail gunner's relentless fire. The Heinkel-He 111 gunfire had a surprising range, with bullets carried by the prevailing wind. Herman, a seasoned combat pilot, adjusted his aim, aiming high to compensate for the wind, expertly leading the target. His Spitfire rounds struck the enemy bomber's fuel tanks, resulting in a spectacular eruption of flames, painting the sky in a brilliant display of orange and red hues. The Heinkel-He 111 disintegrated into three distinct sections, spiraling down into the depths of the English Channel.

Herman pulled up gracefully, watching the trailing plume of smoke from the wreckage. The three fragments of the Heinkel disappeared beneath wispy clouds. Regaining altitude, Herman rejoined the squadron formation, now heading home. He couldn't help but

German Heinkel-He 111 Bombers

notice that his fuel gauge was perilously close to empty, apparently punctured by the Heinkel's bullets. Herman knew he had to make a quick decision; it was time to bail out.

Herman Bails Out:

In a matter of minutes after inspecting his aircraft's fuel gauge, Herman realized he was running on empty. He was acutely aware that his flight time was measured in mere minutes. If the unfortunate event occurred where he had to eject over the English Channel, he had to steer clear of the French coastline, where German troops maintained a vigilant watch. Their sole duty was to scan the horizon for low-flying planes or English spies attempting to infiltrate occupied France. His best chance of rescue lay in the open sea, although it remained a toss-up between an English or German vessel. Before making the daring leap, Herman relayed his final known coordinates and counted on Air Command to track his plane through its transponder.

Bailing out was his sole recourse; he had to make the most of this dire situation. Memories of Mr. Goodwin's training came flooding back. He had been right all along – sooner or later, a parachute would be indispensable. Herman was deeply grateful that Mr. Goodwin had insisted they master the art of bailing out before even learning to fly. His thoughts briefly drifted to Karina, and he clutched her photograph displayed on the instrument panel before tucking it into his flight jacket. The engine sputtered, and the moonlit sky revealed the propeller's silhouette, signaling his readiness to open the cockpit canopy and prepare for his exit. But as he grasped the canopy handles and pulled with all his might, it remained stubbornly sealed. Evidently, the same bullets that had pierced the fuel tank had also damaged the canopy's slide rail. The propeller ceased turning, relying solely on the Spitfire's forward momentum as it glided through the air. The nose of the aircraft gradually veered towards the sea.

With time running out, Herman swiftly drew his .45 handgun from its holster, racked the slide, and chambered a bullet. He fired two shots at the canopy, one at the front and one at the rear. The howling wind filled the open cockpit as he attempted to escape, but the fierce forward momentum, reaching 300 mph or more speeds, made it impossible to break free. Karina consumed his thoughts, and he braced himself for imminent death, mere minutes or perhaps seconds away.

Yet, as fate would have it, occasionally, unforeseen events work in one's favor. As the aircraft streaked across the sky above the English Channel, it entered denser air, causing the plane to roll onto its back. Suddenly, gravity became Herman's ally. He exerted every ounce of strength to push himself, and within moments, he hurled out of the cockpit and into the open air. Reaching for the ripcord, he pulled it with all his might. However, the main parachute only deployed halfway, as the jagged edges of the damaged canopy had severed some of its cords. Herman spun uncontrollably; his parachute lines tangled like a spaghetti nest.

Once again, the parachute training that Mr. Goodwin instilled saved Herman's life. Swiftly, he reached up to his shoulders and unfastened the J-hooks securing the main parachute. The primary chute soared towards the French coastline while Herman pulled the ripcord on his reserve parachute. It unfurled just 250 feet above the sea. Herman had another stroke of luck;

had he hit solid ground at his current velocity, he would have been killed or, at the very least, suffered severe leg injuries. Instead, he landed in the water.

Acting quickly, Herman unhooked the J-hooks on his reserve parachute and inflated his Mae West life jacket. As the jacket inflated, he understood why it earned its name – it kept him afloat remarkably well. He drifted in the water for a while, losing consciousness.

When he regained awareness, Herman found himself aboard a French fishing vessel, the unmistakable scent of fish and saltwater in the air. Grateful for his high school French lessons and prior Spanish knowledge from his time in New Mexico, he was well-equipped to communicate with his rescuers. Plus, his grandmother's heritage, a mix of Spanish and Indian blood, explained his original name, Heronimo, which had been anglicized to Herman.

***

After over thirty minutes of attacking the bombers and dogfighting with the Bf-109s, Ski transmits on the Operational Channel, "Squadron 204, check your fuel, reassemble at 22,000 feet, and return to Airbase."

Of the original twenty-five Spitfires, twenty-one form their tight flight pattern for their return flights. As they begin their one-hour flight to home base, squadron 519 from Air Base Sutton-Bridge transmits on the radio, "On our way to join the fight."

Ski. "Careful, you have lost the element of surprise. However, the Bf -109's should be running low on fuel. They will not be flying escort for long."

"Roger thanks."

Soon after the exchange of comms with the 519, Ski does not see the "El Bambino" in the flight pattern.

Ski hears the transmission garbled, "May Day, May Day."

He then sees that Herman's plane is losing altitude quickly. Herman's plane turns on its belly, and a dot the size of a pinhead drops out of the cockpit. Within seconds, a malfunctioning parachute opens. The black dot at the base of the parachute cords is spinning like a top. Ski sees the main parachute sail away, and the reserve parachute opens. The black dot and the reserve parachute hit the water's surface within seconds. Ski turns his plane and does two flights over Herman, who had deployed his Mae West life jacket. As Ski flies over Herman, he dips his wing. Herman waves his arms, trying to tell Ski I am alive.

***

Air Squadron 204 flies back to their airbase. The twenty planes land, refuel, and take off again to attack the German Luftwaffe on their way back to France. After another five hours, sixteen planes return home. It has been a long and rough day; nine aircraft have been lost. But more tragically, nine pilots have also been lost. The pilots all know that the chances of any pilots surviving are very low. After twelve hours of grueling tension and g-forces, the temperatures varied from minus 20 degrees to over 100 degrees in the cockpit within seconds of passing out. The pilots of Squadron 204 are given twelve hours for rest and recuperation (R & R). At the end of the twelve hours, Captain Alfons Kowalski (Ski) must provide a written and an oral report to the Flight Wing Commander, Colonel Petro Harr.

Captain Kowalski, "Colonel, we lost nine good men yesterday."

"Yes, that is my understanding, but the reports are that we destroyed over 100 of their bombers and over 50 of their Messerschmitt's. I call that an excellent hunt.

"Sir, I have to tell you that one of my nine fighters lost was Lieutenant Herman Hutchinson."

"I am sorry to hear that; I understand he was like a son. War is hell. The sooner we kill all of these bastards, the better."

"Yes, Sir, I agree. Sir, may I ask a question."

"Of course, what is it?

Lieutenant Hutchinson's plane went down due to the fuel tanks taking a bullet. He was able to parachute and landed in the sea. I broke formation and did a couple of pass-overs; I saw the lieutenant floating in the water. I could clearly see the yellow Mae West life jacket. What are the chances that he is alive and will be rescued by the resistance?"

"Captain, I need to be straight with you. It would probably be best if he is dead. Should the Gestapo get ahold of him, he will likely be tortured for months and killed."

"Thank you, sir, but if anyone can escape the bastard Germans' hands, it will be Lieutenant Hutchinson."

The Colonel shakes his head, rubs his chin, and, with concern, says, "I hope you are right."

French Fishing Boat:

Pierre Le Monde had been a fisherman all his adult life. His father and his grandfather had been fisherman as well. He was a stout five feet eight inches with robust legs that looked like tree trunks, his hands were strong and callus, and he had a thick neck. His face was round, with piercing black eyes and cheer pink cheeks and a short square nose. It appeared like it had broken more than once. He always wore a stocking cap pulled tight over his head. He was always joking, and at the waterfront taverns, he was known as the *"Taueau"* (Bull). One thing he did but hid it from the Germans---he hated that a foreign power was occupying his country. He lived in the lower *arrondissement* of Cherbourg. In this neighborhood, they are ordinary people, mainly merchants. Since the Germans had occupied the city, the citizens were either silent, obeyed the conquerors, or collaborators.

However, there is a small fraction of the populace that is resisting the German occupation. Captain Pierre Le Monde and a handful of his friends are in the resistance. Pierre had a perfect cover; he was a fisherman. Early in Britain's Battle, it seemed like pilots were falling from the sky like raindrops, both Germans and Englishmen. By happenstance, he had pulled up two pilots from the sea, one was a German, and one was English. Upon docking his boat, the Gestapo came and took both pilots. After the S.S. Colonel put a bullet in the head of the English pilot, the Colonel walked up to Pierre, slapped him on the back, and called him a hero. He turned and told the German Harbor Police to reward Pierre with twice his daily rations. From that point forward, Pierre knew what he needed to do. He would continue to rescue English pilots, but he would turn them over to Lizzette Raymond, who was with the local *resistance* cell. Once the pilots were given to Lizzette, Pierre was not told where the pilots were being taken. The resistance worked in cells. One cell did not know what the other was doing. This way, if a cell was penetrated by the Germans or the *Malice* (French police) working with the Germans), only that cell would be sacrificed. What Pierre did know was that somehow the pilots were being returned to England to continue the fight.

Because Pierre had rescued a German pilot, the Harbor Patrol incorrectly saw him as a collaborator. He would rescue German Pilots from that point forward, but he would promptly put a bullet through their head, weigh them down, and drop them back into the ocean. However, to remain on the good graces with the German's he would occasionally turn over a rescued German pilot. From the beginning of the air battle against the British to September 1940, Pierre had rescued eight British pilots, killed fifteen Germans, and rescued five German pilots. This was a perfect cover, as the harbor patrol saw Pierre and his crew as loyal subjects to Herr Hitler.

On the fishing trip that rescued Herman, Pierre had fished out two English pilots and killed three Germans. Because that evening, so many planes had flown over the English Channel, he was returning one German Pilot that was so severely injured that he was unconscious. He docked his boat, and the Harbor Police held him as a hero, The Chief of the *Malice* stated that he personally was going to tell the *Ober Kommandant* of Pierre's unselfish aid to the Third *Reich*.

After the commotion had died down, the two English pilots were smuggled onshore, hidden in a macerals pile. Two miles offshore, Herman and the second Pilot, Tommy, were transferred from the horse-drawn wagon to an old beat-up bus. The bus had been used during the war with the Germans as an ambulance. During the entire rescue operations, it had been made clear to Herman and Tommy to remain absolutely quiet. After three hours of secretly moving the English pilots, Herman is taken to a convent run by a nun's group. The convent was well hidden in the forest and had been built in the 1600s. It had served as a French headquarters in the 100-year war. Thus, it had secret tunnels and hidden underground rooms. It was an ideal place to hide people and contraband.

When Herman and Tommy were safely in a hidden room of the convent, Sister Patricia and Lizzette prepared Herman and Tommy a lentil soup to warm-up their bodies. Sister Patricia, who was also a nurse, gave both the airmen a thorough examination. Herman was the worse of the two airmen. Due to the high speed of his descent into the English Channel's waters, his knees were highly strained. Herman had great difficulty standing up. Only time would heal his strained knees.

Convent in Forest

Sister Patricia now questioned both airmen, "Sir, we need to get word back to your command that you are in the hands of the free French. Your loved ones will be most happy to hear that you are alive. We will make every attempt to get you back to England. But the road is long and hard. It will require that you be in the best of health and that your body be strong,"

Herman, "How will you notify my command that I am in the hands of the free French?"

"We have contacts with the British Special Operations Executive (SOE); through this means, we will contact your command."

"Will this be through the radio network?"

"This I cannot tell you; it is best that you do not know how the information will be passed. To pass the information, I will need two things from you. One, your military identification number from your dog tags and the code word given to you in case you were rescued. We have your I.D. from your dog tags, now I need your pre-arranged Password."

Tommy, "I love my grandmother's mince pies."

"And you, *Monsieur*?"

Herman says his Password, "The Spanish did not find gold in Orogrande."

Sister Patricia, "Please spell Orogrande, the password needs to be perfect; otherwise, the British will believe that it is fake, and the resistance cell has been compromised."

Herman spells Orogrande.

Sister Patricia writes down the I.D.'s and Passwords and gives them to Lizzette.

Lizzette, "We will do our best to get word back to your command in England."

Lizzette did not tell Herman or Tommy how the information would be communicated to their command. Herman had been told by Ski that the French resistance had hidden transmitters that were used to communicate with the British SOE.

The French resistance:

Lizzette Raymond was a young French woman who had been working the French government as an administrative clerk. Her husband Filipe was a lieutenant in the French Army and had been captured by the Germans early in the battle in the Ardennes Forest. Lizzette answered the call to arms be-coming an ambulance driver. Lizzette drove a beat-up old school bus, which had been transformed into an ambulance. Lizzette drove the makeshift am-bulance to the front lines and designated field hospitals. During her time transporting the wounded Lizzette was forced to witness the atrocities of the Germans. The German Luftwaffe had no regard for civilian life. The German Messerschmitt's and Stuka's would come down and strafed the long columns of refugees: women, old men, children, babies in strollers, and cattle were killed mercilessly along the packed roads.

After the Germans occupied France, she was conscripted to work in the office of the *InspektorKirminell.* This office had the responsibility of inves-tigating and prosecuting criminal offenses for the French Police under Ger-man control. Initially, when Germany took control of the country, most ar-rests consisted of French thieves, burglars, and murderers. However, as time went on, the Germans started arresting Frenchmen who were in violation of the occupation laws, such as, writing graffiti on walls and buildings, tearing down posters, and other minor infractions. Because of Lizzette's position, she was in an excellent place to know what the German's intentions were, the most valuable spy amongst the resistance.

Her work in the French resistance, was to provide information on the German intentions. On the night that the two pilots were rescued, Anton Fau-quier, a member of the resistance, contacted Lizzette that the two pilots would need to be transported to a safehouse. Anton provided the horse-drawn wagon that would secretly transport the pilots. The wagon was filled with mackerel in order to hide the two pilots from being observed. From the wagon, the pilots were then transferred to an ambulance bus driven by Liz-zette. Anton needed help transporting each of the pilots to a safehouse. Liz-zette was familiar with the safehouse, a convent in the countryside outside of Paris. It was dangerous work, but the pilots needed to be moved that even-ing. If they were to remain on the fishing boat, it was likely that Pierre's cover as a *resistance* fighter would be blown. Pierre's work in the rescue of downed pilots was too important. Anton and Lizzette delivered the two pilots to the convent and quickly departed to avoid raising any suspicion. After the pilots had two weeks to recuperate, Lizzette visited the convent late on a Saturday evening. Her assignment was to assess the two airmen's health and then report her findings to her contact. She needed to assure that they were healthy enough for the arduous trip through France and into Spain.

The Safehouse, the Convent:

Lizzette arrived at the Convent at nine p.m., one hour before curfew. She would spend the evening there and then journey back to her home the following day. This was nothing more than a routine visit for her volunteer work through the church. One of the pilots was a young Canadian and the second was British. During her evaluation, both pilots were very nervous and worried, they still were not sure that they were safe from the Germans. Thankfully, after each meeting with Lizzette they seemed to calm their nerves, allowing them to provide valuable information regarding the war effort.

Lizzette and nurse Patricia pull up two chairs next to the Canadian pilot's bed. The only news they have is Nazi propaganda; they would like to know if the Germans have conquered England and if France will be forever an occupied territory? The German's claim that Germany will rule the world for 1,000 years.

Patricia, "The war is going very well for the Germans, according to the German radio broadcast, England is ready to surrender, and Russia will be conquered quicker than France. Is that true?"

The Canadian pilot, "No, England will never surrender. England has withstood the German Luftwaffe, and the bombing of the English cities has made the determination of the English, even stronger."

Lizzette inspected the dog tags, "I see on your dog tags that you are in the Canadian Royal Air Force and your name is Heronimo Hutchinson. That is an unusual name for a Canadian. Are you really, Canadian?"

"No, Madame, Heronimo is my given name. My grandmother is half Mestizo and half Apache. Her great uncle was an Apache Chief by the name of Geronimo. The name Geronimo in Spanish means a great Indian warrior. The name Heronimo sounds like Herman-i-o; thus, my friends called me Herman when I was growing up."

"Oh, I see, it is only a shortened name for your real name. The name 'Herman' is not well-liked in France. It is German. The equivalent to Herman in France is Armand---that will be your name while you are in France."

"Armand, yes, I understand, better in French, *Merci beaucoup.*"

"The German radio says that all Americans are in support of Germany; they will never join the English."

"Yes, there is a strong sentiment in America for supporting Germany. However, President Roosevelt strongly favors the Allies."

"Then why does America not join us and England on the war against Germany and Italy?"

"I really do not know, but I can tell you that there are many Americans like me that know that the war with Germany is inevitable."

Armand (Herman) now shows a picture to Lizzette. "This is my fiancée, Karina, we crossed the border into Canada and joined the Canadian Air Force."

"*Oui,* but you are but a few, this will not defeat the Germans. I am afraid that Goebbels in his radio broadcasts is right. Germany will rule the world for 1,000 years."

Sister Patricia, "This will not happen. The sisters and I pray every night that America will join the war and help defeat Germany. You see, the Lord is already answering our prayers. You are like an angel that has fallen from the skies. It is an answer from God that America will soon answer the call."

Lizzette, "Is it true that your American hero Charles Lindbergh is a Nazi. In my office, the Germans have a picture of Lindbergh with Hitler from the 1936 Olympics games. He is shaking hands with Hitler. It is being said by the Germans that Lindbergh will be the next American President."

Armand, "*Oui,* it is true that Lindbergh loves everything German. He is being hoodwinked when he visits Germany. The Germans show him all their advancements in aviation and war machines. He believes in the German theory of *Ubermenschen*; after all, he is from Aryan ancestry."

"So, do you think that Lindbergh will become the next President of the United States?"

"No, it is my belief that President Roosevelt's primary objective is to win the election in November of this year. He has already, under his executive authority, given England thirty surplus destroyers and tons of surplus equipment. There are rumors that he will ask Congress for a historic bill that will provide ships, tanks, aircraft, and weapons to the Allies once he is elected President."

Lizzette is no fool. She knows and understands what wins wars. She says with a dejected mood, "All of this will help, but the Germans will prevail in the end. We need the might of the American Army. If America does not enter the war soon, it may be too late."

Armand shakes his head looks directly at Lizzette, "Madame, I understand that you work in the German Criminal Division, is that correct?"

"Oui, that is correct."

"What are the Germans saying regarding their future plans?"

"I am not privy to their closed-door sessions, but I do hear the non-commissioned officers talk about the German plans for world domination. They even talk about where their next assignment will be. They talk about London and Moscow. They hope that they will be in the armies that attack America."

"Do you hear anything about the plans in Russia?"

"*Oui,* they joke about how the French were idiots when Napoleon attacked Russia. The Russians did not defeat Napoleon. It was the Russian winter. Hitler and his generals are too smart. Operation Barbarossa started in June to avoid the Russian winter. The Germans will not be fooled like the French."

As the conversation with Lizzette continues, Armand recognizes the value of the intelligence that Lizzette has. He asks Lizzette, "Do you know where I can find a radio for transmission to England?"

"*Non,* having a radio transmitter is punishable by death. I will pass the information to my contact."

"Who is your contact?"

"This, I cannot tell you. Our cells are all stand-alone. I only know him by his cover name. We all use cover names."

"*Oui,* I understand. Can you tell your contact that if I can send a message to the British MI5, that they will likely send transmitters and operators to work with the resistance?"

"*Oui,* I can tell him, but he will need to make that decision."

The contact was *El Renard*; 'The Fox'. He was named El Renard for obvious reasons; he would always out-fox the Germans. El Renard was twenty-five years old but had more than eight years of battlefield experience. When the war broke out in September of 1939, El Renard quickly drove through the Sahara Desert, crossed via ship to Marseille, and joined the French Army. He was an officer in the French Foreign Legion and had served with a colony in central Africa. During Renard's eight years in the legion, he had learned German and English, but his forte was covert operations and the many ways of killing the enemy. This allowed Renard to be smart and know of the German military tactics. Based on this experience, he was promoted to *Capitaine.* By the winter of 1939, he was captured by the Germans after his company fought bravely in northern France. Fortunately, he and six others escaped from the German guards on their captive march to Germany. During their escape, they killed six German guards, took their weapons, and disrobed them. As Renard's team escaped, they were in excellent shape and kept to the rugged mountain ranges between Germany and France. Using the uniforms and weapons that they had stolen from a raid on a German weapons depot; Renard found it easier to traverse through the German countryside before entering France:

Renard now needed additional weapons to arm other French citizens who would become his Army of the resistance. Renard and his men fought and found a well-stocked armory on the outskirts of Strasburg. They approached the German guard who was posted at the front of the armory. Using his German command voice, he stated the rank of the guard and handed the guard the papers from the pockets of the uniforms they stole from the Germans. As the guards were examining the papers, Renard quickly reached over and broke the guard's neck. As if on que, the other five members of Renard's Group instantly killed the remaining four guards. Renard and his team stole Sten guns, Mauser Rifles, PO-8 lugers, hand grenades, and ammunition. In order to avoid the road, Renard also took four healthy pack mules. This cache of weapons was what initially armed the resistance. After crossing into France, Renard chose to make his hideouts in a series of mountain ranges. Each hideout would be located in the southwestern part of France, near Lyon. By the fall of 1940, Renard had cells throughout France, all his cells were insulated from each other. If one cell was compromised the remaining cells would survive. The resistance cells now had weapons but lacked in radio equipment. They had limited resources to communicate amongst each other and had only two transmitters for communications to the outside world.

When Renard heard that his covert agent *Papillon* (Lizzette's cover name) had rescued an American pilot, he decided to meet with the pilots. These pilots appeared to have connections with the British SOE, who could contact the British MI5, and obtain the much-needed communications equipment and additional arms that Renard needed to expand his resistance army. Renard traveled from southern France to Normandy in disguise, along with his associate, Marcin. They both made the trip to meet with the pilots through the use of designated safehouses. Before their meeting in the Convent, they staked out the area and made sure that it was not being watched by the Germans. For security purposes, Renard had told no one that they would be visiting the Convent. Using the skills that Renard had learned in the legion, they scaled the convent walls and entered through the ceiling unannounced. Moving through the attic space, they moved quietly. This was a more difficult task than it should have been as wild pigeons also use the attic space as their home. As they carefully crawled and walked through the area, Renard could feel the crunching of years of pigeon droplets under their knees and feet. After quietly moving down from the attic and to the chapel, they waited until one of the sisters had come for prayer. As sister Patricia was kneeling at the altar, Renard came from behind and said in a soothing voice, *"N'ayez pas peur, nous sommes amis."* (We are friends, do not be afraid).

Sister Patricia turned and simply said, *"Oui,* we have been expecting you."

"Can you take us to the pilots?"

"Oui, follow me." Sister Patricia takes Renard and Marcin through a series of private rooms, hallways, stairs, and down to an underground tunnel. The tunnel gave the feeling that it was older than the church itself. As the nun led the two men, the style and types of mortar and temperature seemed to change. Also, the humidity in the cave starts to rise but quickly drops once they arrive at the second set of stairs. They take the second set of stairs and come up into a small infirmary with four beds. One man is lying in bed, and the other is sitting in a chair, both legs splinted with wooden pegs.

Sister Patricia points at the pilots, "The one in bed is an Englishman, his name is Tommy McGuire. The one sitting is the Canadian American, his name is Heronimo Hutchinson."

Renard, "What's wrong with the two?"

"The Englishman has a concussion. Hopefully, time will heal his wound. Armand (the Canadian pilot) strained both his legs when he hit the water. He also will recover in time, but they are in no condition to travel hundreds of kilometers to Spain."

"Merci Beaucoup."

Renard and Marcin walk over to the American, *"Bonjour, je m'appelle Renard, et quell est votre nom?"*

Armand knows enough French from high school and answers in French, *"My name is Heronimo Hutchison, but Sister Patricia says it is best to use the French name, Armand."*

Renard says, *"Oui, Monsieur,* us French do not take kindly to the name Herman," as Renard says the word 'Hermann,' he picks up a bed pot, spits, and says, "Hermann Göring, may he rot in hell!"

"Monsieur Armand, I will need to ask you a few questions to confirm your identity. I am sure that whom you say you are true. That you are the Canadian American pilot who parachuted into the sea."

"Sur Bien Monsieur, ask me anything you wish."

"Très Bien, Armand, I was in the French Army when we were fighting the Germans. During those short four months, we had the honor of having some Polish pilots flying in our Airforce. You have told *Papillon* that you were with the Polish Squadron the 204. Is that right?"

"Oui Monsieur."

"Who was the most decorated Polish fighter with the British Royal Air Force?"

Armand smiles and speaks. "Kowalski is the most decorated flier in the RAF. He took me under his wing. I treat him like my own father."

"Monsieur Armand, you, as well as Kowalski, are the most wanted Spitfire pilots. The Germans have thousands of marks on your heads. They despise and hate you with all their guts. But we congratulate you for killing over thirty German Messerschmitt pilots and hundreds of *Boche* flying in those bombers. It is indeed a pleasure to meet you."

"Merci Beaucoup, I hope to help you fight the *Boche* with your resistance."

"Now that we have established whom you are, let's get down to business," says Marcin.

"How can I help you while I gain the strength required to make the journey to Spain?" Asks Armand.

Renard, *"Oui, Monsieur,* we have only one transmitter; the Germans have new equipment and a well-trained team that can direct find our transmitters in minutes. In the last month, the Germans found one of our transmitter teams. Our fighters destroyed the transmitter and committed suicide as the Boche encircled them. We transmitted the information to the SOE regarding yourself and the English flyer. In less than five minutes we picked up the equipment and moved. Within ten minutes, a team of twenty SS troops was at the transmit site. We need more and better transmitters plus arms. Do you think that we could somehow get you to England and see if something could be done?"

Armand, "Perhaps, but waiting for me to get well and for the journey to Spain will take time. Sister Patricia says that I will be able to walk within two weeks with the help of crutches. She believes that in one month, I will be fully recovered. Perhaps we can send a quick message to have a Lysander plane come pick me up. These planes require only a short takeoff and landing."

"Oui, Monsieur, the English will only fly such a dangerous mission to rescue a flyer such as yourself."

"Then we do it, come back in two weeks and bring your transmitter. We can move down the coast away from the convent. I will transmit an encoded message; they will know it is I. Then, I will ask for either a Lysander or a submarine rescue mission."

"Merci Beaucoup Monsieur."

Armand, *"Madame* Sister Patricia, do you have a copy of the *Count of Monte Cristo."*

"*Oui, Monsieur,* we have all eighteen volumes here at the convent. Shall I bring them to you?"

"*Oui,* Madame, please bring them to me at once."

Armand now tells Renard, "You will not have to return in two weeks. I will prepare the encoded message tonight, and you can take it to your transmitter operator. Only the SOE in London will be able to decode the message, so when the response is received, please bring it back to me so I can decode it for you."

"Très bon," says Renard.

Sister Patricia brings the eighteen volumes of *The Count of Monte Cristo*. Armand tells Renard and Marcin that it would be best if he could work alone. They say, *"Très Bien"* and leave the room.

Armand must now decide on which volume, chapter, page, paragraph, and sentence to use in *The Count of Monte Cristo* to create his message. The message will need to be simple. It needs to be transmitted in two minutes or less. Having the message longer than two minutes will allow the Germans with their new equipment to locate the transmitter.

Armand writes, "Need to have rescue, air or water, I have important intelligence Info. Please provide time, place, and method."

Armand now encodes the message. He then hands it to Renard and Marcin and tells them, "Remember to bring the response to me for decoding."

Renard and Marcin nod and leave the same way they came in. They take the stairs to the roof and rappel down to the ground. Sister Patricia pulls up the rope, and Renard and Marcin covertly travel back to southern France.

As they are traveling through the French countryside, Marcin asks Renard, "Do you think that Armand will be able to help? We need to have the SOE provide us weapons and transmitters."

Renard, "If I had a choice. I would prefer the transmitters. The weapons we can steal from the Germans, but transmitters, we need our own."

"Oui, transmitters are what we need."

"We must concentrate on having the Canadian American flyer getting back to England. He seems like someone who could really help us."

Chapter Two
Hutchinson Extracted
French Coast

SOE received the encoded message from the French resistance. Colonel Susan Phillips, Branch Chief for logistic support, assembles her team to discuss the latest message received by the SOE. She begins the briefing, "Gentlemen, we have received a message from the French resistance. The message is short but to the point: Lieutenant Hutchison from the 204th Air Wing has been rescued by the French resistance. Lieutenant Hutchinson has contacted a main cell of the French resistance. We must make all attempts to rescue the Lieutenant. He would bring valuable information regarding how we would assist the French resistance. Do we have any recommendation on how best to rescue the Lieutenant?"

Captain Alfons Kowalski speaks up. "There are several ways to rescue Lieutenant Hutchinson. One, we fly a short-range land and take off the plane and bring back the Lieutenant using a Lysander; two, we use the resistance network and move him overland to Spain; and three, use the Navy to send a submarine for the pick-up."

"And what are the odds of success for each method?"

"First method will only be successful if we move the Lieutenant south to an area not controlled by the Germans. This will take time to move the Lieutenant somewhere near Lyon. As of now, we have not been active in flying aircraft into and out of occupied France. Thus, our success will rely on unknown assets."

"And what about the second and third methods?"

"I would not recommend the second method. It will take time, and traveling incognito through hundreds of miles and crossing the Spanish border is risky. The best. The best method would be via submarine; we control all of the assets, and it can be done within weeks, not months."

"Very well, Captain James, contact the Navy and see if they can support the mission."

"Colonel, the Navy will only support such a dangerous mission if the order comes from high up."

"Yes, I agree. I will contact Colonel Richardson from MI6 and have him support my request."

Captain Kowalski now stated some concerns, "We cannot afford to have the Lieutenant captured by the Germans. Although he is in the Canadian Air Force, there is some risk that he will be found to be an American. As you know, America is not at war. It would be a great propaganda coup for the Germans. We need to be careful how we rescue the Lieutenant."

Now, Colonel Phillips understands the importance of the mission. "We need to contact the OSS representative and see if they have any suggestions on the rescue team."

The Plan to Rescue Herman (Armand):

After an exchange of several messages and phone calls, the American office of the OSS has a recommendation. "We use two covert operatives who have extensive special operations training. They are Hispanic, born in Mexico and Argentina. If captured, they have instant deniability. It will be apparent that they are not Americans."

Colonel Phillips accepted the offer and transferred the two special operations individuals to the SOE. Within two days, Francisco Vargas and Andres Valencia report to the SOE. They are briefed on the mission, and within two weeks, they are on the English submarine, the HMS Patmore.

One week after leaving the convent, Renard and Marcin reached their mountain hideout and transmitted the message to the British SOE. Two days later, they received an encrypted message. They quickly journeyed back to the convent, and Armand decodes the message. The rescue will be by submarine on the coast of the Bay of Biscay. The latitude, longitude, and time are given. It is near Bordeaux, 115 kilometers south along the coast. It will be two weeks from the day that Armand decodes the message.

Renard rubs his chin, thinks quietly, and says, "We have much to do. We must get you and the Englishman passports and the German *Ausweis* (ID card). We will need sister Patricia to take official photos of your passports and travel papers. I must contact the cell south of Cherbourg and arrange for the *passeurs* (smugglers). They will be your guides to the required point on the coastline."

Armand, "I could pass as Spanish. I can speak the language."

"*Oui Monsieur*, excellent *idee*." What about the Englishman?"

"No, only English with a cockney accent."

"Very well, he will need to be a deaf-mute. We will have an older *paaseur* woman acting as his mother. As for yourself, your *paaseur* will be a fellow Spaniard returning to Spain. You have been working as a common laborer in the textile factories in the Cherbourg area. The Spanish angle is perfect. You will have no problems with the Germans. At this time, Franco is Hitler's lap dog. Spain has sent 50,000 men to join the *Wehrmacht* on the Russian front. When the tide turns, Franco will come running to the Western Allies for help."

Marcin screams, "That goddamn Franco is an opportunist." Marcin then continues to give a five-minute tirade of every cuss word in French.

Renard looks at the pilots and says," Marcin is a Frenchman with Spanish blood. He fought in the Spanish Civil War against Franco."

"*Très Bien*, we will leave and return in one week with the papers. Both of you need to be in excellent shape. We will be using the trains for Bordeaux, but we may need to make some walking trips around some checkpoints. Marcin nor I will accompany you on your journey. *Papillon* will bring your *passeurs*. Your *passeurs* will know the country in southern France. *Bonne Chance*, (Good Luck) we need all the help we can get."

In one week, *Papillon (Lizzette)* arrives at 9 p.m. with the *passeurs*. Armand will travel with Juan Rodriguez. Armand's passport and travel documents have him as Pablo Martinez. They are both from Barcelona and are textile workers returning home. Tommy's *paaseur* is a woman in her mid-thirties, but her makeup has been applied to make her look like she is in her forties. Tommy's name is Thomas Fennell, and he travels with his mother, Marguerite Fennell.

Juan and Armand, now identified as Pablo, can easily travel by train from Cherbourg to Bordeaux. As predicted, the Germans are in high spirits with the successful war in Russia. The German guards congratulate Juan and Pablo twice for supporting the Third Reich. Thomas and Marguerite have also made it to Bordeaux; however, they had harrowing experiences that made the journey take longer. The guards had a difficult time believing that Thomas was mute. Thomas, not fully recovered from his brain concussion, didn't help. Although he is still glassy-eyed and disoriented, he fully understands the predicament. Twice, the Germans scream at Thomas, trying to get some reaction. Thomas hugs his mother and shakes like a two-year-old. He mumbles and cries with a distinct stammer. After these two performances, Marguerite asks, "Are you *Très bien*?" To which Thomas gives a wink and says, "I am fine, acting my part." He performs so well that even Marguerite believes that his brain concussion is much more severe than she was told.

After arriving in Bordeaux, Armand, Thomas, and their two *passeurs* take a bus to a small fishing village eight kilometers from the designated pick-up spot. The group meets with the local resistance cell in a barn outside of Bordeaux. The farmer hides them while they sleep with the horses and cows. During their two-day stay at the farmhouse, they use this time to clean their single-action World War I surplus Mouser rifles and some old .38 caliber six-cylinder revolvers. Thomas would joke around, saying he looked like a Sheriff in the American Wild West.

As they wait for the submarine, Armand takes control and discusses their various options once they approach the beach. First, they will need to collect some Intel on the German patrols. Armand and Marguerite stake out on a tall mountain ridge, viewing the patterns of the patrol boats. Armand, using his knowledge of engines, and Marguerite, using her knowledge of the German patrol boats, determined that the boats have two BMW 300 horse-power engines. Generally, the patrol boats cruise at what they estimate to be 5 to 10 knots and about 100 meters from the shoreline. The patrol boats have five crewmembers. The pilot, captain, navigator, and two guards appear to carry heavy machine guns. As Marguerite scans the patrol boats with her binoculars, she tells Armand, "*Monsieur*, take these spy glasses and view directly over the patrol boat."

Armand takes the binoculars and scans the horizon. He quietly whispers, "Trouble, German destroyer."

"Will that be a problem for our submarine?"

"*Oui,* but I am sure the submarine captain will first bring up his periscope and scan the waters. If he sees a German destroyer, he will seek deep waters and wait for the next night."

"*Oui, Oui, Monsieur*, if we need to wait until the coast is clear, then we wait."

Armand thinks *that we will not have a destroyer in the area. If we do, the submarine captain will abort.*

The Group Moves to the Coastline:

On the evening of the pick-up, Armand, Thomas, and the *passeurs* leave the safehouse at 9 p.m., one hour before the German curfew. The four walk away from the coastline and traverse across the dense forest. They wear black stocking caps, high-top waterproof hiking boots, and tight-hand gloves. Their faces are also painted with lampblack to keep them hidden. They are all armed with surplus Mauser single-action rifles and Wild West six-shooters. By midnight, they are only one mile from the coastline pick-up point.

At 2:30 a.m., behind several thick clouds, the moon cast a dark shadow over the forest. The traveling team hopes it stays that way: the darker, the better. Juan leads the way to the coastline, slowly climbing onto a fifteen-foot rock formation along the coastline's edge; he lays flat on his stomach and signals the others to follow. Armand, Thomas, and Marguerite follow, lying on their bellies and only using hand signals to communicate. They survey the area. It is now 2:50 a.m., and they use their watches to time the patrol boats. Every twenty to thirty minutes, a patrol boat slowly cruises north or south. They can hear the engines' low murmur and the bow splashing against the water. They can also hear a song by Marlene Dietrich singing a German ballet. The song is sexy, and they hear the German sailors laughing and imagining that they are bedding Marlene. Armand, Thomas, Juan, and Marguerite do not say a word, but they hope this patrol boat will be patrolling at 3 a.m.

On Board the English Submarine:

Captain Marion Connally has been a submarine captain for twelve years. He is an English Naval War College graduate and is one of the British Navy's best skippers. The pick-up of English pilots is a process that takes time to become routine. This operation is perilous and carries a high probability of failure. Captain Connally knows that the British Navy is very cautious with its submarines and crew. Thus, Captain Connally knows that whoever is being rescued must be a valuable asset. So much so that they likely have information that may turn the battle against the Germans in favor of Great Britain. Captain Connally was the one who selected the pick-up point. This section of the Bay of Biscay was the least patrolled by the Germans. He has also requested that a diversion be created on the Normandy peninsula's tip to send all destroyers in that area towards Normandy. There were no German destroyers within 50 miles of the pick-up.

The diversion has worked.

Prior to surfacing, the captain orders for the submarine to be brought to periscope depth and has the periscope raised. As he does a complete 360-degree check of the surrounding area, he sees a couple of patrol boats. He uses the submarine periscope to determine that the boats are German.

The captain has carefully timed the surfacing of the submarine between the patrol boat shifts. He knew he had only ten minutes to surface and launch the rescue boats.

At 2:45 a.m., the HMS George Patmore submarine surfaced two miles off the coast at 50 feet of depth. Two SOE members, Francisco and Andres, are dressed in wet suits, flippers, and goggles and are fully armed with Sten guns, .45 caliber pistols, hand knives, and a pull-out rubber raft. The rubber raft is known as a Rubber Inflatable Boat (RIB). They pull the air cord; the RIB inflates. The SOE operators jump in the RIB and install a small two-horsepower motor to the rear of the RIB. In five minutes, Lieutenant Vargas and Valencia are headed to the coast of France. When the rubber raft was twenty yards from the HMS George Patmore, the submarine submerged and was out of sight. Slowly but with powerful strokes, the SOE operatives and the two-horsepower engine closed the distance to the coastline.

Armand, Thomas, Juan, and Marguerite continued to scan the horizon. Juan signaled to the others that he had seen the submarine, but by the time the other three turned their binoculars, the HMS George Patmore had submerged. They waited patiently and thought that perhaps the mission had been aborted. Then suddenly, three quick flashes of light appeared at their 10 o'clock. It was the rescue crew. Juan quickly returned the three flashes with his torch, and the RIB turned to the port side, sailing towards the group's location.

Juan, *"Très Bien,* gather your gear, and let's move down to the beach, *"Vite, Vite, equipe*!" (Fast, fast, team.) The team reached the beach, waded into the water, and pulled the RIB onto the shore. Francisco, Andres, and two watertight cylinder drums were inside the RIB.

RIB Boat with a small engine

Francisco tells the Frenchmen, "Quickly, we need to move the rubber raft and containers behind the rocks."

Armand translated for Juan and Marguerite. Vargas and Valencia immediately recognized the accent as American.

In his cockney accent, Thomas says, "Mates, it sure is good to see you."

Vargas glanced at Thomas and said, "We can catch up later, mate; we need to move the containers and RIB."

The four-man team and one woman moved the RIB and its containers behind the rocks in less than four minutes. One minute after moving behind the large rocks, they heard the low rumble of the German boat engines. The searchlight passed over the top of the rocks as they hunkered down and waited for the patrol boat's sound to dissipate. After the engine's sound fades, Vargas takes his hand knife and opens the container's lid. He continues to pull out an eighty-pound rucksack from container one. Each rucksack contains time pencil detonators, fuse cords, plastic explosives, German lugers, and a Motorola Bakelite radio receiver.

Juan and Marguerite have completed their mission; as they leave, Armand and Thomas say, *"Au revoir."*

Marguerite pats her rucksack with the weapons and explosives and says, *"Merci Beaucoup."*

Francisco marvels at Marguerite's strength, "Quite a lady, good she is on our side."

Thomas, "Yeah, mate, intelligent and a real badass. She has a few German kills to her credit. Good thing she is on our side!"

Armand, Thomas, Francisco, and Andres must now make their way to the HMS George Patmore. They quickly gather the RIB, the small two-horse-power motor, the propeller, the empty tubes, and two large rocks. After they are out to sea, the rocks will be inserted into the packing tubes and sink them. The first 500 meters go well; Francisco has used a small VHF radio and communicates with the submarine that they have Arman and Thomas and are on the way to the submarine. ETA is twenty minutes.

An unexpected interruption occurred as the small engine silently propelled the RIB toward the submarine. The sound of a drone emanated from one of the patrol boat's engines. Vargas promptly shut down the small motor, and they carefully placed their paddles flat on the raft's floor. Vargas, Valencia, Armand, and Thomas all assumed a prone position in the rubber raft as the drone grew louder. Soon, it transformed into a high-pitched whine when the searchlight swept over the raft, followed by a deafening roar, indicating that the patrol boat was now circling the rubber raft. The searchlight stopped as it illuminated the raft and the four Allies lying face down in the RIB, their hearts racing. The patrol boat's engines idled.

Armed with a bullhorn, the patrol boat's captain shouted, "Achtung, capitulation, oder du wirst getotet!" Then, in a thick German accent, he added, "Lay down your weapons, or I will order my men to start shooting."

Vargas conveyed to the group, "We must surrender or face certain death. The German demands we lay down our weapons."

Valencia whispered to Armand and Thomas, "When Vargas and I stand up, slowly and quietly roll over the raft's side and into the water. Take the torch, point it in the direction of the submarine, and signal SOS."

Vargas and Valencia rose to their feet slowly to buy some time. The SOE operatives raised their hands high, concealing their Sten guns strapped behind their backs. As they hesitated, the German Captain yelled into his bullhorn, "Remove your gun belts!" They deliberately struggled with unstrapping their gun belts, further delaying the inevitable. Eventually, the gun belts dropped into the boat.

Once more, the boat captain bellowed into his bullhorn, "I know that others are in the boat. I will count to five, and if they do not stand, I will order my men to shoot you and riddle the rubber boat with bullets."

For a tense ten seconds, nothing happened. Vargas thought, "Surely, our sub has seen the SOS, and the German patrol boat is lit up with search-lights—come on, come on, fire at the son of a bitch!"

Now, the German captain, growing increasingly impatient, began the countdown to have his crew open fire, "Funf, vier, drei,"—but from a dis-tance, the unmistakable sound of the submarine's 53-caliber Mark 18 (150cm) gun was heard: thump, thump, thump, followed by the whine of 53-caliber shells streaking toward the patrol boat. The German captain heard the distant thumping and knew what it meant. Before he could utter 'zwei,' a 53-caliber shell struck the patrol boat on the starboard side. Two more rounds suddenly struck the boat, causing it to explode into a giant fireball. The Ger-man crew members were thrown fifteen feet into the air as the patrol boat was engulfed in flames.

Armand and Thomas managed to pull themselves back up into the RIB. Vargas started the motor and turned the knob to full speed. He handed control of the RIB to Armand, saying, "Aim the boat for the sub."

Vargas and Valencia grabbed the paddles and rowed with all their strength toward the submarine. Their muscles and bones ached from the sus-tained resistance and the cold seawater. Adrenaline pumped through their shoulders and backs as their lungs struggled to keep up with the oxygen de-mand. As they drew closer, they cheered each other on with words of encour-agement, pushing themselves to keep rowing. "Don't stop! Keep going!"

Upon reaching the submarine, the crewmen threw them a line, and with their hearts still pounding, they quickly climbed aboard and descended through the deck hatch. Captain Connally had been monitoring the horizon and knew the explosion's noise would likely attract another patrol boat.

Once the rescue party was safely on board, the hatch was sealed. The captain ordered, "Full speed at 120 degrees south-southwest, dive to thirty feet. Dive, Dive, Dive." The submarine's horn blared its dive alarm as the me-chanical behemoth beneath the water blew its ballast and disappeared. The HMS Patmore glided through the water and then sank swiftly and efficiently.

Ten minutes after the HMS George Patmore had safely retreated to sea, German Luftwaffe anti-submarine aircraft began patrolling over the Bay of Biscay. The flight crews assumed that the submarine was heading north towards England, but Captain Connally had anticipated this move and had initially sailed west, then south for 50 kilometers. It was a longer journey back to Plymouth, their home port, but it was a safer route.

Vargas, Valencia, Armand, and Thomas were allocated berths roughly the size of walk-in closets. Clean clothes, underwear, socks, dungarees, shirts, and tennis shoes of various sizes had been neatly arranged on the bunks.

The sailor who had escorted them to their berths informed them, "The Captain would like you to join him for tea in thirty minutes."

"Thank you, Ensign, we will be there," replied Vargas.

Soon, the four joined the captain for tea, biscuits, tuna sandwiches, and assorted cheeses. Red and white wine bottles adorned the table.

The captain spoke, "Welcome aboard the HMS George Patmore. While our accommodations may be slightly more cramped than you are used to, you can be assured that this submarine has the best chow in the British fleet."

Armand was surprised that the captain knew his name and asked, "So you knew who it was that you were sent to rescue?"

"Of course," the captain replied, "your name is well known in the British Armed Forces. You may be an outlaw in the United States but a hero in Great Britain. Thank you for your service. You and Kowalski are the most decorated foreign fighters in the RAF. I can only assume that you have important intelligence to assist in our fight against the Nazis."

"Thank you, Sir," Armand acknowledged, "but the mission would not have been possible without these two SOE operatives. And yes, I do have some very sensitive information."

The captain refrained from asking further questions at the mention of sensitive information. Intelligence was invaluable in war, and the captain understood the importance of the need-to-know principle. His duty was to return both Hutchinson and Maguire safely to their homeland.

Chapter Three
Francisco Joins the Army
El Paso, Texas

Francisco graduated from El Paso High School in 1937. In the fall of the same year, he enrolled at the Texas College of Mines. He chose the engineering route to become a metallurgical engineer. His brother Arnulfo is a student at the college and is due to graduate in the spring of 1939. Francisco and Ramon have a common bond, Ramon's sister, Avelina. Francisco has lived with Ramon's sister since he was ten, and he sees Ramon's sister as his mother.

On a Saturday afternoon, both Ramon and Francisco have a free afternoon.

"Let's go to the movies. There is a new Cowboy movie showing at the Crawford Theater." Says Ramon.

"Good idea, let's go."

The Crawford Theater is in downtown El Paso. The film is a Western movie with the Sheriff and his deputies, who are the good guys (white hats) and the bad guys (wearing black hats). The bad guys are holding up stagecoaches and robbing banks. In the end, the Sheriff prevails against the gang of outlaws. After the movie, Ramon asks, "Could I ride with you to go see my sister?"

"Of course, my car is parked right around the corner."

That afternoon, they visit *Tía* Avelina. By 1939, Jose and Avelina had four children: Petra (Pat) was seven, Jay was five, Jose Jr. was three, and Chata was one. The small house where Jose and Avelina live is a madhouse of children playing and babies crying. Francisco and Ramon helped with the kids. They take Pat and Jay for a walk along the irrigation ditches and the farmlands. After helping *Tía* Avelina with the children, Francisco and Ramon sit beneath a large cottonwood tree and have one of their long conversations about the newsreel they had seen when they saw the Western movie at the Crawford Theater.

With much concern, Francisco asks Ramon, "Do you think that the Germans will ever invade America?"

"No, I think that the Germans only want to rule Europe. Once they conquer Poland, they will stop. They only want to be the major power in Europe."

"Well, we will see if they conquer Poland. The Germans may then turn to the west and attack Belgium, Holland, Denmark, and France."

Ramon says, "The owner of the laundry where I work, who was in WW I, says that the French will stop the Germans; they have heavy fortifications along their border with Germany. These fortifications have been built to stop any attacks using tanks."

Francisco still needs to be convinced. He says, "I don't know, there is a WW-I veteran, Mr. Utterback on Glenwood Drive, who was an officer in the Army during WW-I, who thinks differently."

Ramon thinks about the two different opinions of the two WW I veterans. He then suggests, "It's early. Let's go over and talk to Mr. Utterback."

The Utterback family lives four houses from Francisco's home on Glenwood Drive. Mr. Utterback is in his fifties, but it looks like he is in his seventies. He is a grizzly older man who knows everything happening in the neighborhood and the world. Mr. Utterback always has his stand-up radio tuned to the news. He always listens to the fireside chats from President Roosevelt. Mr. Utterback is also known for his salty language, which he uses frequently to express his opinion. On a warm summer day, he always sits in his rocking chair, looking out toward the street and waving at all the pedestrians walking along the road. He knows Francisco well, as the model-T makes a racket as it drives down the road.

Francisco and Ramon walk the short distance to see Mr. Utterback. As always, Mr. Utterback is sitting in his rocking chair. He sees Francisco and Ramon approaching and says, "Francisco, good to see that you are not driving that Goddamn car of yours; it makes too much racket. Should be a law against making that loud noise."

"Sorry, Mr. Utterback, I will try not to accelerate the car when I pass by your house."

"Yeah, you need to keep the Goddamn noise down. It scares my chickens so that they don't lay eggs."

After the customary "How are you?" and Mr. Utterback asking how Francisco's aunt and her children are doing, the conversation turns to the events in Europe. Francisco asks Mr. Utterback's opinion, "Sir, the Germans have invaded Poland. Do you think they will stop there?"

"No way in hell. The Germans want nothing more than to dominate the world."

Ramon. "How they gonna do that? They are but one nation. Surely, they cannot be more powerful than the combined armies of England, France, and the United States?"

"The Germans are not alone; they have formed a union called the Axis Powers with Italy and Japan. The Italians with Mussolini started their dictatorship in the 1920s. They invaded Ethiopia, and they would like to return to the Roman Empire of two thousand years ago. The Japs now control half of China and the Pacific Rim. They have set their sights on the rich islands of the Pacific and Australia. The Germans are the real problem. The Germans will soon have their troops in North Africa, and they will march to the rich oil fields in Saudi Arabia."

"Why Saudi Arabia, it is nothing but sand and camels?" asks Francisco.

"You see, that's the problem. Most Americans are idiots when it comes to the world. The sands of Saudi Arabia have oil!"

Francisco feels a little stupid that he did not know why the Germans would want Saudi Arabia; he says, "OK, I get it; without oil, their tanks won't run."

"Yeah, you think that Junker you ride uses gasoline? The modern tanks use hundreds of gallons to travel twenty miles. The Germans need oil, and they are going to get it if we do not stop them."

Ramon then says, "We are stronger than the Germans. Because of American troops, we won World War I."

"Look, you little knuckleheads, we did not win the war."

"Yes, we did; the President said we won the war."

"President Wilson was a big fuckin liar, but so were the Brits, Frogs, and Krauts. They all said they won! What happened is that they all got tired of fighting, half the men in the trenches had that damn Spanish Flu, and all four sides said, enough, let's shake hands and go home."

"OK, I see it was like when two kids get in a fight in the playground, and they both fight to a draw, and one kid says, "Let's shake hands and be friends.""

"Yeah, kind of like that, but one kid still is pissed, wants to beat up on the other kid, and jumps him after school."

Francisco and Ramon now have their answer; Ramon says, "Francisco, that Mr. Utterback sure is smart."

"Yeah, he is a decorated veteran of WW I. I think he was a Colonel and was assigned to Intelligence."

Francisco goes to Fort Bliss:

In May of 1940, Germany attacked the nations to the east. Holland, Belgium, Denmark, Norway, and France. The conquest was completed by June 25, 1940. Francisco is deeply affected by the newsreels showing German tanks rolling through the cities of the conquered countries. He looks in abhorrence as the Stuka dive-bombers and Messerschmitt's firing at the long lines of refugees attempting to flee the front lines. Mr. Utterback's prediction is coming true. He now knows that he must do his part to fight against German aggression. Francisco decides to drive his Junker to Fort Bliss and join the Army.

He parks his Junker at the parking lot of the recruiting office and walks in. He will ask that he be assigned to either Intelligence or to a paratrooper division. He knows what paratroopers do but not Intelligence. However, if he becomes as intelligent as Mr. Utterback, then the Intelligence field will be OK. Francisco likes the movie scenes where the paratroopers would jump behind the enemy lines and attack the Japs and Krauts. He will ask to be an Intelligence Officer if he cannot be a paratrooper.

At the recruiting office is a sergeant who stands six feet three inches with a square jaw, broad shoulders, crew cut, blue eyes, and a tapered body. He is the soldier in the recruitment posters that every American boy wants to look like. On his nametag is his last name, Armstrong. Francisco thinks, *bet his first name is Jack?*

The Sergeant introduces himself with a ramrod posture, "Welcome, young man, my name is Sergeant Armstrong, and to whom am I speaking?"

"Thank you! My name is Francisco Vargas, and I would like to know more about the Army."

"Of course, I am here to answer any questions you may have."

"My first question is, if I join, can I be a paratrooper or maybe in Intelligence?"

"The first thing we need to do is have you fill out this form. After you fill out the form, we will ask you a few questions. We need to ensure that we assign you to an occupation code matching your skills."

This makes sense to Francisco. He takes the forms and starts filling out the paperwork. Sergeant Armstrong returns to an office, which he shares with Sergeant O'Connor. He sits down and gives O'Connor a short laugh, "Ha, Ha, got another Beaner that looks like a Chinaman that wants to be a paratrooper or be assigned to Intelligence.

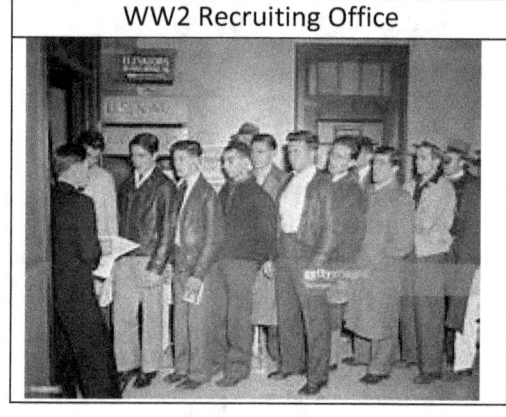
WW2 Recruiting Office

O'Connor looks out the office window and sees Francisco filling out the forms, he says, "No need to worry, he probably has the Intelligence of a burro. He will never pass the arithmetic quiz. Hell, not even I can pass it. I only know the answers because they were given to us."

"Yeah, you are right---we got another cook. Those Mexicans can cook".

This time, they both laugh----"Ha, Ha, ha."

Francisco completes the forms in twenty minutes and knocks on the window. Armstrong tells O'Connor, "He already has a question."

The Sergeant comes out and says, "You got a question? Have you quit?"

"No, Sir, I am finished."

Sergeant thinks *no way; the best anyone has done is thirty-five minutes, and even then, the recruit barely passed with a 73.*

The Sergeant takes the completed forms and takes them back to his desk, "Vargas, go ahead and have a seat; this will not take long to grade."

Sergeant Armstrong goes through the first page, and all answers are correct. He completes grading the test, and Mr. Vargas gets a 100! Sergeant Armstrong cannot believe what he sees. He then returns to the form Mr. Vargas filled out with his name, residence, date of birth, and place of birth. He sees the black mark---he was born in Mexico. He checked for his citizenship, and it was written, "Mexican, a legal alien with a residence permit." The Sergeant then asks O'Connor, "Is there any way we sign the Beaner? We need some numbers to meet our quota."

"Yeah, we can sign him up as a cook; that's the only way he can join."

The Sergeant now has the job of convincing Francisco to join as a cook. He knows he is not dealing with an ordinary Beaner; he is dealing with a Smart Beaner. The Sergeant tries every trick taught at the recruiting school. The Sergeant tells him that being a cook is the most important job in the service.

"The Army marches on its stomach; without food is like being without gasoline for the trucks and tanks,"

Nothing works, and Francisco does not join the service----at least not yet.

Sergeant Armstrong makes a copy of Francisco's forms. He gave Francisco the other copy and said, "We will keep a copy here at the recruiting office should you change your mind."

"Thank You." Francisco knew where he needed to go. He drove straight to Mr. Utterback's house. As usual, Mr. Utterback was watching the world go by on the front porch. Francisco lifted his foot off the gas pedal and coasted into the Utterback driveway. Francisco quickly gets out of his clunker. And at a quick step, he went toward Mr. Utterback.

Mr. Utterback saw Francisco walking at a fast pace toward him. He said, "Slow down, young man, where's the fire?"

"Mr. Utterback, I need your help?"

"OK, slow down now. What's the problem?"

Francisco went on to explain the problems he had with trying to enlist. Francisco showed Mr. Utterback a copy of his test's perfect score and explained that being a registered alien would not allow him to enlist with what they called an "Occupancy Code" for anything but a cook. They said, "It was army policy, and they could not fight city hall."

Mr. Utterback, with some consoling, said, "OK, tomorrow you and I go see General Edwards, the commanding General at Fort Bliss. He owes me a few favors; I think I can straighten this out."

"Wow, you know General Edwards?"

"Yes, he was my lieutenant when I was a Colonel in the war. I know him well."

"Yes, Sir, I will be here at sunrise tomorrow."

"Make it 8 a.m. I am sure the General has some other things on his mind early in the morning."

The following day, Francisco and Colonel Utterback arrive at the Fort Bliss Commanding Generals Headquarters at 8:45 a.m. Colonel Utterback is wearing his uniform from WW I. It fits him to the "T." The difference is the pants are long, and the shoulders of the Ike jacket are a bit big. Otherwise, he looks very distinguished. Unknown to Francisco, Colonel Utterback was active in the Veterans of Foreign Wars. He and General Edwards were on a first-name basis. They continued their friendship after WW I. General Edwards was now a two-star Major General. As soon as Colonel Utterback walked into the General's front office, the General's aide stood at attention, saluted, and said, "I will tell the General you are here; please be seated."

It did not take long; the aide came out in fifteen minutes and said, "The General will see you in his conference room. Please follow me."

"Thank you, Lieutenant."

The Colonel turns and tells Francisco, "You stay here, but give me your test papers."

The Colonel comes back in fifteen minutes; it is all arranged you will not join as a cook. We are going to assign you to what is the most critical mission of the war. You will be assigned to the Quarter Master Corps."

Francisco is disappointed *but will listen to what the Colonel has to say.*

"Francisco, I could not let you come with me because the General will speak freely about the war effort when we are alone. President Roosevelt signed a classified executive order, which supplied arms to the British and French. It is the Quarter Master Corps who is in charge of supplying these items. Francisco gets the hint: the items are weapons.

Now Francisco knows why the Colonel had to talk to the General privately. Colonel Utterback tells Francisco, "The General said to wait another week and return to the recruiting office. The recruiters will not know why you are being assigned to the Quartermaster Corps. They will follow the orders as written."

Francisco waits ten days and again goes to the recruiting office at Fort Bliss. In January 1940, Francisco Vargas joined the U.S. Army Quarter Master Corps as a private.

Chapter Four
Office of Strategic Services (OSS)
Rockefeller Center, New York, New York.

During the twenty years between the First and Second World Wars, the U.S. had no centralized or coordinated method for collecting and analyzing enemy intents. Previous code-breaking operations of the State Department, the MI-8 run by Herbert Yardley, had been shut down in 1929 by Secretary of State Henry Stimson, deeming it an inappropriate function for the diplomatic arm because **"gentlemen don't read each other's mail."**[1] The FBI had retained the responsibility for domestic security and anti-espionage operations. However, due to the scuttling of the espionage activities of the State Department, the U.S. was flying blind when the Italians, Germans, and Japanese were rolling through Africa, Europe, and Asia. The U.S. had to rely on the news reports by the New York Times, London Times, Le Monde, Das Reich, La Voce D'Italia, and Japanese newspapers from Tokyo.

The only reliable Intelligence Report came from the British. The British had a long history of Intelligence collection. They had established two departments under the Government Communications Headquarters (GCHQ) umbrella. MI5 was responsible for counterespionage, and MI6 was the spy agency collecting enemy activities and intents. Both departments required a high degree of security. Major events occurred well hidden from both the general public and the enemy. One of the greatest successes of the British Intelligence Service was the invention of radar. This new technology played an essential role in the British being able to defeat the German Luftwaffe. Early in the war, the German Luftwaffe outnumbered the British Army Air Force by a factor of 5 to 1. Using radar, the British Air Force would know when and where the German planes were headed. The British went to great lengths

---

[1] Stimson, Henry L. *On Active Service in Peace and War* (1948). *Per Bartlett's Familiar Quotations*, 16th edition.

to keep the secret of the radar from the Germans. The German air raid that was known by the British and was allowed to go unfettered was the bombing of Coventry. On the night of November 14-15, the Germans launched a major bombing campaign against the city of Coventry. Over one hundred Luftwaffe bombers rained thousands of bombs on the city. British Intelligence was aware that the raid was to take place, but on the orders of Churchill, the raid was allowed to take place with no advanced warning to the citizens of Coventry. The British MI5 agents in France had sent secret coded messages that the Germans suspected the British had a *Funkmessgerat* (Radio Measuring Device). When the air raids occurred with no adequate air counterattacks by the British, the Germans incorrectly concluded that the British did not have this *"Wunderbar"* weapon.

While the Italians and Japanese were conquering territory in Africa and Asia, Roosevelt knew it was only a question before Europe would be engaged in a war. When the British Prime Minister Neville Chamberlain met Hitler in Munich, Germany, he came away with a piece of paper that satisfied Hitler's appetite. The Munich Agreement gave Hitler the region of Sudeten, Czechoslovakia. Chamberlain arrived in London, waving the agreement to the British people that he had tamed the bear. Hitler had told him that Germany was a peace-loving country, and he believed him. Churchill, who was in the British admiralty, knew better. Churchill and Roosevelt were longtime friends, dating back to WW I.

Roosevelt and Churchill knew that war was inevitable. President Roosevelt had significant domestic problems. One, most Americans did not want war, and two, America had a large population of German descendants. A good number of these German Americans sided with Germany. President Franklin D. Roosevelt was concerned about American intelligence deficiencies. On the suggestion of William Stephenson, the senior British intelligence officer in the western hemisphere, Roosevelt requested that Colonel William J. Donovan draft a plan for an intelligence service based on the British Secret Intelligence Service (MI6) and the Special Operations Executive (SOE).

In 1940, Roosevelt met with Colonel William J. Donovan. Roosevelt gave the green light to Donovan to begin the recruitment of agents who would work in the field, similar to British MI5 and MI6. Donovan began to lay the groundwork for a centralized intelligence program. He organized the

Coordinator of Intelligence (COI) with the headquarters in Room 3603 of the Rockefeller Center. The Center was ad hoc and based on the ideas of some of the junior officers; recruits were being enlisted in the three branches of the Armed Forces and placed in the Quartermaster Corps (QC). The QC was a perfect cover-up for both domestic and foreign concealment. Beginning in 1939, the United States was providing weapons to the British. The big-ticket items were naval warships, technically being "loaned." After the war, many of these ships were obsolete or had been sunk; thus, the loan became a grant.

In October of 1941, Allen Dulles was appointed to head the COI. The offices were located on the floor immediately above the operations of Britain's MI6.[2]. Evan Thomas has described the OSS as an "informal" and "freewheeling" place where rank meant little." David Bruce later recalled, "Woe to the officer who turned down a project because, on its face, it seemed ridiculous or at least unusual. He is referring to the officers in the OSS, contrasting with the regular Army officers who turned down such projects. Imagination was unlimited. Ideas were his plaything. Excitement made him snort like a racehorse." Throughout the war, the OSS would endure criticism by segments of the U.S. media and by many highly placed figures in the U.S. government and military. General George Marshall was an early critic but later changed his mind. Eisenhower was always supportive, as was George Patton.[3]

----

[2] Waller, Douglas (2011) Wild Bill Donovan: The Spymaster Who Created the OSS and Modern American Espionage. New York Free Press ISBN 104165-6744-5 pp352

[3] "Interview with "Wild Bill" Donovan Biographer Douglas Waller" History Net September 8, 2011, Retrieved.

Chapter Five
Training Begins
Logistic Center, Ogden, Utah

As the recruits arrived at the Ogden Logistic Center, they first received a thorough physical examination. They were first marched into an auditorium resembling a basketball gym. The floor was wood, and the walls were bare cinder blocks. The building was equipped with fifty folding chairs with no padding. Evidently, it was previously used as a warehouse and, by the smell, most likely hay bales. When the recruits arrived, they were lined up outside and marched to a fitting room. A supply clerk measures their height, waist, wingspan, and shoe size. At the end of the line, they receive two changes of clothes with four pieces of underwear, four T-shirts, six pairs of socks, and two pairs of boots. They receive a kit with soap, shaving cream, a razor blade, a hair tonic, and a comb. All their belongings are placed in a bag, and their last name is stenciled on the duffle bag.

After receiving their wardrobe, they march uniformly to the barbershop. There are eight chairs, so it takes two minutes for each recruit to have his haircut. In four minutes, all twenty recruits have their hair cut to a short butch cut. Next, they march to their sleeping quarters. There are ten rooms. Two recruits to a bedroom. Each bedroom has two standup closets and two small desks with a table lamp. On the desk is a typewriter. The beds are comfortable, but anyone over six feet two inches would have their feet dangling over the edge of the bed. The bed has a small pillow, a bedsheet, one wool blanket, and a second blanket folded at the foot of the bed. Francisco's roommate is Andrew Valencia. Andrew (Andrés) Valencia is from San Antonio.

After being acquainted with his roommate, the twenty recruits are marched back to the warehouse. A neatly dressed Army sergeant directs them to sit on the right side of the auditorium. They all sit in the first five rows: four to a row. After taking a seat, twenty recruits walk in from the left side. Francisco takes a double and a triple look; they are all women: twenty women, ages eighteen to twenty-five.

Francisco thinks *that makes sense; women make good supply clerks.*

After all are seated, the tall Sergeant addresses the group of forty recruits, "Ladies and Gentlemen, welcome to the U.S. Army Logistics Center. My name is Staff Sergeant Wilson Vorster. All of you have been chosen for your unique skills. Everyone here speaks at least two languages besides English. All of you speak German, Italian, or Japanese as a second language. That is why you are here. I will speak in increments of ten minutes, and then open the floor for ten minutes of questions and answers. After today and tomorrow, we want you to understand why you are here fully. So, let us begin."

A hand goes up, "Sir, I have a question."

Sergeant, "My ten minutes are not up. Have a seat!"

The Sergeant looks annoyed and says, "Let's start with the obvious and learn to follow instructions. This is the U.S. Army; we are not at your *Tía* Lupe's house for Thanksgiving dinner! OK, let me start by telling you why you are here. All of you have undergone a background investigation by the FBI and have been cleared to the Secret Level. This means that what you hear or do here at the Logistics Center stays at the Logistics Center." The Sergeant now introduces Major Malcolm Berkshire.

Major Berkshire has an English accent and begins to tell the group why they are here, "You are here to conduct counterespionage activities against the enemies of America and Great Britain. The world is at war with the Axis Powers. Your country has been supplying my country with weapons of war to fight against the dictatorships of Germany, Italy, and Japan. You are going to be trained to infiltrate the networks of these Fascist countries and find the spies in the U.S., England, France, and if necessary, in, Germany, France, and Japan." Major Berkshire carries on for ten minutes.

Sergeant Vorster interrupts, "Sir, shall we open the floor for questions?"

The major looks at his watch and says, "Yes, of course, we can have ten minutes of questions." He points, "You there, ask your question?"

A stocky, brown-skinned recruit stands and starts to state his name---Sergeant Vorster interrupts, "Recruit, there is no need to state your name.

There is a number on your desk. We will address you by the number on the desk."

"Yes, Sir, number on the desk." Sergeant Vorster lets it pass; he is not an officer, and there will be no need to address him by Sir.

The standing recruits ask, "What can we tell our families when we write to them, or they ask questions when they write back?"

Now, Sergeant Vorster realizes that all this spy work is new to the recruits and the teaching staff. He confers with the Major. The English Major takes over and begins from scratch.

"I will answer your question regarding letters. All letters will be sent to and from an Army Post Office (APO) Box Number in New York City. The APO will, in turn, route your letters to and from your relatives. All correspondence will be strictly censored when you write your letter, 'do not seal the envelope.' A censoring staff will read the letter to determine if any classified material exists in the letter. If classified material exists, the letter will be returned to you. The censor will mark the material that is classified. You will only get two strikes if you try and send a second letter containing classified material---you will be a washout."

"What will be considered classified?"

"Where you are and what you are being trained for is classified. When you receive your assignment, it will carry a higher classification. Your mission will be restricted to a need-to-know basis."

Major Berkshire summarizes the mission of the group, "Our mission is to find and eliminate the enemy spies, both domestic and foreign, who are interfering with the lawful movement of goods, supplies, and services to Great Britain, France, and any of our allies." After the mission statement, the Major gives a summary of the training. The training will be an intensive four-month course on Spycraft. After the general training, recruits will be placed in select groups. You will receive specialized training to complete your cover story in your select group."

A recruit raises his hand, and Major Berkshire says, "Yes, go ahead; what is your question?"

"Can you give us examples of cover stories?"

"Yes, let me give you a couple of examples. One, we are shipping aircraft parts to England. Those who have shown a skill for engines, machines, or anything mechanical will be trained to be mechanics. Two, some of the women may be typists or nurses. These are but a few examples. Once you complete your basic training, we will decide individually what will be your trade. This trade needs to be real. You will need to be an expert. We cannot have you having a diploma in mathematics and not know a damn thing about Calculus."

All forty recruits laugh but now understand and are ready to begin. Major Berkshire directly addresses the group, "You will learn the following."

- Sending and receiving encrypted messages
- How to encrypt and the decryption key
- Establishing contact
- How to look for facial signals of lying.
- How to extract knowledge without the subject knowing
- Learn the habits of the persons you are investigating.
- How to make drop location safe
- Tracking and recognizing voice patterns. Inflections
- Clothing, shoes, shirts, pants, socks
- Hairstyles. Hairdos
- Group behavior, how to single out the strong and the weak
- Learn all of the details of vehicles and motorbikes.
- How to tail a subject, alone or with assistance
- How to hot-wire a car, which ones are the easiest. Hardest
- Separate courses will be taught of explosives.
  - o Making your own
  - o Fuses
  - o Time belays
  - o Explosion Cone
  - o Using Dynamite Safely
  - o Where and what types of dynamites are used by the enemy
  - o Explosive for doors, safes, large buildings
  - o Concealments
  - o How to carry explosives safely
- A separate course will be taught on weapons

- o   Handguns, German, Italian, British, French, Russian, Japanese, Chinese, and American
- o   Rifle, single-shot sniper
- o   Making your own bullets
- o   Automatic, German, English, Italian, Japanese, Chinese and American
- A separate course on knife fighting
- Map reading
- Lock picking
- How to defeat handcuffs, rope ties, leg ties
- How to survive underwater
- How to endure torture

While these courses are being taught, all students will start the day at 6 a.m. sharp. Breakfast at 7 a.m. One hour of calisthenics, running, jumping, obstacle course, and a five-mile run in under thirty-six minutes.

Daytime training courses end at 3 p.m. One hour of Martial Arts.

Dinner at 5 p.m.

Nighttime courses start at 6 p.m.

Lights out at 9 p.m.

The next day starts over. At the end of four months, if you survive, you will be given your assignment. Now, are there any questions?"

Fifteen hands go up, "OK, number 1018."

"Is shooting graded?"

"Yes, pass or fail."

"What happens if you fail?"

"Washout, you become a cook."

"OK, number 1522." It is a woman.

"Do women have the same tests as men?"

"Yes."

"Will there be conversational language tests?"

"What an excellent question! I will add that to course curriculum."

"Can you explain the language course?"

"Yes, at both MI5 and MI6, we found that the enemy will try to uncover your identity by asking questions about where you claim to come from.

50

For example, if you claim to have come from Augsburg, they will ask to name the towns surrounding the main town, like Gablingen, which has a Messerschmitt factory."

"Another example is your accent; all languages, especially German, have distinctive accents and expressions, depending on the region in Germany. A Berliner and a Bavarian speak with different accents and express themselves differently. The Berliner may say, '*Jawohl mein Herr*, and the Bavarian may say *Bitte, Bitte, Ya.*'"

After six weeks of basic training, all recruits receive their regular uniforms. Each recruit had been issued two pairs of pants, four pairs of boxer shorts, four pairs of black socks, four 'T-shirts, two Ike jackets, two black ties, two types of hats, square

Recruits Receiving Their Uniforms

and peaked, two belts, two pairs of boots, one pair of dress shoes. After all recruits are dressed, the drill sergeant orders the recruits to muster on the parade ground for inspection. With a commanding voice, the drill sergeant inspects every recruit respectfully but offers a critique of all dress errors. As the Sergeant inspected the troops, he slowly circled behind each soldier and asked that the right leg of the trousers be lifted. He wanted to ensure the socks had been pulled to their full length. Other errors corrected were the belt buckle not being centered, the tie not being tied to a square knot, shoes not being sufficiently polished, and hats not being placed squarely on the head.

After completing the inspection, the Sergeant addressed the troops and barked, "I expect tomorrow's inspection will have no dress malfunctions. dismissed."

Chapter Six
Selecting the Candidates
Logistic Center, Ogden, Utah

In the spring of 1940, Francisco completed his basic Spycraft training. The war in Europe had turned for the worse. Germany now controlled all of mainland Europe, German panzers were advancing toward Moscow, and the Japanese had taken control of the Pacific Rim and marched toward Australia. From the late 1930s to March of 1941, the United States had been providing aid to Great Britain on an ad hoc basis. In March of 1941, Roosevelt introduced the Lend-Lease program to Congress. Despite opposition from isolationists, President D. Roosevelt signed the Lend-Lease Act on March 11, 1941.[4] The Act provides aid to Great Britain.

Due to the signing of the Lend-Lease Act, the number of ships carrying supplies to the embattled British Island increased by a magnitude of 10 to 1. However, with the increase in ships sailing the Atlantic trade routes, the German submarines were taking a toll on all shipping that was not on American ships. Hitler does not wish to antagonize the Americans and bring America into the war. However, the Germans have many sympathizers and clandestine networks. These German agents provided information to the German Navy on ships departing to the British Isles. The English admiralty must devise a plan to eliminate these spy networks on American soil. The British have attempted to have the American FBI intervene; thus far, the FBI has resisted. America is technically not at war, and having the FBI arrest German sympathizers without any legitimate reason may further tip the scales in favor of the Germans.

In February of 1940, elements of the MI5 and from the U.S. Coordinator of Intelligence (COI) with the headquarters at the Rockefeller Center met to discuss the possibility of having assistance from the newly formed

---

[4] *Ebbert, Jean; Hall, Marie-Beth; Beach, Edward Latimer (1999). Crossed Currents. p. 28. ISN 9781574881936.*

counterespionage corps trained in the western United States. The problem of Americans assisting the British on U.S. soil needs to be treated with utmost secrecy.

Colonel Richard Burkhead of the British MI5 has made an exciting proposal to his American counterpart, Colonel John Rubenstein; both Colonels are on a first-name basis.

Richard presents his plan, "John, as you know, Americans have been volunteering to fly our Spitfires in Defense of our nation. We are extremely grateful for their aid. With their aid, we could not have defended our country."

John responds, "Yes when we called for trained pilots to answer the call for help, more than five hundred stepped forward from many countries. Some were from America. I am glad to hear they are providing some of the help you require."

"We cannot sustain the continuing bombing by the German Luftwaffe. Just in January and February, more than one hundred cities and towns have been bombed. Our supplies are being lost, and we cannot replace the supplies faster than the Germans are destroying them. If the Lend-Lease Act is ever passed, it will certainly help."

"Yes, I agree the Lend-Lease Act will certainly help. But, according to my aides, you wanted to discuss other means where we may be able to help; is that correct?"

One problem: where you may be able to help is to find and root out the German networks in America that are providing the German Navy with information on our shipping. Last week, the British admiralty reviewed the information on the tonnage that has been sunk. However, based on data from September of 1939, it is evident that the Germans knew the routes of our ships. We have tried sailing north to the Arctic and south to the Bermuda Islands. The Germans always know where our ships are sailing. Without question, the Germans are receiving information from American ports on the shipping schedules."

Colonel Rubenstein takes a few minutes to review the data. He sees the pattern. The German submarines operating in Wolf Packs are sinking more ships than expected. John says, "I agree the Atlantic Ocean is too big to have the Germans guess where our ships are sailing. So, what is your recommendation?"

Richard, "We pattern the help similar to your fliers."

"Hmmm, interesting, but flying and ship protection are two different things," says Colonel Rubenstein.

"Not really; both will be using Yanks; one protects the skies, and one protects the waters."

"Here is my proposed plan," says Burkhead.

"Our Signals Department Intercepted radio communications from the Florida Keys to South America last month. The transmission was encrypted with low-grade encryption; thus, we easily decrypted the message. The message was to a supply company in Argentina requesting parts for fishing boats. As you may know, there is a strong movement in Argentina for a Fascist type of government. We have known for some time that Hitler has aspirations for forming an allegiance with the South American countries. His master plan is to jump from Africa to South America and run his panzer divisions up to Mexico and eventually the United States."

Burkhead continues, "Based on our analyses of the radio traffic, these fishing boats are using the port of Bayonne, New Jersey. These fishing boats are being used as sentries to provide the data to the German submarines."

Rubenstein immediately sees the problem, "I see since we are technically not at war with Germany since the crews on the fishing boats are technically not breaking any laws in the United States."

"That's correct. We must infiltrate the fishing boat network and root out these German sympathizers."

"So why not use your navy shipmen to infiltrate and expose all network members?"

"Yes, we would normally do that. If we had enough time, we would select and train our agents. They would penetrate the network, and we would eliminate the German spies. However, time is of the essence. Should Hitler conquer Moscow and heaven forbid England, there may be no stopping the Germans and the Japanese."

"So, you propose using some of our newly trained agents to infiltrate this fishing crew?

"Yes, that's correct."

"No doubt you have given this possibility some thought?"

"Yes, we have. MI5 decided that I first discuss this with you if you agree we can move forward with the plan."

"OK, makes sense. What are some of the details?"

"First, the cover story. The intercepted radio communications are asking for new engines and repair parts, and the boat company sends two trusted boat mechanics to install the new engines to repair the malfunctioning boats. MI5 could move forward and apprehend the owners and workers at the Argentina boat factory, or after we further analyze the communications, we may decide to apprehend the two mechanics and replace them with our own. This operation will be low risk and high reward. It will occur on U.S. soil or the high seas; thus, we see no need for kinetic action."

"So, if we use U.S. citizens, how do we cover for them in case some FBI agent trips across our investigation?"

"The chosen agents will have Argentinian passports. They will replace the boat mechanics."

Rubenstein is impressed, "I see, we not only fool the Germans but the American government as well. Looks like a great plan."

"By the way, if the FBI does pick up your two agents, they will not need training. Compared to the German Gestapo, your FBI is a neophyte."

Rubenstein thinks for a few seconds and says, "I will ensure they are the best we offer. Once we have the plan's details, they will receive any required specialized training."

Selection Begins:

Colonel John Rubenstein takes the Silver Star Union Pacific train from New York City to Ogden, Utah. The train travels for 48 hours and covers over two thousand miles. The train ride starts in New York, with the tall skyscrapers seen to the train's left. It travels through the Pennsylvania coal country. After leaving Pennsylvania, the train travels through Ohio and Illinois and crosses the Mississippi River. The journey goes through the breadbasket of America. Iowa and Nebraska have large farms with corn, hay, and soybeans. After the Great Plains, the train starts climbing the Rocky Mountains. Majestic snow-covered peaks are seen on both the left side and right side of the train.

Soon, the train rolls along the Great Salt Lake, and Ogden, Utah, is the last stop.

The Colonel has telegraphed Sergeant Wilson Vorster and Major Malcolm Berkshire to expect him this Thursday. Both the Vorster and Berkshire conclude the Colonel is coming to inspect the progress of the training.

The Silver Star arrives right on time at 3:34 p.m. Colonel Rubenstein is tall and thin, his body is ramrod straight, and he carries himself like a distinguished Colonel. He is dressed in a three-piece suit from Fifth Avenue's finest men's store.

Both Vorster and Berkshire salute, and Rubenstein returns it. Rubenstein thinks that if we *need to get rid of this saluting, it is best to stay in the shadows because saluting puts a spotlight on individuals.*

The Training Center has a couple of cars reserved for dignitaries. It is a four-door 1937 Chevrolet Sedan. The Sergeant drives the vehicle, and the Major and Colonel sit in the back seat.

Colonel, "I have heard great things about your training program, and I am looking forward to seeing the recruits in training."

"Yes, Sir, the recruits are now in their specialized training program."

Before inspecting the agents, Colonel Rubenstein tells the Sergeant, "From this point forward, do not address me as Colonel Rubenstein; do not salute. Call me only by my first name, either John or Johnny."

"Ah, ah Y, y, y, ----yeah, if you don't mind, I prefer John."

"Good choice. John is OK, and I will call you Will."

The Sergeant thinks briefly and says, "Yeah, I like Will. My grandmother used to call me Will."

For the remainder of the first- and second days, Will escorts John through the specialized training. John pays closer attention to engine repairs, communications, and encrypting messages; it is evident to Will that John is knowledgeable in all of the areas because he always asks the recruits in-depth questions. The fact that the stranger was inspecting their training was not unusual; they all assumed that he was probably some accountant from Washington who wanted to know how the money was being spent.

After the second day, John asked Will, "Tomorrow, I want to meet with you and Malcolm to discuss my findings. Will thought nothing of it and assumed it would be another ATTABOY or chew-out session. He did not know it would be a chew-out session but probably would talk about what changes needed to be made, and he hoped that John would bring some news about the agents' future.

At 7 a.m. sharp, Will, Malcolm, and John meet in a makeshift conference room. John starts the conversation, "Gentlemen, I am here to discuss and plan for a mission. The mission is to infiltrate what we suspect is a German intelligence network on the Eastern Coast of the United States. We believe that the network is run out of Bayonne, New Jersey. I will give you a summary of the mission. Tomorrow, Mr. Richard Burkhead from MI5 will be here to discuss what we know. After Richard presents the mission's parameters, we will ask you to recommend four men and four women. Richard and I will interview the eight candidates and make the final selection."

Malcolm asks, "Would it be possible if you could give us the primary requirements and skills required for these eight individuals?"

"Yes, of course. Number one, they must speak fluent Spanish and conversational German. They need good English, but we can accept that English is their second language. Two, they need to be mechanically oriented; their cover will be boat mechanics. Third, they need to look Hispanic."

"OK, I can think of eight candidates right now. "

"Good. Also, they need to be in excellent physical shape and know how to swim; they will be around boats and water."

Will asks, "What about marksmanship?"

"Only average. They will not need to engage in combat or become involved in a firefight. However, they will be issued handguns that may be easily concealed."

"Secondary requirements are the things I have witnessed today. Map reading, using a sextant, lock picking, and all of the general items a good surveillance agent must have."

Malcolm, "Will and I will go through the test scores of all recruits and recommend eight for you to interview tomorrow."

John says, "One more thing; they need radio communications skills."

"No problem; we teach that in our basic course."

John, "One last thing: Richard will also conduct the interviews. I would like to have the resumes of the selected eight by 7 a.m. The interviews will begin at 10 a.m. We will have each candidate for one hour with a one-half-hour break and continue until we finish. That will be nine to ten hours, so we intend to finish between 7 p.m. and 8 p.m."

"We are on a fast track; thus, Richard and I will make our decisions the following day and begin the specialized training the day after Tomorrow. We will be working through the weekend."

"If there are no further questions, we start Tomorrow at 7 a.m. Thank you, gentlemen, and have a good night."

That evening, Will and Malcolm work late into the night reviewing all 40 resumes, and by 11:30 p.m., they have selected eight candidates.

Interviews:

The next day, John and Richard have the eight chosen resumes delivered to their room. They have a quick breakfast at the training cafeteria and scan the eight resumes. As they suspected, they all look excellent. They always do on paper, so person-to-person interviews must be conducted.

Richard, who has more experience, tells John, "What we need to look for is how well a person will perform under stress."

John, "How do we determine how an agent will react under stress? Unless you consider taking this interview as stress?"

"You are right; experience has shown that you must dig deep into the candidate's life. Ask them how they felt about the death of a family member. We will need to dig into different events or circumstances of their lives that they would rather not talk about."

"OK, you certainly have more experience than me. I will follow your lead."

Richard says, "At MI5, we have what we call 'Bad Guy---Good Guy. Ever heard of that?"

"No, what is that?"

"It's used in interrogations, but it can also work here. I will be the Brit asshole, and you will be the understanding Yank."

"Sometimes you can get good reactions when using this technique."

"OK, it is now 9:45. I suggest we take a latrine break and prepare for our first interview."

At 10 a.m., the interviews begin. The interviews last until 10 p.m. It is a long day, but at MI5, long days are the norm and not the exception. John and Richard have the resumes and have pages of notes ready.

John says, "We will sleep late Tomorrow and start the selection process at 8 a.m.

After breakfast, they meet at 8 a.m. in a training conference room. John and Richard start the process of down-selection. After a back-and-forth of all eight candidates' pros and cons, they selected three recruits on the shortlist.

The number one candidate is Andrew (Andrés) Valencia. John says, "He fits the requirement to the 'T'. He is twenty-four years old and born in Penito Moreno, Argentina, a small town along the Chilean border. His mother was German, and his father was Chilean. He was educated in Karlsruhe, Germany, until the age of ten. His mother wanted him to have a German education. When his mother died, his father returned him to Argentina. In 1932, his father remarried an American woman of Hispanic descent. His father has a degree in mathematics, and because of the depression, there were no jobs in Argentina. The family immigrated to the U.S. Upon arriving in the U.S., Valencia attended Trinity University in San Antonio and received a degree in international studies."

Richard, "Yes, I agree, he has a pilot's license and overhauled the engine on his biplane. He hates the fucking Germans because they screwed his father out of a job and blackmailed him in Argentina. The Germans ran a Mafia in Penito Moreno."

John, "The next candidate is Juliette Santiago; her father is Spanish, and her mother is a German Jew. The father fought in WW I in the American Army and received his U.S. citizenship due to his service during the war. The family lived on the French-German border until 1932. When Hitler was elected as the Chancellor of Germany, due to her mother being a Jew, they immigrated to Argentina. In 1939, she immigrated to the United States. She was living in New York City, attempting a career on Broadway. She was working part-time as a barmaid on the waterfront bars. She has a salty language and is very sexy. You know that women make the best spies. Most people find women to be less aggressive. Also, men think that they do not have the brains to be a spy. I see her working with Valencia; they make the perfect waterfront couple. The type that does not take shit from anyone."

"So far, we agree. Who is your third?" asks Richard.

"I like the kid that looks Chinese. His name is Francisco Vargas, but he goes by the name Chico. He was born in Meoqui, Mexico. For being only twenty-one, he had a tough life. He lost his father in a railroad accident; his brother was murdered; four women raised him: his mother, aunt, sister, and grandmother. He was very close to his brother, so the murder of his brother was very stressful. He passed this stressful situation with composure and self-control. I looked at his resume, sharp as a tack. He scored 100 on his recruiting examination; no one ever does that. Speaks fluent German, Spanish, French, and English. But what impressed me was when he and his good friend, Ramon, overhauled that old model T-Ford. I know how hard it is to overhaul a Model T. I tried it myself and gave up. I also liked that he knew how to use his connections; He went to some old Colonel who knew the base commander, and he was then assigned to the Quarter Master Corps. He was a top athlete in High School; his resume said he was a tailback on the high school football team. He was also the city 100-yard champ."

Richard was now satisfied, "OK, we have our team; I think those three are perfect. We will tell Will and Malcolm that we have our team and meet with them at 7 a.m. tomorrow."

Chapter Seven
Nazism in American Pre-WW-II
American East Coast

During the 1920s and 1930s, there was great turmoil in the United States. Following WWI, America entered a period of wealth and excess. Building on post-war optimism, rural Americans migrated to the cities in vast numbers. Throughout the 1920s, Americans hoped to find a more prosperous life in the ever-growing expansion of America's industrial sector. While American cities prospered, the heartland was producing required food on mega-farms. The industrial revolution was manufacturing farm equipment that would allow fewer men to farm more extensive tracts of land.

From the late 1920s to the early 1930s, the heartland of America suffered an unusually long drought. The drought, high temperatures, farms practicing poor agricultural practices, and wind erosion all contributed to the making of the Dust Bowl. The Dust Bowl further amplified the movement of the population from the rural areas to the major cities on the East and West Coasts.

The results of this under production of foodstuff resulted in prices increasing, creating widespread financial despair among the American public. In addition to the food shortage, the stock market crashed. Investors and speculators widely believed that the stock market would continue to rise forever. On March 25, 1929, after the Federal Reserve warned of excessive speculation, a small crash occurred as investors started to sell stocks at a rapid pace. The selling of stocks at such a rapid pace exposed the market's shaky foundation. In order to shore up the stock market, the National City Bank of New York provided $25 million in credit to stop the market's slide. The bank's move brought a temporary halt to the financial crisis. However, the American economy showed ominous signs of trouble. The production of steel declined, construction was sluggish, automobile sales went down, and consumers were building up high debts because of easy credit.

Despite all the economic warning signs, the stocks resumed their advance in value. This gain continued almost unabated until early September 1929 (the Dow Jones average gained more than 20% between June and September). The market had been on a nine-year run that saw the Dow Jones Industrial Average increase in value tenfold, peaking at 381.17 on September 3, 1929.

In late September 1929, the London Stock Exchange crashed when a top British investor and a number of his associates were jailed for fraud and forgery. The London Exchange crash greatly weakened the optimism of American investment in overseas markets: the market was severely unstable in the days leading up to the crash. Periods of selling in high volumes were interspersed with brief periods of rising prices and recovery. On October 24, 1929, the stock market crashed.

Breadline in Early 1930s

By the early 1930s, Americans were out of work, and bread lines appeared throughout all American cities. Soon, the depression spilled to the European continent. Germany suffered the worst. The rapid deterioration of the German economy gave rise to Adolf Hitler; Hitler gave massive rallies where he would rant, yell, and scream. *"Machen Deutschland Weider Grossartig!"*[5] (Make Germany Great Again) Hitler was referring to the times before WW-I, and the Great Depression. He demonized the Jews and Bolsheviks and blamed them for the plight of the Germans.

These conditions of 1930 gave rise to Americans of German descent who were against the policies of Franklin D. Roosevelt. They called Roosevelt a Communist and a Jew lover. As Hitler in Germany grew stronger, the German American descendants formed groups called *Bunds* (Federations). These

---

[5] Hitler Speech, 1940

Bunds grew in size and political power and had German Americans in various elected positions from the school board, mayors, congressmen/women, and powerful, well-known Americans. One of these Americans was Charles Lindbergh, who opposed the intervention of the United States aid to Great Britain.[6]

Based on the conditions that existed in the 1930s, the German Americans who were sympathetic to Nazi Germany were attempting to influence the American Government to side with Germany. The German American *Bund* soon grew in power and prestige.

History of the *Bund*:

In 1932, Heinrich "Heinz" Spanknöbel founded the original German group, "The Society of American Friends of Germany." Initial support for American fascist organizations came from Germany. In May 1933, Nazi Deputy Fuhrer Rolf Hess gave Spanknöbel the authority to form an American Nazi organization.[7] Shortly thereafter, with help from the German consul in New York City, Spanknöbel formed the Friends of New Germany by merging two older organizations in the United States—the Society of American Friends of Germany and the Free Society of Teutonia; both were small groups with only a few hundred members.

In 1936, the *Amerikadeutscher Bund* was formed. The new *Bund* was now more closely affiliated with the Nazi Party. They started wearing the black uniform of the Storm troopers, marched with the goose step, and adopted the Nazi salute.

The *Bund* consisted mainly of American citizens of German descent. However, they would accept Americans who looked Aryan and had a hatred for Jews. Initially, the goal was to promote a favorable view of Nazi Germany. As the organization grew, some of the outlying members of the *Bund* were adopting the same treatment of Jews as they saw in the newsreels. They started beating up Jews and began painting swastikas on synagogues. Soon

---

[6] Charles Lindbergh's September 1, 1941 Speech, URL, historyontheinternet.com. Archived from the original on June 21, 2019. Retrieved September 12, 2019,

[7] "American Bund." *Archived from* origination on *January 24, 2018. Retrieved March 2, 2011.*

after the founding of the *Bund,* he promoted himself to its *Bundesleiter.*[8] Spanknöbel carried himself as Hitler and dreamed that he would be the Chancellor of the United States.

Spanknöbel was an employee of the Ford Motor Company.[9] Nazi Deputy, Fuhrer Rolf Hess, gave Spanknöbel the authority to form a new and more powerful American Nazi organization.[10] Shortly after that, with help from the German consul in New York City, Spanknöbel had an office in Yorktown, Manhattan. He soon had a robust presence in Chicago, with memberships in the thousands.

As the American Nazi party became more robust, they presented as openly pro-Nazi and engaged in activities such as storming the German-language New Yorker *Staats Zeitung* with the demand that Nazi-sympathetic articles be pub-

American Nazi Party Marches in New York City

lished. Spanknöbel attempted to infiltrate and influence other non-political German-American organizations, such as the United German Societies. One of the Friends' early initiatives was to counter, with propaganda, a Jewish boycott of the business in the heavily German neighborhood of Yorkville.

The organization existed into the mid-1930s. Although it always remained small, with a membership of 5,000 and 10,000, it mainly consisted of German citizens living in the United States and German emigrants who only

---

[8] "American Nazi Organizations Rally at Madison Square Garden 1939." *Rare Historical Photos. February 19, 2014*

[9] *Van Ells, Mark D. (August 2007). Americans for Hitler, The Bund. America in WWII. 3. pp. 44–49. Retrieved May 13, 2016.*

[10] "American Bund." *Archived from* origination *on January 24, 2018. Retrieved March 2, 2011.*

recently had become citizens. In December 1935, Rudolf Hess ordered all the *Bund* leaders to return to Germany to strengthen Hitler's cutthroat army.[11]

In 1936, the German American *Bund* was established as a follow-up organization for the old German *Bund.* The new Bund elected a German-born American citizen, Fritz Julius Kuhn, as its *Bundesfuhrer.* Kuhn was a veteran of the Bavarian Infantry during World War I. He was seen as an *Alter Kampfer* (old Fighter) and, in 1934, was granted American citizenship. Kuhn was initially effective as a leader and was able to unite the organization and expand its membership. He was a strong leader but was arrogant, egotistical, self-centered, and ruled with an iron fist.

The organizational structure of the *Bund* mimicked the German Nazi Party. The German American *Bund* divided the United States into three *Gaus* (Districts), *Gau Ost* (East), Gau West, and Gau Midwest. Together the three *Gaue* comprised 69 *Ortsgruppen* (local groups): 40 in *Gau Ost* (17 in New York), 10 in *Gau Westen,* and 19 in Gau Midwest. Each *Gau* had its own *Gau-leiter* and staff to direct the *Bund* operations in its region of operation by the *Fuhrerprinzip*. The *Bund's* national headquarters was located at 178 East 85th Street in the New York City borough of Manhattan.

The *Bund* established several training camps, including Camp Nordland in Sussex County, New Jersey; Camp Siegfried in Yaphank, New York; Camp Hindenburg in Grafton, Wisconsin; Deutschhorst Country Club in Sellersville, Pennsylvania; Camp Bergwald, and Camp Highland in New York State. The Bund held rallies with Nazi insignia and procedures such as the Hitler salute. It attacked the administration of President Franklin Delano Roosevelt, Jewish-American groups, Communism, "Moscow-directed trade unions," and American Boycotts of German goods.[12] The organization claimed to show its loyalty to America by displaying the flag of the United States alongside the Flag of Nazi Germany at Bund meetings. It declared that George Washington was "the first fascist" who did not believe democracy would work.

---

[11] Ibid

[12] *Patricia Kollander; John O'Sullivan (2005)." I must be part of this war", a German American's fight against Hitler and Nazism. Fordham Univ Press. P.37.ISBN 0-8232-2528-3.*

The most influential of the *Bund's* activities was a rally held at Madison Square Garden in New York City on February 20, 1939.[13] Some 20,000 people attended and heard Kuhn criticize President Roosevelt by repeatedly referring to him as "Franklin D. Rosenfeld," calling his New Deal the "Jew Deal," and denouncing what he believed to be Bolshevik-Jewish American leadership. The rally was filled with speeches that advocated violence and the demonizing of Jews and blacks. The hate-filled speeches resulted in an outbreak of violence between protesters and *Bund* stormtroopers. The stormtroopers used the same tactics as in Nazi Germany. NYPD had to use more than 1,500 police officers and 100's horse-mounted police to quell the fighting between the stormtroopers and the anti-Nazi groups, who were also equipped with clubs and knives. Dozens of Nazis and anti-Nazi protestors were arrested, and hundreds were taken to the area hospitals.

Pro-German Rally

The rally, which attracted 20,000 Nazi supporters, was the subject of the 2017 short documentary *"A Night at the Garden by Marshall Curry."*

At the outbreak of the war in early 1942, Kuhn was arrested by New York State. While Kuhn was in prison, his citizenship was canceled. On June 1, 1943, Kuhn was released after serving 43 months in prison. Kuhn was re-arrested on June 21, 1943, as an enemy alien and interned by the federal government at a camp in Crystal City, Texas. After the war, Kuhn was interned at Ellis Island and deported to Germany on September 15, 1945.[14] He died on December 14, 1951, in Munich, Germany. [15]

---

[13] "Bund Activities Widespread Evidence Taken by Dies Committee Throws Light on Meaning of the Garden Rally." New York Times. February 26, 1939. Retrieved 2015-

[14] "Fritz Kuhn Former Bund Chief, Ordered Back to Germany." The Evening Independent." September 7, 1945.

[15] Ibid

The activities of such groups as the German Bunds created splinter groups that would carry out their activities to assist Germany in winning the war. The German Bund acted with impunity for two years from September 1939 to December 1941. The Second Amendment of free speech protected them. Americans of German descent could voice their opinions as long as they did not demonstrate violence. During these two years, the United States was assisting England, France, and Russia to fight against Germany. This assistance infuriated these pro-Nazi groups. A number of these pro-Nazi groups took it upon themselves to aid and abet Germany since it was not against the law.

Chapter Eight
Pro-Nazi *Gau* (District)
Camp Nordland, Sussex County New Jersey

Wilhelm and Hilda Müller lived in the small town of Helmstedt, Germany. Wilhelm and Hilda were married in 1908, and he had been offered a job in Bremen, Germany, by Hilda's uncle Gunter Schneider. Uncle Gunter was a fisherman on the North Sea. The North Sea provided harsh sailing conditions; thus, Wilhelm needed to be strong and healthy. When Uncle Gunter attended Wilhelm's wedding, Wilhelm asked, "*Onkel* Gunter, it is my understanding that you are always looking for sturdy young men to sail on your ships."

Onkel Gunter, "Yes, I can always use some strong men to put to sea. What makes you think that you have what it takes?"

"Perhaps you did not know I served four years in the German Marina."

"Oh, what were your responsibilities?"

"I served on a frigate; we patrolled the German coastline."

"Did you ever go out to the open waters of the North Sea and the Atlantic Ocean?"

"*Jawohl*, more than one."

"Did you get seasick?"

"The first time I did. But after that, I was fine for the rest of my four years in the Marina."

"Impressive, Hilda did not tell me you served on a small frigate. Be at my office after your *Flitterwochen* (Honeymoon), and we will determine if you can be a good fisherman."

"*Dank Onkel*, I will be there."

The week after his honeymoon, Wilhelm took the train to Bremen and met with *Onkel* Gunter. Gunter had his reservations that his nephew would not work out, so he had a direct and stern talk with Wilhelm, "If after your first working assignment on the fishing boat, you cannot handle the sea waves, I will dismiss you, and that you will accept my decision."

Wilhelm fully agreed. He knew that the North Sea would be fine. As a mariner on the German Frigate, he enjoyed the rough seas. He especially liked being on the bridge and rolling through swells three to five (10 Feet) meters (16 feet) in height.

After the first fishing trip, which lasted five days at sea, *Onkel* Gunter knew he had an excellent, strong seaman. Within one year, Wilhelm was the captain of one of his best boats.

In 1910, Wilhelm and Hilda had a young son they named Fritz. Wilhelm was called back to duty when WWI started in November of 1914. He served on German Submarines. Due to his previous four years in the Marina, Wilhelm was made the executive officer of a submarine. Wilhelm completed twenty-five missions on an SM U-23. The U-23 was credited with the sinking of eighteen Allied ships. One month before the end of the war, the U-23 was sunk by British destroyers.

Fritz was nine years old in 1919 when the Treaty of Versailles was signed, ending the battlefield hostilities. Frau Müller was left a widow at the age of twenty-eight with three children, Fritz, Gisela, and Emma. In 1922, the Müller family immigrated to the United States. They sailed into New York Harbor carrying over 3,000 persons from Italy, Ireland, Germany, and a dozen other countries. All immigrants were processed through Ellis Island.

Hilda had some distant cousins who had been in America since the 1880s. This was the Jurgen Brunner family. The Brunners lived in Woodbridge, New Jersey, twenty miles south of New York City. Herr Brunner was a fisherman sailing out of Bayonne, New Jersey. Fritz, then twelve, worked for *Onkel* Jurgen during the summers and after school. Fritz mirrored his father; he was tall and strong, with broad shoulders, blue eyes, blond hair, and a tapered body. Fitz completed his education at the age of sixteen. Upon completing his education, he continued working for Onkel Jurgen. By 1928, *Onkel* Jurgen was in his mid-fifties and could no longer captain a ship in the high seas. In 1930, at age twenty, Fritz was now in command of three fishing boats.

The Great Depression and the stock market crash were good for the Brunner Fishing Company. Fish were plentiful, and the Dust Bowl had reduced the supply of fresh products; thus, the demand for fish grew exponentially. By 1934, Fritz had eight boats, five forty, and three fifty-footers. Six to eight seamen crew the boats. Fritz had bought his boats from the *Schaefer GMBH Boot Branchen,* built in Buenos Aires, Argentina.

In 1934, Fritz joined the Pro-German branch in Nordland, New Jersey. Initially, Fritz joins because he thinks ---*It is the right thing to do.* He joins to see if he can help his fellow brothers of German descent. The leader of the *Gau* is *Hauptman* (Captain), Fredrick Grossman. Grossman works as an accountant. He has an excellent command of English and German and gives logical and well-researched speeches. Through his leadership, the number of active members has increased from a handful to over three hundred. From 1934 to 1937, the membership concentrated on outreach programs to show the American public German culture. The yearly events emphasize classical music, composers, songs, traditional dances, yodeling, and Oktoberfest. During these three years, German and non-German families with children attended the festivities in a carnival-type atmosphere.

In the beginning of 1938, the *Gau* is now addressed as a *Bund. Joseph Schenkel* has been assigned as the new *Gauleiter.* Schenkel is the opposite of Grossman; Schenkel is over six four-three inches and overweight. He is demanding and gives long-winded, rambling speeches. He ends his speeches with the *"Heil Hitler"* salute. Fritz notices that the crowds have thinned out from three to two hundred. They are mostly men in their twenties and thirties, with women and men in their fifties and sixties. The theme now is Germany First, *"Deutschland Uber Alles."* (Germany over all else). The members of the *Gau* are extremely infuriated over President "Rosenfeld" favoring the British, French, and Russians. Before the signing of the Lend-Lease Act, all materials were being carried by ship, not flying the American flag. The American State Department still wants the U.S. to at least appear to be taking a neutral stand; The U.S. Army Air Force is extending leave of absence for any pilot who wishes to travel to England and fly the British Spitfire against the *Luftwaffe.*

Fritz sees all of this one-sidedness and thinks *there is something I can do for my country, Germany.* At the next *Gau* meeting, he waits until *Gauleiter* Schenkel completes one of his two-hour speeches. Tonight, Schenkel was even more bombastic than usual. He is right on the edge of calling all German-

American citizens to take up arms and throw that Jew-loving President out of the White House. He orders that the members of the *Nordland Gau* attend the pro-Nazi rally scheduled for Madison Square Garden.

After the *Gau* meeting, Schenkel and six of his cronies are drinking imported German beers at the back of the meeting hall. Fritz walks to the back room and is stopped by one of Schenkel's guards, *"Halten Sie, was is Los?"* (Stop, what do you want?).

Fritz understands German, but he cannot speak it. He

Gau USA Training Camp

answers, "I have some important information to discuss with our *Gauleiter."*

"Haben Sie Ausweis."

"Yes, I have an I.D. card."

"Sitz Hierher Dich und warte." Fritz takes a seat and waits. He has been waiting for over an hour and sees that five of Schenkel's friends have exited; they are stammering and half-drunk.

The guard tells Fritz in German, "You may go in, but our leader is very busy; he can only see you for five minutes."

The one thing Fritz is not is dumb; he knows he needs to get Schenkel's attention in the first five minutes. He walks into the meeting room. Schenkel is busy and is shuffling through a stack of papers; he looks up and asks, *"Ja, mein Herr?"*

Fritz does not speak German but knows that Schenkel said, "Go ahead and tell me what you have." Fritz stands at attention and says in the clearest and phonetically correct English language, *"Mein Gauleiter*, I have a plan to help the German Navy sink those English boats."

Now, Schenkel pushes the papers to his left and says, "You may sit, but this better be a solid plan. I am a very busy and cannot waste my time on frivolous ideas."

"Jawohl Mein GauFuhrer. "

"Proceed."

"I own a fishing company in Bayonne, New Jersey. My company has eight boats, three of which are 50-foot boats and will be able to handle the rough seas of the North Atlantic. Twice, when fishing 200 miles from the New York coast, I have noted the shipping lanes of the supply ships to England. We could radio this information to my office in Bayonne, New Jersey. Then, using the connection of the *Bund,* we could relay the information to our consulate in New York; indeed, they can relay this information to our submarines in the Atlantic.

Schenkel asks, "Does that mean you cannot do this now?"

"Sir, I must order three larger diesel engines with dual propeller shafts from the boat factory to do this properly. We must find out how long to stay in the deep waters to survey the ship convoys. We may need to stay In the deep waters of the Atlantic for more than a week before we pick up the convoy. That's why I will need bigger engines."

"I see why don't you go ahead and place the order? Would not this help your fishing company?"

"No, sir. The engines I have now will get me to 150-200 miles from the coast and back in two days. If I ran into a storm, I could not make it back into port. Also, each engine is $5,000. The only way I can upgrade my three boats is with the help of the *Gau.*"

"It's a good plan, but I must contact our headquarters in New York and see if they can get the money."

"Jawohl Mein Kommandant."

Give me two or three days; I will contact headquarters. If this is as big as you say, we should have no problems getting the funds from the German consulate."

As Fritz leaves, Schenkel says, "Should this operation be accepted and funded, I will board the boat with your crew. I would like to see the operation firsthand."

"Ja Mein Kommandant." Fritz *thinks. I hope he changes his mind; there is no time for land lovers.* The seas will have swells of 15 or 20 feet, which can cause seasickness.

Bund Boat Surveillance:

Schenkel receives word from the *Gau* headquarters that the funding for the new engines has been approved. Schenkel lives within a two-hour drive from Fritz's boat company. He decides that driving to Bayonne, New Jersey, would be safer and let Fritz know that the funds have been approved for the new engines. He drives his 1932 Plymouth coupe to the Fritz offices of the Boat Company.

Schenkel says, "Herr Müller, we have arranged for the funding of the boats. To not alert the FBI, we have arranged for a loan of $15,000 through the National City Bank of New York City."

Fritz responds, "Good with the loan, but will I need to pay for the loan?"

"No, cash will be provided to allow you to pay for the loan. The loan is for five years, so pay off the loan every month, and the entire transaction will appear like a normal business loan to upgrade your boats."

"Yes, I understand, that should work."

"I have the papers for your signature. Once I return the paperwork to the bank, you will have the money transferred to your company account."

"I understand, I will send a telegram to the offices of the *Schaefer GMBH Boot Branchen* in Buenos Aires, Argentina."

In one week, the loan amount has been transferred to the bank account of the Brunner Fishing Company. The next day, Fritz places the order for the three engines.

The Schaefer GMBH of Argentina confirms the receipt of the order. Delivery will be in four weeks, and the shipment will be via an ocean freighter, which will arrive in Miami, Florida. An additional four weeks will be required to sail to Bayonne, New Jersey. Before arriving in Bayonne, New Jersey, the ship must offload supplies in Jacksonville, Charleston, Virginia Beach, Baltimore, and Philadelphia.

Departure will be from Buenos Aires. Additional information on the personnel will be at your facility, who will be arriving with the three engines. Company personnel are Engineers Rafael Torres and Eduardo Almanza. Mr. Almanza will be traveling with his wife, Marie Elena. Señor Torres and Almanza have identification cards. Both are expert mechanics and are required to guarantee proper installation and operation. The price of technical support is included in the cost for the three engines. The telegram is signed, *"Gracias por su negocio."* (Thank you for your business). *El Presidente,* Jose Esquival, *Schaefer GMBH.*

Fritz drives from Woodbridge to Nordland, New Jersey, and tells Schenkel that an additional month will be required to transport the engines from Miami to New Jersey. Schenkel tells Fritz to have the engines offloaded in Miami and transported overland to New Jersey. This will only require an additional three days to the schedule.

The agreement states that two mechanics from the South American Company will supervise the offloading and shipment to New Jersey. Then, they will follow the shipment and supervise the installation of the engines.

British MI5, Signals Intercept Station
The British Virgin Islands:

The British have a very robust Signals Intercept capability. The ability to intercept radio communications has been the mainstay of surveillance operations from the Government Communications Headquarters (GCHQ) in Manchester, England. The requirement to intercept enemy radio communications has been assigned to the MI5 division of GCHQ; the Chief of MI5 radio intercepts is Colonel Berkeley Baker, a veteran of the Signals Intercept Division. Colonel Baker was a Lieutenant in WW I. He worked in the code-breaking section of MI5.

At the outbreak of WW-II in September of 1939, the British were very concerned with the German submarines. British Intel had estimated that the German Navy had sixty to seventy-five submarines. Colonel Baker was tasked with determining where the German submarine fleet sailed in the Atlantic. Submarines in WW II were all diesel-powered. When submerged, the submarines operated on batteries. However, batteries had short life spans, and a submarine would need to surface to charge the batteries. These batteries were charged using diesel generators, which produced deadly carbon monoxide; thus, the charging of the batteries could only be completed on the ocean's surface. When the submarines were on the surface, the captain of the ships would receive his orders. The standing orders were to receive only; the Germans knew that the British would use any transmissions from the submarines to locate their submarines.

By the late 1930s, the British had installed radio intercept sites in Bermuda, Tortola Island in the British Virgin Islands, Ottawa, Canada and in Bude, England. These sites were all highly classified. The intercept systems were intercepting High-Frequency transmission, which required antenna systems installed on one or two acres of land.

The MI5 site in Tortola, British Virgin Islands, intercepted unusual radio traffic from the eastern United States to South America. The locations of these two sites could not be triangulated because the two sites were only being intercepted by the Tortola site. Seaman Edwards was on duty when the first intercept occurred, "Lieutenant Mason, I have an intercept that is being transmitted from the eastern United States. Should I maintain on the frequency and copy the transmission?"

Lieutenant Mason walks over to the intercept station and places a pair of headsets on his ears; he listens to the manual Morse code. The Lieutenant immediately recognizes that the code is encrypted, "Continue with the intercept and record the entire transmission."

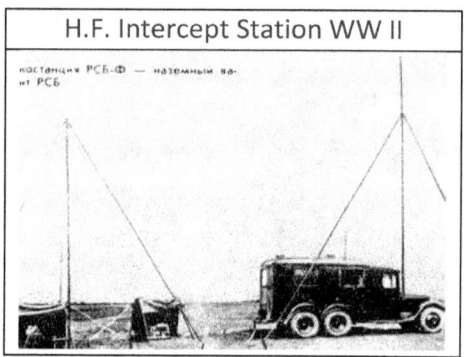

H.F. Intercept Station WW II

"Yes, Sir."

The transmission is between a site in the Eastern United States and from South America. Lieutenant Mason recognizes that the encryption is a low-grade cipher, and the location in Tortola can decode. After four hours, the two decoders assigned to the Tortola site have decoded the messages. The Brunner Fishing Company in Bayonne, New Jersey, is discussing purchasing three boat engines from the Schaefer *GMBH* factory. The intercept site in Tortola has a standing order that all communications will be reported to GCHQ in Manchester. Lt. Mason is a trained Intel Officer who knows that Intel comes from all sources. The Intel group at GCHQ needs all of the information. After they collect all Intel from all sources, the puzzle pieces will be fitted, and the entire enemy operation is unveiled. GCHQ sends a message to Tortola and gives the intercepts of the transmission a code name *"Rompecabeza."* (Puzzle). The message reads, "All *Rompecabeza* info shall be treated as classified on a need-to-know basis."

Lieutenant Mason assigns Seaman Edwards, Fitzgerald, and Donald to monitor all communications from the American East Coast to South America on a 24-hour basis. Within one week, the monitoring produces a clear picture of the communications between both sites. The boat factory, *Schaefer GMBH,* located in Buenos Aires, manufactures three large boat engines for three 50-foot boats belonging to the Brunner Fish Company in Bayonne, New Jersey. Usually, the purchase of the three boat engines would go unnoticed. The British MI5 has undercover agents monitoring the actions of Herr Joseph Schenkel, the *Gauleiter.*

The travel of Schenkel to New Jersey and the communications between the Brunner boat company and the South America Company has been elevated to the highest levels of interest. Colonel Baker is now informed. Operation *Rompecabeza* now needs to have a counterespionage mission.

Chapter Nine
MI5 Plan
Virginia Horse Farm, Charlottesville, Va

At the beginning of 1939, the U.S. Coordinators of Intelligence (COI) and the British GCHQ had a joint agreement allowing each to use the facilities of the other to conduct counterespionage missions. Colonel Richard Burkhead of the GCHQ MI5 Division Chief recognizes the significance of the radio intercepts from the Tortola, British Virginia Islands. He has communicated his concerns with GCHQ in Manchester, England, and has been given the green light to proceed with a surveillance mission. The Director of GCHQ, General Elliot Penrod, has clarified that the mission is only surveillance. The use of deadly force is not authorized unless it is self-defense.

In coordination with COI Director Colonel John Rubenstein, Colonel Richard Burkhead from the New York office of MI5 began the detailed preparation for *Operation Rompecabeza*. The three chosen operatives are on a train scheduled to arrive in Richmond, Virginia. The three operatives selected from the Ogden Logistics Center have been given a new identity. Francisco is Emilio Fonseca, Andrés Valencia is Carmelo Torres, and Juliette is Yolanda Maldonado. Before leaving Ogden, the three operatives have been given background information on their new identities. They need to know all of the details of their new identities, year born, place of birth, father, mother, brothers, sisters, uncles, aunts, cousins, and pertinent information such as schools attended and any special talents.

Emilio, Carmelo, and Yolanda have been instructed to disembark the train in Richmond, and each is to go to a separate monument. The city of Richmond was the capital of the Confederacy. During the early 1900s, dozens of Confederate memorials were installed in the city.

Colonel Berkshire from MI5 gives the following instructions, "When arriving in Richmond, each will go to the monument designated in your information packet. After you read your instructions, memorize the information, then burn the sheets. You will sit at a bench reading the Richmond Times-Dispatch. After sitting on the bench, an individual will approach you and ask for a cigarette. You will have a pack of Lucky Strikes and offer him a cigarette. If the individual takes the cigarette and lights up, follow them at a distance of 40 to 50 yards. He will have a vehicle. Enter the vehicle, and you will be driven to a safe house in Virginia."

Berkshire continues, "If your contact takes the cigarette and DOES NOT LIGHT UP, then do not follow your contact. Go to the motel as provided in your information packet and wait for further instructions."

"Questions?"

"Yes, Carmelo asks, when we travel by train, do we travel as a group or as separate individuals, not knowing each other?"

"Good question, it would be best to travel as separate individuals."

Emilio, "How long will we be in Virginia?"

"We estimate three to four weeks."

Yolanda, "When do we receive our new identity cards?"

"Your new identity cards will have passports from Argentina. The passports will be stamped at the port of entry in Miami, Florida. You will be in the United States on a work visa. Good for sixty days. All of these details will be covered at the Virginia location."

The three operatives arrive at the Richmond train station with no issues. Each walks or takes a taxi to their designated meeting location. Their travels continue with no issues. After meeting their points of contact, they are driven to a large house with a series of barns and silos at a home near Charlottesville, Virginia. The property is a working horse farm, and the main house has been restored to the façade of a southern plantation. The property belongs to an Englishman who has an American wife. The IOC, MI5, and MI6 use it. The owner is an Englishman, Sir Theodore Raleigh. He is a decorated veteran of WW-I and was knighted due to his heroism in the battle of Somme, France.

After arriving at the Virginia farm, Emilio, Carmelo, and Yolanda are given separate rooms. Sir Raleigh and his wife Margaret host a dinner for the group. For dinner, they have southern fried chicken with mashed potatoes and grits. For dessert, they have apple pie; iced tea and coffee are also served. After dinner, Sir Raleigh states, "Tomorrow, my good friend, Colonel

Burkhead, will be here. The Colonel and two associates will be here at 9 a.m. to begin your training. My wife and I will not be involved in your mission as it is strictly a need-to-know. Both my wife and I thank you for your service."

Carmelo, Emilio, and Yolanda all thank Sir Raleigh and his wife.

The next morning, breakfast is served at 8 a.m., and Colonel Burkhead and two associates arrive at 8:45. The group assembles at one of the barns. From the outside, it looks like a barn, but from the inside, it is a well-equipped technical laboratory.

Colonel Burkhead briefs Emilio, Carmelo, and Yolanda on the current information. After detailing the intercepts from the Tortola intercept station, he gets to the point, "The freighter with three engines and the spare parts is scheduled to arrive in Miami in three weeks. On board the freighter are the two mechanics and a woman. Our intercepts indicate that to save time, the two Argentinian mechanics will disembark in Miami along with the engines; they plan to load the engines on an eighteen-wheeler and drive them to Bayonne, New Jersey. We estimate driving the engines to New Jersey will take three to four days."

Emilio says, "Sir, when do we replace the mechanics?"

"We have a team who are experts in kidnappings. The team has been transported via air in the newest Douglas C-47. They will arrive in three days. They need to scout the roads between Virginia and Miami, Florida. They will track the transport truck. Most likely, the apprehension will occur near the North Carolina-Virginia border. The abduction will be carefully coordinated with the mission team. From the point of abduction, the mission team will take full command."

Yolanda asks, "Can you tell me what exactly the woman is doing with the two mechanics?"

"Yes, she is an accountant at the ship factory; apparently, she is the daughter of a Nazi Sympathizer. We believe that her grandfather immigrated to Argentina in the early 1900s. She has been sent on a different mission. The intercepts that we have from Tortola indicate that she is to explore a link between America and the Argentina Nazi Parties. She is quite beautiful as the intercepts refer to her as 'La Muñeca'" (The Doll).

The Colonel looks at Yolanda, "That's one of the reasons you were selected."

Emilio sees that Yolanda is blushing, adding, "Yes, but she was excellent on the technical subject; she was outstanding on all the automotive subjects."

This provides the Colonel an excellent segue into the boat engines, "Where we need a great deal of training is on the subject of the newest boat engines. The Brunner Fishing Company has purchased these engines in Bayonne, New Jersey. Starting Tomorrow, Mr. Gregory Timmons, an expert on the Shaefer engines, will start the training. There will be ten days of classroom and ten days of hands-on training."

Carmelo, the most experienced of the three operatives, asks, "Where did we find the engine?"

The Colonel has a sly smile and says, "The P-47 has a big cargo compartment. It seems like our Navy captured a German freighter trying to run our blockade on the North Sea."

Carmelo shakes his head and says, "Good thing, we need to be experts; only with the hands-on experience will we be able to fool the fishermen."

Burkhead now shifts to the mission, "I will provide the mission's objective. Only after you have infiltrated the fishing company can we plan for the details. These details will be determined by the three of you once you have gathered sufficient data. Carmelo, as the most experienced, thus, you are assigned as the team chief."

The objective is, "To determine if Fritz Müller is surveying the ships leaving ports from the eastern ports of the United States. Second, how is he transmitting the information to the submarines?"

Then, Emilio makes an important observation, "Sir, if the boats are out to sea near the 200-mile mark, there is a need for instantaneous communications to provide the information to the submarines."

"Yes, we believe that to be true. We have not intercepted traffic in the HF spectrum from an unknown source in the Atlantic to a station on the East Coast. This is a riddle that must be solved."

Emilio, *"A sí, ahora entiendo por qué la misión se llama "La Rompecabeza."* (Yes, now I understand why the mission is called "The Puzzle."

"Yes, you are right, it is a puzzle." Says the Colonel.

Preliminary Planning:

The Colonel then gives the team an overview of the plan. "From 08 to 16 hundred hours, you will be receiving classroom training on the boat engine."

"Additional training will be provided on the areas that you may need: lock picking, hidden messages, sextant, reading the stars, coded messages, hand signals, radio comms, and recognition of facial expressions to indicate when a person is not truthful. In three days, there will be a special toolbox. Certain tools will be used for covert radio transmissions," says the Colonel.

Carmelo, "Sir, if you do not mind, we want to clear our calendar after dinner. We want to design our plans based on what we know and present this plan for your review and comment."

The Colonel now knows that he has a very dedicated team at his side. He notes that Carmelo did not say, "For your approval, he said for your comment." He thinks *it is a big difference; they can improvise and think independently.*

Carmelo, Emilio, and Yolanda meet every night and discuss all possible contingencies and actions; when pulling the boats to dry dock, examine the boats for areas where eavesdropping equipment could be installed, have conversations with the fishermen as to where they sail, number of times they have encountered heavy storms, how far they go out, where is the best fishing?

Yolanda may produce the best Intel. She will start discussions with Fritz regarding his association with the *Bund.* Yolanda knows the history of the German people. If you did not know any better, she could convince anyone that Hitler's policies were just and proper. She may need to give Fritz the history of the Nazi Fascism and parrot all of the propaganda that he hears from his leader Schenkel. Fritz could lower his guard and tell Yolanda how he gathers the Intel and how it is reported to the German submarines.

Yolanda says, "I need to ask the Colonel to give me a bio on Fritz and Schenkel. If I am convincing enough with Fritz, he may give me an audience with the *Bundesleiter."*

Carmelo says, "Careful with Schenkel, I hear he is arrogant and is an egomaniac."

"Even better, most men think of women as being stupid, and they do not pose a problem. I have run across these types before. They are at times the easiest to extract information. They like to show how important they are and impress the ladies."

"Maybe, but if you go see Schenkel, I think I need to go with you."

"R-R-Really *un hombre macho.*" (Yolanda extends the Rs for emphasis. "You-u-u going with me will shut Schenkel quicker than an FBI agent. No, I will go alone."

Emilio, who has been listening, responds, "I think it is a good idea; remember we were taught in Ogden that women make better spies."

The idea of Yolanda going out independently to extract info from Fritz or Schenkel is tabled, and they move on to the next set of ideas.

Emilio says, "The Colonel said that no radio intercepts are occurring from the fishing flotilla to anywhere on the eastern shore, but somehow the information is getting to the U-boat commanders."

"Yeah, that's what he said; what are your ideas?"

"Only two ways: radio comms directly communicate to the U-boats."

"The Colonel already said that the Brits have not intercepted radio comms. They are the best, so if he says no radio comms have been intercepted, then we have to believe there is no comms."

Emilio thinks for a few minutes, rubs his chin, and combs his hair with his right hand.... *Hmmmm.... got to be away.* Carmelo and Yolanda are discussing surveillance methods, and Emilio interrupts excitedly, "I-I-I got it!"

"Got what?" asks Carmelo.

"The comms. There is only one way to use radio comms. Fritz has a flotilla of eight boats. The boats fish at intervals of twenty-five to thirty miles. Six boats at twenty-five miles give you 150 miles. Two additional boats give you an additional 200 miles."

Carmelo and Yolanda look perplexed. They still do not get it.

Emilio then says they are using their boats as relays. Emilio then explains that the VHF and UHF range radio frequencies are direct line of sight. Unlike the HF frequency, these radio waves cannot follow the Earth's curvature.

Carmelo says, "I thought you said that the Brits have the best Signals Intercept Systems in the world."

"Yes, that's correct, but physics is physics. HF frequencies are used for long distances. These radio waves bounce off the Earth and then are refracted in the ionosphere back to Earth. They continue bouncing using the ground and the ionosphere of the sky. They can move great distances." Emilio sees that Carmelo and Yolanda are confused and "What the hell is he talking about? Emilio then finishes his explanation of radio waves. "Think of the HF wave following a ditch or a channel."

"Está Bien, ya yo entiendo" (I understand now).

The three continue their discussions and agree they will alternate speaking only German one night and English the next. They agree Spanish will not be necessary since it is their native tongue.

At the end of the first week, the three engines arrive. The kidnap team has also come, but in the interest of security and safety, neither Carmelo, Emilio, nor Yolanda meets the kidnapping team from MI5.

Gregory Timmons, a maintenance tech from the boat department at the Plymouth Naval Shipyard, has been teaching using the engine manuals for the first four days. On the fifth day, the engine is placed under some crossbars with two hoist jacks to allow the raising and lowering of the engine. Timmons first goes over all of the parts of the engine. He begins by removing each part and explaining what function the part performs. The three operatives caught on quickly as they were selected because they scored the highest in the technical and automotive tests.

By the third day, each can remove all parts and reassemble. Timmons now goes over common problems associated with the engines: low power, engine misalignment, exhaust buildup, broken intake valves, and other normal malfunctions of wear and tear.

On the fourth day, Timmons shows areas where they can cause the engine to run at reduced speed and power. This is the area where they will likely need to inject a malfunction if they need to convince Fritz to allow them to be on the fishing trips. It is the only way to determine how to make the boats faster and to provide better maintenance procedures.

Last week, Timmons showed what will be required to install the larger engines; newer and larger propellers will need to be installed. The driveshaft needs replacement, and the bushings and seals must be changed. After the new engines are installed, sea trials will be required. Timmons goes over all the tests that must be performed on the upgraded boats and the five remaining boats. The idea is to stay at the fishing company as long as possible. The more time, the more Intel they can collect.

The engines arrive in Miami:

Two weeks and one day from departing Buenos Aires, the three engines and parts arrive at the Miami port. The MI5 kidnapping team is in place and surveying the engines' unloading. Soon, the truck departs from Miami; the transport truck and a 1937 four-door black sedan follow the transport truck. The MI5 team does not expect any problems. A man and a woman drive in a 1937 two-door Chevrolet; the third man drives the transport truck; the two men and the woman are not professional Intel agents. They expect minimal resistance. Once they have the identification of the transport and chase the car, they pull back and follow at a safe distance. The MI5 team is a professional hit team; thus, they know all the proper procedures of surveillance tracking. There are four in the group, and they alternate following the transport truck and the chase car. The instructions are to abduct the three targets near the North Carolina-Virginia border.

After two days, they remained 100 miles away from the Virginia border. On the evening of the second day, the MI5 team will kidnap the three Argentinians. The transport and the chase car stop at a motel for the night near High Point, North Carolina. At 3 a.m., the kidnap team quietly picks the locks of the motel. They place a towel soaked in Propofol over the mouth of the Argentinians, they pass out, and discreetly place them in their vehicle.

Carmelo, Emilio, and Yolanda are waiting two miles from the motel. The transport truck and the chase car are driven to the designated location. The truck and the chase car drive away, with Emilio driving the truck and Carmelo and Yolanda in the chase car. All of this is accomplished in twenty-two minutes. During the twenty-two minutes, not a word was spoken. The Ogden threesome now joins the MI5 team as professional counterespionage agents.

Chapter Ten
Brunner Fishing Company
Bayonne, New Jersey

Emilio drives the transport truck, and Carmelo and Yolanda drive the chase vehicle. They depart from the High Point, North Carolina border and drive on U.S. Highway One through Richmond, Virginia, and on to New Jersey. It is a two-day drive, and the team encounters no problems. They arrive at the Brunner Fishing Company on the morning of the third day. The buildings are as they were depicted in the photos provided by MI5. As they arrive at the site, a big man with a scruffy beard wearing a soiled shirt, unkempt long hair, and military-style boots greets them at the front gate. The transport truck stops, and the man with the scruffy beard steps forward. "I am the security guard. You must be the mechanics with the new engines, and we expect you. I need to check the load you are carrying and show me some identification."

Emilio jumps out of the truck, goes to the back, and uses a skeleton key to unlock the doors. The doors swing open, and the guard gives a glance and says, "I need some I.D., and then you can drive in."

Emilio shows the guard his driver's license. The guard looks at the driver's license and says, "You got something with your picture?"

"How about my passport?"

"Yeah, that will do."

After inspecting the passport, the guard looks back at the Chevrolet sedan with a man and a woman and asks, "Are they with you?"

"Yes."

The guard walks to the sedan and motions to roll down the windows; Carmelo and Yolanda have their passports ready. The guard looks perfunctory at the passports and waves the truck and the sedan through the gate.

As the truck and sedan come rumbling to the main building, two men walk out to greet them. The company supervisor, Karl Schneider, and the head boat mechanic, Walter Needleman, have big smiles.

As Emilio jumps out of the truck, Karl greets him with a big bear hug and says, "Welcome, *Amigo*; good to see that you made it."

"Yes, we had no problems; the roads in America are better than in Argentina."

Carmelo and Yolanda exit the sedan and come forward to greet Karl and Walter. They introduce each other, and Karl says, "First, we need to have you meet the boss, Fritz Müller."

Carmelo, "Yes, we would like to meet him and then get right to work."

Walter, "As soon as you meet *Herr* Müller, we can begin with a walkthrough of the repair area." Walter looks at Emilio and says, "If you give me the keys to the transport, we can begin unloading the engines and spare parts."

Emilio reaches into his pockets and gives the key to Walter, "You may need to pull the choke a couple of times; it is a diesel truck."

Walter signals to one of the workers, throws the keys to the worker, and tells him, *"Fahren sie den Lastwagen in die Reparaturbucht."* (Drive the truck into the repair bay) The worker takes the keys and drives the truck to the repair bay area.

The three team members, Karl and Walter, walk to the main building. The receptionist, Gisela, greets them and says, *Herr* Müller will meet you in the conference room. I will tell him you are here."

Karl escorts the group to the conference room. Gisela brings in French coffee and macrons. After two minutes, Fritz walks in. They greet each other and exchange names. Fritz, who, by nature, is not a trusting person. He decides that he will test these Argentinians with his German. He begins, *"Wie war deine Reise von Buenos Aires?"*

Carmelo answers in what Fritz believes is perfect Berlin German, *"Unsere Reisen...* (the answer continues in German) was without problems. The voyage on the ship went well, and we transferred the engines to Miami without any problems. Your roads are all paved; thus, we made excellent time from Miami to New Jersey." Carmelo notices that Fritz has glassy eyes and a muddled and confused face. It was evident to Carmelo, Emilio, and Yolanda that Fritz was not a German speaker. Karl and Walter already knew that, but they only laughed internally without showing their emotions. After more than five minutes of Carmelo describing their journey in German.... Carmelo finishes his dissertation and says....*" Es ist sehr gut, hier zu sein und wir schatzen ihr Geschaft!"* (It's good to be here; we value your business!)

Karl, who speaks passable German, gets Fritz out of an embarrassing situation; he answers in English Carmelo's description of the trip from South America, "Gentlemen and Lady, it is good to have you here. I will now escort you through our company and the maintenance and repair facility."

The group exits the conference room, and Emilio says *Danke und Auf Wiedersehen."* (Thank You, and we will see each other again.)

Fritz also wanted to talk to Yolanda, but after the embarrassment of him not knowing German, he thought it best to move on. He will let some time pass and ask her for a separate audience later.

Walter now takes over. Walter gives the group a facility tour for the next two hours. Walter is very open and answers any questions the group has; at this time, all inquiries are related to the performance of the boats. The group wants to establish trust between the fishery workers and themselves. After the tour, they drive to an All-American cafeteria and have lunch. During lunch, they talked about the need to install the new engines.

Emilio asks, "How will the larger, more dual-powered engines help in your business?"

"The idea for the newer engines was to allow our boats to remain further out to sea. In the fishing business, you need to chase the fish. Sometimes, you get lucky and catch all the fish you can carry in one or two days. Most of the time, the boats must stay out five to seven days before we can return to port. Now, we do not need the larger engines to fish; we need the larger engines to return to port. Last year, we lost a boat and crew when we hit a hurricane. The hurricanes can have winds of over 100 miles per hour. In the open sea, the winds can be over 150 miles per hour, with swells over twenty feet. Then is when we need the bigger, stronger engines."

Emilio says, *"Danke, Herr* Needleman."

Now that the group has finished lunch, they head back to the fishery and install the new engines. Walter and three of his workers have been assigned full-time to install the engines and upgrade any of the remaining five boats. The Brunner crew has one of the 50-foot boats in dry dock. The engines with dual propeller shafts are uncrated and move to the dry dock area using dollies. The spare parts crates are opened, and all of the items are laid out in a logical pattern. First, the driveshaft and the propellers must be removed. All of the engine bushings and nuts are unscrewed. Water lines and electrical connections are disconnected. The bottom of the boat and the back panels are removed. A special jig mounted on wheels is inserted under the boats, and the engine is lowered using hydraulic jacks. The smaller engines are still good and can be sold as used engines for 50% of the original value.

Now, the reverse process takes place. As the new engines are being installed, it is evident to Karl and his workers that the two Argentinians are experts in the new dual-shaft engines. Connections and installation of new items are thoroughly explained. As a bonus, some maintenance workers speak better German, and some speak better Spanish. Both Carmelo and Emilio talk to German and Spanish fluently. Karl makes it a point to tell Fritz that he (Fritz) made an excellent decision when he insisted that the Schaefer Company send some expert installers.

He tells Fritz, "Herr Müller, you made an excellent decision on the Argentinians. "They are experts; without them, we may have made some dumb mistakes."

Fritz is the type of person who likes to be stroked, "He says, sometimes you get lucky."

"No, Sir, I don't think it was luck. You could look forward and anticipate problems."

"Walter, when you complete the first boat and have sea trials, I would like to go with you. When do you think that the first boat will be ready?"

"Two, not more than three days."

"Excellent. Can *Fräulein* Yolanda come by my office tomorrow at 3 p.m.?"

"Jawohl mein Herr, 3 p.m. tomorrow."

As Carmelo and Emilio are preparing the first boat for sea trials, Walter asks Carmelo, "Please ask *Fräulein* Yolanda to go by and see *Herr* Fritz tomorrow at 7 p.m." Walter gives Carmelo the address of the meeting place; it is a French restaurant on Ocean Avenue on the waterfront.

That evening Carmelo tells Yolanda that Fritz wishes to see her tomorrow at 7 p.m., Yolanda assumes that Fritz will likely want to discuss the possibility of the connection between the Nazi movement in Argentina and in the United States. This is the reason for her trip to the United States.

The following day, Yolanda dresses in her most exquisite red silk dress, medium-high heels, leg stockings, and low-cut dress to accent her bosom. She wears her hair long with a small jewel crown over her head with sparkling earrings to match her bracelet. Yolanda wears only a slight touch of lipstick and touches her eyebrows with a black eyebrow pencil. Her skin has a light olive complexion, and she wears a pinch of the most expensive French perfume. She wishes to express opulence, beauty, confidence, and strength of character.

The correspondence between Fritz and South America has indicated that Yolanda has a strong character and likes the finer things in life. Yolanda's grandfather immigrated to Argentina from Germany in the early 1900s and always maintained a strong tie to the Fatherland. Yolanda's father fought in WW I and was a decorated German soldier in the Wehrmacht.

Yolanda was sent on the mission because of her beauty; men could not resist telling her no, ---they all wanted to bed her.

Yolanda must play the role described to her; the real Yolanda is presumptuous, spoiled, and flirty. She has average intelligence and, based on her relationship with her father and grandfather, has been sent on a mission to explore the likelihood of a working relationship between the American and Argentinian Nazi parties.

Yolanda meets Fritz at 7 p.m. at the waterfront restaurant. Fritz is at the table when Yolanda walks in. She simply looks stunningly beautiful. In her red dress, she is ravishing. Fritz quickly gets up and pulls out her chair to have her sit down. Yolanda can see in his eyes and expression that she had the intended effect. Now she needs to be coy, flirty, and move Fritz to the sexual line but not cross it. Fritz knows that Yolanda knows German, so he will avoid making the same mistake he made with Carmelo and Emilio. He tries to appear suave and debonair; he says, *"Mademoiselle, liken sie du Vin."* (Which is a cross of French, English, and German).

Yolanda knows what he is asking, saying, "Oh yes, I would like to have some wine, *Danke."*

Fritz signals the waiter and asks for the wine list. Fritz looks at the wine list and asks the waiter to recommend a wine. The waiter recommends an expensive 1937 Château Marie Elon wine, and Fritz says, "Yes, that will be fine."

The waiter returns with the bottle of wine and pours a small amount into Fritz's glass; Fritz looks at the waiter and says, "Go ahead and fill it to the top." His only experience is drinking beer; he always fills the glass to the top.

Yolanda knows she is having dinner with someone who wishes to seem important; she will oblige and praise him repeatedly throughout the evening. The dinner menu comes, and the waiter asks, *Mademoiselle,* what would you like?

"I will have the Chateaubriand with a béarnaise sauce and asparagus risotto."

Fritz looks through the menu and recognizes the fish entre, he says, "I will have the salmon with a baked potato and also asparagus."

Waiter, "Excellent choice." The waiter brings out freshly baked bread and places a small dish between Yolanda and Fritz. The waiter pours olive oil in the plate. Yolanda tears off a piece of the bread and dips it in the olive oil. Fritz does the same.

When two people are having dinner, they start talking about each other and their lives. Yolanda now primes the pump. She gives a small bio of her life and asks Fritz to tell her how he became so successful with his fishing company. Fritz now goes non-stop about how he worked for his uncle as a twelve-year-old and worked his way up the ladder. Fritz is now drinking wine as if it was beer. He orders a second bottle of wine. Nothing was given to him; his success came from hard work. Yolanda inserts little tidbits: that is wonderful, that's amazing. Germans are such hard workers and other aggrandizing statements.

At 9 p.m., dinner is complete, and after-dinner drinks are ordered. Yolanda orders a Grand Marnier. Fitz now shifts to beer.

Fritz, "You know us Germans like our beer. Did you know that the world's best beer party is in Germany---- *J.A., auf dem Oktoberfest in München?"*

Yolanda thinks *his German gets better the more he drinks*. By 11 p.m., Fritz is mumbling and stammering. He gets up to go to the men's room, and he staggers from one chair to another, and he falls on the lap of an old lady and says, "*Bitte, Bitte, Entschuldigung."* (Sorry, Sorry, excuse me).

As Fritz is in the men's room, Yolanda pays the tab. Fritz now comes out smiling. Yolanda now knows that when Fritz gets drunk, he has a happy face. She now knows that it is likely that when he is drunk, he will answer any questions that she asks. Tonight was a good night, establishing a connection between the two. She is sure that there will be more nights like tonight.

Sea Trials:

The first 50-foot boat is complete. The dry dock is flooded with water, and the first boat is now ready for Sea trials. On the boat are Carmelo, Emilio, Walter, and two maintenance crew members. The boat will be tested for maneuverability, speed, and engine endurance. The boat easily maneuvers to port and starboard. Walter captains the boat. The boat makes circles, racetrack loops, and sharp port and starboard, which places the boat at a fifteen-degree list. Speed is determined from a straight standstill. The boat accelerates to the top speed of 40 knots in forty-five seconds. The endurance is to determine how long the boat can sail at maximum speed and not harm the engines. This will require that special measuring equipment be placed in the engine. The oil pressure, oil temperature, and cylinder expansion will need to be measured. This test is essential; it will allow the crew to know at what speeds they can sail through hurricane-type winds and waves.

As they begin the endurance test, Emilio asks Walter, "What's the furthest that you take the boats out to find the fish?"

Walter, "Lately, Frits has been on all fishing trips, and we have gone out to 150 miles."

"So, if I figure correctly, that would be about 4 to 5 hours at top speed."

"What we will do to simulate the endurance test, we drive the boat for five hours at 90% speed and return at the same speed."

"That's a good idea, but when we need the big engines is in a strong storm. The seas are relatively calm now. Not a very realistic test."

Carmelo says. "Let's take the boat out to six hours. That would be about 200 miles. If the engines hold, then we have a good test."

"Agreed, we can do that with the next boat. We should have the engines installed in two days."

Second Meeting with Yolanda:

On the evening that Fritz had dinner with Yolanda, Fritz arrived at his home at 11:30 p.m. He was drunk and came in staggering and singing the Munich beer hall song. He went up to his bedroom and his wife said, "Fritz you're drunk, I left some blankets and a pillow downstairs on the sofa."

"Come on, honey, give me a kiss.

"No, I said go downstairs and sleep it off!"

This is not the first time that Fritz comes home drunk. He always comes home drunk from one of his so-called *Bund* meetings. As far as Mrs. Müller is concerned, it's just a bunch of rowdy men waving flags and bitching about the President. As long as Fritz puts food on the table and earns the money so the family can pay the bills and clothe their two girls, she is happy.

Gisela, the receptionist, had told her, that a team was visiting from Argentina. So, Mrs. Müller assumed that Fritz had been partying with the South Americans. She always believed that Mexicans and people from Latin American countries were drunks, so when Fritz arrived late, she had placed blankets and pillows on the downstairs couch.

The day after their dinner, Fritz arrives at his office at 10 a.m. Gisela assumed he had a hangover. Fritz enters the office and asks, "What is my schedule today?"

"Your schedule today? You do not have one---remember you were going out for sea trials. Walter and the South Americans left this morning at 8 a.m."

"Dammit, your right. I forgot all about it."

"They return in two days; shall I schedule you in?"

"Yes, go ahead, Goddam Germans always efficient, always on schedule. If we say we leave at 8 a.m., we leave at 8 a.m.," says Fritz.

Fritz thinks *Hmmm...in two days. I need to contact Yolanda and see if she can meet me in my office either this afternoon or tomorrow.*

Fritz tells Gisela, "Contact Yolanda and see if she can come by my office this afternoon."

The South Americans left all of their contact information with Gisela when they first arrived at the Brunner Fishing Company. Gisela contacts Yolanda at her motel and asks if she is available this afternoon. Yolanda does not want to appear too eager, she tells Gisela, "I have some appointments this afternoon, I will contact you later. I will see if I can move some things around."

She waits one hour and calls back, she tells Gisela, "I can see Mr. Müller at 4 p.m., but I have an appointment at 6 p.m."

"I'm sure that will be fine, I will tell him that you will be here at 4 p.m."

Yolanda thinks *this is working out perfect*ly; the meeting at his office will be all business. At 4:05 p.m., Yolanda is at the Brunner Fishing Company parking lot. She wants to arrive ten minutes late purposely. Yolanda was correct; the meeting was all business. Gisela sees Yolanda arrive ten minutes late; she does a "tsk, tsk," looks at the clock, and says, "Fritz will see you now."

"Well, glad you could make it Fräulein Yolanda," Fritz does not attempt to hide his displeasure with her tardiness.

"Most sorry, I am late; my meeting with a previous appointment went longer than expected."

"Well, first I apologize for my behavior last night, it will not happen again. One thing we need to discuss is your Nazi activities in Argentina."

"Of course, that's why I am here, but this information is very sensitive and cannot be discussed here. I was told by my father, that the German Americans had organized themselves in Bunds, this is what I would like to discuss."

"I should be able to give you any information that you desire."

"Do you think that it is safe that this is discussed here in your office?"

"Of course, discussing our German American' activities is perfectly safe to be discussed in my company."

"Are you sure?"

"Of course!"

Yolanda now uses her training in extracting information from subjects without the subject knowing that information is being extracted. One method is to present or discuss how the Nazi groups are organized in Argentina. She will purposely describe the groups as being inferior to the American organization. The idea is to have Fritz comments that, "We in America organize differently." In other words, we are better, "We have better security, etc."

Yolanda begins by first explaining her position in the Argentina Nazi *"Grupos."* She is the secretary/treasurer. After two minutes of Yolanda's description of the Argentina *"Grupos,"* Fitz takes the bait and tells Yolanda what he knows about the German-American *Bund.* He emphasizes that he is only a Nordland *Bund* member and only knows what the *Bundesfuhrer* has told him.

Fritz, "I will need to ask my *Bundesfuhrer* if he wishes to give you an audience."

"Very well, I understand; you are merely a soldier. You take orders. You could accompany me to your headquarters in Nordland. I also have some information from our *Patron* that can only be discussed with your leader."

Fritz does not understand what "Pay-Tron" means, but he assumes it means some leader. Fritz has one free day before the next sea trail is scheduled; he drives to Nordland and seeks to talk to Herr Schenkel. Schenkel agrees to meet him immediately. Schenkel assumes that Fritz is there to update him on the new engines. Fritz meets with Schenkel at the Bund headquarters building, which is a dilapidated warehouse in central New Jersey.

After their perfunctory, "*Heil* Hitler's, Fritz's gets down to business. He tells Schenkel that the Argentinian team has a woman who is the secretary-treasurer of the Argentina Nazi *"Grupo."* She is here on instruction from her leader to address the possibility of having a mutual agreement between the American and Argentinian friends of Nazi Germany.

Schenkel, "It cannot hurt to talk, yes, when can you and her be here and enter into preliminary discovery discussions?"

"Mein Bundesfuhrer, we can be here in two days."

"This must be kept secret, let us meet in the back room of the *Deutsche Bierhalle* on Antwerp Avenue."

"Jawohl mein Bundesfuhrer! The appointment is set the day after tomorrow at the German beer hall."

Sea Trials Continue:

Fritz drives back to Bayonne, New Jersey. He gives instructions to Gisela to tell Yolanda that they have an appointment with the *Bundesfuhrer* at 8 p.m., the day after tomorrow.

Gisela reminds Fritz, "Remember Sea trials tomorrow at 8 a.m."

"Danke, tell Walter that I will be there."

At precisely 8 a.m., the second 50-foot boat departs for Sea Trials. Walter takes the boat through the maneuverability tests. Fritz is impressed by the performance of the double prop engines. Walter explains to Fritz that they will be running the engines at 90% efficiency for five to six hours until they are 200 miles out. They will then return to the company docks. Walter explains that this is the best they can do with driving through a hurricane with winds of 150 mph and swells of 20 feet.

The long day of twelve hours gives Fritz, Walter, Carmelo, and Emilio time for discussions in the stateroom. Carmelo expertly moves the talks to the methods of fishing. Fritz volunteers that the three boats with the larger twin engines will allow for fishing to occur at the 150 to 200 miles. Fritz, "The 200-mile range will allow for the fishing of marlin. Marlins bring in top dollar for their meat. They are also large and thus have good ratios of fish to dollars. Two Marlins will equal two boats with the fish tub full of tuna. Plus, they bring in twice the dollars."

When the boat reaches the 200-mile border, Fritz, Karl, Carmelo, and Emilio move up to the bridge. Karl says, "From here we can see for miles."

After thirty minutes top side, the group goes back to the stateroom. Fritz stays top side for an additional fifteen minutes. He unlatches a secret compartment, removes a special radio provided by the German consul in New York, and keys the radio, "*Brunner boot, and kannst du mich horen?*" (Can you Copy).

"*Ich horen.*" (I can hear).

Fritz quietly turns off the radio and places it back in the secret compartment.

As the discussion continues, Emilio asks, "Do the smaller boats also go out to the 150 and to the 200-mile border?"

"My fishing flotilla will always go to the fish. During the hurricane season, if there is a report that hurricanes are in the warmer waters of the Atlantic, the smaller boats will stay closer to shore."

"Yes, it looks like you have a good plan."

Fritz likes to be told that he is a good planner and always looks to the future for the betterment of his company. At the end of the day, the Sea trials are successful. The next day, he readies for the appointment with the *Bundesfuhrer*.

Meeting with the *Bundesfuhrer:*

Fritz and Yolanda leave at 4 p.m. for their meeting with Schenkel. Gisela has arranged for two rooms at a local motel. Fritz and Yolanda arrive at the motel at 6 p.m. and agree to depart to the Beer Hall at 7:30 p.m. Yolanda knows that she will need to shake Fritz off after their meetings. Yolanda correctly assumes that Fritz will want to share her bed. She has been through this before, and one week of brushing off unwanted advances was taught at the Ogden Training Facility. Now she has a real live test lab--- the real thing.

At 7:30 p.m., Yolanda meets Fritz in the lobby of the motel. Yolanda again looks stunning; she is wearing a low-cut light purple blouse and match-ing skirt, lace stockings, high heels, and a necklace with matching earrings. Her hair is tied in a Spanish Bun, her nails are painted with a light pink color, and she is wearing the latest perfume from Fifth Avenue in New York City. Fitz looks at Yolanda and thinks *Herr Schenkel is going to be pleasantly sur-prised!*

After Fritz and Yolanda arrive at the beer hall, the receptionist escorts them to the private room reserved for Schenkel. As Fritz walks with Yolanda, all the men turn their heads and follow the woman with Fritz. She is what men call a "Real head-turner."

Schenkel is waiting at the table; he arrives at 7:30 and has already drunk two beers. Schenkel thought Yolanda would be a short, fat woman with a square face, sandals, and a long dress. She would look like the house clean-ers he always sees in the movies. He never expected to see a Marlene Die-trich. He immediately stands up, pulls out a chair, and offers Yolanda a seat at the table. Schenkel had the evening planned. They would order a Weinersnitchel and beer and be done with the dinner. Talk about how great he has organized the America *Bund*. Advise the Argentinian and the evening would be over by 9:30, by 10 p.m. Now everything changed.

Yolanda knows that her appearance has surprised Herr Schenkel; she needs to have Schenkel lower his guard. He must think with his brains be-tween his legs and not in his head.

Yolanda, "Herr Schenkel, allow me to introduce myself." She gives her name and her title to the Argentinian Nazi *Grupo* and then, to his surprise, asks. "Do you wish to talk in German or English? I am equally comfortable in both."

Schenkel has now recovered. He was born in Dusseldorf, and as such, he is a native German speaker. He decides to see if she can speak in German. "Fräulein Yolanda, I am most impressed with your offer, *Ich bin in Deutschland Geboren. Deutsch ware also mein perfekte Sparche.* (I was born in German, so German is my preferred language). For the next fifteen minutes, the conversation is in German. Yolanda describes the Argentina Nazi *Grupos*. The structure is very similar to the American Bund. The main difference is the connection that the Argentina *Grupos* have with Hitler and the Nazi high command. Schenkel is impressed with the Argentina organization. Schenkel then recognizes that Fritz has been left in the dark. He then suggests that he and Yolanda should speak in English so that Fritz can join the conversation.

Schenkel tells Fritz, Fräulein Yolanda has excellent German. She speaks with a Bavarian accent, but nonetheless, she is of Aryan stock."

"Herr Schenkel, may I remind you that it is Frau Yolanda."

"Yes, Yes--- of course, Frau and not Fräulein."

Fritz notices the distinction between married and not single.

After fifteen minutes of the German conversation, Schenkel asks for the menu; red and white wines are ordered. The three order their meals and continue with their discussions. Both Fritz and Schenkel drink the wine as if it is beer. After the two bottles of wine, two more are ordered, after the two bottles, two more are ordered. By the time they finish their meals, the dessert is ordered. Yolanda has been sipping her wine; Fritz and Schenkel have continued drinking the wine as if they were drinking their beer. With the dessert, Yolanda orders a Sherry wine; Fritz and Schenkel now switch to all beer. By 10 p.m., Fritz and Schenkel are drunk. When drunk, Fritz has a meek personality, and Schenkel is the opposite; he has become boisterous, animated, and authoritative.

When Schenkel states the obvious, Fritz agrees. *"Jawohl mein Bundesfuhrer."*

Schenkel asks Fritz to give him the status of the boat upgrades. Fritz answers similar to a private giving his company commander a status of the battlefield. Schenkel then asks. *"Hauptman* Müller, have you tested the direct VHF link to my headquarters?"

"Jawohl Bundesfuhrer, the link was tested yesterday, and all functioned in accordance with the specifications."

The conversation between Fritz and Schenkel is occurring as if Yolanda is not even present. She is only a woman; she does not have the intelligence to understand the actions that the *Bund is taking.*

The conversation continues until 11:30 p.m. Schenkel holds his liquor much better than Fritz. All three leave at midnight, Schenkel drives his car home. Yolanda drives Fritz's car to the motel. She helps Fritz into the vehicle. At the motel, she helps Fritz out of the car, helps him to his room, and throws him on his bed.

The next day, they leave the motel at 10 a.m. Fritz has a hangover with a big headache. Yolanda drives the car back to Bayonne, New Jersey.

Debrief, Yolanda, Carmelo, and Emilio:

By the end of the second week, the third boat had been upgraded, and Sea Trials had been completed. The collection of data has also been completed.

As the team chief, Carmelo summarizes the investigation's findings, "One, all boats work as a team. Relays are used." The comms from the 150 to 200-mile range use a new radio designed by the Germans in the low VHF frequency band. The transmit frequency is in the 50 to 60 mega-frequency range. Direct line of site comms exists between the Brunner boats and *Bundes* Headquarters. The receiving station is near the Nordland Bund headquarters. They were likely installed along the coast. The team will recommend that MI5 covertly install receiving stations along the New Jersey coastline when a ship convoy is departing. Once intercepting the signal, the frequency could be jammed, or intelligence gathered to be used accordingly. Once the convoy direction is known, and the information is transmitted to the Nordland *Bund* Headquarters, the information is sent via landline to the German consulate in New York City and then to the German submarines.

Chapter Eleven
German Network Uncovered
Virginia Safehouse

In June 1940, the mission completed, the team drove from Bayonne, New Jersey, to the Virginia Safehouse. Colonel John Rubenstein and Richard Burkhead, MI5 are waiting for them at the Safehouse. Colonel Rubenstein welcomes the trio, "Team, we are anxious to hear your findings. Here are the keys to your rooms. After a few hours of rest, we would like you to debrief us in the conference room."

Carmelo, "Two hours will not be necessary; we can be ready in thirty minutes."

Colonel Rubenstein looks at Yolanda and asks, "Thirty minutes good with you?"

"I prefer two hours."

"Two hours it is."

The conference room has an early dinner prepared. Country fried chicken steak, mashed potatoes, grits, green salad, and iced tea. As they are having their early dinner, the debriefing begins. Carmelo being the team chief, "Colonels Rubenstein and Burkhead, we are happy to report that we have the information on how the fishing boats are reporting the schedules and routes of the ships destined for England. Emilio will provide the method of communications."

Emilio, "Sir, we are fairly confident that Fritz Müller is communicating with someone on the coast and transferring the ship locations and the routes taken."

Colonel Burkhead, "And how do you come to that conclusion?"

"After installing the new double prop engines, the boats needed to be tested for endurance. This required that we drive the boats to the 200-mile marker. Müller insisted that we wait one hour before returning home. He stated that he wanted to simulate the actual conditions. The fishing trips will always be at the fishing location for some time; thus, the engines need to cool down. During the one hour, Walter, the boat captain, Carmelo, and I met in the stateroom. Walter had some details to go over regarding the engine upgrades. During this time we think that Müller communicated with someone on the eastern coast."

"That's hardly any evidence. Did you see Müller communicating?"

"No, as I said, we were discussing technical details with the captain in the stateroom. Now you need to hear the Intel obtained by Yolanda."

Yolanda now describes her evening discussions with Müller and Herr Schenkel. She leaves out her sexy dresses and flirting with Müller and the *Bundesfuhrer.* She did not need to describe her methods to the Colonels, it was understood that it was her M.O. "On my first dinner with Müller and also my meeting with him in his office, Müller concluded that I had some very valuable information regarding the Argentina Nazi *Grupos.* Müller then drove to Nordland and convinced Herr Schenkel that he needed to discuss the possibility of an alliance between the U.S. and Argentina Nazi organizations."

"And how did the meeting with Müller and Schenkel determine the communications link?"

"Coming to that part."

"Sorry, just that this is very important."

Yolanda skips the part of the two getting drunk: "During our five-hour dinner, Schenkel cut to the chase and asks Müller if they had tested the new radios provided by the German Wehrmacht?"

"Hmm... interesting, what are these new radios?"

Emilio now interrupts, "Sir, after Yolanda told us of the conversation between Müller and Schenkel while Carmelo distracted Walter, I was able to find the hidden compartment and confirmed that a radio was well hidden in a cubicle on the bridge."

"Did you take a photograph of the radio?"

"No sir, but I turned on the radio and noted that the frequencies ranged from 52 to 54 megacycles. I also completed a sketch of the radio." Emilio reaches into his rucksack and hands the sketch to Colonel Burkhead.

Burkhead looks at the sketch and compliments Emilio, "Well done, gentlemen, and, of course, to Yolanda."

Carmelo, "Sir, if I may ask, what we are doing with the kidnapped crew?"

"They will be released. Since you accomplished your mission in total stealth mode, the crew will return to Argentina with accolades for a well-done job. Even if they decide to tell anyone of their mysterious kidnapping, no one will believe them."

Colonel Rubenstein now offers some unsolicited comments, "This mission shall remain secret, and you are not to discuss this mission with anyone. Once you leave this Virginia facility, you will not even discuss the mission amongst yourselves. Is that understood?"

Carmelo, "Yes, Sir."

Emilio, "Yes, Sir."

Yolanda, "Yes, Sir."

"Operation *Rompecabeza* never happened."

MI5 New York Office:

Colonel Burkhead communicates with the GCHQ office of intercepts and codes, "Need assistance in America. Information obtained through counter surveillance has indicated the Germans have a new radio system operating in the low VHF band. Request that a radio team be flown to America ASAP and investigate."

Return message, "Radio team, flying to America with intercept equipment. Expect them at your office within one week."

In ten days, MI5 has radio intercept teams stationed at the British New York consulate, Washington Embassy, and one van roving station. Five days after the three stations are operational, a flotilla of ten ships leaves New York harbor with supplies for the embattled island of England. Within nine hours of the flotilla departing New York, the New York Consulate and the roving van intercepted encrypted communication at 53.2 megacycles. The intercepted communications are in the form of data bursts. The communications have a low level of encryption. The Germans do not trust their newest enigma encryption to third parties. The MI5 code breakers at the New York consulate decrypt the message.

Colonel Burkhead quickly informs the British Navy that the flotilla is in peril. Orders are given to sail for another fifty nautical miles and change course to a more southerly direction. The flotilla of ten ships is delayed for two days but arrives in Plymouth with no ships lost.

Colonel Rubenstein now informs Francisco, Andres, and Juliette, "Effective immediately, you are being transferred to Milton Hall, Scotland. Milton Hall is the training site for the British commandos. There you will continue with your training as covert agents. The British commandos being trained at Milton Hall are the best of the best."

Francisco is excited about being transferred to the European theater. He asks, "Are we going to see action against the Germans?"

"That I do not know, but if you are to see action against the Germans, you will need the type of training being conducted at Milton Hall."

In June 1940, Francisco, Andres, and Julieta are promoted to sergeants, and they board a troop carrier headed to Plymouth, England. After two weeks aboard the ship and two days on the train, they arrived at Milton Hall, Scotland, in late June 1940.

Chapter Twelve
Herman, and Karina
La Mesilla, New Mexico

In 1922, Alfred Hutchinson and Concha (Conchita) Ojos had a son named Heronimo in honor of Conchita's grandfather. Heronimo. Conchita was the granddaughter of the great Apache warrior Geronimo. The Mexicans had given the great Apache warrior the name "Heronimo," which in Spanish means the brave one. As Heronimo is growing up, on the farm next to the Hutchinson farm is a family of two sons and one daughter. The younger of the two sons is one year older than Heronimo, and the sister is one year younger than Heronimo. The brother's name is Reuben, and the sister's is Karina.

As they were growing up, Reuben and Heronimo were best of friends. Reuben's little sister, Karina, always wishes to follow the boys. The boys are always trying to shake Karina; they run off and hide behind trees, bushes, irrigation ditches, old, dilapidated barns, and the arroyos. After a few minutes, Karina always finds them. Reuben and Heronimo finally conclude that they cannot shake Karina. When Karina was three, and Heronimo was four, Karina had difficulty pronouncing "Heronimo." She found the name too long; besides, Heronimo thought that his name sounded too grown up. Karina started calling Heronimo "Herman." The name stuck, and Heronimo was soon being called "Herman." by all his friends.

The three were inseparable from the ages of seven, eight, and nine. Karina could run as fast, climb trees, and swim in the Rio Grande as the boys. At the age of ten, their parents gave each of them their horse. John Solemn, Karina's father, had a horse farm. The quarter horse business was very profitable in the Rio Grande Valley. Strong quarter horses would bring top dollar for use on the cattle farms. Alfred Hutchinson, Herman's father, had fifty acres of farm that grew cotton, corn, soybean, and alfalfa. Alfalfa was an excellent crop to return the soil to its natural fertilizing properties.

Herman, Reuben, and Karina loved riding their horse along the Rio Grande. Fertile fields existed for miles to the west and east of the "Big River." The river had brought life to the area since before the Conquistadors had ridden through the region seeking gold. To the east of the river, across from Las Cruces, was the Orogrande Mountain Range.

As Herman looks east, he sees the jagged peaks of the Orogrande Mountains and asks Reuben and Karina, "Do you know that the Spanish believed that those mountains contained gold?"

Karina, "Did they ever find the gold?"

"Yes and No. There is a legend that the Spanish did find the gold, but the expedition was overcome with greed. Two of the soldiers killed the captain and three of the fellow soldiers. The two thieves carried as much as they could stuff in their saddlebags. In the fight to steal the gold that killed the captain and the three other soldiers, the mules, which were part of the expeditionary force, ran off. The weight on their horses was too much, and the horses collapsed. An old Indian legend says that the thieves died of thirst and dehydration in the Sonora desert."

Reuben, "That's a bunch of hogwash. The history books say that the Spanish never found the gold. These are the lost seven cities of Cibola."

Herman, "So, you two eggheads think that the Spanish did not find the gold? They did, but they were overcome with greed. Greed is what killed them all, and with their death, the secret of the Orogrande gold is buried forever".

Herman continues, "I know because my grandmother told me the story. I wear a necklace today with a gold stone." Herman pulls out his necklace and shows Karina the small, flat stone. It shines in the sunlight with a bright golden color. "This is the stone given to me by my grandfather, Geronimo."

Reuben pulls the reins on this horse, mildly kicks it with his spurs, and comes next to Herman, "Wow, that's pure gold, bet it is worth a fortune."

"I have an idea," says Karina, "Let us ride out to the Orogrande Mountains. Maybe we can get lucky and find some gold?"

"Yeap, let's ride," says Reuben.

The Rio Grande Valley is about ten miles from the foot of the Orogrande Mountains. As Herman, Reuben, and Karina ride their horses through the sagebrush, they see smoke rising from the east. As the plume rises, they hear the delayed sound of the rocket blast. The horses hear the explosion, and they are startled and rear their front legs. The two horsemen and horsewoman quickly bring their horses under control. They sit high on their saddles and look to the east. The rocket continues to climb. At 600 meters, the smoke contrail discontinues, and the rocket comes crashing down to the earth.

Reuben asks, "What the hell was that?"

Herman, "I don't know, but we will soon find out."

They ride their horses at a full gallop, and within two minutes, they are at the rocket crash site. They dismount and start inspecting the long cylinder with fins. The nose of the cylinder is caved in as if someone hit it with a spatula. Two of the fins have been torn off. The exposed end of the cylinder is smoldering with smoke, and the edges have been blackened. As they inspect the rocket from afar, a British Land Rover comes barreling through the sagebrush. Driving the vehicle is an older man with long gray, unkept hair and a scruffy beard, wearing black hiking boots and a white smock. The truck comes to a screeching halt. Before the truck stops, the old man jumps out and screams, "Do not touch anything!"

The three are taken aback and shake their heads, raising their hands to indicate they have not touched any rocket parts.

The old man says, "You kids stand back; I need to place the rocket pieces in my truck before the park ranger shows up." The old man brings out two pairs of work gloves, looks at Reuben, the bigger of the boys, throws him the gloves, and asks, "Appreciate if you could help me place the rocket in my truck. You can follow me to my ranch, and I can offer you kids some refreshments."

Reuben, Herman, and Karina follow Mr. Goodwin to his ranch, riding their horses. The ranch has five rooms with an elevated porch. The front of the house has five steps leading to a veranda, which then circles the porch. The porch has a three-foot railing. The property has two large barns, a corral, and a small storage shed. Behind the barn is a grass aircraft landing strip.

Mr. Goodwin is now relaxed and introduces himself, he says, "My name is Ronald Goodwin, and to whom do I owe the pleasure of meeting."

Reuben, Herman, and Karina introduce themselves. They dismount and allow their horses to graze in the grass fields before the house.

As Mr. Goodwin goes inside the house, he points to some chairs on the porch and tells the three, "Please have a seat; I will bring some refreshments."

Karina, "Thank you, Mr. Goodwin."

After a few minutes, Mr. Goodwin comes out with a tray with four glasses of iced tea. The tray also has an open dish with sugar and chocolate chip cookies. As the four sit and enjoy the vista of the Orogrande Mountains, Reuben asks, "Mr. Goodwin, can you explain what we saw today?"

"You mean the rocket.""

"Yes, but what is a rocket?"

"A rocket is nothing more than a cylinder with a controlled explosion at the bottom of the cylinder. The cylinder has packed explosives, which act as fuel. The fuel is ignited, and the cylinder flies to the sky."

Herman thinks for a few seconds, "Hmmm …. You mean like a bullet exiting the barrel of a gun. When I go hunting with my Dad, we pack our shells with gunpowder. I know how the bullet is propelled out of the barrel. It is pushed with an explosion, and the bullet exits the barrel at a high velocity."

Mr. Goodwin, "Excellent Herman, you are starting to understand the Physics of rocketry. After the three pepper Mr. Goodwin with hundreds of questions, Mr. Goodwin raises his hand and says, "Are you three interested in rocketry? Most people think I am nuts and that rockets have no use for the modern world. They couldn't be more wrong!"

The three are in awe and answer, "Yes, sir, we are most interested."

"Very well, let me give you a summary of rockets." Mr. Goodwin tries to keep his explanation simple so the three kids can understand. He starts with his summary.

"A rocket is like a balloon. Let us say we blow up a balloon and then release the air. Who knows what happens?"

Karina answers, "We blew up hundreds of balloons for Reuben's eighth birthday. Do you remember Reuben?"

"Of course, I remember."

"Well, more than once, when we tried to tie the nozzle, the balloon would get away, and Wham! The balloon would fly all over the room. We even had a contest to see which balloon would stay in the air the longest."

Mr. Goodwin, "Karina, what you had in those balloons were rockets! The air in the balloon blew out the nozzle, and the air rushing out propelled the balloon forward. Now, when you were having your balloon contest, did the balloons travel in a straight line?"

"No, the balloons flew in all sorts of crazy patterns. They were fun to watch."

"Well, what if we could somehow make the balloon travel in a straight line? Would the balloon achieve distance?"

"You mean like go ten or twenty feet?"

"Yes."

"And how would we do that."

"Does anyone know why the Indians put feathers on the back of the arrows?"

Herman says, "Yes, I know. Without the feathers, the arrow zig zags and does not go in a straight line."

"Exactly, we could make the balloon be like an arrow with feathers on the back. This would guide the balloon in a straight line."

Reuben, "That's crazy; we could never place feathers on the balloon's nozzle."

Herman now thinks *of the cylinder they had seen rising to the sky* and says excitedly, "Oh, I get it; the cylinder had compressed air, and when the air was released, the "rocket" shot straight up."

"Now you are starting to understand the science of rocketry. What happens is that the rocket has a small engine, and the engine burns fuel. The burning fuel creates a hot gas. The burning fuel then pushes the gas out the back of the cylinder, and the cylinder, which is the rocket, moves forward."

Reuben, "Yeah, I get it. Are you the first to have invented what you call a rocket?"

"No, rockets have been with us for hundreds of years. The first rockets we know were used in China in the 1200s. These rockets were used for fireworks. Armies also used them in wars. In the next 700 years, the world's armies made improved rockets. Rockets were used in the American War of

1812. Think about our national anthem....and the rockets' red glare, the bombs bursting in the air...."

Karina asks, "So, rockets have been used for all these years. What makes the rockets that you are testing different?"

"Yes, good question. What I am trying to design is a rocket that has a payload. Think of it as a letter being mailed to El Paso. The rocket lands in El Paso, and the citizens of El Paso now have the letter."

Herman is starting to see the use in war; he says, "Mr. Goodwin, if I understand you correctly, the rocket will not have a letter. It would have a dynamite bomb and explode. Is that right?"

"Yes, that would be one use, but there are other more friendly uses?"

Karina, "Like what?"

"Someday, man will explore the planets and the universe. Rockets that carry their fuel will be needed for space travel."

"How do you know so much?"

"Rock science was not my original idea. There is a man named Robert H. Goddard, who pioneered the science of rockets. He is a Clark University graduate with degrees in engineering and chemistry. He was chased out of his home on the east coast. His neighbors were complaining that his rockets would fall on their homes. Lucky for me, Dr. Goddard moved to Roswell, New Mexico. I have visited him twice in the last two years. He has been my mentor in the science of rocketry."

For the remainder of the day, Mr. Goodwin and the three discuss rockets, the cylinder's design, fins, fuel types, fuel ignition, guidance, and length of burn, direction, recovery, and other pertinent items.

The time passes very quickly; before they know it, it is after 6 p.m. Karina looks through the window and sees a clock on the wall of Mr. Goodwin's home. We need to get on our way. It will be dark before we can get home."

Mr. Goodwin asks, "How far are your homes?"

Reuben, "We live in La Mesilla."

"That's a good three-hour horse ride from here. It will be dark in one hour. I can drive you in my Land Rover; you can board your horses here. Have your Dad drive you back out tomorrow, and you can ride back during the day."

Herman, "Our families do not have cars. We will need to ride at night."

"I got another idea; why not stay here overnight, and you can ride tomorrow."

"Good idea, but we must tell our families that we are safe and will return tomorrow."

"That's not a problem. I have a radio connecting to the Las Cruces sheriff's office. We can contact the Sheriff, and he will inform your parents that you are safe and staying at the Goodwin ranch. You need not worry; Sherriff Mason is a good friend of mine. He will vouch for me when he calls your parents. He will tell them you are staying with a good, reputable old man."

Mr. Goodwin makes the radio call. Ten minutes later, Sheriff Mason calls Mr. Goodwin and tells him both families have been informed.

"Yeah, they are good to stay with you one night."
After receiving the call from the Sheriff, the horses are boarded in one of the barns. As they remove the saddles and give the horses water and hay, they notice two bi-winged planes. They will ask Mr. Goodwin about the planes af-ter they finish their rocket discussions.

As they are boarding the horses, Mr. Goodwin has prepared dinner. Dinner is a soup with pork and beans. It is not exactly a seven-course French dinner but a typical Western dinner in southern New Mexico. As they are hav-ing dinner on the veranda, they see a flock of sheep bleating in the distance as they walk toward the house. Behind the sheep is a burro and a sheepdog. They are herding the sheep to the ranch house.

Mr. Goodwin, "My sheep go out to pasture every morning and come back at sundown. The burro, Amigo, and the dog Compadre are my sheepherders. I was losing sheep to wolves until I got Amigo. Since then, I have not lost a sheep. After a few months, I got the dog to keep Amigo com-pany. Hence the name Compadre, which means close friend in Spanish. Amigo and Compadre work well as a team. They even sleep in the shed next to the sheep corral. I could not ask for two better guards. I only pay them with food and let them know I appreciate the service. As the sheep are headed to the pasture every morning, I pet both Amigo and Compadre. I let them know that I appreciate their service. I can tell by the look in their eyes and the wag of their tails that they like being appreciated."

Karina, who loves animals, says, "Mr. Goodwin, what a wonderful story, I would love to meet Amigo and Compadre."

"As soon as they have the sheep in their corral, we can go down to the shed, and you can meet my two employees."

For the remainder of the evening, the science of rocketry continues, but Herman now has his eyes on the biplanes sitting in the barn next to the horses.

Biplanes:

The following morning, Karina wakes up with the bleating of the sheep. She quickly gets dressed and runs outside to bid farewell to the flock, Amigo, and Compadre. Mr. Goodwin is supervising the sheep as they exit their corral. As he holds the gate open, Amigo and Compadre are standing guard over the sheep, almost as if they were counting. Karina went over to the burro and the dog.

Mr. Goodwin looked at Karina and said, "Go ahead, you can pet them on their heads, they will like that."

"Thank you, sir." Karina went over and tapped both Amigo and Compadre on their heads. Soon after, the burro and the dog ran after a stray sheep and brought the sheep into the flock.

Mr. Goodwin then said, "OK now that we have completed our first chore young lady, let's go have some breakfast."

Karina and Mr. Goodwin prepared scrambled eggs, bacon, toast, coffee, and orange juice. The aroma of the bacon permeated throughout the house, and soon Herman and Reuben are up and eager to go.

Herman tells Reuben, "I cannot wait and ask Mr. Goodwin about those planes in the barn."

"Planes, my brain is full of all that talk about rockets, don't know if I can take another lecture on 'How Planes Fly.'"

"I am not interested in how they fly. I am interested in learning 'To fly,' one of the planes."

"I don't think you are old enough to fly a plane?"

"I read where you don't need a flying license. Not like a car!"

Herman and Reuben are dressed, and they walk out to the veranda where Karina and Mr. Goodwin have set up the breakfast table. The two boys, Mr. Goodwin, and Karina, enjoy a good breakfast. Both the boys have six slices of bacon and three scrambled eggs.

Karina tells the boys, "Slow down. Mind your manners."

Mr. Goodwin says, "Go ahead, and eat all you want. I can remember when I was a growing boy. My mother would say that I could eat an entire cow!"

After breakfast, Karina has prepared a fruit salad. Mr. Goodwin drank coffee, and the boys and Karina drank orange juice. Herman did not wait for a segue; he went right to the subject, "Mr. Goodwin, you think I could learn to fly one of those planes you have in your barn?"

Without hesitation, Mr. Goodwin said plain and simple, "I don't think so."

"Why not? My Dad has taught me all kinds of mechanical things. No reason why I cannot learn to fly a plane."

"OK, let's go out to the planes and see if you could fly the plane."

Reuben and Karina hold their laughter; "No way does Herman know how to fly a plane!"

They get to the first plane, and Mr. Goodwin looks at Herman and says, "Jump into the cockpit." Herman scurries up to the cockpit and sits in the pilot's seat.

Herman's eyes barely see over the cabin wall of the cockpit. Mr. Goodwin asks, "How you gonna fly if you cannot see?"

Herman stands up, looks around, and tells Reuben to throw him a cushion on the ground. Reuben throws him the cushion. Herman places the cushion on the seat, sits, and says, "I can see now."

"OK, see those two paddles on the floor. Those are the rudder controls. Reach down with your right leg and push down on the pedal."

"OK, I see your point, I need to grow taller, and then I can learn to fly."

"You got it."

The four retire back to the veranda, and Mr. Goodwin is very impressed with the thirst for knowledge of the three kids. As with the rocket, they start asking hundreds of questions.

Mr. Goodwin, "I have always had a love for flying. In the Great War, volunteers were being asked to fly the newest war machine, the two-winged airplane. The airplane has seen many advancements since the Wright brothers first flew in Kitty Hawk, North Carolina. The Wright brothers tried to sell their idea to the U.S. Army, but our generals were not far-sighted and laughed at the idea of flying machines being used in war. Hell, even the Mexican General Álvaro Obregón knew better; he used a biplane to bomb his enemies. Nevertheless, the French and the Germans quickly knew how the airplane could be used in warfare. The Germans and the French became the leaders in aircraft design. They also had the best pilots."

Herman says, "Yeah, but we had the Red Baron. He was the best pilot in the war!"

"You are right about the best pilot, but he was German. The American movies make him out to be an American hero, but he was German. I should know I was there."

"Really, Mr. Goodwin, you were there?"

"Yes, I was there. I joined the U.S. Army in 1916. By 1917, I was in an infantry unit training in a little village north of London. The village had a small airport and was the home of the company that was manufacturing the British Sopwith Snipe airplane. At the time, the airplanes were not reliable. The British Air Corps was asking for volunteers to fly the planes. I asked my company commander if I could be assigned to the British units that would be flying the planes. I was denied the transfer to the Brits, but I was assigned to a new unit in the U.S. Air Corps that would be flying the airplanes. No one wanted to volunteer for the Air Corps as it was a sure ticket to death."

Reuben, Herman, and Karina are captivated by Mr. Goodwin's story. They are hanging on every word.

Mr. Goodwin continues, "I received my training in 1917 toward the war's end. The plane was a Sopwith double winger. An absolute requirement when a student learns to fly an airplane is the ability to learn how to parachute. We had more training on the parachute than we had on flying. After my training in flying and parachuting, I was assigned to the U.S. Air Corps. I flew a total of nine missions. My missions were all reconnaissance. I flew over enemy lines and photographed the enemy positions. On my ninth mission, I encountered a plane from the German Luftwaffe. It was no match; the

German pilot was very good, plus he had a faster plane with the newest cannon fire. The Germans had mounted their cannons at the front of the airplane. They shot their bullets through the rotating propeller. The Germans, who are experts in engineering, had integrated the propeller turns with the firing of the aircraft cannon. This gave the German pilot better accuracy when shooting at an enemy aircraft."

"So, you engaged and shot down the Kraut. Right, Mr. Goodwin."

Sopwith Double Wing Aircraft

"Yes, I did engage in a "dogfight," but he shot me down as I said it was one-sided—fortunately, all those hours of learning how to parachute paid off. I climbed out of my cockpit and jumped out. Immediately, I pulled the ripcord, and the parachute opened just like in training. However, the fight was not over, at least not for the Germans. The German pilot flew right at me. I braced for the bullets that were sure to come, but nothing came, he flew right past me. The pilot tipped the wings of the plane. It was the Red Baron. So, you see, I did meet the Red Baron."

"So, did you fly missions anymore?"

"No, I fell behind enemy lines and was taken prisoner. The war ended a few months later, and I was released to the American Army."

"So, what happened to the Red Baron?"

"He was not as lucky. He was engaged in a dogfight and flew very low to the ground; an Australian gun was directly under the dogfight. When the German plane came over the gun position, the Aussies fired, and the bullets ripped through the chest of Manfred von Richthofen, the Red Baron."

"And are the planes in the barn the ones you flew in World War I?"

"No, they are not the planes that I flew in WW I. They are, however, replicas of the planes I flew. Since returning from the war, I have bought and traded for the parts to build the type of aircraft that I flew in the war. In 1926, I built the first plane, and by 1930, I had two planes. I use the planes for crop dusting, and two years ago, I was contacted by the flying circus to use my planes to perform acrobatic stunts."

"The two planes have been modified and upgraded with the 9-cylinder, 320 horsepower engines. I also had to lengthen the body by two feet to allow for the installation of a newer and, larger and more powerful engine. The plane has also been modified for a second seat. This was done to allow me to use the plane at the flying circus performances. I charge one dollar for one person and fifty cents for two persons to ride in the plane. On a good Saturday, I can make twenty-five to thirty dollars. Easy money."

"So, can you take us for a ride?"

"Sure, I can take two persons then one."

Mr. Goodwin takes the three for airplane rides for the next two hours. They fly over the Rio Grande Valley and along the base of the Orogrande Mountain Range. All three are hooked on the aircraft. They all want to grow up and fly planes. Mr. Goodwin tells them, "When you can reach the paddles, I will teach you how to fly."

Every year, they visit the Goodwin ranch at least three or four times a year; they climb into the cockpit and test if they can reach the paddles.

Chapter Thirteen
Prerequisite Flight
Santa Fe, New Mexico

From 1932 to 1936, Rueben, Herman, and Karina visited the Goodwin Ranch frequently. They enjoyed their conversations with Mr. Goodwin. As the years went by, Mr. Goodwin had designed and built rockets that are more powerful. The rockets were now obtaining altitudes of 1,000 feet and were traveling distances of two or three miles. The park rangers and Sheriff had designated an area at the base of the Orogrande Mountains, which were miles from ranches, farms, or settlements. The nearest town was Las Cruces, which was thirty miles west of the range. The only things that lived in this semi-desert land were jackrabbits and rattlesnakes.

Karina would stay with Mr. Goodwin at the launch point, and Rueben and Herman would be downrange. The four would communicate using VHF radios, which had a range of five miles. As the countdown would commence,

"Five...Four...Three...Two...One...Blast off."

Rueben and Herman would track the rocket using binoculars. Rueben would carefully note the rise of the rocket and the estimated height where the rocket would flatten and start on its flight downrange. Herman would pick up the flight with the binoculars and note when the rocket would turn toward the ground. Herman's job was to ride his horse to the "crash site" and ensure that the sagebrush would not catch fire. He would then wait for Rueben to arrive on horseback. Mr. Goodwin and Karina would soon arrive on the Land Rover.

After the flight of all rockets, the team would enter a discussion of the rocket flight. Mr. Goodwin had advanced the design of the rockets to where he had integrated gyroscopes. The gyroscopes allowed the rocket to have a sense of the rocket position relative to its vertical and horizontal positions. Mr. Goodwin had also designed a clock timer integrated with the information from the gyroscopes to control the fins on the rocket. The fins would then control the rocket to move from a vertical position to a horizontal position. The downrange team information was of crucial importance making any necessary adjustments to the flight controls.

As soon as the team was seated at the conference table, the debrief of the rocket flight commenced. Mr. Goodwin, "Flight team, it looks like we had a successful flight. Karina, please begin with your observations of the blast-off."

"Yes, Sir, the blast-off went smoothly. From the time of igniting the fuse to rocket lift-off, it was five seconds. The rocket wobbled and turned on its axis but achieved a stable condition at approximately fifty feet. The controls for proper vertical lift-off appear to have worked as designed."

"Karina, what about rocket fuel consumption?" asked Mr. Goodwin. Mr. Goodwin has observed all these flight characteristics but considered it best if a second party observe the flight. This would provide a more unbiased observation.

"The fuel consumption was smooth and continuous. It appeared to have achieved the desired altitude of 1,000 feet."

"Reuben, please report your observation from the midpoint of the flight path," commanded Mr. Goodwin.

"From my survey instrument, the rocket achieved a height of 850 feet. The rocket turned from vertical to horizontal with a point angle of sixty-five degrees true north. This was twenty degrees from the desired forty-five degrees; hence the overhead flight was an approximately one-half mile from my observation point. From the distance of the one-half mile, the rocket was flying at a steady airspeed."

Without being asked, Herman now gives his report from the crash site. "The rocket landed approximately two miles from the designated crash site. Due to the distance from my location to the crash site, I was not able to witness the flight from horizontal to vertical. However, I did hear the crash. I was able to quickly find the crash site. The distance traveled was two miles in one minute; thus, the average speed was 120 miles per hour. Calculating ten seconds to achieve maximum height and ten seconds for the height to the ground that would be one minute and forty minutes to travel the two miles. Estimated airspeed would be greater than 150 miles per hour."

Mr. Goodwin is very proud of his rocket team. He will use this data to make the required adjustment to the control parameters and build the next rocket. Unfortunately, most of the parts to the rocket are destroyed when having a crash landing. The average time between rocket tests is two to three months, depending on parts availability. After completing the rocket test, their attention now turns to flying the biplane.

***

Karina, Rueben, and Herman have been anticipating this day for the last four years. They are now tall enough to reach the control paddles. Mr. Goodwin promised them four years ago that when they grew to the point where they could reach the control paddles that he would teach them how to fly. The three students immediately wish to jump in the plane and start flying. Herman who is the most 'gung-ho.' says, "OK, Mr. Goodwin, I'm ready. Can we start on our lessons today?"

"Yes. we can, but we need some classroom study first."

The three look a little disappointed, but they concede that they do need some book lessons before they jump into the cockpit. Mr. Goodwin begins with an explanation of what makes a plane fly. "It is important that you understand the aerodynamics of flight. The time will come where you will have a malfunction of the engine or to the controls. You will be up in the air, with only yourself. You will need to take corrective actions at the instant that you detect the problem. You will be lucky if you have a minute to act. Most likely, you will have only seconds to make your decision and make the required corrective action."

Herman now understands, "OK, as always, you are right. We will not start our flight lessons until you certify that we are ready."

"Ok, let's begin with what makes a plane fly. In the 1700s, a man by the name of Daniel Bernoulli wrote the equations, which are now known as the Bernoulli's Principles. The Bernoulli Effect is what creates lift to the wings of the airplane. The great navies of the world, the Spanish, English, and Dutch were employing this principle before Bernoulli wrote the actual equations. The navies of the world were using the Bernoulli principle in the front jib of their sailboats. The jib is used to sail into the wind. The boat needs to sail at an angle into the wind, thus the term tacking into the wind. The jib sail will fill with wind; however, the wind at the tip of the sail will split and travel on both sides of the jib sail. Because the sails "fills" the distance traveled by the wind on one side is different. The wind on the outside has a "higher" velocity than the inside wind, thus a force or push to the outside is created. On a boat, the Bernoulli principle will allow the boat to tack into the wind."

Mr. Goodwin goes on to explain, "Bernoulli's principle can be used to calculate the lift force on the wing of a plane if the behavior of the airflow in the vicinity of the wing is known. For example, if the air flowing past the top surface of an aircraft wing is moving faster than the air flowing past the bottom surface, then Bernoulli's principle states that the pressure on the surfaces of the wing will be lower above than below. This pressure difference results in an upwards lifting force.[16] Whenever the distribution of speed past the top and bottom surfaces of a wing is known, the lift forces can be calculated (to a good approximation) using Bernoulli's equations[17] established by Bernoulli over a century before the first man-made wings were used for flight."

Herman, gets it, he says, "Is that why the wings on your planes are fat on top and smooth on the Bottom?"

"Exactly, what else?"

Karina, "The tail has a rudder and elevator flaps. The flaps are controlled by the foot paddles. Flaps are on the wings and are used to control stalls. Ailerons are also on the wings and control the roll using the stick. Elevators are on the tail and control up and down using the foot paddles. The rudder is also on the tail and controls the directions of the aircraft, left or right.

Reuben now gets into the conversation, "So, if you have the flaps on the right wings and left wings to come down or up at different angles, you will cause the plane to turn in a circle."

Mr. Goodwin, "That's correct, but let's not forget the tail."

"Oh yeah, the tail also has flaps." Says Karina.

"Yeah, but I think it is called the rudder?" Asks Herman, "Is that right, Mr. Goodwin?"

---

[16] Resnick, R. and Halliday, D. (1960), *Physics*, Section 18–5, John Wiley & Sons, Inc., New York ("Streamlines are closer together above the wing than they are below so that Bernoulli's principle predicts the observed upward dynamic lift.")

[17] *Eastlake, Charles N. (March 2002). "An Aerodynamicist's View of Lift. Bernoulli and Newton (PDF) The Physics Teacher. 40 (3): 166–173, Bibcode 2002Ph Tea 40. 166E, doi. 10.119/1.1466553."*The resultant force is determined by integrating the surface-pressure distribution over the surface area of the airfoil."

"Yes, that's correct. So, you see that the pilot needs to control the wing flaps and the tail rudder. The pilot also needs to control speed. And who can tell me how the speed is control?"

"Easy says," Herman, "That's controlled by the speed of the propeller, which is controlled by throttling the engine."

"Yes, that's correct. The pilot also controls the pitch of the propeller blade. Pitch is measure as one looks at a cross-section of the aircraft. As the pitch is increased, more upward thrust is given to the plane."

Herman, "Mr. Goodwin I can see your point, a pilot needs to fly in three dimensions. Driving a car is like playing checkers. Flying a plane is like playing chess!"

The classroom instruction continues for two days. Mr. Goodwin teaches them about the engine, weather conditions, how to read the clouds, avoid bird flocks, how to glide the plane, and how to use a parachute.

Mr. Goodwin, "After your two days of instruction, we are going to visit my friend in Santa Fe, New Mexico. He has a company that performs at the state fairs. He has a tower that is 150 feet tall. My friend Roger Marshall's company also has a training school for pilots. Flying clubs and the New Mexico Air Corps use the training school flight training and parachute practice. It is very important that you know how to jump from a plane. If you are going to be flying throughout your life, it is only a question of time when you will need the parachute. The saying is 'It is better to have it and not need it, than not to have it and need it.'"

Parachute Practice:

The following Friday, Mr. Goodwin, and the three students travel in Mr. Goodwin's Land Rover to Santa Fe. They leave at 1 p.m., for a five-hour car drive. On the way to Santa Fe, Mr. Goodwin explains to his students. "School begins at 9 a.m. There will be ten to fifteen students, including you. In the morning, you will be learning how to land from your parachute jump. If you are going to get hurt, it is on the landing. You will jump from a four-foot riser and land of a mat. You will learn to slightly bend your knees to cushion your landing. Upon landing, you will roll with the landing. The idea is to distribute the force of the landing throughout your body.

"Herman, "That should be easy; we have been jumping for heights of six feet or more."

"Good, then you shouldn't have a problem. After you learn how to fall, you will climb the 150-foot tower. There is a rope from the top platform to the ground. From 150 to 100 feet, the rope is inclined at between five and ten degrees. You will attach yourself to the rope with a snap harness. The harness will be securely tied to your body. You will jump, and the rope will guide you slowly to the first 50 feet mark, at the 100-foot mark, the descending will approximate the actual parachute drop. The first 50 feet will get you the sensation of the downward motion. As the ground comes up, you will flex your knees and be ready to absorb your body hitting the ground."

Reuben, "Will a heavier person hit the ground faster than a lighter person?"

"Yes, at the 100-foot mark, the slope will be corrected to the weight of the student. They will give you a number. The instructor on the platform will hold a sign with your number. The ground instructor will adjust the slope for your weight calculation. In other words, do not jump out of sequence. For example, Karina will have a higher degree to her slope. If you jump with Karina's slope calculation, you will arrive at a higher speed than would be normal."

Herman, "Sounds like they have their act together when do we actually jump?"

"The jumps will be on the second day. Your parachute will be folded by a professional. The class will first perform static jumps. You will have the ripcord tied to the rail on the plane. You will be lined up fifteen persons deep. All of you will hook to the track. The instructor will know when you are at the 1500-foot elevation. A green light will come on, and each student will jump out of the door on the plane. The instructor will literally push you out of the plane door. For the first two or three seconds, you will hear nothing then---- bang your parachute will open. You will use your left and right arms to pull on the parachute cords. When you pull on the cords left or right, the parachute releases air, and you have an ability to direct your fall. At this time, your parachute landing is not in danger. You will be landing in a large grass area."

The team arrives on schedule, 10 p.m. They have a good night's sleep. Have breakfast at 7:30 a.m., and arrive at the school at 8:30 a.m.

They register, their height and weight are measured, and each is given a number. Reuben, Karina, and Herman's numbers are 7, 8, and 9. They are led to a classroom, and the instructions begin. The instructor is a good looking, square jaw, broad shouldered, crew cut, no-nonsense having, military-type young man. He looks like he is in his twenties, He introduces himself as Sergeant Kilgore, and his assistant is Sergeant Mendoza. Mendoza looks like he came out of the same mold as Kilgore, but he was left in the oven to long, he has a dark brown complexion. Both are very professional.

Sergeant Kilgore begins, "The course you are taking, "Parachute Jumping" is very exact and is very safe if you follow the instructions. There will be no 'Cowboys' in my class. You will follow our instructions to the 'T" --- is that understood? OK, you all have a number, and I will address you by the number. I will ask each of you to answer in the affirmative that you understand and will follow the instructions."

Sergeant Mendoza now takes the podium, "I will state your number. You will stand and state in the affirmative that you will follow the instructions. Student number one."

Student Number one stands and says. "I understand and I will follow instructions." Students two through fifteen all stand and state that they will follow instructions.

Sergeant Kilgore then explains, "Jumping from 1,500 feet can get you killed. It is a matter of life and death that you follow the instructions. This flight school has been in operation for five years, and no one has ever been killed. We intend to keep it that way."

The classroom instruction occurs as described by Mr. Goodwin. By 10:30 a.m., they are jumping from four feet and learning the parachute landing roll. At 12 noon, they break for a one-hour lunch. The students are all marched to a cafeteria where their lunch is being served. They have a choice, meat, fish, or salads with apple, pecan, or lemon pie. Drinks are iced tea or water. After the students have been served, and desserts are being offered, Sergeants Kilgore and Mendoza address the students. Kilgore explains the afternoon exercise. A controlled jump from 150 feet. The training will continue for the afternoon until all fifteen students have perfected the landing.

Sergeant Mendoza explains the activity and states, "If you do not wish to proceed, this will be the time to excuse yourself. When you climb to the 150-foot level, it will seem like a long-distance down ---and it is. If you jump from this height, you will be killed. However, the speed of your fall is controlled by the guide rope. Before the exercise, Sergeant Kilgore and I will demonstrate."

From 1 p.m. to 5 p.m., the fifteen students practice the parachute landing. Each student has five jumps. What takes the longest is climbing the steps to the 150-foot platform. Each needs to take at least ten minutes to re-coup. The heavier persons are the ones having a problem, both climbing the stairs and making a perfect landing. Although not graded; Herman and Reuben would get A's, and Karina would get an A+. After the first practice jump, Karina becomes the darling of the camp. Also, the only woman. When the students are surprised that she is learning how to fly ---she simply responds, "Have you ever heard of Amelia Earhart?"

The first time Karina gave the Amelia Earhart response, the male students said, "Touché!"

That evening dinner is served at 7 p.m. At the dinner, Mr. Goodwin and the owner of the Flight School each give a small speech. Mr. Goodwin talks about his experience in flying Biplanes in WW-I. The students are enthralled and captivated by the story of the Red Barron. Mr. Goodwin places emphasis on his parachute jump ---it saved his life and the fact that the Red Barron did not shoot at him when he was descending.

Now the founder and the owner of the Marshall Flight School takes the podium. He congratulates all the students on the first day of training. He goes on to tell them that tomorrow will be an important day. It will be the real deal. He talks about his wartime experience. He also flew the Biplane, "But unlike my friend Edward Goodwin, I did not have the privilege of being shot down by the Red Barron." All the students laugh. Mr. Marshall ends his small speech, "A few years ago we had another aviatrix complete the flight course, and we wish that Karina Solemn have the same success as the first." Mr. Marshall allows a few seconds to enable the students to wonder who the first was, and he says, "Amelia Earhart!"

If Karina ever had any doubts of her being a pilot, they disappeared that night, she thinks, *wow an aviatrix just like my heroine Amelia Earhart!*

The following days are the real deal. Before boarding the cargo plane, a simulated rail with a doorframe and a two-foot drop has been built in a

Quonset hut. The students line up by numbers, one thru fifteen. Sergeant Kilgore is at the simulated door. He barks out an order. "Jump time ten seconds and counting "Five...Four...Three...Two...One."
Sergeant Kilgore places his hands directly behind student number one and gently 'pushes' him to jump through the simulated aircraft door. The simulation goes without a hitch.

They all go to the building to be fitted with their parachutes. The parachutes are numbered to account for the height and weight of the student. Each student picks up his or her parachute and is assisted with the placement of the parachute harness on their bodies. They have two parachutes, the main parachute, which will automatically open with the ripcord tied to the rail on the plane. The second parachute is used as a safety, in case the main parachute malfunctions.

After all the students have their parachutes properly installed on their bodies, Sergeant Mendoza barks an instruction, "Listen up, in case the main chute malfunctions, you pull this handle. However, this is very important, before you pull the handle for your safety parachute, reach above your shoulder and un-snap the J-hooks to your main parachute. Do not open your safety parachute until you have released the main chute. Does everyone understand? OK, starting with number one, let me hear the affirmative."

Student number one says. "Affirmative." All students from two to fifteen barks out, "Affirmative."

Sergeant Kilgore. "OK, gents and lady, follow me."
The fifteen students duck walk to the cargo plane. They all take a seat, and the plane takes off. The noise of the twin propellers is deafening. Sergeant Kilgore, who normally has a loud and deep voice, has problems being overheard from the noise in the plane. The students have been told of the noise; thus, hand signals are being used. In ten minutes, the plane is circling over the drop point. The light on the plane turns from red to yellow. Sergeant Kilgore signals with his hand to stand and hitch up. Each student has been instructed to ensure that the student in front of him has snapped the j-hook of the ripcord to the plane rail. After each student has checked for the connection, the student gives the student being checked a strong pat in the rearend. Karina is between Reuben and Herman, so Herman gives Karina a small pat. Karina turns and shouts, "Are you sure."

Herman gave her a 'Man-Sized' pat and then shouts, "Is that better?"
"Yeah, no time to treat me differently!"

They are all standing, hooked up and ready, the light changes to green and Sergeant Kilgore, motions with his right hand, five fingers, he counts with his fingers, "Five...Four...Three...Two...One...-----Go."

In fifteen seconds, there are fifteen-parachute openings. Reuben, Herman, and Karina all have the same sensation; immediately upon jumping from the plane there is absolute silence, the deafening roar of the plane engines is no longer present. **Then for a fraction of a second,** you then hear the Swoosh of the wind **and** ---WHAM--- the opening of the parachute. With the opening of the parachute, the body is pulled back toward the plane. The snap opening feels like the shoulders are going to be extracted from the body. The pain of the snapping of the parachute is only temporary, soon the pain is gone, and a new sensation is felt. It is a feeling as if you are in a fairy tale ---- you are Peter Pan or the Fairy Godmother, you are floating through the clouds. You see the earth as you have never seen it before. Floating through the air feels like you will stay up there forever. You see the mountains surrounding Santa Fe. The town of Santa Fe looks like playhouses, with the cars looking like ants. You cannot feel it, but you know that soon you will reach the ground. After what feels like forever, the earth is rushing up to you between six and eight feet per second. You must prepare for the landing. Reuben, who was number seven, reaches the ground first. He flexes his knees and braces his body as he was taught and prepares for the landing. He pulls on the parachute cords to alter the flight to be parallel to the earth. He slowly lands; he cushions the landing by doing a parachute landing roll. He quickly gets up and starts collecting his parachute. As he is drawing in the parachute, Karina makes a perfect stand-up landing. She also starts gathering her parachute into a **four-foot** ball. Soon after Herman lands, he makes a parachute landing roll, and in one motion, he is standing and pulling in his parachute. They look around, and all fifteen students have made a safe landing.

Two multi-passenger vans collect the students, and they are driven to the classroom. The parachutes are all dropped off with the jumpmaster. He and his assistant will prepare the parachutes for the next jump. After a thirty-minute debrief, they again will have their parachutes applied, and a total of five jumps are completed.

Sergeant Kilgore, "It is now 4 p.m. One more jump will be completed. The jump will be from 2,500 feet. This added height is to allow for the use of your safety parachute. The main parachute will be discarded while in flight, and the safety parachute will be used. However, due to the danger of releasing the main parachute, this exercise will be completed in three flights. Flight one will have students one through five, flight two will have students six through ten, and flight three will have students eleven through fifteen. Also, the time between the individual jumps will be thirty seconds. The thirty seconds clears the discarded parachutes. This is very important, unbuckle the main parachute within the first fifteen seconds after your main parachute has opened; your safety parachute is smaller than your main parachute, so you need more time to slow down the descend. One advantage that you have with the smaller parachute is maneuverability. You will be able to pull on the cords as you get ready to land and further cushion your landing."

Student number five raises his hand. Sergeant Kilgore, "Yes, you have a question?"

"Yes Sir, since we are now jumping at intervals of thirty seconds, and I will jump at two minutes and thirty seconds after the first jumper. Will this not have my landing outside of the landing zone?"

"Excellent question, No, the plane will be flying what we call a racetrack pattern; thus, we will always maintain our required flight pattern to ensure that the students land in the designated landing area."

The Sergeant looks around and says, "OK, group one prepares to board." Group one walks to the jumpmaster. They have their two parachutes applied, and they board the plane.

Groups two and three will watch from the ground. The plane flies a racetrack pattern. At thirty seconds, the parachute from student one comes flying off, and five seconds later, the safety parachute opens. Two trucks are picking up the discarded main parachutes. All five safety parachutes are seen at three minutes from the first jumper. Within ten minutes, all five are on the ground. The process is repeated three more times, and all fifteen students land safely.

On the evening of the second day, all fifteen students receive their stage one-flight diplomas. Tomorrow the instruction on how to fly a biplane will begin.

Chapter Fourteen
Learning to Fly
Goodwin Ranch, New Mexico

Upon completing the parachute training, Reuben, Herman, and Karina return to the Goodwin Ranch. The art of flying the aircraft will require actual time in the cockpit. Mr. Goodwin believes that with his two Sopwith biplanes, the three can learn faster and better under his tutelage. Mr. Goodwin allows the three to take a one-week break and let their parents know that they will be staying at his ranch for one week beginning next week.

One week from the start of their Santa Fe trip, the pilot training begins. As with the parachute, training on the first day is to review and understand all the cockpit instruments and the flight controls. Unlike the training in Santa Fe, the training occurs in the barn alongside the two planes. Mr. Goodwin has prepared a drawing of the instrument panel. The sketch has the following gauges and meters.

One, Air Speed
Two, Horizontal plane Indicator
Three, Altimeter
Four, Compass with True North
Five, Climb Rate
Six, Fuel Gauge
Seven, Turn Indicator
Eight, Red Line Indicator

Mr. Goodwin then explains each instrument and asks the students, "Reuben, is the Air Speed the same as ground speed?"

"No, Sir, the airspeed is the plane's speed through the air. This will differ from ground speed since it considers the speed of the wind as the plane flies through the atmosphere."

"Good answer, Herman. Can you give me an example of when the airspeed would differ from ground speed?"

"Yes, Sir, the combination of a tailwind speed and the natural push of the aircraft engine will be faster than a ground speed. If you are flying into the wind, your air speed will be slower than ground speed."

Mr. Goodwin, "Karina, can you tell me why the horizontal bar indicator is important?"

"Yes, Sir, the horizontal bar indicator will tell you the level of the wings relative to the ground. You will use the indicator to stabilize the plane."

Mr. Goodwin continues to ask questions to his three students. He then urges Herman to enter the cockpit of plane number one and Reuben the cockpit of plane number two. He and Karina will be the grading instructors. Mr. Goodwin randomly calls out one instrument. Herman and Reuben will point out the instrument. Herman tells Karina the purpose of the instrument. Reuben tells Mr. Goodwin the purpose of the instrument.

Mr. Goodwin, "OK, let's all return to our seats." The three take their seats around a makeshift table in the barn."

Mr. Goodwin brings out a second drawing. It is a detailed mechanical drawing of all the controls of a biplane. The drawing has the yoke, foot paddles, sprockets, pulleys, gears, cables, connection points, wing flaps, tail flaps, and tail rudder. Each item is identified, and a discussion is held regarding each item's function.

Again, Mr. Goodwin goes through a series of questions, "Karina, how is the rudder controlled? And what function does it perform?"

"The foot pedals control the rudder. Foot pedals normally control the rudder for left and right turn control. The position of the tail flaps also called the elevators, allows for small constant adjustments for elevation for up and down drafts or a steady state climb or descent. This will allow the plane to rise or to fall in altitude."

"Very Good," answers Mr. Goodwin.

"Herman, what is the yoke?"

"Yes, Sir, the yoke will respond by turning the wheel. The plane flies left and right, and the plane turns left. Also, the yoke will control the angle of the plane; pulling up will result in the plane to rise, and pushing away will cause the plane to fly down."

After discussing the controls and their functions, Mr. Goodwin says, "OK, I think you are ready to fly the plane. As I have explained before we drove to Santa Fe, I have modified the plane with two cockpits. The back cockpits have parallel controls. Thus, the plane can be flown from the front or back cockpit. I will start with Reuben since he is the oldest. Before we take off, we check the radio comms. At all times, we will be in communications. Reuben and I will fly the first plane. After we achieve a safe altitude, Reuben will take over the controls."

Mr. Goodwin and Reuben mount the cockpits and take off. At 5,000 feet, Mr. Goodwin gives the controls to Reuben. Mr. Goodwin speaks on the radio channel. "Turn the yoke left to achieve a slight left turn."

"Copy, turning left."

"Stabilize at 5,000 feet."

"Stabilizing at 5,000 feet."

Mr. Goodwin and Reuben remain in the air for forty-five minutes, and all the primary controls, left, right, up, down, circle, and change altitude, have been completed. Mr. Goodwin takes control and lands the plane. Herman is next, followed by Karina. For a total of two hours, Reuben, Herman, and Karina lodge each. After their first flight lesson, they are all excited about their flying ability. Mr. Goodwin hands each a logbook and tells them to log their hours and their actions. Mr. Goodwin means to them that they each will need twenty hours of flight time before they learn to take off and land.

Herman asks, "Is the twenty hours required by some government regulation?"

"No, I have imposed the twenty hours. Our government needs to catch up on regulations related to aviation. The Germans, French, and English are way ahead of us in aeronautical engineering. In the 1920s, the Wright Brothers tried to interest the U.S. Army, and they laughed at him. Soon after Wilbur and Orville had achieved flight, they went to the Paris Air Show and were a big hit. They secured contracts with the French, English, and Germans."

"Why were the Wright Brothers so much ahead of the French, English, and Germans?"

"The Wright Brothers had built a wind tunnel in their garage, and by trial and error, they shaped the wing as written by Bernoulli," said Mr. Goodwin.

Karina. "After we log the twenty hours of flight time, will you teach us to take off and land? "Yes, you should be able to log your twenty hours of flight time within a month. After your twenty hours, we will take off and do touch-downs and lift-offs."

Herman, "How many take-offs and landings do we need before we can solo."

"That will be my call. When you are ready, I will let you know. There will be one more thing before you solo. Anyone wish to guess as to what that will be?"

"I think I know," says Karina. "Bet it will be parachuting from the back seat of one of the biplanes?"

"Yes, you are correct. If you ever need to parachute from your plane, it will be because you are in trouble. Thus, your plane will likely not be flying in a straight horizontal plane. You will likely be pointed down. It will require a certain amount of strength to climb out of a plane when you are flying down to pull yourself out of the cockpit. I will be flying the plane, and each of you will need at least two jumps from a plane with a fifteen-degree down slope. This will at least give you an idea of what you must do. Knowing how to escape from a cockpit and jump is important. My ability to parachute from my plane in WW I saved my life. Many a time, the Germans shot down my fellow pilots, and they did not bail out. When a pilot does not bail out, we never know why. The plane usually will burst into a fireball when it hits the ground."

Herman thinks briefly and says, "Mr. Goodwin, we thank you very much. I am happy we ran into your rocket testing four years ago. You are like a father to us."

Mr. Goodwin says , "Herman, the winds of war are blowing hard in Europe. It is only a question of time before the United States will be at war. We will need accomplished pilots like yourself to fly our newest planes. Next to learning how to fly the plane, parachuting will be the next most important task."

Reuben and Karina echo Herman's words of thanks.

From 1936 to 1939, the three became accomplished flyers. Herman, who has always been the most enthralled and fascinated with flight, joins a traveling flying circus and performs acrobatic flights using the circus planes. Karina and Herman have also grown fonder of each other. They are now boyfriend and girlfriend. By 1939, Herman was nineteen and Karina eighteen. They are now adults, and their parents recognize that they have their own lives to live. Besides, Karina's parents think the world of Herman and believe it is only a matter of time before they marry.

Chapter Fifteen
The Flying Circus
Northeastern USA

In the winter of 1938. Reuben **was** nineteen, Herman was eighteen, and Karina was seventeen. Reuben was in his second year at New Mexico College of Agriculture and Mechanical Engineering (NM A&M). Herman and Karina loved flying. Herman and Karina had upward of 500 hours of flying Mr. Goodwin's Biplanes.

On a warm spring day, they flew one of Mr. Goodwin's planes to the flight school in Santa Fe. Although it was a warm day, when flying at 5,000 feet and speeds over one hundred mph, Karina and Herman had to dress warmly. They wore woolen overalls, aviator hats covering their ears, gloves, goggles, and wool-lined inner leather boots to keep them warm.

Upon arriving in Sant Fe, they found Sergeants Kilgore and Mendoza. As soon as they landed and parked their plane in a hangar, Sergeant Mendoza welcomed them heartily, "Congratulations on your flying expertise. I have heard some good words through Mr. Marshall that both of you are now expert fliers."

Pilot Dressed for Flight

Herman, "Thank You Very Much."

"What can we do for you?"

Karina, "We are seeking some advice on how to further our flying experience. Mr. Goodwin suggested we fly to your flight training center and seek advice?"

"OK, why don't you come in get comfortable, and I will see if Sergeant Kilgore and Mr. Marshall are available?"

"Thank you," says Herman. "You guys can make yourselves at home. Go to classroom number one, and I will get Sergeant Kilgore and see if Mr. Marshall is available."

Karina and Herman walk to classroom number one. They take off their woolen coats, flight overalls, and leather helmets. Underneath their overalls, they are dressed in presentable clothes; Karina uses the lady's room to brush her hair and place it in a ponytail. She wears a New York Yankee baseball cap with a ponytail through the back hole in the cap. Herman and Karina wear long-sleeved baseball sweatshirts, mainly to keep warm when flying at 5,000 feet.

After thirty minutes, both Sergeant Mendoza and Kilgore enter the classroom. Sergeant Kilgore, "Man, it's good to see you. We are always proud of our students who take up flying as a hobby."

After twenty minutes of catching up with Herman and Karina, Karina summarizes what they have been doing. Sergeant Kilgore sees Karina's engagement ring. "Karina, I got to ask you who is the lucky guy." Kilgore and Mendoza had noticed the ring but thought it best that she volunteered the information. They were concerned that she might be engaged to someone other than Herman.

Karina now says with much joy, "Well, of course, Herman and I are engaged to be married. We have always known since we were ten years old that we would get married."

"And do you have a date?"

"No, not yet."

Herman then says, "In a way, that is why we are here."

Mendoza says with a chuckle, "You gonna ask us for permission? After all, we did adopt Karina during the parachute flight school."

"Yeah, we should.

"Well, you got our permission!" says Kilgore.

"Thanks," says Karina.

Herman, "Guys, that's not why we are here. Karina and I have been flying the biplane for three years. We each have over 500 hours of flight time. We are interested in flying for a living, like one of those Flying Circuses."

"OK, I see; we do have some contacts with a flying team in New York."

"Do you know of any flying team in New Mexico or maybe Arizona?"

"No, not really; you see, the Northeastern United States is more heavily populated, thus more opportunities for performing aerial acrobatics."

"Would you know how to get a hold of them?"

"Yes, they often come west and perform at the state fairs. The next one is in California, outside of Los Angeles. I believe it is in Orange County."

"How do we contact them?"

"The best thing is to have Mr. Marshall write you a letter of introduction. Mr. Marshall will write a letter and give them your *bona fides.*" Both Herman and Karina look puzzled.

Mendoza says, "Bona fides means that the letter will establish your credentials."

"You mean like the letter will state that we have over 500 hours of flight time?" asks Karina.

"Yes, that's right, but the letter will get you an audience with the flight director. You will need to take your plane and show the flight director that you can fly in loops, dives, dives without the propeller turning and reengaging as the plane comes down."

Kilgore, "You sure you can do all of that?"

"Yeah, not much we cannot do. It is worth a try. The most they can say is no. Besides, we can visit Hollywood and perhaps meet Clark Cable," says Karina.

Herman, "How far is the Ryan aircraft factory from Los Angeles?"

"If you mean the Ryan Aeronautical Company, it is in San Diego. San Diego is only a half-hour flight from Orange County."

"OK, how soon can we get the letter with the *bona fides*?"

Flying Circus Poster

"Mr. Marshall will be in later this afternoon. I know he thinks the world of Karina....eh, eh, a, a, a-- you also Herman. I am sure he will have the letter written tonight, and you can take it with you next month when the Albany Flying Circus is performing at the California State Fair."

"Do you know why they are called the Albany Flying Circus?"

"Probably because they are based out of Albany, New York."

The following day, Karina and Herman have their letter of introduction.

It is now March 1939, and the California State Fair is held at the Orange County Fair Grounds, thirty miles south of Los Angeles. Karina and Herman fly their biplane to California. They landed in Tucson and Indio, California, to fuel up. The next stop is the Ryan Aeronautical Company in San Diego. They landed at an airstrip maintained by the company. Herman had wired ahead to request a viewing of the Pt-22 Recruit Trainer. The aircraft company received the request as a potential customer. The company then wired back that they had an appointment two days before the start of the California State Fair.

As they landed their biplane at the company landing strip, a salesperson, Mr. Robert Longman, met them. Robert was impressed by the exceptional maintenance of the biplane. His confidence was boosted immediately, and the chances of a sale were now higher. Mr. Longman waited for his prospective buyers to exit from the plane's cockpit and was mildly surprised to see that one of the pilots was a woman. Mr. Longman knew that women were piloting planes, especially since Amelia Earhart had been flying planes built by Ryan Aeronautical. The plane that his prospective buyer, Herman Hutchinson, had expressed interest in was the Pt-22 Recruit. The P22 was a single-wing aircraft trainer that sold for $10,000. Mr. Longman had the Pt-22 available for inspection.

As Herman and Karina approached Mr. Longman, Mr. Longman welcomed them to Ryan Aeronautical.

"My name is Robert Longman, and I will be your company representative while you are here at Ryan Aeronautical."

"Thank you, Sir," replied Herman and Karina.

"If you follow me, I can show you the plane you are interested in."

Herman and Karina followed Mr. Longman to a hangar, and the Pt-22 was in full view. It was a beautiful single-wing plane used by the U.S. Army Air Branch. Mr. Longman went through the specifications.

Herman, "What is the top speed?"

"The cruising speed is 150 mph, with a top speed of 200 mph. Of course, when flying downward, our test pilots have achieved upwards of 250 mph speeds."

"Would it be possible to fly it?"

"Yes, of course, but you must have one of our test pilots be in the second cockpit. I am sure you understand this is for your safety and our insurance. Once the plane reaches altitude, our test pilot will allow you to take the controls."

"That's perfectly understandable." Says Herman.

"Can we fly the plane today?" asks Karina.

"Of course, please step into my office and sign a waiver that relieves us of any potential injuries regarding your test flight."

Both Herman and Karina sign the waivers, and within thirty minutes, Herman is sitting in the cockpit of the Pt-22 trainer. The pilot is in the back seat; his name is Roger.

Roger explains, using the radio Intercom system, "I will take the plane up to 5,000 feet, and then you can take the controls. You can fly the plane in a normal flight pattern: no stunts or aerobatics. If we encounter any problems, I will take control. Is that understood?"

"Yes, Sir, understand."

The Pt-22 takes off and climbs to 5,000 feet. Herman takes control and flies the plane for thirty minutes. The plane flies north to Orange County and turns west toward the coast. Herman flies the plane along the coastline and increases the airspeed to 220 mph with a tailwind. At ten minutes from the Ryan Aeronautical landing strip, Roger takes control and lands the plane.

The plane taxis to the hanger; Herman jumps out of the cockpit and Karina jumps in. Roger explains the processes, and Karina also flies northeast toward Riverside. The plane turns and flies south toward the Mexican border. Again, ten minutes from the Ryan Aeronautical landing strip, Roger takes control and lands the plane.

Having complete the test flights, Mr. Longman says, "Shall we go to my office and complete the sale?"

Herman and Karina say nothing. They follow Mr. Longman to his office. After Mr. Longman gives them his well-prepared sale pitch, Herman says, "Mr. Longman, we were very impressed with the Pt-22 plane. We are on our way to our new employment for the Albany Flying Circus. After we complete our discussions with our new employment, I am sure that an aircraft will be recommended. After that, we will contact you, and if required, we can complete the purchase. I assume that you have financing available?"

Yes, we can arrange for financing, it will require a twenty percent down payment. Also, we have a second plane, which you may be interested in. It is the Dt-13A; it has a 450-horsepower engine with a top speed of 250 mph. It is the fastest aircraft in America today."

"What is the price?"

"The Dt-13A sells for $15,000, but I am sure I can get you a 20% discount."

"Very well; we thank you for the opportunity to test your aircraft. Both Karina and I were very impressed. I am sure that you will be hearing from us soon."

"Thank you very much, and I wish you the best in your new employment."

As Herman and Karina walk back to their biplane, Karina tells Herman, "You know we don't have that job yet. Are you counting our chickens before they hatch?"

"Yeah, but I did not want to tell Mr. Longman, 'We are not interested.' You never know. We might get lucky and have a job next week."

Herman and Karina fly their biplane to the Orange County Fairgrounds the following day. They land at a grass airstrip next to the county fairgrounds. Their biplane is very well kept. The plane's name is "*El Bambino,"* in honor of Babe Ruth. It has the latest Rolls Royce 250 horsepower engine, and stainless-steel cross cables stabilize the wings. The cockpit has the latest Westinghouse instruments. The plane is painted a Cherokee red with a yellowtail. When in flight, the plane resembles a cardinal. Upon landing at the state fairgrounds, the workers immediately go to the airfield to see the plane. When they see that one of the pilots is a beautiful young lady, they are all smitten with the aviatrix and the plane.

One of the flying circus ground employees assumes that '*El Bambino*' and the lady pilot are part of the flying circus. He tells his fellow workers, "Looks like we will get a good turnout. The lady pilot herself will attract droves. Yeah, after losing Amelia Earhart in the Pacific, the country is starving for a heroine."

After landing, Herman inquiries regarding where to find the flight director, Mr. Thomas Harper. He asks one of the ground workers to direct them to Mr. Harper. The ground attendant walks them to a portable trailer. He knocks on the door, and Mr. Harper sees his worker, Johnny; he asks, "Yes, Johnny, what can I do for you?"

Mr. Harper, two of the pilots just landed; they ask to speak to you."

"Hmmm--- my two pilots were not expected until this weekend. Who are these two pilots?"

"They are waiting in the van. Should I ask them in?" Thomas thinks there is *nothing to lose; I can talk to them and let them know that I have no openings.* He tells Johnny, "OK, show them in."

Karina and Herman walk into Mr. Harper's trailer office. Immediately, he sees Karina's beauty and a strong young man. Both Herman and Karina introduce themselves. Mr. Harper is also a pilot and is in his early thirties. He accepts the letter of introduction from Herman and assumes that Herman is the pilot and Karina came along for the ride. She must be his girlfriend. After some pleasantries, Mr. Harper asks the two to have a seat while he reads the letter from his friend, Edward Marshall. He is surprised that both are pilots. He thinks everything looks good on paper. I need to see them fly their plane. He takes the next step and tells them, "Mr. Marshall thinks the world of you, but flying in a circus is not like flying as a hobby."

Herman, "Yes, Sir, we were told that by Mr. Marshall and Mr. Goodwin."

"You mean Ronald Goodwin from Las Cruces, New Mexico?"

"Yes, Sir, he has a ranch outside of Las Cruces and is also a rocket engineer."

"Yes, Ron and I go back a few years; he taught me how to fly. How is Ron doing nowadays? I do not hear much about him. He used to come to the air shows, but I have not seen him in the last couple of years."

"Yes, Sir, he spends all his time designing and testing rockets. He says rockets are the future."

"You know," Ron says, "Rockets are the future, he is probably right. You will not find a smarter man than him. OK, I am busy today, so let us see what you can do tomorrow. Do you have your own plane? "

"Thank Sir, what time should we be here tomorrow?"

"How about 10 a.m."

"Yes, sir, we will be here."

After Herman and Karina leave Mr. Harper's office, Johnny walks into the office and is very excited. He says, "Mr. Harper, I gonna hand it to you. Hiring that beautiful young lady is a stroke of genius. Already, there is a buzz; everybody wants to see her fly, or better yet, they all want to fly in her plane. Having a woman join the flying circus will double our attendance. Every mother will want to bring her daughter to see the beautiful aviatrix. Yes, Sir, a stroke of genius."

Harper thinks *all I need to see is if she can fly. Johnny is right. I am running a business, and having a beautiful young pilot will improve the bottom line.*

The morning comes, and Karina and Herman are not only good fliers; they are excellent. Plus, they are bringing their plane. After the test flights, Mr. Harper invites Karina and Herman into his office trailer. He has a simple one-page contract. The contract states that they will be paid **twenty-five dollars** per flight during an appearance. On an average day, they each will make four to six flights. The usual length of an appearance is one weekend and four or five days. Thus, they each can make over 500 dollars per weekly appearance. Mr. Harper explains that they must pay for their expenses to and from the site's location. Mr. Harper explains that most flying circus appearances are on the East Coast. Most are centered on the major metropolitan cities of New York, Boston, Philadelphia, Baltimore, and Washington. Occasionally, they perform in the Canadian cities of Ottawa, Toronto, and Montreal. Mr. Harper suggests that Herman and Karina move to the New York area. From there, it will be a one-day flight to any appearance. Living in southern New Mexico will not only eat up their salaries, but they will not be able to perform for any appearances that are unscheduled requests.

Mr. Harper, "Karina and Herman, let me tell you the obvious. Both of you will be the star attractions. You are both young and have Hollywood-type looks. Especially you, Karina, you are a beautiful young lady. We have very few women pilots. Amelia Earhart was America's darling. Her disappearance in the Pacific Ocean was a real blow to the American mental state. Having Karina appearances as a young aviatrix will help to boost American morale."

Herman and Karina signed the contract. They are both delighted. They fly home to New Mexico and tell their parents the good news. **They tell Mr. Goodwin the good news and confirm that they can now pay for the plane.**

Mr. Goodwin said, "No need to pay; consider it your wedding present."

"Thank you, Mr. Goodwin, that is very kind of you," says Karina.

Herman, "Karina and I have talked it over; we plan to fly through the summer and fall seasons. By then, we will have money saved to get married."

"That's wonderful. I look forward to the wedding."

Chapter Sixteen
Great Britain Call for Pilots
Ottawa, Canada

In 1933, the German Reichstag passed the Enabling Act of 1933, which began the process of transforming the Weimar Republic into an autocratic Nazi Germany. The Nazi party now controlled the Reichstag and was a one-party system. With the one-party system, Germany became a dictatorship. Hitler aimed to eliminate Jews from Germany and establish a 'New Order' to correct what he saw as the injustice of the post-World War I. The Treaty of Versailles was written to favor France and England, and in the 1920s and early 1930s, Germany fell into an economic depression. Hitler's first six years in power resulted in rapid economic recovery from the great depression.

Hitler blamed the Jews for the loss in **World War I** and for the economic depression. He held massive rallies where he ranted, raged, fumed, and demonized the Jews, Gypsies, and Communists. Hitler denounced the restrictions imposed on Germany by the Treaty of Versailles. He annexed the territories that were inhabited by millions of ethnic Germans, which gave him substantial popular support. Hitler preached that Germany needed living space *(Lebensraum)* for the German people in Eastern Europe, and his aggressive foreign policy was the initial cause **for World War II**. Hitler ordered the invasion of Poland due to his *Lebensraum* policy. He felt that both France and England were too weak and that they would turn the other cheek. His bullying tactics in Munich against Neville Chamberlain had worked, and he saw no reason why his continuing aggression would not continue to work in his favor. From September 1939 to April 1940, the German Army conquered all of mainland Europe. Italy was his ally, and Franco in Spain was his lap dog. Japan had joined the Axis Powers. In the spring of 1940, Hitler believed that he would conquer the world within three to four years. The Third Reich would be the second coming of the Roman Empire. Germany and the Aryan people would rule the world for 1,000 years.

In April of 1940, Hitler set his sights on Great Britain. Initially, Hitler believed that Great Britain would likely join the Axis Powers of Germany, Italy, and Japan. However, with the election of Winston Churchill, the English Prime Minister rejected all offers of a peace treaty.

Hitler then ordered the German High Command to draw plans for the invasion of the British Isles. In the spring and summer of 1940, the Germans had amassed their entire Army on the North Sea overlooking the cliffs of Dover. The distance between Calais and Dover is eighteen nautical miles, and on a clear day, the white cliffs of Dover may be seen from Calais.

However, before an assault from the shores of France and Holland could begin, the Germans needed to control the skies. Field Marshall **Hermann Wilhelm Göring** was ordered to destroy the British Royal Air Force (RAF). Göring was arrogant and egotistical, much like Hitler. He had a military plan that was brilliantly designed. He had a superior Luftwaffe with ten times more planes than the British. He also had experienced pilots from the wars with the Poles and French. Neither the Poles nor the French had proven a match for his Luftwaffe. He saw no reason why the RAF would pose any serious problem. It was only a matter of time. He felt confident that the Germans would have a beachhead in southern England by late summer. Once they had a beachhead in south England, the Wehrmacht would land their tanks, dive-bombers, and superior Army to use their new blitzkrieg tactics to conquer England by Christmas of 1940.

The Battle of Britain started on July 10 and ended on October 31, 1940. Historian Stephen Bungay cited Germany's failure to destroy Britain's air defenses to force a truce or outright surrender as the first major German defeat in World War II and a crucial turning point in the conflict.[18] The Battle of Britain takes its name from the speech given by Prime Minister Winston Churchill to the House of Commons on June 18: "What General Weygand called the 'Battle of France' is over. I expect that the Battle of Britain is about to begin."[19]

---

[18] Bungay 2000, p. 388
[19] Stacy, 1955, p.18.

As planned by the German High Command, the Battle of Britain commenced with the bombing of the RAF landing strips. The German Luftwaffe had intended to surprise the British Air Force while the planes were on the ground. However, much to the surprise of the Germans, the RAF Spitfires and Hurricanes would always engage them before the German Pf-109 Messerschmitt's and the Heinkel's would reach their designated targets.

Unknown to the Germans, the British established a series of 'Communication Towers' used as Radar. As the battle over the skies of Great Britain and the North Sea waged, the British and Germans were losing planes at an alarming rate. The battle became one of attrition. At the beginning of the war, the Germans had an advantage in aircraft and pilots. The British could manufacture the Spitfires and Hurricanes at the rate they were being lost. What the British could not do was produce experienced pilots at the rate that were being killed. British men as young as eighteen were being trained in two weeks to fly the Spitfires and Hurricanes. These young men were being killed during training, and when they did attack the German planes, they were no match for the experienced German fighter pilots.

A solution had to be found. The RAF, using the BBC and other means of broadcasting to the world----Britain needed help. They needed to gain experienced aircraft pilots.

In June 1940, the Albany Air Show performed in Ottawa, Canada. Herman and Karina were the star attractions on their *'El Bambino'* biplane. Karina flew dozens of flights with two children in the rear cockpit. She would stay until nightfall to ensure all the kids got a ride. The young girls and grown women all wanted a ride and an autograph. Herman had learned to fly the Dt-13A. He, like Karina, dazzled the crowd with the aerobics of the single-wing plane. Herman made simulated bombing runs and flew the plane in what appeared straight up

Poster Calling for Pilots

to the sky. He would turn off the engine. The plane would come twisting, turning, and twirling only to have the engine reengage, and the plane would again soar into the sky. As the plane came down, twisting and turning- sure to crash onto earth- the plane would suddenly regain its engines and do a horizontal roll. The crowd loved the show, and crowds of over 5,000 people were soon attending.

In the audience was the British Ambassador to Canada. The Ambassador immediately went to the embassy air attaché and ordered Colonel Susan Mildred Phillips to find the pilot of the acrobatic plane and see if he would enlist in the Canadian Air Force. Pilots were desperately needed in the Battle of Great Britain. After witnessing the pilot's skills, the Ambassador was sure he could defeat his share of the German Pf-109 Messerschmitt.

On the day the Air Show ended, Colonel Phillips arranged to have Herman and Karina visit the British Embassy. A Rolls Royce limousine was waiting at their hotel and was driven to the embassy. They first met the Colonel and had their initial discussions. Colonel Phillips was surprised to find the couple so young; Herman was six foot even, and Karina was five foot seven, tall for a woman. They were both dressed in their best wardrobes. Herman wore a tuxedo and Karina an elegant evening dress; they **made** a strikingly beautiful couple.

Colonel Phillips was dressed in her 'Dress Blue Uniform.' She had six medals on the left side of the jacket and carried herself like a distinguished and decorated British Colonel. After talking about Herman and Karina's flying experience, the Ambassador entered the sitting room. After the introductions, the Ambassador says, "Mr. Hutchinson, that was quite a demonstration this week. I have never witnessed such a flight performance, such as I witnessed on Wednesday. Where did you learn to fly like that?"

"Yes, Sir, thank you. Karina and I have been flying since 36. We learned how to fly in southern New Mexico. Our adopted uncle, Mr. Ronald Goodwin, taught us how to fly on his biplane."

"Interesting, hmmm....is this the Ronald Goodwin that the Red Baron shot down? And the Red Baron waved at him as he came down on his parachute?"

"Yes, Sir, I believe that's the one. Why do you know him?"

"No, I was also in WWI, flew planes myself. I heard about the American ace pilot who met his match with the Red Baron. Legends are sometimes made of what you do not do----rather than what **you do**. So, yes, I heard about the legion of Ronald Goodwin and the Red Baron."

Karina, "So you also flew biplanes?"

"Yes, I did. I flew the Sopwith Model 2. They only flew two missions over the battlefield as an observation post. I was shot down, but I was lucky to have bailed out and landed with the Canadians. I spent one year in the hospital. When I was released from the hospital, the war was over. Soon after that, I joined the British Diplomatic Corps. I have served in Australia, New Zealand, and now Canada."

After each telling each other of their careers, Herman and Karina's careers are short, but the Ambassador could have talked for another four hours.

A formal servant approaches the group and announces, "Sir, dinner is served."

The four adjourned to the dinner table and had an eight-course French meal with a Canadian red and white wine. For dessert, they have a Cherries jubilee. After dinner, they retire to the veranda overlooking the city of Ottawa. After some small talk, the Ambassador gets to the point of the evening. "Mr. Hutchison and Miss Solemn, I have invited you to our Embassy to ask you to consider joining the Canadian Air Force to help us, the British, fight the German Luftwaffe."

Herman, "We thank you very much for your consideration, but U.S. law currently does not allow U.S. citizens to fight for any country that is engaged in warfare. We have been told that as U.S. citizens if we aid the British, we will lose our citizenship and not be able to return to our country."

Herman, who stays abreast of the situations in the world and the United States, says, "Sir, President Roosevelt is a very astute and wise man. As you know, there is a presidential election in November of this year. I believe the President does not want to antagonize the pro-Germany population. This section of the population supports Lindbergh and Willkie. The President is concerned that any overt action favoring England may **backfire**."

Karina, "Sir, Herman and I have discussed the possibility of us helping the British people. You may not know that my maternal grandparents are Jewish. They emigrated to the U.S. from Russia in the 1870s. So, I have Jewish blood. We believe that what Hitler is doing to the German Jews is wrong. Last year, my parents helped a cousin and her family immigrate to the U.S. through Mexico. They told us of the persecution of the Jews in Germany. They said that it is only going to get worse."

The evening ended, and the Ambassador told the Colonel to see if something could be done to allow Herman and Karina to join the Canadian Air Force. Colonel Phillips made some inquiries at the U.S. Embassy in Ottawa, but she was told by the U.S. State Department that the situation was very delicate and that it would be best that no 'formal' agreement be reached. On her own, the Colonel then crossed the border using her diplomatic passport and located Herman and Karina in their apartment in Albany, New York.

Colonel Phillips, "I am afraid that your government has the official position of not allowing U.S. citizens to fly for the RAF. However, I bring word from the Ambassador that it is only a question of time before the U.S. enters the war on the Allies' side. I am authorized to tell you that our Prime Minister and your President continue to have informal discussions. Should you decide to enter Canada and fly with the Canadian Air Force, we can assure you that you will be treated with the utmost respect. We can give near 100% assurance that when the U.S. enters the war, your ability to return home will be reinstated."

Herman, "We thank you very much for your travel to Albany. This will be a serious decision on our part. You understand that should we join the Canadian Air Force; it will be both of us."

"Yes, we understood that from the beginning. Women, especially women with flight experience, such as Karina, are being accepted into the RAF. They are essential as they perform the critical jobs of flying planes from factories to airfields."

"We will need some time to think it over---but no more than one week. Where can we contact you?" asks Karina.

"Here is my contact information. If you decide to join the Canadian Air Force, leave all your flight gear at the Albany Airshow office after you contact me, and I will come by and pick it up. When you cross the border, you may be questioned by FBI agents. You should not have a problem; no one will suspect too young lovers to be fliers if they ask what you will be doing. Tell them you are visiting a friend; give them this number I will answer and vouch for you."

"Thank you. We will need to discuss this amongst ourselves. We will contact you within the next week," says Herman.

The following day, after their surprise visit by Colonel Phillips, Herman and Karina discuss their dilemma. Herman has always known that Karina's grandparents were Jewish. However, this was never addressed. It was just not that important; Karina was who she was, and Herman had known her and Reuben all his life. She was the girl next door, and he had fallen in love with her. He asked her to marry him because he could not imagine life without her for the rest of his life. Once when they had gone to the movies in Las Cruces, they had seen in the newsreels the persecution of the Jews in Nazi Germany. That evening they had discussed what they had seen, and abhorred, loathed and found it revolting what they had seen. They both agreed that, in time, the U.S. would have no choice but to enter the war on the side that was against egomaniacs and lunatics like Hitler and Mussolini.

Karina and Herman had the following discussion the evening after the Colonel left their apartment. Karina, "For the past two years, I have always felt that we should be doing our part to defeat such maniacs as Hitler."

Herman, "Yes, I agree. Now is our chance to help the just cause."

"If we decide to go to England, we must tell our parents."

"Yes, I agree, I am sure both our parents will agree and wish us a safe return. I know that both our parents are strongly opposed to the treatment of Jews in Germany."

"Yes, my grandmother prays every day for all of the persecuted people in the countries conquered by the Germans."

"Karina, I think we should go. We have a talent that is much needed to fight the Germans. Besides, I would like to fly that new plane the Brits have, the Spitfire!"

"Well, then it is decided. We need to arrange to leave our *'El Bambino'* with the Air Show."

"Yes, I am sure that Mr. Harper will take good care of *'El Bambino.'*"

Karina, "Wait a minute; we must tell our parents about our decision. We can fly our plane to New Mexico and leave the plane with my brother at Mr. Goodwin's ranch. Besides, we need to talk to Mr. Goodwin about our decision."

"I agree; let us contact the Colonel and tell her to give us seven to ten days to tie up all our loose ends. We will contact her and inform her of the expected date to cross the Canadian border."

That same evening, Herman and Karina contacted Mr. Harper at the Air Show that they were taking a leave of absence. An emergency occurred in New Mexico, and they will return in seven to ten days. Mr. Harper thinks nothing of the notice. The next Air Show is scheduled for Philadelphia in two weeks. The days after the Colonel's visit, Karina and Herman fly *El Bambino* to New Mexico. They alternate piloting the plane. It is 2,200 miles from Albany to Las Cruces. Flying at an average of 125 mph, the flight is completed in twenty-four hours, allowing for fuel stops.

Herman and Karina land at the Goodwin Ranch landing strip. They meet with Mr. Goodwin and inform him of their decision.

Mr. Goodwin, "I support your decision; the U.S. will enter the war sooner or later. Both of you are at prime military age and might as well control what and where you will be fighting. That evening, they stay at the Goodwin ranch. For a better part of six hours, they listen to Mr. Goodwin impart his expert knowledge of fighting planes in dogfights to Herman and Karina. He stresses the following items: "First, see the enemy before he sees you; second, attack with the sun behind your back; third, attack from above; fourth, practice and practice both your attack and getaway flight patterns; and finally, have the fastest plane."

Herman, "What do you know about the Pf-109 Messerschmitt?"

"Knowing the Germans, it will be a good fast plane. I have studied both the specifications of the German plane and the Spitfire. From what I have read, they are both equally excellent planes. They have speeds up to 350 miles per hour. The Spitfire has a smaller turn radius. You can use that to your advantage. The biggest advantage will be tactics; based on my experience in **World War I**, the Germans will follow a strict pattern. Learn what the tactic is and anticipate their moves. In other words, think ahead as you engage in a dogfight----anticipate where the enemy will be and fire your cannons before he fires at you."

After meeting with Mr. Goodwin for more than six hours, Mr. Goodwin stands, turns, and walks back to his work room. He comes out with a special parachute harness. He explains, "Herman when you end up flying the

Spitfire and engage in aerial combat, wear this special harness. This will allow you to have a reserve 'emergency' parachute. You see these J-Hooks? Connect your main parachute to the harness using these specially designed J-Hooks. Should you ever be in trouble you can disconnect the main parachute and open the emergency parachute."

After thanking Mr. Goodwin, **Karina** and Herman use Mr. Goodwin's Land Rover to drive to La Mesilla and inform their parents of their decisions. As anticipated, they are supportive and wish them well. Karina's grandparents are concerned but also give them their blessings. Reuben is now a senior at New Mexico A&M and states in no uncertain terms that he will join the war effort in 1941 after he graduates. He has been told that he can pick his choice of the armed branches and will be commissioned as a second lieutenant.

After three days in their hometown, Reuben drives them to the Union Railroad Station in El Paso, and Herman and Karina are on the Southern Pacific Silver Liner headed east. In three days, they arrive at the Albany, New York train station. On the train trip east, they stopped in Dallas for one hour, and they called Colonel Phillips, who said that they would be crossing the border in four days. They ask her to come by and pick up their flight gear. Colonel Phillips is very punctual and arrives five minutes before the appointed time. She picks up the flight gear and drives them to the Buffalo train station.

In Buffalo, Herman and Karina board the train for Ottawa. Herman and Karina tried to look as inconspicuous as possible. They understood that if they were caught, they would not be able to proceed to join the Canadian Air Force. It was likely that they would be denied entry. If that happened, they were prepared to try again from a different city and take the train to Montreal or Toronto. There was also the possibility that they could be sent to prison, as well as fined. It was unlikely that both Herman and Karina had confidence in their ability to talk themselves out of any situation. At the Canadian border, the train stopped, and two men wearing business suits with ties and crew cuts boarded the train. Immediately, all the passengers knew they were G-men. Herman never understood the dress code of the FBI. If they wanted to be undercover, they needed to do a better job.

One of the G-man asks, "May we see your passports?"

"Yes, Sir." Both Herman and Karina displayed their passports.

One of the agents looked at their passports and did a double take on Herman and Karina. He then said, "Are you two the fliers from the Air Show?"

"Yes, Sir," says Karina.

G-man number two hands them back their passports and then surprises them with his response, "I was at the Albany Airshow, and my two daughters rode on one of your flights. They think the world of you. You two are heroes to my daughters. Especially you, Miss Solemn. Soon, we will be in the war and need fliers of your caliber."

"Thank you very much Sir. Glad your daughters had a good time."

"You two watch yourselves and be safe." The FBI agents looked at Karina and Herman and said, "Here are our business cards, should you need any help from the FBI."

The agents disembarked, and the train proceeded to Ottawa. Herman looked at Karina, "Well, that was a surprise. Do you think they knew that we were on our way to join the fight in England?"

"Well, if they didn't, they will soon figure it out when we no longer perform at the Air Shows."

Within two hours, the train arrives at the Ottawa station. Colonel Phillips is waiting at the station. She is dressed in civvies, "How was your crossing? Any problems?"

"None whatsoever; the FBI agents wished us well, even gave us their cards; they said if we had any problems to let them know; perhaps they can help," said Herman. Colonel Philipps smiles and thinks *that the U.S. will join the war against the Axis Powers within the year.*

Chapter Seventeen
The Royal Canadian Air Force (RCAF)
Ottawa, Canada

Upon arrival in Canada, Colonel Phillips had arranged for Herman and Karina to stay at the Ottawa Canadian Hotel for two nights. She had also informed Colonel Emmitt Page from the Royal Canadian Air Force that she was bringing two experienced pilots from the United States to join his Air Force. The day before Karina and Herman arrive at the Canadian Airfield, Colonel Phillips discusses the two new recruits.

Phillips, "Sir, I will bring two experienced United States recruits."

Page, a straight, laced, no-nonsense Colonel, says, "Are they experienced?"

"More than 800 hours on the DP-3XA Ryan Aeronautical aircraft."

"Where the hell did they learn how to fly that plane? I understand the DP-3XA is as fast faster than the Spitfire or the Messerschmitt.

"They have been flying for an Air Show."

Colonel Page now eases his adversarial posture and asks, "When will they be here?"

"Day after tomorrow."

"And are they aware that they are breaking the U.S. law?"

"Yes, but they are very levelheaded young fliers. They know that England cannot fall. This would create an untenable situation for the U.S. They would be left alone to fight the Axis Powers."

"It is too bad that one of these two young persons is not the President of the United States; it seems they have a pretty good head on their shoulders.

"Sir, I will have them here the day after tomorrow at 9 a.m."

"OK, it is always good to have good, experienced pilots. Have them report to Captain Gregory Baker. He oversees initial training. We need to make sure that they are experienced. Our counterparts in Great Britain are having over fifty percent of their new pilots being killed within their first week of combat. This is due to the need for more experience. Our Canadian Pilots do much better. And we need to keep it that way."

Herman and Karina arrive at the training site. They are two of twenty recruits who have volunteered to fly for the Canadian Royal Air Force (CRAF); Captain Baker is a little older than Herman; Baker is twenty-four but looks younger. Captain Baker introduces himself and tells the recruits that this is not a flight school. England needs experienced fliers.

Captain Baker, "It is my duty to ensure you know how to fly. We have ten trainers in our inventory, and we do not intend to lose any of these trainers; the first day, you will fly in a two-seater trainer. The flight instructor will verify that you know how to fly. If you pass the first day, you will fly our most modern plane, the Ryan Aeronautical DP-3XA. This plane closely resembles what you will be flying in England. If there are no questions, we begin today. First thing, we outfit you with your Flight suits."

Herman raises his hand, "Yes, you have a question?"

"Yes, Sir, if we have our flight suit, may we use it?"

Baker grimaces and says, "You will be flying the advanced Ryan Aeronautical DP-3XA if you have the right equipment." Baker thinks, *dumbass, he will no doubt be the first one to wash out.*

The twenty recruits are marched to the fitting room and given a flight suit, boots, gloves, and a leather helmet. Both Herman and Karina take the issued equipment and walk to the changing room. Herman and eighteen recruits use the general changing room, and Karina uses the cleaning closet. As they wait their turn for the initial 'test' flight, Herman and Karina have on their professional flight suits from the Air Show. They are immediately tagged as real pros or idiots; they will soon find out. The initial fights are completed in two hours with ten trainers and five test pilots. Four recruits have failing grades. Twelve have passed, two are excellent, and two are outstanding.

After the tests are complete, Captain Baker reviews the chart, calls out the failed pilots by number, and asks them to report to building number 2015.

After they depart, "Congratulations, you have now entered the two-week prep program to be inducted into the Canadian Royal Air Force. You may proceed to build number 1010. There, you will receive meal tickets and bunk assignments. Recruit numbers 57 and 58; please remain in your place. All others may leave."

Captain Baker now relaxes and asks, "Where did you learn to fly the DP-3XA? As far as I know, we are the only Air Force with the plane."

"Yes, Sir, you may be the only Air Force, but the Albany Air Show purchased the first two to three months ago."

"Oh, I see, so you are the stunt pilots at the Albany Air Show. Is that right."

"Yes, Sir."

The captain looks at Karina and says, "You know that women cannot fly missions?"

"Yes, Sir, but we can fly the planes from the factory to the airfields."

"Correct, the Brits have the Air Transport Auxiliary (ATA), which has women pilots delivering aircraft from the factories to the airbases. Also, the women pilots will move aircraft around the bases as needed, sometimes because of losses due to air combat, and for general purpose maintenance."

"OK, starting tomorrow, we will have physical exercises in the morning and flying simulated bombing missions and aerial dog fights in the afternoon. After two weeks, you will ship to England."

"Yes Sir, we will be ready."

"Majors Gillespie and Burns will teach the combat missions; they are our most advanced fighter pilots."

"Do we have any pilots here with actual wartime experience?"

"Unfortunately, no, all experienced pilots are required for the war effort. What we have done in the past is if we have outstanding pilots with considerable experience, we will use them to provide guidance. The two of you may fit into that category.

Herman, "Yes, if we can help, we certainly will."

For the next two weeks, it was physical exercises in the morning: running, swimming, evasive techniques, parachute jumping, hand-to-hand combat, and weapons training. These courses were usually taught in three months; however, there needed to be more time. The primary item was flying. Thus, more than half the daylight hours were used on flying techniques.

After the first two days, it became obvious that Herman and Karina had above-average skills. They were designated as the lead students.

In the evening, after a forty-five-minute dinner, the students assembled in the training room, and Herman and Karina would provide flying instructions. Initially, some of the older men (twenty-five to thirty) objected to having two of the youngest students give the instructions. Still, after the initial sessions and the actual demonstrations of flying the DP-3XA on the edge of its flying ability, the team quickly accepted their expertise and fell into line.

All the instructions and the actual flights performed by the students were essential lifesavers. The most daring and likely the one that would be very useful in a dogfight was the need to fully understand the plane's ability and the pilot's ability not to lose consciousness. First was the straight dive down toward earth; the pilots had to know when to pull up and miss the ground by tens of meters. This would be very useful to evade a German plane on your tail. The Second was knowing the turn radius; the tighter the turn, the better. This needed to be practiced at high altitudes as the turn taken at speeds of over 350 mph would produce blackouts. The key was knowing the speed and radius where the pilot was on the edge of not passing out. The third was a barrel roll, with quick downward and back-up acceleration. This would be needed to move from being the pursued to the pursuer.

In addition, the normal lessons of attacking from altitude with the sun behind your back were exercised in daylight. Nighttime attacks were also exercised, using the reflections from the moon. Reveille was at 6 a.m. and lights out at 11 p.m. The seventeen-hour days were packed with three hours of physical exercises in the morning and flight training at night. The days were long, and all nights were well spent resting and recharging both body and mind.

***

After two weeks of training with the Canadian Royal Air Force, sixteen pilots are ready to be flown to England. The pilots, including Herman and Karina, fly in a C-47 transport plane. The plane departs the Ottawa area with refueling stops in Newfoundland, Greenland, and Iceland. After a twenty-hour flight, the group arrives at a non-descript landing airfield in Scotland. Officers of the Royal Air Force are there to greet them with much enthusiasm. They are driven in four land rovers to billets on the base. Karina was shown to a Quonset hut serving as her temporary quarters. Herman and the men were led to a men's semi-permanent building, which had been used as a barn before the war. After one hour of washing up and changing clothes, the new arrivals are directed to a building used as the past Command Center.

After all sixteen pilots are seated, the briefing begins; Captain Ian Williamson addresses the recruits, "Gentlemen and lady, welcome to Scotland. My apologies for not allowing you more than one hour of rest. I am afraid that we do not have the privilege of time. Time is of the essence; we have been engaged in a battle to the death against the German Luftwaffe. We thank you for volunteering to provide us with assistance. Canadians are only one of many who have answered our call for help; other nationalities include personnel from outside the United Kingdom. Many of these volunteers are British subjects, thus, citizens from territories that comprised part of the British Empire. Additionally, a significant number are refugees and exiles from German-occupied and American emigrants. If there are Americans amongst you, I salute you for your bravery."

All the Canadian pilots understand that the two Americans have defied their government and, under penalty of imprisonment and heavy fines, have volunteered to assist England in a time of great need.

Captain Williamson continues, "As of today, we have had experienced pilots who have answered the call from Poland, France, Australia, New Zealand, South Africa, India, Mexico, the United States, and numerous other countries. Your number now exceeds 300 flyers and counting. Now, you likely want to know your training schedule. Tomorrow morning reveille is at 6 a.m. Breakfast at 6:30, Classroom at 7:30, and we intend to drive you to the air base at 9 a.m. You will be training on the Spitfire Camel Model XP-700A. Are there any questions?"

"Yes Sir, how long do we train on the Spitfires?"

"Two weeks."

"Will we be stationed in Scotland?"

"Due to security concerns, the locations are classified."

"Will the non-British flyers remain as a unit?"

"Yes, your Squadrons have been named the Eagle Squadrons."

"Do we know if we will be on bombing runs, escorts or seek and destroy the enemy aircraft?"

"The Command Center in London determines the actual mission. Herman, your mission will be in reaction to what the Luftwaffe does. If you have a direct line to Herr Hitler, you can ask him?" All of the pilot's laugh.

One of the pilots says, "If I get a hold of the bastard, I will arrange for a hunting trip and put a bullet between his eyes."

Captain, "Well, good to see that we are all in the fighting spirit."

The captain looks at Karina, "Young lady, I have seen your resume, which is quite impressive. After training at camp 1207, you will be driven to the Spitfire factory. There, you will bivouac, and with other women, you will be critical in flying the new Spitfires to the more than 100 bases throughout England."

"Thank you, Captain Williamson."

Chapter Eighteen
Herman Joins the Polish Squadron
Air Base, Outside of London

The day after their arrival, Captain Williamson addresses the arrivals. "Fellow Pilots welcome to Kirknewton Royal Air Force base. We are just east of Edinburgh, Scotland. We are out of the range of the Luftwaffe. This will be your home for seventeen days. After your training on the Spitfire, you will be assigned to one of the three Eagle Squadrons. The Eagle Squadrons are stationed in RAF Abbots Bromley, Binbrook, Fitwell, Kidlington, Lisset, and Kemble. Where you will be stationed will be based on need. The RAF will make that decision two days before your assignment."

Captain Williamson displays a map of the RAF bases.[20] "As you can see, we have many fighter bases. We also have bomber bases, but these still need to be shown; the initial three days will be classroom instruction on the theory of flight, radio communications, understanding Morse code, and engine design. Usually, these subjects are taught over months. We, however, do not have the time."

Williamson continues, "After the initial three days, the morning will be instructions on the Spitfire. Afternoons and evenings will be actual flight time on your Spitfires." One of the Canadian pilots raises his hand. "Yes, Sir, you have a question?" asks Williamson.

"Are the planes we will be training on also the planes we will be flying in combat?"

"Yes and no, the planes you will be flying will also be assigned to your unit. We do this for expediency; the pilot flies the plane to his designated airfield, thus saving precious time."

---

[20] Map of RAF Stations WWII, Wikipedia

"Gentlemen, may I introduce Sergeant Gilliam? He is an expert on radios and Manual Morse."

Gilliam, "Radios and the Manual Morse code will be your only connection to the world outside your cockpit. Next to your plane and fuel, they are the most important tools that you will have." Sergeant Gilliam explains the theory behind using the VHF and UHF radio bands. VHF is used to communicate with the base operations, and the UHF band is used for aircraft-to-aircraft communications. Sergeant Gilliam explains that all communications are encrypted; thus, the Germans cannot decrypt the communications."

RAF Fighter Bases

A pilot states, "Sir, I am a Ham radio operator, and I use Manual Morse. I don't think we can fly the plane and tap all the dots and dashes for manual Morse."

Sergeant Gilliam says, "You are correct. Manual Morse is not used when flying the plane. It is used when you are on the ground. I must be honest; some of you will be shot down in enemy territory. The chances of you surviving more than ten missions are only 60/40. Our foreign pilots, like yourselves, have a better ratio of 90/10. This means that after all of you have completed ten missions, one of you will not return. If you are shot down behind enemy lines, you will receive survival and evasion tactics to better your chances of returning home. Fortunately, we do have friends in Holland and France. If you are shot down over France, your chances are good that the Free French or the resistance fighters will find you first. They have underground networks to get you back through Spain if they do. After the initial three days of orientation, the real flying begins. Flying will take on a different aspect. It will become a matter of applying the knowledge of flying and the theory of flight to war processes. The theory needs to be applied to the Spitfire. Usually, the students gradually learned to apply the theory using trainer aircraft, but the Germans' war did not allow the time. Great Britain's and the world's fate depends on 'fighter pilots.' As students, you must learn what typically takes six months in two and one-half weeks."

Captain Williamson first took the podium and addressed the group. "This morning will be your initial flight instructions. First, you need to **learn all** the Spitfire's instruments, gauges, and controls. We have experienced Spitfire pilots; all have seen action in the war. They have volunteered to use their three-day leaves to provide flight orientation. After the three days, you will fly the Spitfire as a solo. Lieutenant Harrington will now explain your next three days."

Harrington, "After learning the cockpit instruments, you will sit in the back seat of a Spitfire, which has been modified as two-seaters. On the second day, we will learn to fly in close formations. Close formations need to be mastered. This is necessary to take our planes through the thick and dense cloud cover. The English coast, North Sea, Holland, and France have extreme weather conditions, and you will find yourselves flying through the dense fog and clouds. Second and equally important, the clouds can be your best friend or your most ardent foe. Clouds can be used to conceal **yourselves** from enemy aircraft, and they, in turn, conceal themselves from you. Flying in close formations offers protection and being able to fight without the tedious necessity of making a rendezvous over a featureless cloud mass."

"You will be trained to fly under a canvas hood to simulate dense fog or clouds such that you cannot see out and be forced to fly on instruments. It would help if you learned to trust your instruments. When flying in the clouds, you will easily lose your sense of direction. We have lost pilots due to the pilots believing in their instincts. Do not do this--- believe in your instruments. This will save your life."

After Lieutenant Harrington, Captain Bigelow took the podium; he briefed the group on high-altitude flying. "High-altitude flying will be a very revealing and difficult experience."

"The temperature in the atmosphere will drop by 3 degrees Fahrenheit for every thousand feet of altitude. Now, flying at four or five thousand feet or less means little, but the process is miserable and unwelcoming when the altitude is stretched to twenty thousand feet in an open cockpit with no heat. At this height, the temperature is 60 degrees below the temperature at sea level. So, flying in the North Sea with the sea level temperature at 40 degrees Fahrenheit, your temperature in the cockpit will be 20 degrees below zero. Adding to the miserable conditions will be the wind flying around your cockpit at upwards of 300 mph."

"During wartime operations, you must climb to altitudes of fifteen to twenty thousand feet. At these altitudes, the wind density will decrease; thus, your plane will gain the last thousand feet very slowly and painfully. Two-hour bombing trips into Germany and France are not unusual, and by the time you return, you will be very cold and dying for warmth."

After Captain Bigelow, Lieutenant Meriwether took the podium. Meriwether was the most RAF decorated pilot; he was only twenty-one years of age but had been through the RAF flight school and was one of the original Spitfire pilots from the onset of the Luftwaffe attacks. He had been credited with the first 'Kill' when his Spitfire had shot down a German Dornier Do-17 bomber. Lieutenant Meriwether had twelve confirmed 'Kills' and ten unconfirmed in two months.

As the Lieutenant came to the podium, the entire group listened intently. "I am going to discuss dogfighting, dive-bombing, and air-to-ground gunnery.

Dogfighting:

Lieutenant Meriwether now discusses dogfighting, "Without question, you will be involved in dogfights with the Germans. Two things are to your advantage: speed and surprise. Early in the war, the Germans were flying to the shores of England at high altitudes. They have since then learned of our radar. With radar, we could detect them when they left their bases in Holland and France. Now, they attacked at low altitudes to evade our radar. This has helped us; our intelligence service has collaborators in the occupied territories. Using covert communications, these spies transmit to us as the German planes are flying to our shores."

The Lieutenant continues, "Once Air Command has detected or been informed of the Germans' attack, we will scramble our Spitfires to attack the pending wave of German Bombers and Fighter planes. Our Air Controller will vector you to your attack position, and using the dive techniques, we attack the enemy from above. The Germans will have Pf-109 Messerschmitt's flying bomber protection. It is these planes that you will engage in dogfights. Your flying skills will be taken to the limits. Learn to shoot where the enemy will be, not where he is. Also, try and attack going downwind; the range of your bullets will double, while the guns from a tail gunner on the Heinkel's will be cut in half. Learn the barrel roll to become the hunter and not the hunted."

The Lieutenant clears his throat and continues, "When flying over enemy territory and you are shot down, bail out over Holland or France. In the next two weeks, you will memorize locations with passwords in these two countries. If members of the find you, they will arrange to move you through France and into Spain. From Spain, you can be shipped via sea vessel back to England. If at all possible, avoid parachuting in Germany. Currently, we have an unwritten agreement with the Germans. We treat their flyers humanely, and they reciprocate. In Germany, you will be taken to a POW camp. Once you are there, we will try for a prisoner exchange. However, by all means, do not get captured. If or when the war starts turning bad for them, there's no telling what they will do."

Dive Bombing:

Lieutenant Cornell stepped up to the podium and began, "Dive bombing is an intricate and potentially dangerous maneuver that demands precision. Approaching the target requires a gradual descent, typically between two to three thousand feet, depending on cloud cover. As you draw near, the aircraft's nose should be angled into a steep 45- to 50-degree dive, creating a sensation akin to a vertical 90-degree plunge. At this point, it feels like your stomach has been left behind at that initial altitude. The aircraft will rapidly gain speed, and you'll notice vibrations and protests from the plane itself. However, it's crucial to have faith in the aircraft's construction; it's designed to endure these intense vibrations. The plane will howl and shake, which can be quite unnerving. The art lies in firing the guns or releasing the bomb at the lowest point of the dive, then executing a timely pullout to avoid crashing into the ground. The closer you get to the target before releasing your payload, the better your chances of hitting it, increasing the risk of crashing.

Finding a sensible compromise is imperative. This exercise will reveal the temperament differences among all of you. Nervous pilots may pull out too high, while the reckless might go dangerously low. In your actual flight training, instructors will monitor your dives, starting at a safe altitude and gradually decreasing the distance to the target."

Lieutenant Meriwether, who had thoroughly reviewed the pilots' resumes, inquired, "I understand we have a stunt pilot among us. Is that correct?"

Herman, who had been keeping a low profile, responded, "Yes, Sir, that would be me."

"Could you share your simulated diving experience?"

Herman, a confident individual, came to life. "Certainly, Sir. I can provide valuable insights. I was initially trained on a Sopwith biplane by my uncle. Miss Solemn and I flew that plane for two years at the Albany Air Show. We even visited the Ryan Aeronautical Factory in San Diego and piloted the new experimental DT-13A aircraft, which shares flight characteristics with the Spitfire. I've since learned that many of the DT-13A's specifications influenced the Spitfire's design."

"Did you fly the DT-13A?"

"Yes, Sir, I logged over 800 hours of flight time in it, and Karina has over 500 hours."

"And did you perform dive-bombing simulations at the Air Show?"

"Yes, we did. The Air Show acquired two DT aircraft. During the shows, we simulated dive-bombing runs, which the audience enjoyed. Tommy and I, along with another Air Show pilot, often completed up to ten dive-bombing runs per day. We also simulated dogfights and executed aerial acrobatics over the crowd, including barrel rolls."

"Excellent. I'll inform your instructors to include these acrobatics in your training. They'll serve you well against the German Luftwaffe."

"One more thing, Sir."

"Yes, please go ahead."

"Trust your instruments without reservation. It doesn't matter what your instincts tell you. After a dive, you'll lose all sense of direction when you pull up and execute a double barrel roll. Consult your instrument panel and trust its readings. All my Air Show flights were in daylight, with clear skies and no rain or clouds. My uncle, a World War I biplane pilot, was my initial instructor. He also emphasized that 'the enemy has a say in things.' Be prepared, practice diligently, and anticipate your enemy's moves. Study and learn their tactics."

"Well said, Mr. Hutchinson. We'll be honored to have you join our ranks."

***

In August 1940, Herman was assigned to the Squadron 204, which had Polish and Czechoslovakian pilots. The Polish and Czech fighter pilots had fought bravely when the Germans invaded Poland. Still, the German Luftwaffe had overwhelmed the Polish Army and Air Force with superior weapons and more significant numbers. As the Polish government surrendered, over fifty pilots flew their Dewoitene fighter planes to France. After the fall of France in April of 1940, the Polish and Czech pilots again flew their aircraft to England and offered their services. These pilots were Godsend; they all had years of experience. After a few weeks, they mastered the Spitfire and Hurricane fighter planes.

When Herman joined Squadron 204, a Polish fighter named Alfons (Ski) Kowalski was an Ace fighter pilot. Ski had twelve confirmed killings and ten unconfirmed. Ski was a bit older than the young twenty-somethings; he was thirty-two but looked forty. He was slim, with red cheeks, and his hair was prematurely turning gray. He always wore a beaked cap, aviator jacket, and work boots that smelled of engine oil; if one did not know any better, a sane person would tag him as a greasy car mechanic. Although he did not look the part, there was no one better when it came to mechanical items, like car engines, water pumps, electric motors, and plane engines. But he was the best at flying fighter planes. He had a knack for flying fast aircraft. His knowledge and inherent aviation skills had allowed him to escape the German Luftwaffe in both Poland and France. He had bested the best German aces and was both feared and respected.

When he heard a young Canadian with air show experience was being assigned to the Squadron, he immediately sought the stunt pilot. Ski was always searching for new ways to fly his plane. He had seen films of the Air Shows in America and was looking forward to meeting this daring young man. Ski and Herman hit it off, and they were inseparable for the next four months.

Herman showed him all the Air Show aerobatics, but more importantly, Ski took Herman under his wing and taught Herman the German fighters' tactics. The Squadron Fight Commander saw the bonding between the two fliers and assigned them to the same missions.

Twice a month, Herman and Karina would visit each other. Ski then became a father figure, reminding Karina and Herman of their beloved Mr. Goodwin. Karina would spend hours with Herman and Ski watching the sunset and tell him of their home in the Rio Grande Valley. Ski would often ask, "Why are you here?" After Karina gets to know Ski, she finally confides in him that she has Jewish blood and that Herman and she are fighting for their people. After Karina's confession, Ski told Karina and Herman that he also was a Jew.

Ski, "The things that Hitler and his thugs are doing in Poland are atrocious. These Germans are hideous people. I witnessed the killing of women and children being killed point-blank just because they were Jews."

Karina, "Is it true that the Jews are being herded into ghettos and being starved to death?"

"Yes, the city of Warsaw has been destroyed by the Nazi Luftwaffe. I tried to shoot down as many of these bastards as possible, but they were like a swarm of angry bees. One week before Poland surrendered, I had made plans to fly my family out of Poland on a Westland Lysander Aircraft. After ten hours of fighting on my French Dewoitene D-250 aircraft, I gathered my family, my wife Helene, and my two children. I had a small house on Warsaw's outskirts, and I felt they would be safe there. But the German Wehrmacht advanced more quickly than I had anticipated. When I was one kilometer from my home, I saw the smoke billowing from my home. When I got home, there was nothing but ashes, burnt wood, and a collapsed roof. A passing neighbor in tattered rags and swollen-teary eyes came up to me and said, "Your family was burned alive. They chained the front door and boarded the windows and back door. Then they set fire to the house."

"Do you know which regiment of the Nazi Army did this?"

"No, all I know is that they were wearing black uniforms, had lightning bolts on their lapels, and wore jackboots. I hope that they all burn in hell!"

"Do you know what became of the bodies?"

"Yes, yesterday three young men from the came by and carried the bodies out. I could tell that one was grown and the other two were smaller. I assume that those were the bodies of your wife and children. I asked him where they had been taken; the older man said over the hill and to the valley of the butterflies. There they would be buried."

"I thanked the old man and told him that I was flying my plane to France and continuing the fight, so you see, I am fighting for my family, Poland, and the free world."

By September 1940, Herman had completed over twenty missions with the 204 Squadron. He had six confirmed kills and four unconfirmed. His expert knowledge, which he had acquired when flying in the Albany Flying Circus, served him well. Herman, Ski, and the other fliers had established a lifetime bond when fighting the German warplanes and waiting outside the Quonset Huts for the call to man their Spitfires and intercept the incoming German bombers.

Chapter Nineteen
State of the Union, 1940-41
Washington D.C.

From September 1939 to June 1940, the nations of Europe were engaged in World War II. Germany had successfully conquered Poland, Norway, Belgium, Holland, and France. Only Great Britain remained to be conquered. The general world consensus was that it was only a matter of time before Great Britain would also fall to Nazi Germany. In the United States, there was a strong movement to remain neutral. Most of the American public wanted no intervention in the European wars. Roosevelt had a difficult situation to manage. The 1940 elections were in five months, and he had to thread a needle not to antagonize the American population to turn against him. He had to manage the situation until after the election expertly. The President had managed to supply small arms, weapons, and war material to Great Britain through Canada. Still, the destroyers that Britain desperately needed were being blocked by powerful Congressmen who were strong isolationists.

The article appeared in the Atlantic Magazine in 2018. The following events of 1940 were written. "On the evening of Sunday, May 26, 1940, days after the Germans successfully conquered mainland Europe, Roosevelt delivered the dire events in Europe. In his speech, Roosevelt explained that the greatest threat was from within. He explained that the threat to the nation came in different sizes and shapes. One group constituted a Trojan horse of pro-German spies, saboteurs, and traitors. While not naming names, he singled out those who sought to arouse people's "hatred" and "prejudices" by resorting to "false slogans and emotional appeals." These fifth columnists sought to "divide and weaken us in the face of danger," Roosevelt declared, "We must deal with them vigorously."

This first group included the German Nazi groups who were now active in spreading German propaganda, such as the BUND (German American Federation) in several eastern cities of the U.S. This group organized mass demonstrations with the primary objective of creating favorable policies toward Nazi Germany. These organizations were a threat in plain sight. Parades were held in a number of the major cities of the U.S., such as New York, Philadelphia, and Chicago. Charles Lindbergh was a supporter of these Nazi groups. He would give speeches often denouncing the policies of President Roosevelt. The leaders of the BUND would often call the President "Mr. Rosenstein."

The second group was the isolationists; included in this group was Charles Lindbergh, who was openly supporting Nazi Germany. The President explained that a certain number of individuals opposed his administration's policies simply for the sake of opposition -- even when the nation's security stood at

Lindbergh with Herman Goring

risk. The President recognized that some isolationists were earnest in their beliefs and acted in good faith. Some were afraid to face a dark and foreboding reality. Others were gullible, eager to accept what some told them of their fellow Americans, that what was happening in Europe was "none of our business." These "cheerful idiots," as he would later call them in public, naively bought into the fantasy that the United States could continuously pursue its peaceful and unique course in the world."

"They "honestly and sincerely" believed that the many hundreds of miles of saltwater would protect the nation from the nightmare of brutality and violence gripping much of the rest of the world. It might have been a comforting dream for FDR's "shrimps." FDR called people without a backbone "Shrimps." The President argued that the isolationists of the nation were dreaming that the United States was in a safe oasis in a world dominated by fascist terror. The overwhelming majority of Americans were not dreaming of a beautiful world but a "nightmare" of a people without freedom -- the nightmare of a people lodged in prison, handcuffed, hungry, and fed through the bars of a jail.

Two weeks after that fireside chat, on June 10, 1940, Roosevelt gave another key address about American foreign policy. This time, it was in the Memorial Gymnasium of the University of Virginia in Charlottesville to an audience that included his son Franklin, Jr., who was graduating from the Virginia Law School. That same day, the President received word that Italy would declare war on France and was sending four hundred thousand troops to invade the French Mediterranean coast. In his talk, FDR deplored the "gods of force and hate" and denounced the treacherous Mussolini. "On this tenth day of June 1940," he declared, "the hand that held the dagger has plunged it into the back of its neighbor."

"But more than a denunciation of Mussolini's treachery and double-dealing, the speech finally stated American policy. It was time to "proclaim certain truths," the President said. Military and naval victories for the "gods of force and hate" would endanger all democracies in the western world. In this time of crisis, America could no longer pretend to be "a lone island in a world of force." Indeed, the nation could no longer cling to the fiction of neutrality. "Our sympathies lie with those nations giving their lifeblood in combat against these forces."

Then, the President outlined his policy. America was simultaneously pursuing two courses of action. First, it was extending to the democratic Allies all the material resources of the nation; and second, it was speeding up war production at home so that America would have the equipment and workers equal to the task of any emergency and every defense." There would be no slowdowns and no detours. Everything called for speed, "full speed ahead!" Concluding his remarks, he summoned, as he had in 1933, when he first took the oath of office, Americans' "effort, courage, sacrifice, and devotion."

It was a "fighting speech," wrote *Time* magazine, "more powerful and more determined" than any the president had yet delivered about the war in Europe. But the reality was actually more complicated.

On the one hand, the President had taken sides in the European conflict. No more illusions of "neutrality." And he had delivered a straightforward statement of the course of action he would pursue. On the other hand, he was not free to make policy unilaterally; he still had to contend with isolationists in Congress. On June 10, the day of his Charlottesville talk, with Germans about to cross the Marne southeast of Paris, it was clear that the French capital would soon fall. France's desperate Prime Minister, Paul Reynaud, asked Roosevelt to declare publicly that the United States would support the Allies "by all means short of an expeditionary force." But Roosevelt declined. He sent only a message of support labeled "secret" to Reynaud. In a letter to Winston Churchill, he explained that "in no sense" was he prepared to commit the American government to "military participation in support of the Allied governments." Only Congress, he added, had the authority to make such a commitment."

"We all listened to you last night," Churchill wired the President the day after the Charlottesville address, pleading, as he had done earlier in May, for more arms and equipment from America and paring down his request for destroyers from "forty or fifty" to "thirty or forty."

"Nothing is so important," he wrote. In answer to Churchill's urgent appeal, the President arranged to send what he cleverly called "surplus" military equipment to Great Britain. Twelve ships sailed for Britain, loaded with seventy thousand tons of bomber planes, rifles, tanks, machine guns, and ammunition-- but no destroyers were included in the deal. Sending destroyers would be an act of war, claimed Senator David Walsh of Massachusetts, the isolationist Chairman of the Senate Naval Affairs Committee. Walsh also discovered the President's plan to send twenty torpedo boats to Britain. Flying into a rage, he threatened legislation to prohibit such arms sales. Roosevelt backed down -- temporarily -- and called off the torpedo boat deal.

Adding to the President's troubles was the glamorous public face and articulate voice of the isolationist movement of the charismatic and courageous Charles Lindbergh. His solo flight across the Atlantic in May 1927 had catapulted the lanky, boyish, 25-year-old pilot onto the world stage. "Well, I made it," he said with a modest smile upon landing at Le Bourget airfield in Paris, as thousands of delirious French men and women broke through military and police lines and rushed toward his small plane. When he returned to New York two weeks later, flotillas of boats in the harbor, a squadron of twenty-one airplanes in the sky, and four million people roaring "Lindy! Lindy!" turned out to honor him in a joy-mad city, draped in flags and drenched in confetti and ticker tape. "No conqueror in the history of the world," wrote one newspaper, "ever received a welcome such as was accorded Colonel Charles A. Lindbergh yesterday."

On May 19, 1940, a week before the President gave his fireside chat denouncing isolationists and outlining plans to build up American defenses, Lindbergh made the isolationist case in his radio address. The United States was not in danger from a foreign invasion unless "American people bring it on" by meddling in the affairs of foreign countries. The only danger to America, the flier insisted, was an "internal" one.

"I am absolutely convinced that Lindbergh is a Nazi," FDR said melodramatically to his secretary of the treasury and old Dutchess County neighbor and friend, Henry Morgenthau, in May 1940, two days after Lindbergh's May 19 speech. "If I should die tomorrow, I want you to know this." The President lamented that the 38-year-old flier "has completely abandoned his belief in our form of government and has accepted Nazi methods because apparently, they are efficient."

Others in the White House shared that assessment. Lindbergh, Harold Ickes sneered, pretentiously posed as a "heavy thinker" but never uttered "a word for democracy itself." The aviator was the "Number one Nazi fellow traveler," Ickes said. The delighted German embassy wholeheartedly agreed. "What Lindbergh proclaims with great courage," wrote the German military attaché to his home office in Berlin, "is certainly the highest and most effective form of propaganda." In other words, why would Germany need a fifth column in the United States when it had the nation's hero, Charles Lindbergh in its camp?[21]

---

[21] 1940: FDR, Willkie, Lindbergh, Hitler--The Election amid the Storm, by Susan Dunn, published by Yale University Press, 2013.

Chapter Twenty
Covert Transmitters
MIT Labs

Andrew (Andrés) Valencia, Francisco (Chico) Vargas, and Juliette Santiago had completed their counterespionage assignment on the New Jersey *Bund*. They were now to report to Milton Hall, Scotland, to receive advanced commando tactics. On the way to Scotland, they were ordered to visit the MIT laboratories in Boston, Massachusetts. The three were to inspect and report to the OIC the status of the advanced HF radio transmitters. These transmitters were classified as surplus radio equipment; thus, they were destined to be shipped to the British to assist with the war against Germany.

Colonel Moore from the Quartermaster Corps and Colonel Rubenstein from the Office of Information Communications (OIC) had decided that electronic technicians would need to be sent to England to instruct the English on using the new advanced communications equipment. Dr. Peter J. Fry invented the communications system from the Massachusetts Institute of Technology (MIT).

Dr. Fry was a 1931 immigrant from Poland. He wanted to immigrate to a country where he could continue his research in radio communications. Dr. Fry was fifty-one years of age and even six feet tall, but he looked taller based on his small frame. He weighed only one hundred and fifty pounds and had a slim body. He had a pointed head and was prematurely bald. He had long, curly hair that circled his bald head. The bald head and the curly hair appeared like a bird nest on his head. He always wore a white smock and wore open-toed sandals. His only purpose in life was radio communications. Underneath his smock, he always wore denims and a white t-shirt. Wearing the smock relieved him from making a decision about what to wear on any given day. He said that he had more important things in life to him and the world. He ate and drank radio communications.

In late 1939, after the Germans had invaded Poland, Colonel Burkhead from the New York British consulate visited Dr. Fry. At first, the Doctor did not want to be disturbed, but after he was told that the Brits needed his help with the war against the Germans, he readily accepted.

Colonel Burkhead, "Dr. Fry, we need your help in radio communications."

"Yes, of course; what is it that you need?"

"We are at war with the Germans. Germany has conquered Norway, Holland, and Belgium and will soon overrun France. Many resistance fighters in the countries used guerrilla tactics against the Germans. We are starting a program to arm these freedom fighters and need a method to communicate with these resistance cells. We do have short-wave radios that we can parachute to these resistance fighters. However, based on our intelligence, the Germans have state-of-the-art direction-finding equipment. We need some method where these resistance fighters can communicate with us and not be DF'd."

The Doctor goes into deep thought, rubs his chin, and walks around his laboratory. He thinks and says, Hmmmm----yes, yes, I see the problem. Give me two days, and let me know what I can design. Please give me your address and how I can contact you."

Colonel Burkhead writes down his address in New York and a phone number on a paper sheet and hands it to Dr. Fry.

The Doctor looks at the sheet of paper and says, "No, No----you need an address here in Boston. I may have the design for your solution by tomorrow."

"Yes, Sir, I will make arrangements for a hotel here in Boston. I will call your assistant and let him know where I am staying."

"That's better; now I have work to do."

On the morning of the second day, Colonel Burkhead was contacted by a courier. The message read, "Come by my laboratory today at 1300." The Colonel felt a rush of confidence that the wily old Dr. Fry had a solution to the comms problem. The Colonel entered the Doctor's laboratory promptly at 1300 hours. As usual, Dr. Fry wore his white smock, thick Coke bottle glasses, and disheveled hair. When he heard the knock on his laboratory door, he shouted, "Please enter, Colonel." He had been around the military for years and was grateful they were always punctual. He likes punctuality----and not wasting time.

The Colonel opened the door and stepped into the laboratory, "Hopefully, you have some good news."

"Yes, of course, I have some design plans. I can have a working prototype in ten to fourteen days if you approve. First, we must describe the problem and then apply a solution. The problem is that the Germans use their newest radio direction finding (DF) equipment to locate the transmitters. The solution is simple, but implementation is complicated. The Germans need at least two DF locations to have a good transmitter location. However, it is best to have three. The DF equipment must first intercept the transmit frequency and point to the directional antenna or antennas to achieve maximum signal strength. The direction of maximum signal strength becomes a vector on the map. The three vectors are plotted on the map using the vectors from the three-intercept stations. Where the vectors intercept is where the transmitter is located."

The Colonel remains silent; he knows the theory of DF, but he needs a solution. Hopefully, the solution is coming. No sooner does he think about a solution when the Doctor speaks, "The solution is not to let those bastard Germans intercept the RF frequency or at least make it difficult. Colonel, I will dispense with the physics behind radio HF communications using the Earth's ionosphere. Suffice it to say that radio waves at certain frequencies bounce between the Earth's ionosphere and the ground, thus achieving long distances. Some frequencies are better than others at certain times of the day and night. Here comes our solution: first, the transmitter's frequency will change at a predetermined time interval and select different frequencies every three to five minutes. Second, make the transmissions as short as possible, using short bursts of communications."

"How is that possible? The operator uses Manual Morse coding, and as we know, that takes time to transmit a message. Tapping the dots and dashes takes time to transmit the message."

"Excellent, Colonel, but you need to understand the problem before applying a solution. This is where I can be of great help. Let us move over to my blackboard. I will describe the implementation using my drawing. You will also see mathematical equations; these you can ignore. They are how the

172

solution is applied, but we need only to concentrate on the physical implementation."

The two move over to the blackboard, and the Colonel sees that the three blackboards are covered, withdrawing, and mathematical equations.

The Doctor begins the lecture; he points to some drawings on the blackboard and says, "The operator will first transmit in code the time sequence and frequencies to be used. The receiving location will automatically switch to these frequencies at the designated times. All of the switching will be done automatically by an electrical box that I will design."

The professor uses his pointer to some drawings and mathematical equations at the far end of the blackboard. "This alone will defeat the Germans, but knowing the Boche, sooner or later, they may figure out what we are doing. So, we add a second element to obfuscate the transmission. The transmissions will be in short, condensed packets. I have designed an electrical circuit for both the transmitter and receiver. The transmitter operator will first prepare his transmission offline."

The Doctor continues, "Recently, an entertainment company in England manufactured discs that had the property to record simple things like dots. The length of the dots can be controlled to signify a dot or a dash. Using this technique, the operator can prepare his transmission on the aluminum discs. He would then transmit the message in bursts. The shifting frequency and the burst transmission will make it extremely difficult to DF the transmitter location."

The Colonel thinks about the proposed solution and says, "In theory, that all sounds very good, but I see two problems with the solution: first, how does the operator know what set of frequencies to use, and second, in a combat situation, the operator will not have time to pre-record the message."

"Yes, you bring up excellent points; knowledgeable operators can only solve the first problem. Most operators using the HF spectrum know what frequency to use based on their location, the receiving station's location, and the time of day. To aid in the solution to this problem, I will prepare a reference handbook. The handbook can be used when training the operators. The second problem is ideal for a command post, where the operator has the time to prepare the aluminum disc cards. Frankly, the first solution will solve the problem. If the transmitter shifts frequencies every two or three minutes, the DF equipment will have problems with two or three sites intercepting and coordinating the intercepted vectors."

Colonel Burkhead is satisfied with the solution; he asks, "How soon can we have a prototype?"

The Doctor answers, "I have already made a list of the required parts. The time will depend on your ability to acquire these electrical parts. I have purposely used known components that are used in radio and vehicle electrical manufacturers. When you deliver these components, my laboratory assistants and I will work twenty-four hours daily to build and test the devices. It will likely take two days to build the prototypes, and we can test them immediately after the black boxes are ready. So, my best estimate is seven to ten days, depending on us receiving the components."

"Excellent; I will begin immediately to order the parts. I will have some of my technicians deliver the parts. The three technicians delivering the parts are trained operators with technical backgrounds. They will likely be reassigned to the operating theater and will train the field agents."

"Very good; I suggest you start immediately to locate and order the required components."

After days, all required components are delivered to Dr. Fry. By the ninth day, the systems are ready for testing. On the morning of the tenth day, Andrew (Andrés) Valencia, Francisco (Chico) Vargas, and Juliette Santiago arrive by train from Ogden, Utah. Accompanying the three is Colonel Burkhead. The Colonel introduces Andrés, Francisco, and Juliette.

The Colonel assures the Doctor that the three operatives have clearances and are experienced field operators. The Doctor thinks I will soon find out if they are some nit-wicks. Dr. Fry explains, "High Frequency (HF) radio waves provide long-distance communications using the ionosphere's properties. The technicians assigned to me for the research and testing need above-average radio communications knowledge."

Yes, yes, of course, the three technicians all have a good understanding of radio comms."

Before Francisco, Andrés, and Juliette meet with Dr. Fry, Colonel Burkhead gives the three a quick description of the Doctor. He tells them that he has an eccentric and peculiar personality. He is like an absent-minded professor but brilliant in all scientific and technical fields. He is an expert when it comes to RF communications. As a teenager in Poland, he built his own HF radio systems and was one of the Ham Radio Amateur Club founders. He will like you if you are into the scientific and technical areas. If he thinks you are interested, he will quickly fall into his professor mode and talk all night if you allow him. The best way to communicate with him is to be inquisitive. He says, "The only dumb question is one not asked."

After listening to the Colonel describe the "Professor," they feel like they already know him.

The Colonel and the three techs walk into Dr. Fry's laboratory early on a Monday. As always, the professor is wearing his white smock. For a man with a slim frame, he has a bullfrog's voice, "Welcome to my laboratory; please take a seat on these bench stools. Colonel, could you please introduce your technicians?"

"Yes, of course," the Colonel introduces, "Francisco Vargas, Andrés Valencia, and Juliette Santiago."

After some small talk, the group gets down to testing the covert HF communications. Dr. Fry explains the theory regarding frequency hopping and burst transmission. The Doctor starts a dissertation and lecture on the theory of HF communications using the ionosphere. He explains the reason that HF may be used for long-distance communications. HF frequencies bounce from the Earth to the ionosphere and back to Earth, thus traveling long distances. As he explains, Francisco raises his hands, "Sir, I have a question?'

"Yes, of course, ah, Francisco, right? What is it?"

"Thank you, Sir; you said that the signals bounce off the ionosphere. If I remember my radio propagation theory, they bounce off the Earth's surface but are bent or refracted by the ionosphere.

"*Bravo maestro!* You are quite correct."

The professor thinks for a few seconds and asks his assistant questions. Colonel Burkhead told me that you were all quite knowledgeable regarding RF communications. You should tell me a little about yourselves and your background in RF communications.

"Yes, Sir, answers Andrés. When the Quarter Master Corps recruited us, it was because we all had a technical background. I have a background in

HF radios. I have a Ham radio license and fly small planes as a hobby; thus, I know plane engines."

Francisco says, "Sir, I also have a Ham Radio license. You might say that we are 'Radiohead.' I have been rebuilding car engines for years. I rebuilt an old model-T Ford in El Paso when I was twelve and drove it throughout the city. I also helped my uncle Amador with plumbing, carpentry, roofing, and electrical circuits and worked as a general-purpose handyman."

Juliette followed Francisco, "I am not a licensed Ham, but my father in Venezuela had a small shop selling and repairing radios. He taught me everything about how the radio worked and how to determine the best frequencies for long-distance communications. I often sat for hours talking to strangers in Australia, Germany, England, America, and Russia."

Francisco says, "Also, when we had basic training in Ogden, we all specialized in radio communications; thus, we all had to learn manual Morse."

After learning his assistants' qualifications, the lecture/discussions of the theory of HF communications proceeded very rapidly. The main thing that the professor needs to teach the assistants is how to decide on what frequencies to use depending on the conditions of the ionosphere. The ionosphere properties will change depending on the weather, time of day, the direction of the radio wave, transmission over land or water, and other variables.

The professor needs to ensure that his assistants understand the theory behind the ability to have HF long-distance communications. With a full understanding, his covert methods communications obfuscation will work. He asks Francisco, "Can you explain the layers of the ionosphere?"

"Yes, Sir, there are three layers, the D, E, and F layers."

"Very good. what is the difference, and how does each affect the radio waves?"

"Sir, the first region, known as the D region, affects the low frequencies below 5 megacycles. These frequencies are used when communicating short distances. For example, from Boston to Hartford." The second region is known as the E region. This region of the ionosphere will affect frequencies between 5 to 20 megacycles and is the area that will be the most used. Frequencies in this range would be used to communicate with New York. Philadelphia or Baltimore. The third region is the F region. A person would use frequencies above 20 megacycles to communicate with Denver or Los Angeles."

The professor asked, "If we can communicate with these far distances, why do we need more transmitter power for this long-haul communication? Can anyone tell me the reason?"

"Yes, sir, I believe I can," said Juliette. As the radio wave travels through the ionosphere, two things happen. One is attenuation, and the second is the dispersal and diffusion of the energy in the radio wave. As the radio wave travels through the trough created by the Earth's surface and the ionosphere, the radio wave's energy is slowly reduced."

The professor now strongly emphasizes the skip distance and the skip zone. He says, "These will be very important when determining what frequencies to use. You must learn how to calculate the following."

"The skip distance for a signal using HF propagation via the ionosphere is the distance on the Earth's surface between the point where radio signals from a transmitter, transmitted to the ionosphere, and refracted downwards by the ionosphere, to the point where they return to earth and are received."

The professor continues, "When signals are transmitted in the HF spectrum, they will only extend for a small radius around the transmitter via the ground wave. Beyond this, they are not audible until the sky wave is returned to Earth. The skip zone or silent zone is a layer where a radio transmission cannot be received. The zone is located between layers covered by the ground wave and where the sky-wave first returns to Earth."

The professor then says, "The key aspect of HF propagation is to use the right frequency. It may be possible for propagation to enable communications to exist within one area but not another. Because the higher frequency signals can pass through the lower layers, signals on different frequencies will travel different distances. As the higher frequencies tend to be reflected by higher layers, these can reach much greater distances due to the geometry."

In summary, the professor asks each of his assistants. "Why it will be essential to calculate the proper frequencies, type of antenna, and time to transmit.

Andrés answers the question for the group. "Sir, the operators will be functioning in enemy territory. They will need to get it right first and get out of there before the bastards can DF them. It is a matter of life or death."

"Very good; now let's put the theory to work in the field." Dr. Fry now explains the 'black boxes' which he has designed. "First, you must consult this manual which I have written. Based on the time of day, the year's season, and the distance between the transmitter and receiver sites, this will tell you what frequency to use. You determine the appropriate frequency range after you turn to the pages that refer to your frequency parameters."

"Next, you decide the number of different transmit frequencies and the times to switch frequencies. Do not make your switching times greater than five minutes. You do not want the Boche to DF your transmitter. Enter the frequencies and switching time in the 'black box.'"

For this to work, you must have a predetermined coding system. Our predetermined coding system will be the book "The Count of Monte Cristo." The preamble in our message will be CMC-12-3-2. This will indicate the book, chapter, paragraph, and beginning sentence. The primary key is the book; thus, the CMC might be a number, for example, 1, 2, or 3. These are the books that the sender and receiver have pre-arranged. For example, book number one would be "*The Count of Monte Cristo*, book two, "*The Tale of Two Cities*," and so forth."

Next, the professor says, "The black box will convert your message to the manual Morse dots and dashes. This black box will record the dots and dashes on this aluminum disc. The good thing is that the manufacturer of this disc is the **Amusement Equipment Company Ltd of Wembley, England.** Your command in England should be able to get you a stack of discs. If they can parachute in weapons, they should be able to send the disc. However, switching frequencies is the most important of the methods not to be located."

"For our field testing, we will begin with three frequencies, two discs per frequency, and switch time to be two minutes; thus, a normal thirty-minute manual Morse message will be transmitted in six minutes using three different frequencies. Remember to code the frequencies used in the setup message's initial preamble. This will be a burst transmission of less than one second; thus, DF'ing the frequencies and switch times is impossible," says the professor.

On the weekend of the first week, the team prepares for the field testing. Juliette stays in Boston. Francisco travels to New York, and Andrés travels to Philadelphia. Francisco and Andrés are using the work vans from MIT and have worked overall with the MIT letters on the back of the overalls. They also have business cards identifying them as employees of MIT. When testing the comms, the professor instructs Francisco and Andrés to park the vans in roadside parks. Do not try to hide from the public but try not to cause any undue attention. The testing will all be conducted from inside the van, with only a small wire antenna strung across the top.

By Monday of the second week, Francisco stops outside of New York City in Westchester County, and Andre stops outside of Philadelphia in a roadside park in Chester, Pennsylvania. Both consult their frequency manual prepared by Dr. Fry and conduct successful tests at different times of the day. After testing in New York and Philadelphia, Francisco travels to Pittsburgh, and Andrés travels to Cincinnati. Again, the tests are conducted at different times of the day, and all tests are successful.

By the end of the second week, Francisco and Andrés return to Boston; Colonel Burkhead is present for the debrief. Francisco gives the debrief, "Sir, all tests were successful. We now can communicate with our operatives in the field, with the Germans unlikely to find our transmissions."

Colonel Burkhead looks at the professor, "Well done, when we can have fifty of the transmitters and receivers?"

"I have provided your team with a complete bill of materials and instructions. Once the materials are obtained and technicians are trained. One system consists of a transmitter and receiver and may be built in less than four hours."

"Thank you very much. These HF communications systems will be of great value in our war against the Nazis."

Immediately upon the four leaving the MIT laboratory, all materials are ordered for building the fifty HF comms systems. The materials will be delivered to the Quarter Master facility in New York. There, they will be assembled and shipped directly to Milton Hall, Scotland.

Chapter Twenty-One
Herman Returns
Plymouth, England

The HMS George Patmore arrived in Plymouth, England, two days after Armand (Herman) and Tommy's rescue. As is the case with all military operations, a debrief is performed. Heronimo (Herman) Hutchinson's debrief has attracted the interest of the highest officers in MI5 and MI6. Colonel Susan Mildred Phillips is the officer in charge of developing a counterintelligence network in occupied France. Colonel Phillips had been assigned to the British Embassy in Canada and was responsible for recruiting Canadian citizens who spoke French for Germany's war effort.

The debrief of Herman and Tommy will consist of two parts. Part One is for the benefit of the RAF. Part Two will be regarding the French resistance. Colonel Phillips knows Herman from when she assisted with his border crossing from the United States to Canada.

HMS Patmore Returns to Plymouth

Herman and Tommy arrive at the large naval base and are given separate quarters with proper RAF uniforms and civilian clothing.

Their escort informs them, "Sirs, Colonels Phillips and Harr will see you in one hour. Please change into your RAF uniforms. I will return and escort you to the conference room for your debriefing."

Herman, "Thanks, Sergeant."

At precisely one hour, the Sergeant returns and escorts Herman and Tommy to a conference room.

"Please, Sirs, take a seat. Colonels Philipps and Harr will be here shortly."

Herman wonders if Colonel Phillips is the same Colonel Phillips he met in Canada. After waiting in the Conference room, he has his answer. Colonel Phillips walks in and says, "Lieutenant Hutchinson, it's a real pleasure to see you again!"

"Likewise, Colonel Phillips."

Colonel Harr, the Commander of the Polish Squadron 204, "Lieutenant Hutchinson, a job well done on the German bombers, and most happy to see you back in England."

"Sir, it's good to be back."

"Before you ask, we have informed your fiancé, Karina, that you are now safe and back on English soil. As soon as we complete the debriefing, you will be sent to the hospital to ensure that you do not have any permanent injuries, and then Karina will be welcome to see you."

"Thank you, Sir."

Lieutenant McGuire, "Your parents have been informed of your safe return; likewise, they will be able to visit you at the hospital."

"Thank you, Sir."

"We will begin with the air battles and your need to parachute into the English sea. We begin with Lieutenant Hutchison. Your Air Wing will conduct Lieutenant McGuire, your debriefing after we complete the resistance debriefings today."

After Colonel Harr had provided an overview of the proceedings, Captain Alfons Kowalski was requested to participate in the air battle debriefing. As soon as Captain Kowalski entered the room, there were handshakes and bear hugs, "Karina knows that you are being debriefed, and as soon as we complete the formalities, she will join us."

"Thank you, Captain Ski."

Colonel Harr, "Lieutenant Hutchinson, can you describe in detail your encounter with the German Luftwaffe and what precautions and new tactics we should take to prevent the loss of our pilots and planes."

Herman describes the shooting down of the Heinkel-He 111 bombers and the Messerschmitt. He explains how the second bomber shot him down and that one of the bomber guns ruptured the gas tank on his Spitfire.

Herman recognized that he had been shot down due to his fuel meter, indicating the loss of fuel, and therefore made a quick decision to fly to the designated zone, where the fishermen had retrieved English pilots.

"Is there anything you may have done differently that would have prevented the Heinkel's gun from hitting your plane?"

"Yes, two things. One, a faster plane, and two, if there is some way of knowing the wind direction, that would be extremely useful. If we do figure out how to give the pilot the direction of the wind on a real-time basis, this would extend our bullets' range and decrease the range of the German planes."

Colonel Phillips, "Do you not know the wind direction when you first engage the enemy?"

"Yes, but once the battle starts, you lose all sense of direction. Only with the instruments do we know the aircraft's position relative to the earth."

The debriefing continues, analyzing the aircraft performance and safety measures that could be improved. Colonel Harr, again, thanks Herman and Tommy for their service to the King. He then turns to Colonel Phillips and says, "Colonel Phillips, Captain Kowalski, and I will depart so that you may continue debriefing on the French resistance."

The French Resistance:

Colonel Susan Mildred Phillips was a decorated veteran of the British Intelligence Service. Her mother was French, and her father was in the British diplomatic service. Colonel Phillips was born in Paris when her father served as the British ambassador to France. She attended International Schools and learned French and German early; thus, she was fluent in both languages. In 1930, Colonel Phillips joined the British Army and attended the Army War College where she specialized in Intelligence. In the early 1930s, she was assigned to the English colonies in Africa. In 1935, she was appointed as the military attaché at the British Embassy in Berlin. When the war broke out in September of 1939, the British Embassy closed, and she received a new assignment in Canada. Her position was vital, as the British needed all Commonwealth countries to join in the fight against Germany. Upon the surrender of France, Colonel Philips was assigned to build and assist the resistance network in France.

In the mid to late 1940s, the office of Special Operations Executive (SOE) was assigned the responsibility of assisting the French resistance with the obstruct of the German war production in France. The idea was to harass and disrupt the supply of materials being moved to counter any allies' attack along the Atlantic or Mediterranean coasts. The SOE encouraged the French Civil Administrative clerical staff to slow down normal tasks such as driving and building permits, electrical and water bills, marriage licenses, medical appointments, judicial proceedings, and other functions of the government. The SOE encouraged that in all of these civil administrative issues there be a requirement to dot every "i" and cross every "t" and to flood the local governments in red tape. The SOE did not have the eyes and ears that it would need to direct the resistance's activities. The resistance required organization. It would need to communicate amongst themselves and with the SOE. The SOE would need to provide the means to achieve these objectives. This could only be accomplished by providing the equipment and the financial resources.

Lieutenant Herman Hutchinson's being shot down and his subsequent rescue was a God-sent opportunity that could be used to create a window of opportunity through his contacts. Colonel Phillips was anxious to begin her debriefing on both Lieutenants Hutchinson and McGuire.

Colonel Philips, "Lt. Hutchinson and McGuire, how were you introduced to the French resistance?

Herman, "We were both picked up by a fisherman from Cherbourg."

"How did he hide you in his boat?"

"Under a stack of fish."

"Did the German shore patrol search the boat?"

"No, apparently, the Germans think that his loyalty is strictly to the German occupation of France. Had I not witnessed him shooting a German pilot and dropping him in the sea, I would have thought he was a German collaborator. He is an outstanding actor. When he is with the Germans, one would think that he is Hitler's lapdog."

Tommy, "Yes, he is a great actor. He fished out a German pilot and kept him unconscious during our rescue. When arriving at the port, he turned the German pilot into the Shore Police. The Shore Police thanked him and said he was a hero of the Third Reich. This was a diversion to keep the Police

from searching his boat. In the evening, we were transferred to a horse-drawn wagon. This is how we were transported to a convent."
Now, Colonel Phillip's interest is really piqued.

She asks, "Do we know who runs the convent?"

Herman, "It is run by Sister Patricia."

"Was she the one that drove the horse-drawn wagon?

"No, it was a woman who goes by the name *"Papillon."* Based on my high school French, it means Butterfly."

"What do we know about *Papillon*?"

"Most I can tell is that she works in the office of the *Kriminaldirecktor.*"

"But she is French?"

"Yes, she was the one that coordinated all of the movements."

"Herman, don't forget *El Renard* and *Marcin*," says Tommy.

"Tommy calls Marcin 'The Wolf," he has the personality of a wolf on the prowl. He has a deep hatred of the Germans. When he speaks of the Germans, he refers to them as animals. They deserve to be shot like a dog with rabies!" says Herman.

"Interesting tell me more about the "Fox' and the 'Wolf',"' says Colonel Phillips.

Herman continues, "El Renard and Marcin are with the resistance. They were away for two or three weeks before we had the arrangements made to travel south to Bordeaux. They run one of the resistance networks. We only touched base with them when we first arrived at the convent and then left for Bordeaux."

Tommy, "It was *Papillon* and *El Renard* that made the arrangements with our *passeurs*."

"So, who were the *passeurs?*

Herman, "A different group. I was accompanied by a Spaniard who went by the name of Juan. I was given fake papers and was given the name Pablo. We acted as textile workers working in the Cherbourg area. We encountered no problems. Apparently, Franco and Hitler are the best of friends. The German guards treated us as if we were one of them. Being Hispanic in France provides a good cover."

"Interesting, I will need to keep that in mind. What about you, Tommy?"

"We had a few problems, but my *passeur* was a woman who went by the name of Marguerite. She acted as my mother, and I was her deaf-mute son with brain damage. The German guards tried to trick me by shouting in my face, but I played my role and never broke character. Marguerite was a doll. She embarrassed the Boche and took no shit, even when they were criticizing me as her mongrel son. She spoke some German and told them I had brain damage due to fighting against the resistance of the Vichy government. Something like that, couldn't understand shit, but then again, I was a deaf-mute. However, I did witness the Boche kicking an old man on the train. After they kicked him, they dragged him to the train door and threw him out. As the train was leaving, German troopers dressed in black were loading the man's body into the paddy wagon. Later, Marguerite told me that the only crime the old man had committed was that he was a Jew."

Herman continues, "We arrived at Bordeaux's outskirts and spent two nights at a safe house. The safe house was a barn, so we slept with the cows and horses. The second night, we were rescued by Captain Connally."

Tommy, "Do we need to describe the firefight and the sinking of the patrol boat?"

"No, not necessary; the SAS operatives will provide a detailed report. Is there anything else you would like to provide?"

Herman, "Yes, the French resistance has the will, the guts, and the determination to fight the Boche to their deaths. They need weapons and, most importantly, the means to communicate amongst themselves and the outside world. They need direction and encouragement. The German propaganda machine is working 24 hours a day, seven days a week. The Germans have already flooded the radio airwaves, the movies at the cinema, school-books, magazines, books, posters, and speeches. They are brainwashing the French public. Ninety percent of the French population already believe this propaganda: the Boche lies, lies, lies, and lies, every day."

Colonel Phillips, "If there was one thing that we could provide, what would you recommend?"

"Radios, to communicate amongst themselves and with us at SOE. I was told that the Germans have the latest in radio direction finding. They have found two of their transmitters and four operators in the last month. They will not take the resistance fighters alive. The Germans will turn over any resistance fighters to the Gestapo. The Gestapo is ruthless; they will torture them for days and then kill them. The resistance fighters will not surrender. The standard procedure is to kill as many of the Boche as possible, then leave one bullet in their handgun and kill themselves."

"Next would-be weapons, like Sten guns and German handguns. They need to be German-made. The resistance can steal the ammo. Also, they need plastic explosives with time-pencil detonators. Ink and paper to be used in the hidden printing presses would be of great value. They would then be able to print leaflets and distribute the news being broadcast by de Gaulle and the "Free French."

Colonel Phillips, "How do you recommend we provide these items?"

"Good question; we can provide these items by parachuting into drop zones. However, before we start dropping any items to the resistance, we must fly or parachute SOE agents with transmitters to coordinate subsequent airdrops."

Colonel Phillips then addresses the issue of how to deliver the weapons to the resistance. "We have three good agent, being provided by the American OSS. They are Francisco Vargas, Andres Valencia, and Juliette Santiago. I believe you know Francisco and Andres. They were the agents that rescued you from the Germans."

"Yes, I know them well. They did an outstanding job in the performance of the rescue mission. Both Thomas and I would not be here if it was not because of their expert knowledge of covert extraction operations. If there is any way they can be honored, they should be."

"Yes, I understand, but with America not in the war, we need to handle the use of American agents with the utmost care."

"Well, if at all possible, you should consider using them as your conduit to the French resistance."

"Your recommendation is noted, thank you."

Homecoming Herman and Karina:

Once Herman was safely on the HMS George Patmore, the 204th Air Wing was informed. Colonel Harr informed Captain Kowalski to call Karina to let her know Herman had been rescued. Karina then immediately told Kathy and Kerrie of her fiancé's whereabouts. Katherine and Kerrie were two good friends Karina had made at the ATA-GIRLS Club; they called themselves the 3K gals. All came from aviation backgrounds and had learned to fly on bi-planes. They were married: Kathy to a Navy man and Kerrie to a Special Air Service (SAS) soldier. Karina was not, but they treated her like she was mar-ried. The girls had rented a small cottage in the country near the Spitfire fac-tory because their husbands were away for long periods. Keeping each other company seemed like the right thing to do.

Upon Herman's release, Karina informed the girls that they would be moving to their own cottage. Kathy and Kerrie understood as they would have likely done the same. To surprise Karina and Herman, the ATA women fliers quickly reconfigured and cleaned up a Quonset hut, which was being used as a storage warehouse. With the help of more than twenty female and male pilots, they converted the warehouse into a dance hall within two days. Once Karina was told that Herman was coming home, she took every flight that required Spitfires and Hurricanes in order to be flown to the Airbase. This worked well for Kathy and Kerrie as they moved out of their cottage and fixed it up as a 'Honeymoon Suite.' Ski had the job of creating a reason as to why Herman had to go to the Quonset hut warehouse as soon as he was released from his hospital appointment. Herman would need to be waiting at the cot-tage while the girls picked up Karina from the airport. The ruse had to be car-ried out with military-like precision. Karina and Kathy would walk through the back door, and Herman and Ski would walk through the front door, and at precisely 8 p.m., the lights would come on and say, "Surprise, Welcome Home!"

Finally, at 8 p.m., Herman and Karina walked through opposite doors, and when the lights came on, they looked at each other and ran to meet at the center of the dance floor. The dance hall was decorated with streamers and balloons. Handwritten signs welcomed Herman home, and all the guests were told that it would be a BYOB party. The 204 Air Wings quickly assembled a ten-piece band, and three ATA girls performed an excellent rendition of the Andrews sisters. Karina and Herman kissed each other passionately as Her-man lifted Karina off her feet, twirling her around. This was one military cam-paign that worked out perfectly. Karina began to cry as they continued to kiss, and Herman's eyes started to tear up. The band started playing "For He's a Jolly Good Fellow." After more than ten minutes of cheers and applause, Colonel Harr and Captain Kowalski gave Herman a toast, and the Quonset hut broke into jovial dancing and cheering until early the next morning. The band played songs by Glen Miller and Tommy Dorsey, and the 'Andrews Sisters' look-a-likes sang all the songs that were popular during World War II.

That evening, Herman and Karina retired to their 'Honeymoon Cottage.' Herman and Karina retired from the impromptu welcome home party and arrived excited at their makeshift honeymoon suite prepared by Kathy and Kerrie. They both walked to the edge of the bed. Karina started to unbutton her blouse, and Herman carefully helped her with the unsnapping of her brassiere. As Karina's brassiere slowly fell to the floor, Herman could see Karina's full breasts. Herman gently started kissing her breasts, and Karina started to unbuckle Herman's pants belt. Karina then kicked off her medium military issued high heels and Herman laid on the bed. Karina then pulled off Herman's aviation boots. They both fell on the bed and started undressing each other.

Herman and Karina had been living together during their flying days in the Albany Flying Circus. It was not the first time they had made love. However, when Herman had been in France, Karina did not know if she would ever see Herman again. When Herman knew that he was likely to die when his plane hit the cold waters of the Atlantic, his thoughts were only about Karina. This evening was special. They made love like they never had before.

They fell asleep at 7 a.m. At noon, Karina awoke, and she made breakfast. Herman awoke to the smell of bacon and eggs. At the breakfast table, Karina had placed two candles. As Karina had her back to Herman, dressed only in his long-sleeved shirt, he decided to ask Karina to marry him. The only question that needed to be answered was when.

The Marriage of Herman and Karina
English Countryside

Once Herman has been released from the hospital, he is under strict orders not to fly. He is ordered to report back weekly to undergo further testing. Herman has had some dizzy spells, but he tells no one. He knows that he will be permanently grounded if he indicates to the nurse that he has reoccurring spells. He thinks nothing of his occasional disorientation and believes that, eventually, they will cease.

Once his one-week appointment has arrived, Herman walks into the clinic and reports for his examination.

The receptionist asks, "Please fill out the form and take a seat."

Herman does as he is ordered; ten minutes later, a nurse comes out with a notepad and asks, "Lieutenant Hutchinson, please follow me." Herman stands and follows the nurse into a laboratory; the nurse points to a chair and says, "Lieutenant, please have a seat. A technician will be with you momentarily."

Herman looks around the lab and spots roughly ten men, all with bandages wrapped around their war wounds.

He thinks *I am lucky I have no physical injuries and should be cleared for flying soon.*

A nurse walks in next to Herman and silently takes his blood, measures his pulse rate and temperature, and wraps a blood pressure band around his right arm.

She writes all the readings on the tablet and says, "Please follow me." They arrive at a room with a small table, a medicine cabinet, and two chairs.

The nurse then tells Herman, "Please be seated. The doctor will see you shortly."

After waiting for only a short period, Dr. Walker walks into the room. He introduces himself, sits next to Herman, and examines the data taken in the laboratory. Dr. Walker is in his fifties and is a World War I veteran. He looks at Herman's background data and says, "I see that you are a flier.... hmmm.... Spitfires. Thank you for your service to the country. Can you tell me how you were injured?"

"Yes, Sir."

Herman tells the doctor about his plane being shot down in the English Channel and his parachuting into the water. Herman then tells him about his rescue by the French resistance. Dr. Walker listens, and when Herman is finished, he asks, "Are you having dizzy spells and momentary loss of equilibrium?"

Herman is surprised that the doctor went straight to the problem and says, "Yes, but I simply sit down or grab onto a steady object, and in a couple of minutes, I am okay. I never pass out."

"Yes, I figured that you may have these symptoms. Your blood pressure is too high. This is often caused by stress periods that can last for days or weeks. I see from your background history that you not only suffered the crash but that you also had a firefight with the German patrol boat. I am afraid that I cannot release you for any flights until you have stabilized your blood pressure and no longer have dizzy spells for forty-five days straight. Lieutenant Hutchinson, I am a veteran of the First World War, I flew the Sopwith biplane for the RAF. I flew over the French battlefield, and I, too, was shot down by the Germans. I am well aware of the conditions that exist when flying. If you were flying one of our new Spitfires at 350 mph and descending on a German bomber, you would likely pass out, and your plane would slam into the ground. I am sure you can understand why you cannot fly under your present conditions."

"Yes, Sir, I completely understand, and I also thank you for your service."

"Good luck, Lieutenant; there are other ways that you can serve England. We need as many good men as possible. And thank you for your support."

"Yes, Sir, I will certainly continue in any way possible.

Herman leaves the clinic and wonders if his grounding is God-sent. Now would be the time to ask Karina to marry him; he would be assigned to ground duty and not be in immediate harm's way. He starts to think of the venue where he will ask. He knows that Karina will be flying Spitfires to a base in northern England, and she will be taking the train back to South Hampton. He will ask her to stop in London for the evening, select a romantic setting, and pop the question.

Karina flies one of the newest Spitfires to an RAF base near Edinburgh and returns on the train. Herman meets her at Piccadilly Circus Station, and they walk to an underground French Restaurant, the "*Moulin Rouge*." Since Herman was going to ask Karina to marry him, he was dressed in his RAF blues with his ribbons on his left chest. Karina still has her ATA flight suit. Herman orders the best red and white wine. He orders a Chateaubriand, and Karina orders the fish of the day: mackerel. How poetic of Karina to order the mackerel: Pierre, the French fisherman, had hidden Herman in a pile of mackerel. During their evening conversation, Herman tells Karina of his visit to the doctor. He tells Karina that he will likely be assigned to a non-flying duty. Karina is very sympathetic, but deep down, she is glad that he will no longer be in danger of being shot down by the Germans.

As Herman reaches into his pant pocket to pull out the ring, the sirens indicate that the bombing is starting to blink into a loud whining noise. The waiters guide all customers through the back door and down into the tube tunnel. Herman and Karina find themselves in the Piccadilly tube station with hundreds of citizens of London. Herman had the presence of mind to take several of the wine bottles left on the tables as they quickly walked down to the tube station. Immediately upon entering the tube station, the general public recognized the uniforms of the RAF. The couple is seen as the heroes of the Battle of Britain. Churchill had given his famous speech, "Never Have so Many Owed so Much to So Few." The crowd erupted in praises for Herman and Karina and were given the best seats in the tube station. The head waiter, Henri, knew that Herman had planned to ask Karina to marry him. Henri and several of the other waiters went up to the restaurant and brought down a table, tablecloth, candles, and two crates of wine.

As the bombs from the Germans were exploding on London's streets, Herman brought out the diamond ring and asked Karina to marry him. She said yes, and they engaged in a long kiss.

The crowd all shouted in unison, "She said yes, she said yes."
The wine bottles were passed out, and the crowd then started drinking with a toast to the bride and groom. It was a celebration that neither Herman nor Karina would ever forget.

Herman, Karina, and 500 plus London citizens emerged from the Piccadilly tube station early when the all-clear was heard from the sirens. Now the wedding needed to be planned. Karina went back to the ATA bivouac building and showed off her engagement ring. All the women of the ATA immediately volunteered to help in the preparations for the wedding. This was not an ordinary time; many obstacles would need to be overcome, all related to the war.

One, the venue needed to be found where the bombing would not interrupt the service. This would require a daytime wedding and reception. Two, the venue needed to be in the country, where it was unlikely that the Germans would bomb. Three, most of the wedding party and the guests were either Spitfire or Hurricane fliers or ATA women, should they be called to action, they would need to abandon the wedding and drive to their respective bases. The agreement with their respective wing commanders that all fliers would need to be in the second wave of interceptors. Thus, they would need to be within a twenty-minute drive to their respective Airbase. The ATA ladies had it a bit easier. By the time of the wedding, there were now over 100 ATA fliers serving the RAF. The women in the wedding party traded their assignments with others to be free during the two days of the wedding.

Karina and her two best friends, Kathy and Kerrie, found an ideal Bed and Breakfast with eight bedrooms and a large seating area for twenty-five people. The wedding would be held outside and under a large tent, which would accommodate twenty tables: ten people per table. The tent was obtained from the British Army Medical Group. Squadron 204's fliers set up the tent and built a wooden dance floor from scrap wood that came from shipping containers. The same band that had played at Herman's coming home party volunteered to play big band music, and the Andrews sisters look-alike made a second appearance. Colonel Petro Harr, the 204th Wing Commander, would perform the wedding ceremony. The last thing that had to be set was the date. With Ski's help, Herman returned and looked at all the days the German Luftwaffe had attacked. It was learned that the best day was Monday. There was no logical reason why this was, but the 204th wing's fliers claimed it was because the Germans liked to party on weekends and were likely hungover. Therefore, the wedding was planned for 10 a.m., and the reception to follow at 1:00 p.m.

The wedding went as planned, with Kathy and Kerrie being the bridesmaids and Ski and Tommy being the groomsmen. The total number of attendees was over 200, with one-half being British, Canadian, and Polish and the other half being other nationalities. A surprise guest was Colonel Susan Phillips, the British Colonel who had helped Herman and Karina cross from the United States to Canada. Fortunately, the Germans did not conduct any bombing runs on the Monday of the wedding. The festivities ended at 6 p.m., and all attendees traveled back to their barracks sober and ready for the next day of flying their Spitfires and Hurricanes.

As Herman and Karina left the wedding tent and were headed for a taxi to the nearest tube station, Ski handed Herman a set of keys for a 1940 MG sports car. Included with the keys was a telegram from Dr. Ronald Goodwin from Las Cruces, New Mexico. The telegram read, "Congratulations on your wedding, drive safely; driving a car is more dangerous than flying a plane. Your friends, family, and I are all proud of your achievements. Godspeed, and stay safe and healthy. Your friend Ronald." At the bottom of the telegram was a single line... "V, Victory."

Chapter Twenty-Two
Team Meets in Scotland
Milton Hall, Scotland

Colonel Susan Phillips is on a fast track to establish a SOE network that would work with the French resistance. Soon after she heard that Lieutenant Hutchinson had been in France and had established contact with the French resistance, she had to speak with him. The Colonel first contacted the 204th Wing Commander, Colonel Petro Harr. After speaking with the Wing Commander, she talked to Captain Alfons Kowalski. The Captain was the first to inform Colonel Phillips of the situation with Lieutenant Hutchinson. He had suffered some injuries to his equilibrium, and if this condition did not improve, he would not be cleared to fly.

Colonel Phillips contacted Captain Kowalski, "I am establishing a branch of the SOE that will be training and providing continued support for covert agents in France. These agents will work directly with the French resistance. Do you think that Lieutenant Hutchinson would be interested in joining my staff?"

Captain Kowalski (Ski). Ski thinks for a few minutes and says, "Yes, that would be a perfect position for him."

"If I talk to him and if he agrees, would Colonel Harr agree to release him to the SOE?"

"Yes, I think he would; Herman would be an excellent choice to be on your staff."

Colonel Phillips talks to Lieutenant Hutchinson:
Colonel Phillips attended the marriage of Herman and Karina as Major Kowalski's plus-one. Both Herman and Karina were glad to see them at their wedding. Colonel Phillips did not mention anything to Herman about joining her staff during the wedding. It was not the time or place for that discussion. One week after the wedding, Herman contacted Ski and asked what

the Colonel was doing. Ski politely asked Herman to meet him for a beer at the local pub.

Ski says, "Herman, you need to think about how you can provide your knowledge to serve the country. Colonel Phillips is with British Intelligence. She has been appointed to the SOE, in charge of the French branch."

"Yes, I also know Colonel Philips when Karina and I crossed from the U.S. to Canada. At that time, she was the British attaché officer at the British Embassy. She was instrumental in making the arrangements for us to cross the border and later join the Canadian Air Force."

This is the office that you debriefed upon your return from France. I think with the contacts you made in France, you can be of great help in the war against the Nazis."

Herman does not hesitate, "Yes, that would be perfect. I can certainly help while I regain my strength and get well."

Herman loves to fly; next to his love for Karina, there is nothing that Herman loves more. Since Dr. Goodwin taught him to fly along the Rio Grande Valley and the Orogrande mountains, flying is in his blood. Ski and Herman continue talking about the war and their ideas of what needs to be done in both the air and ground wars. They discuss the likelihood of when America will join the war. Herman has been communicating with his family, friends, and Dr. Goodwin via letters. The consensus from most citizens of America wrote, *"It is only a question of time; Roosevelt knows that if the Nazis and Japanese are not stopped, they will rule the world with hatred, racism, intolerance, and bigotry. They must be defeated, So, yes, I will do whatever I can while I am grounded."*

After their conversation at the pub, Ski calls Colonel Phillips and arranges a meeting between Herman and Colonel Phillips. Two days later, Colonel Phillips and Herman meet at the SOE headquarters on Baker Street. Herman is excited that he can assist Colonel Philips while he is convalescing from his injuries. Herman arrives ten minutes before the appointed time and goes through security. After getting through the security checkpoint, Colonel Phillips meets Herman and accompanies him to a secure room with no windows.

Colonel Phillips, "Lieutenant Hutchinson, first congratulations on your marriage, and please give your wife my fondest regards."

"Thank you, Madame."

"I understand that you are willing to assist me in building a branch of the SOE. The branch I establish will provide agents and funding to the French resistance. You are the person with the most knowledge of the key members of the resistance. We will need to recruit intelligent agents who can think independently and easily blend in with the local population. That would be an additional plus if they could speak French, German, and Spanish. They must be in excellent physical shape, have a strong constitution, and withstand large amounts of excruciating pain. The organization must have radio operators, explosive experts, fliers, mechanics, coders, and code breakers, linguists, and many other support talents."

"Colonel, what would be my duties?"

"You will be the person managing the field assets. Initially, you will be in communication with the French resistance and direct the missions of the SOE. Examples would be providing the resistance with radios and weapons. Using our aerial photographs, you will direct the destruction of German assets such as ammunition bunkers, communications towers, command posts, airfields, and bridges. You will evaluate the intelligence reports from the RAF Command, intercepts from MI6, and determine their targets. Lastly, you will select agents to be infiltrated into France. A complete background investigation will need to be completed. We currently have British citizens who have a strong affiliation with Germany. You must carefully select our future SOE agents who will not be spying for the Germans. Once we infiltrate these agents, they must be fully trusted by the members of the resistance."

"Colonel, I will do my best to assume that position."

"One more thing: I have been in contact with Colonel Harr, and we both agree that you should be promoted to Captain. Can you have Karina in my office tomorrow for a formal ceremony? She can then pin the captain bars on the epaulet of your blue dress coat."

"Thank you, Colonel; Karina and I will be here for the ceremony."

"I have invited Colonel Harr and Captain Kowalski to attend as well."

The following day, Herman is promoted to Captain Heronimo Hutchinson. After the ceremony, all attendees get back to the business of winning the war.

Colonel Phillips now addresses Captain Hutchinson on how the resistance will receive the required supplies. First, we need to journey to Milton Hall, Scotland. This is where Francisco and Andres are currently training."

Herman thinks briefly, saying, "Is that the training base for the Jedburghs?"

"Yes, that's correct. Francisco, Andres, and a woman by the name of Juliette Santiago are using the base to train SOE agents."

Hmmm, so we will be using the Jedburghs?"

"No, not initially. SOE agents will need to speak French Sp, Spanish, and German. The agents that are being trained are all native to European countries. They need to blend into the population. The best agents need to speak Spanish. Spain is neutral but strongly favors Germany. Thus, agents who speak Spanish and French are preferred. The Germans will not arrest a person if they think he is Spanish."

"Yes, now I see. When I met Francisco and Andres, they did look Spanish. So how did they learn to speak native German?"

"It's a long story, but they and the woman spoke German when they were young. Francisco was born in Mexico but was educated in German schools. The Mennonites had colonies in Mexico, and Francisco attended a school that taught all subjects in German. Andres was born in Argentina with a large German population; his mother is German, so he grew up speaking German and Spanish. Juliette was born on the German-French border. Her parents immigrated to the United States in the 1930s. They have all received commando training at the Ogden base located in the state of Utah."

"Ok, now I see why Francisco and Andress were seasoned commandos when they rescued me on the French coast."

"Yes, I plan to use the three initially for our first contact with the French resistance. You will be directing the operations from our headquarters outside of London."

"Using Francisco and Andres is a wise choice. I am sure that Juliette is equally prepared."

The plan is to depart for Milton Hall first thing tomorrow morning; we will take the train from Plymouth to London, Edinburgh, and then to Milton Hall. It will be an eighteen-hour train ride."

Milton Hall, Scotland:

After a twenty-hour train ride, Colonel Phillips and Captain Hutchinson arrive at Milton Hall. At the train station, they are met by Francisco.

As they disembark, Francisco recognizes Captain Hutchinson (Herman), and they quickly exchange handshakes. Herman introduces Colonel Phillips, "Francisco, please meet Colonel Phillips; she is the branch chief of the SOE French resistance."

Francisco gives a sharp salute, "Pleasure to meet you. Your reputation proceeds your visit. Looking forward to working on your plans to arm the resistance in France."

"Yes, we have much work ahead of us, but with men like yourself and Captain Hutchinson, I am sure we can get the job done."

Francisco, "I have arranged a conference room at the training center. It will be available to us throughout your state at Milton Hall. Accommodations have been made at the Officers' Quarters."

"Excellent, so let's get started tomorrow at 7 am."

"Perfect, we can have breakfast at 6 am and start our planning at 7 am".

At 7 am promptly, the meeting starts. Francisco, Andress, Juliette, four training instructors, Colonel Phillips, and Captain Hutchinson are seated at the table.

Francisco starts the meeting with introductions and turns the briefing to Sergeant Miguel Montes. Miguel stands at six feet, one inch, with a solid square jaw, well-kept hair, muscular shoulders, and arms. He is dressed in his battle fatigues and wearing combat boots. Francisco then remarks, "Sergeant Montes will now outline the training for recruits regarding the new American transmitters."

Sergeant Montes now explains, "The training will be on the properties HF transmissions. All ten students know manual morse coding and decoding of messages. The new equipment provided by the American Land Lease act uses advanced techniques that do not allow the German DF equipment to locate the transmitter. The transmitter operators must learn the theory behind the ability to have HF long-distance communications without being detected. Without fully understanding the HF covert communications methods of obfuscation, the German DF equipment will easily find the trans-mitters. The students need to know that the ionosphere properties will change depending on the weather, time of day, the direction of the radio wave, transmission over land or water, and other variables."

Sergeant Montes turns the podium to Juliette Santiago, "Juliette is an expert on the use of the new American transmitters, she has worked directly with Professor Peter J. Fry in the development of the transmitters."

Juliette now takes the podium and provides an outline of the course; she explains the following:

Modes of Propagation: *The main radio propagation method used in the MF and HF portions of the radio spectrum.*

Antenna Types: *The Typical antenna used for HF comms.*

The variance of the HF spectrum: *Knowing how HF propagation varies and what influences the ionosphere.*

Levels of Ionization: *The levels of ionization that affect the radio waves. There are a number of layers, as the ionization level does not reduce to zero, but instead, there are several ionization layers.*

Skip and Distance Zones: *This determines which locations may have long-distance communications.*

"You students will be taught about switching frequencies and the need to use burst transmissions. This will require pre-planning, and both the transmitter and the receiver must have a method to send a preamble, telling the receiving station the decoding pattern. You will be taught that there must be a predetermined coding system for coding and decoding for the system to work. For example, using." *The Count of Monte Cristo.* The preamble in our message will be CMC-12-3-2. This will indicate the book, chapter, paragraph, and the beginning sentence. The primary key is the book; thus, the CMC might be a number, for example, 1, 2, or 3. These are the books that SOE and the field agent have pre-arranged. For example, book number one would be "*The Count of Monte Cristo*, book two, "*The Tale of Two Cities*," and so forth."

Juliette continues, "You will learn how messages are sent using alu-minum discs from an amusement company in England. The message will be pre-recorded and inserted into the slot in the black box. The black box will convert the message to the manual Morse dots and dashes and transmit it to the SOE in England. Each disc may contain up to five minutes of communications. Thus, an average of thirty minutes of manual Morse will be included in six discs. For field testing, the students will begin with three frequencies, two per disc. The frequencies switch every two minutes; thus, a normal thirty-minute manual Morse message will be transmitted in six minutes using three different frequencies. The students must remember to code the frequencies being used in the initial preamble of the setup message. This will be a burst transmission of less than one second; thus, there is no way of DF'ing the frequencies at these switch times."

Juliette concludes her briefing, "After three weeks of classroom instruction, the ten students conduct actual field exercises. Followed by combat exercises. I will now turn over the podium to Andres Valencia."

Andres, is five feet ten inches, athletically built with a tapered body and slim but muscular arms, neck and a square jaw. He begins, "Ladies and Gentlemen, all of you will receive and intensive course on combat techniques. You will learn these methods and techniques until you can perform them in the dark and by instinct. Learning these techniques will likely save your life. When you enter into a combat situation with a German soldier, Gestapo, or the French Malice, there are only two outcomes: kill or be killed. You can not hesitate; you must act swiftly and with purpose."

A student raises his hand and asks, "Wiil communications operators also complete the combat course?"

"Absolutely, communications operators are a prime target of the Germans. You must learn how to defend yourselves."

A young lady now asks, "Do the ladies receive the same training as the men?"

"Yes, the enemy will not show any sympathy for women. They are an equal-opportunity killing machine. They treat men, women, and children equally; they murder anyone that they determine is not an Aryan German."

Andres clears his throat and, with authority, explains, "What you will learn is an advanced training program. All of you have already completed basic training. Now, we will engage in advanced techniques that are specific to the Germans occupying Europe. Instruction will be provided by experts who have battlefield experience. Your physical exercises will be rigorous and will extend your capabilities to the limit. You will be inserted into hostile territory. Teams will be in groups of four to six. We will ensure that each team has the experts in all disciplines, but it is imperative that all of you know the special talents of each team member. If any team member goes down, the team must continue operating with little to no capability reduction. All team members must be experts in the following disciplines."

"**Explosives** – *How to use plastic explosives with pencil fuses and remote detonators. How to make explosives out of fertilizer and diesel fuel.*

 You will be taught how to use different weapons – *rifles, handguns, packing your bullets using English and German weapons. The preferred weapons will be the German Sten gun and the Luger. Ammunition can be easily stolen or taken from a killed German soldier.*

Hand-to-hand combat – *How to kill with bare hands, using your knife, belt buckle, sharp object, and body points to kill a person. Using the force of the enemy against him.*

 Physical exercise - *running, weights, swimming, climbing trees, jumping, rappelling cliffs, climbing, using a rope. This is extremely important. You will be using the forest and rugged terrain to your advantage. Our motto is to strike quickly in stealth mode, kill and disappear. The forest and nighttime will be ours.*

Camouflage techniques – *Using trees, grass, the color of clothes, painting the face and arms.*

Escape techniques – *How to free oneself from tied hands, using your elbows, feet, and body parts. Once you have escaped the run-away patterns to use and not use.*

Rivers and bodies of water – *using water to your benefit. Hiding underwater using reeds, swimming underwater to muzzle the force of a bullet.*

Treatment of wounds – *Using blood clotting powders, tourniquets-what to use, and where to apply.*

How to cross a minefield – *look for flat spots, crawl, and use your knife.*

Learn and study your enemy's tactics – *Anticipate his next move and counter.*

Think out of the box – *Use your imagination and do things that are not natural. The one advantage is that the Germans do everything by the book. The Germans are very rigid and will not change easily. Study their habits. Before executing the operation, collect intelligence: Plan, Prepare, and Practice. Have plans A, B, and C. You must be prepared to react to your enemy's moves. Be* *ready that your initial plan may need to be modified based on your enemy's actions."*

The SOE agents begin their training integrated with the British Commandos. After five weeks of the twelve-week course, Colonel Phillips receives word that the Germans will receive the advanced DF equipment that would allow the SOE operatives to be easily found. This was ahead of the anticipated schedule.

SOE Integrated with Commandos

Within two days of receiving word of the advanced DF equipment, MI6 intercepted more disturbing news. The Germans were developing a new and more powerful weapon. This new weapon was using the same technology as the DF finders. The Germans had a code name for this capability, *"Freya." Freya* was *a* mythical goddess of the Germanic tribes. *Freya* was a goddess of magic and could foretell the future. The information provided by MI6 has indicated that the *Freya* and DF systems are due to have operational tests in the French Normandy coast area.

Colonel Phillips calls for a meeting of Captain Hutchinson and Lieutenants Vargas, Valencia, and Santiago.

Chapter Twenty-Three
Fifth Fighter Wing, Gablingen Kaserne
Augsburg, Germany

The Air Battle between Germany and Great Britain continued through the fall of 1940. The German bombers continued their raids in London, Manchester, South Hampton, Plymouth, Birmingham, and cities in Scotland. In turn, the British bombed Berlin, Munich, Stuttgart, Dresden, Hamburg, Dusseldorf, and major troop concentrations in France, Belgium, Holland, and Norway. Adolf Hitler was furious that the mighty German Luftwaffe and Kriegsmarine could not bring England to its knees.

General Heinrich Gort, assigned to command the German Bavarian Army Division, summons *Oberst* (Colonel) Gunter Buchner to his office in Munich, Germany. *Oberst* Buchner is assigned as the intelligence officer of the fifth fighter wing stationed at Gablingen Kaserne near Augsburg, Germany. General Rudolf Hess later used the airfield at the Gablingen Kaserne in 1941 to seek a negotiated peace with England. General Gort has recently returned to Munich from a meeting of the German High Command. At the meeting with Hitler and Göring, it was decided that the war effort would shift from England to Russia. However, both Hitler and Göring wanted to extract a price from England for their dogged resistance to the air campaign. Germany had lost 1,000 planes and hundreds of pilots to the anti-craft batteries and the Spitfires and Hurricanes. At the Berlin conference, Hitler gave his Generals one of his many dress-down addresses. His plans for the invasion of England had been perfect; it was only the execution that had failed him. After two hours of blasting all of his Generals for incompetence and ineptitude, he demanded that the British pilots who parachuted into Germany and the occupied territories be severely punished.

Hitler asked that Field Marshal Göring provide the statistics of all the British pilots captured since the Air Campaign started in July of 1940. The statistics showed that most British pilots had been captured in Germany and held at the Marianfelde Prison in Berlin. However, the statistics showed that very few pilots had been captured in France, Belgium, and Holland. Hitler then asked the obvious, "What is being done with the dead bodies?"

Army General Rudolf Hess answered, "There are no bodies to be found." At, which Hitler erupted with a furious dialog, he called all of his generals' imbeciles and stupid. Hitler asked why we were not capturing more British pilots in the conquered territories, especially France.

General Hess answered, "*Mein Fuhrer*, the resistance is very strong in these conquered territories, especially France."

Hitler then demanded that the problem needed a solution. General Gort answered, "*Mein Fuhrer*, I have the perfect solution, I recommend that *Oberst* Buchner command the Gestapo in France. I am sure we all remember *Oberst* Gunter Buchner, a decorated Messerschmitt pilot who commanded the Luftwaffe's fifth wing. He had over ten confirmed kills and over fifteen unconfirmed. Last month, *Oberst* Buchner was shot down. He heroically crash-landed his plane near Stuttgart. However, Buchner lost his left leg below his knee and serves as the intelligence officer for the fifth fighter wing at Gablingen Kaserne. He has been fitted with a prosthetic leg. His career as a fighter pilot has ended. However, he would be the perfect candidate to head the Gestapo in France. He was the top student at the Bundeswehr Command and Staff College. He was born near the French border and speaks fluent French. His studies at the Military Academy indicate that he had superior grades in the intelligence field."

General Hess, "Is he a dedicated soldier of the Third Reich?"

"*Ya, Mein General*, he was one of the original members from our days in Munich. He has an added despise of the British air pilots. He was shot down by their Polish Ace, Kowalski."

After the Berlin Conference, General Gort will re-assign *Oberst* Buchner to the Gestapo and take command of the Gestapo and the *Kriminaldirecktor* in France.

General Gort summons *Oberst* Buchner to his headquarters in Munich. *Oberst* Buchner takes his command staff car, a Mercedes Benz, to the Bavarian Army Command's Munich headquarters. On his drive to Munich, *Oberst* Buchner is aware that General Gort recently attended a meeting of the High Command in Berlin. He thinks that General Gort will simply provide a status of the war effort and the strategy of attacking on the eastern front. He believes that the conference with General Gort is to move the fifth fighter wing closer to the eastern battlefront, which is closer to the Russian border.

Oberst Buchner arrives punctually at 9 a.m. for the meeting with the General. The General's orderly, *Leutnant* Spitzer, welcomes *Oberst* Buchner. He smartly salutes and clicks his heels, "*Heil Hitler, Guten tag, Oberst*, the General will see you now."

Oberst Buchner returns the salute and says, "*Heil Hitler, Danke Leutnant.*"

As Buchner enters the General's office, the Leutnant barks, "General Gort, *Oberst* Buchner." Buchner grabs his peaked hat and holds it in the armpit of his left arm.

Oberst Buchner salutes and the General returns the salute and tells Buchner to take a seat. General, "*Oberst* Buchner, I have recently returned from a meeting with the supreme commander, Herr Hitler, Air Marshall Göring, and other high command members. The war is now turning to the east against the Russians."

"*Ya, Mein General*, the fifth fighter wing is prepared to fight the Russians. The Russians have an inferior aircraft, and their pilots need more wartime experience. Our Luftwaffe should disseminate the Russian Air Force in a matter of months."

"*Jawohl,* Herr Buchner, we have a vastly superior Luftwaffe and Wehrmacht. Hitler and the war council predicted that we should be in Moscow before the winter months set in. However, you are not here to discuss our war plans against the Russians."

Oberst Buchner says nothing but thinks--- *why the hell am I here if not to discuss the plans for attacking the Russian Air Force?* He remains quiet and allows General Gort to continue.

General Gort, "*Herr* Hitler is not pleased with the high numbers of British pilots that are escaping through Spain. We need to stop this!"

"*Jawohl,* General, I do agree we must stop these pilots from being rescued and returning to bomb our cities." Buchner is now beginning to understand why he is here. He is the intelligence officer of the fifth fighter wing, and he indeed has some ideas.

"*Oberst* Buchner, do you have any idea why you are here?"

"Of course, you would like my ideas on how to apprehend those English Pilots. Is that not why I am here?"

"Yes, of course, since you are—a, a, ---were a pilot, we need your ideas on eliminating the resistance fighters from France. They are the scum of the earth."

"Yes, indeed, truly the lowest of mankind. *Oberst* Buchner, now that you can no longer fly, we could best use your knowledge in counterintelligence to find and eradicate the French resistance.

"Of course, I would be honored to serve my country and use my God-given talents."

Oberst Gunter Buchner:

Oberst Gunter Buchner was born near Strasbourg, Germany, near the French border. Growing up as a teenager, he had several French and Jewish friends. However, when Hitler came to power in 1933, Gunter would listen to his speeches on the radio. Following the defeat of Germany in World War 1, Hitler turned to the writings of the French anthropologist Vacher de Lapouge in his book *L'Aryen*, who argued that a superior branch of humans could be identified biologically by using the cephalic index (a measure of head shape) and other indicators. He argued that the long-headed 'dolichocephalic-blond' Europeans, characteristically found in Northern Europe, were natural leaders. These natural leaders were destined to rule over more 'brachiocephalic' (short-headed) peoples.[22]

Hitler and his henchmen interpreted the Lapouge writings as describing the German people as *"Ubermenschen."* (Superhuman) Thus, Germany was destined to rule the world as a natural order of the human race.

Shortly after the Nazis came to power in 1933, the Nazis passed the Law for the Restoration of the Professional Civil Service law, which required all civil servants to prove their Aryan ancestry and defined "non-Aryan" as a person with one Jewish grandparent.[23]

---

[22] Vacher de Lapouge (trans Clossen, C), Georges (1899). "Old and New Aspects of the Aryan Question (PDF). *The American Journal of Sociology*. **5** (3): 329–346. Doi: 10. 1086/210895.

[23] Ehrenreich, The Nazi ancestral proof, p.10

As the Nazis gained more power, the Nazis also classified people with congenital diseases, deformed body parts, down syndrome, mentally impaired, negroes, gypsies, and dark-skinned peoples of Arabic or Mediterranean descent as *Untermenschen* (Subhuman).

Oberst Buchner believed in the superiority of the blond and blue-eyed German. He was proud that his two sons, Joseph and Franz, were model Germans. Joseph was fifteen, and Franz was ten, and both were in the *Hitlerjugend Vereine* (Youth Clubs). They loved their brown uniforms and adored wearing the swastika as an armband. Joseph was very proud to have his father, a Colonel in the German Army. He wanted to grow up and join the SS. He liked how they looked in their black uniforms and jackboots. His dream was to join General Rommel in Africa. He felt he would be skilled at cleaning the dark continent of all *Untermenschen* black people. He could not wait to grow up and become a high-ranking *Schutzstaffel* (SS) officer. As part of the Hitler youth group, Joseph and his fellow youth members would pedal their bikes in Augsburg and identify any persons who looked to be unfit to be Germans. They would report these "unfit" persons to the *Generalinspekteur* and were proud to adhere to the Nazi Party's principles.

Two months before his father received word that he was to take the Gestapo job in Paris, Joseph started having headaches and loss of appetite. He tried to keep it from his parents, but Joseph came home with bruises on his face and with a strained wrist one afternoon after school. His Mother, Hilda, asked him, "Son, I see the bruises on your face, and you keep rotating your right wrist, are you all right?"

"*Ya*, I am fine; I had an accident at school and slipped down the stairs." His mother accepted the explanation, but Joseph had a fever and stayed home from school a week later. His mother then decided to take Joseph to the doctor.

After examining Joseph, Doctor Hinkle told Frau Buchner that Joseph had a small fever and gave her some medicine for her son. However, he said to Frau Buchner that he would like to talk with Colonel Buchner. Frau Buchner asked, "Why, you can tell me anything regarding my son?"

"*Ya, Ya, Frau* Buchner, but some things are best-discussed man to man." *Frau* Buchner thought that perhaps Joseph had some sickness that had to do with syphilis; after all, Joseph was getting to be a man and was big for his age and had probably been to the red-light district. After her husband confirmed that it was related to Joseph's sexual activities, she would have a good talking to her son.

Colonel Buchner went to see Doctor Hinkle within two days, "*Uber-GruppenOberst* Buchner; I need to give you some bad news. Your son has a congenital disease, a rare sickness called phenylketonuria. It is a congenital disability that rarely shows until the child reaches his teenage years. I am afraid that it will only get worse. He will likely start having convulsions and may pass out at unexpected times. It is likely that he passed out and fell down the stairs."

"Yes, but he claimed he slipped and fell down the stairs."

"Yes, I know, but there is no doubt he has the congenital disease."

Buchner continues, "I don't believe it. You are lying to me. If I take my son to a different doctor and he tells me he is fine, you will be arrested for lying to a member of the German Army! I demand that you retest!"

"*Oberst* Buchner, I know that this is very painful for you. I had Doctor Speckle confirm the laboratory tests. There is no doubt that he has the sickness."

"I don't give a damn; you are wrong. My son is the perfect specimen of an Aryan man. Look at him: large head, blond hair, blue eyes, a perfect masculine body, 175 centimeters in height (5 feet, 10 inches). This cannot be true! I will take him to my doctor on the base. I am sure that they will dispute your findings."

Jawohl, UberGruppenOberst Buchner, that is your prerogative. But may I remind you of our policy of ridding the Reich of *menschen* with deformed bodies and, above all else, congenital diseases. I am required to report the condition of your son. The authorities will remove him from your home and place him in a rehabilitation estate. You, of all people, know what that means; you will never see your son again."

The Colonel thinks about his predicament. He asks, "What do you recommend?"

Doctor Hinkle gets up, heads to the medical cabinet and hands the Colonel a tube with the word *"GIFT"* (Poison). "Place two drops in his drinking solution. He will get tired, sleepy, and die a peaceful death."

The Colonel now has a predicament. He is well known in the German command structure as a dedicated follower of Hitler. Hitler knows him personally based on his excellent record as a fighter pilot. Joseph Goebbels speaks highly of him and is used as a model of the true Nazi. Colonel Buchner was confident that he would be a General within the next year and command an Army that would be fighting on the eastern front. He will faithfully complete his assignment to Paris, eliminate the French resistance, be promoted to General, and be assigned to a fighting Army on the eastern front. With his son having a congenital disease, this problem cannot interrupt his climb in the *Schutzstaffel (SS)*. He thinks about his situation and needs to find a solution.

He cannot use the poison provided by the doctor; instead, he comes up with an idea. His son will be killed fighting for the Reich. He has a thirty-day leave to prepare for his transfer to Paris. He will take Joseph on a preliminary visit to his new assignment. This will be interpreted by General Gort as his dedication to his new assignment. He does not know exactly how the French resistance will kill his son, but the details can be worked once they are underway.

Before his formal report date, Colonel Buchner travels to Munich and requests permission to visit the Gestapo SS Paris headquarters. As expected, the General is elated with the professionalism of *Oberst* Buchner. He is even more impressed when Buchner tells him that his son, now fifteen, will accompany him on his trip. The Colonel makes it a point to tell the General that his son is only three years from military service and a leader in the *Hitlerjugend Vereine*.

Having obtained his superior's blessing, the Colonel now must carefully invite his son to join him for a visit to Paris. His major obstacle will be his wife, Hilda. First, he will tell Joseph about the trip. One evening after dinner, he tells Joseph to join him on the back veranda of their home. The Colonel drinks from a glass of wine. He says. "Son, you are now fifteen; it is time to enjoy a fine glass of wine."

The Colonel did not know that Joseph had been drinking wine with his friends at the Hitler youth club since he was twelve. Joseph simply answers, "Yes, father."

After some small talk, the Colonel begins the conversation, "Son, as you know, I am being assigned to Paris to be the head of the *Schutzstaffel (SS)."*

"Yes, my mother told me so. I am very proud of your promotion. I am sure that you will do an outstanding job. Mother tells me it is a stepping stone to a General position."

"Yes, I believe that to be true. As you know, I have a thirty-day leave before my official report day in Paris. I will drive to Paris before my report date and inspect the troops under my command. It will also give me a chance to assess the situation, and if required, I can request any additional troops or perhaps the latest equipment."

"When will you be leaving, and for how long?"

"I will leave within the next few days as soon as I can arrange for a command vehicle and two armored escort cars. There is some danger when traveling in France. However, I will keep the trip personal; thus, no formal arrangements will be made. This is better for security, should we have spies in Paris, they would not know of my trip."

Before the Colonel can ask his son if he wishes to accompany him to Paris, Joseph asks, "Father, would it be possible to accompany you to Paris? It would be an excellent learning experience."

"Yes, excellent idea, but you know your mother needs to bless the trip first."

"Yes, I know, but my mother will have no choice but to agree. I am now fifteen, and she cannot continue to treat me like a child."

After some anxiety and alarm, Joseph's Mother agrees to allow her son's journey to Paris. She agrees only on the condition that the command car will have two armed vehicles and two guards assigned to each vehicle.

After the Colonel has permission from Frau Buchner, the Colonel, and Joseph take a walk in the forest behind their home. Father, "Son, the border between Germany and France has a very dense forest. As you know, I was born in Strasbourg, a town along the border. There is ample game to hunt, reindeer, geese, wild turkeys, wild boar, and other animals we could hunt. You have been asking when we could go hunting. Well, this is a wonderful opportunity."

Joseph is ecstatic and overjoyed with the idea. He has been practicing with his rifle and handgun at the youth club shooting range. This will allow him to use the skills which he has acquired.

Two days later, Frau Buchner agrees to allow Joseph to accompany his father to Paris. The three-vehicle caravan with the two escort cars departs for Paris early on a Monday morning. Unknown to anyone but Colonel Buchner, the Colonel has packed an English-issued Webley MK IV .45 caliber handgun. The handgun is a war trophy, and gun registration was not required. As they drive to the French border, the Colonel tells his driver to cross it near Strasbourg.

The Colonel knows the area of Strasbourg where reindeer and wild boar reside. They reach the border crossing, and the first escort car shows the papers; the guards click the heels of their boots and give the *Heil* Hitler salute.

As soon as they cross the French border, Colonel Buchner commands the driver, "*Fahnrich* (Sergeant) Muller, drive to the forest reservation approximately twelve kilometers on the right."

"*Jawohl, UberGruppenOberst*, Buchner."

Joseph is excited about hunting with his father and asks, "Do you think we will find wild boar?"

"Yes, but if we do, we need to ensure we have a kill shot. These wild boars have been known to attack the hunter. They are very dangerous. If we see one, we both need to be ready to shoot."

With much excitement, "Please, if we see one allow me to take the first shot."

"Of course, I will only be the backup."

The command car and the two escort vehicles arrive at the hunting preserve. Since France is an occupied country, no hunters are allowed, and all guns have been confiscated. Should the Germans find anyone with a weapon, he or she would be promptly executed.

The Colonel and Joseph donned their hunting attire, complete with camouflage jackets, pants, and hats. Their faces were darkened with burnt cork, and they wore sturdy hiker boots. Both carried bolt-action .308 caliber hunting rifles, with the Colonel discreetly concealing an English hand pistol in the back of his hunting pants. As they readied themselves to venture into the forest, two guards offered their services.

"*UberGruppenOberst* Buchner, we will provide security," the guards proposed.

The Colonel responded promptly, "*Nein*, you do not have the proper attire, and too many people will frighten the game. You are to remain here until we return."

The Colonel and Joseph embarked on their journey into the dense forest. "Son, we'll need to walk for several kilometers; wild boar tends to hide deep in the forest," the Colonel explained.

Despite his prosthetic leg, the Colonel maintained a semi-goose step style. He could bend his left leg, but his right, with the prosthetic limb, remained straight. His unique gait featured a bent step with the left leg and a straight one with the right. The Colonel was a staunch believer in exercise, and losing his right leg below the knee had not deterred him from staying in good physical shape. At the Gablingen Kaserne airfield, a five-kilometer track was around the facilities. Every day, the Colonel walked the track twice using his distinctive semi-goose-stepping style, earning admiration from his subordinates for his unwavering dedication to the German Reich.

Joseph, appearing stronger but physically compromised due to illness, began panting heavily and sweating profusely after covering two kilometers. As the Colonel spotted small hoof tracks in the earth, he recognized them as signs of wild boar activity. Exhausted from the trek in the woods, Joseph commented, "Father, I am getting tired. Can we stop and rest?"

They vanished if the Colonel had any lingering doubts about involving the French resistance in his son's fate. He knew what had to be done. The Colonel turned to Joseph and instructed, "Son, you stay here; I will circle around and flush the wild boar towards you. Climb this tree and position yourself to shoot the wild boar as I drive them in your direction."

Joseph noticed a mix of anger and remorse in his father's eyes, perhaps stemming from his inability to keep up. Determined to prove his obedience, he agreed, "Excellent idea, Father. I will climb the tree as soon as I catch my breath."

"Very well, son. You have plenty of time. It will likely be a good hour before I can locate the wild boar and drive them towards you," the Colonel assured as he disappeared into the forest using his semi-goose steps.

After fifteen minutes of rest, Joseph attempted to climb the tree but lacked the upper body strength to pull himself up to the makeshift hunting blind. He rested for another fifteen minutes and tried again, with even less success. Frustrated by damp branches and blisters on his hands, he opted to lean against the large tree trunk for support. Joseph loaded his rifle, inserted a clip of six bullets, and chambered a round. He held the rifle across his chest and simulated aiming and shooting, feeling prepared.

An hour later, the Colonel located two wild boars and began driving them toward Joseph by breaking branches and striking bushes. Joseph could hear the approaching commotion, with the boars' noises growing nearer. The high-pitched screeches and deep growls heightened his anticipation. As the boars burst through the underbrush, Joseph aimed and fired, but his un-steady grip caused the bullet to graze one boar's thick hide. Injured, it charged Joseph. He managed to shoot a second bullet, which struck a tree behind the boars. Before Joseph could take a third shot, the two wild boars attacked with the ferocity of charging bulls.

The injured boar rammed into Joseph, while the other tossed him around violently. Joseph felt the colossal beast's muscle fibers and coarse hairs as its tusks ripped through his clothing and into his abdomen. The first boar continued its relentless assault, flinging Joseph like a ragdoll. The second boar lifted him with its horns and hurled him against a large oak tree, leaving him dazed and disoriented. Joseph felt the second boar gouging and pushing him with its snout, but he lacked the strength to resist. Within thirty seconds, Joseph lay lifeless, surrounded by the cacophony of forest birds. High above, black buzzards circled, drawn by the scent of blood.

The two gunshots resonated, reaching Colonel Buchner, who felt con-fident that Joseph had successfully killed at least one wild boar. At least when he carried out Joseph's fate, his son would have had the opportunity to kill a wild boar. The Colonel arrived at the tree where he had left Joseph, discover-ing the gruesome aftermath. He holstered his English handgun and quickly deduced what had likely transpired. Joseph's inability to climb the tree led to a deadly encounter with the boars, each weighing over 200 kilograms (400 pounds).

Colonel Buchner returned to his guards, showing no hint of empathy or compassion. He recounted the accident and instructed them to bring Joseph's lifeless body back to the vehicle caravan. After Joseph's body was returned to the vehicles, Colonel Buchner then returned to Augsburg. His wife, Hilda, and their son, Franz, were deeply affected by the loss of Joseph. Although Hilda remained silent, she couldn't shake the feeling that Joseph's lack of strength was connected to a hereditary condition. She suspected that "Down Syndrome" may have existed in some of her distant cousins but had not shared this information with her husband. Joseph received a burial with full honors of the Hitler Youth Corps, and Colonel Buchner earned high praise for raising a son willing to sacrifice his life for the country.

After the funeral, Colonel Buchner flew a Luftwaffe military air transport, Heinkel-He 111, to Paris, landing at the Chateaudun Airfield. A command car, plus two military trucks with sixteen SS troopers, provides the escort to the Gestapo Headquarters in Paris.

Chapter Twenty-Four
Oberst Buchner takes Command.
Paris, France

Soon after *Oberst* Buchner arrived in Paris, he started vigorously with German efficiency to carry out his major assignment to root out the resistance. The Colonel needed to thoroughly understand the problem before proceeding with anything else. The previous Colonel in charge of ridding the resistance had been reassigned to the eastern front as ineffective. The second in Command was *Obersleutnant* Siegfried Rauch. Rauch was a mean-spirited person who enjoyed inflicting pain on others. He grew up in a brothel in Hamburg that his *Onkel* Rupert owned in early 1939. Rauch enjoyed inflicting pain on the prostitutes as he performed his sexual acts. At first, Rupert put up with Siegfried's torture of the girls. One Saturday evening, Gertrude, a prostitute, came down the stairs; she was screaming, "Siegfried is going to kill Gisela!"

Rupert was at his usual corner table, drinking his favorite beer and eating a bratwurst. When he saw Gertrude's eyes swollen, her hair disheveled, her blouse torn, and no shoes, Rupert ran to Gertrude. "What the hell is going on!"

"Siegfried has Gisela in chains; he wants to kill her while he is having sex! Gisela is screaming hysterically and has swollen black eyes and bruises on her legs and arms. Siegfried has an audience watching; he has collected hundreds of marks to watch this gruesome sex act."

Rupert grabs a club and a handgun from behind the bar and races up the stairs. He kicks down the door where Siegfried has Gisela as a captive. As Rupert sees the gruesome scene, he shouts to the spectators, "Get the fuck out of here before I kill all of you."

Siegfried is naked and strangling Gisela as he is mounted on Gisela. Siegfried is so drunk and on drugs that he does not recognize that his Onkel has stormed into the room. Rupert takes the club and strikes Siegfried in the head. Siegfried falls off the bed and passes out. Rupert unties Gisela and orders two workers to take her to a clean bedroom and administer first aid.

Rupert orders another two workers to carry Siegfried to his office and tie him to a chair,

After six hours, Rupert takes a water bucket and throws the wastewater directly at Siegfried's face. Siegfried comes to, spitting the wastewater from his mouth.

Rupert looks directly at Siegfried and speaks to him in an angry voice, "You goddamn sack of shit. If it were not because you are my nephew, I would have killed you last night."

Siegfried now comes to his senses, "Those prostitutes are lower than Jews; someday Hitler will declare them all misfits. I am only doing my German duty!"

Now Rupert is outraged. He orders two of his workers to take the sack of shit and throw him out in the street. Onkel Rupert finally rids himself of his nephew.

For six months, Siegfried lived in the ghettos of Hamburg and made his living by stealing money and food from Jews. After all, Hitler was preaching that Jews were sub-human, therefor stealing or raping any Jewish woman was within his right as a member of the *Ubermenschen* race. Before the war, Siegfried avoided being drafted by the Wehrmacht; however, when the war broke out in September of 1939, he quickly joined the regular army. Siegfried earned a reputation in the ghettos of Warsaw as being ruthless with the Jewish population. By the end of the Polish conquest, Siegfried was recruited by the Gestapo. When Hitler turned his Wehrmacht toward the west, Siegfried and the Gestapo were assigned by Heinrich Müller to rid the captured territories of the 'undesirables.' Siegfried's religious devotion to applying the 'Final Solution' made its way to Müller. Müller promoted Siegfried to *Obersleutnant* and assigned him to Paris. Before Buchner was assigned to oversee the Gestapo in Paris, *Oberst* Schmidt, the Paris commander of the Gestapo, and Rauch had different opinions on how to rid France of the resistance. This difference was communicated through official channels to Müller. Once Müller was informed that *Oberst* Schmidt and Rauch disagreed on how to rid France of the resistance, *Oberst* Schmidt was transferred to the eastern front.

Under these circumstances, *Oberst* Buchner took Command of the Paris Gestapo office.

Within two hours of arriving at the German headquarters at the Majestic Hotel in Paris, Buchner ordered his aide, *Leutnant* Fischer, to summon *Obersleutnant* Rauch to his office.

Rauch enters the office of *Oberst* Buchner, stands in front of Buchner's oversized desk, clicks his jackboots, and extends his right arm, "*Heil Hitler, Oberst* Buchner."

'*Heil* Hitler," responses Buchner. Rauch stands at attention and waits

Entrance to German HQs Majestic Hotel

for Buchner to begin the conversation. Buchner deliberately shuffles some papers, signs a couple of documents, and after two minutes of silence, orders Rauch, "At ease, have a seat; we need to discuss the situation with the resistance."

"*Jawohl mein Oberst, wir mussen diese ratten loswerden.*" (We must get rid of those rats.)

"Explain to me the situation in France regarding these enemies of the state. "

"*Jawohl, Oberst,* these rats are everywhere in France. Our *Abwehr, unsere Buro of Intelligenz,* estimates that there are between fifty and sixty networks of the 'enemies of the state.'"

Oberst Buchner shakes his head; he gets up from his chair. He drags his wooden leg behind, looks out to the street, and asks. "So, what were you and *Oberst* Schmidt doing to find and eliminate these enemies of the state?"

"*Jawohl,* that is the problem, Sir, we cannot find them. I believe that we should randomly pick ten Frenchmen and shoot them. We do this every day until the members of these rat infestations come forward and identify themselves."

"Perhaps, but what are we doing to find their transmitters when they communicate with the English?"

"*Jawohl Oberst*, we do not have enough direction finders, nor do we have trained operators. This would help, but we do not have the resources."

"*Sehr gut, Obersleutnant* Rauch, we shall quickly remedy this problem."

"*Jawohl.*"

"And have we tried infiltrating the resistance?"

"*Jawohl* with limited success. *Oberst* Schmidt and I successfully had a Greek sailor infiltrate. He did provide some useful information on two safe houses. When we conducted a raid on one of the safe houses, it was packed with explosives; we lost six *Schutzstaffel* (SS) in one of the raids. Three resistance members were surrounded in the second raid, and a gun battle ensued. The three members of the resistance committed suicide before we could capture them. We did find one English transmitter, but it was destroyed before they committed suicide, and we found some ashes and burned paper. These papers were probably their encoding and decoding documents. All contents collected from the two raids are at the offices of the *Abwehr.*"

"*Sehr gut*, I will need to inspect the items collected, and we need to think about infiltrating the resistance. Also, can you bring me the Greek that did infiltrate the resistance?"

"That is not possible; we found him in the river *Seine*; he had a bullet to the back of his head."

"Hmmm, he rubs his chin----give me a day to think about our approach. In the meantime, bring me a list of ten Frenchmen to be executed promptly. Also, prepare leaflets, 10,000 francs for information leading to the arrest of any resistance member."

Obersleutnant Rauch now thinks *Oberst Buchner is more in line with my ideas; now we will get things done!*
As instructed, *Obersleutnant* Rauch returned two days later with a recommendation for postings and leaflets. The recommended posting read:

Achtung: *Any male person directly or indirectly helping the French resistance by engaging in subversive activities against the German authorities will be shot immediately. Any woman involved in these lawless activities will be sent to German concentration camps.*

Subversive activities include engaging in assisting any enemy of the state including listening to enemy radio propaganda or using a radio to transmit any messages to the enemy.

Should a person be found to assist enemy pilots in escaping back to England, that person's immediate family will be shot. The bodies of their family will be hung from trees or lampposts to remind all Frenchmen to adhere to Germany's laws.

A reward of 15,000 Francs, and in individual cases, higher, will be given to anyone providing information on these state enemies.

To members of the resistance: you have two weeks from this notice to turn yourselves in. Should you surrender, you will receive a fair trial, and your families will be spared.

Two weeks pass, and no member of the resistance has come forward. *Oberst* Buchner thought everyone would need help to step forward, but he and *Obersleutnant* Rauch had a plan. They would take four prisoners from the civilian prison of the *Kriminaldirecktor, accuse* them of being found with transmitters, and execute them in the public square. As evidence of their criminal activities, they would use the same transmitter, which had been seized in the raid conducted by *Oberst* Schmidt.

Oberst Buchner orders Rauch to wait two weeks before the public executions take place. The French public did not know any better, and *Oberst* Buchner had proved his point---he was going to be ruthless and would pursue the resistance until all were eradicated. However, the one group that was not fooled were the resistance members.

Papillon meets with Renard:

Papillon, who is now firmly entrenched as an accountant with the office of the *Kriminaldirecktor,* uses the prearranged method to communicate with *Renard.* She leaves a message at the designated safe house and by their prearranged signaling method for a meeting. The arrangements have been made that only if required, the code word would be left with the owner of the butcher shop, and a meeting would then occur on the third Sunday evening of the following month. Sunday was considered the best time since it was natural for *Papillon* to attend church at least once a month for confession. As previously arranged, *Papillon* and *Renard* met at the convent.

Papillon, "There is now a new Colonel directing the *Gestapo*. He has replaced Schmidt. His orders are coming directly from Hitler. His primary goal is to find and kill all members of the resistance. Hitler was agitated and mad that he could not bring England down to its knees. He blames the English RAF with having bested the Luftwaffe. He got infuriated when he was told that very few of the English pilots being shot down in France are ever found. The German High Command has assigned a former Luftwaffe pilot, *Oberst* Gunter Buchner, to head the *Gestapo* in Paris. Buchner's only task is to destroy the resistance. Buchner was also a member of the German *Abwehr*; thus, he has contacts in the German Intelligence Service. He is smart, intelligent, cunning, cruel, ruthless, and cold-blooded. To add to our problem, *Obersleutnant* Rauch remains. He personally wishes to implement Hitler's 'Final Solution.' I have personally witnessed Rauch executing an old disabled Frenchman just to rid the undesirables from the *Champs Elysée*."

Renard, "*Très Bien,* we must be very careful how we proceed."

"Yes, *Oberst* Buchner has taken a plane back to Germany. The best I can tell, he is going back to Germany to inspect some new wonder weapons that the Germans have designed to find our transmitters. We need to be very careful. I suggest limiting all your transmissions to less than five minutes."

"Do we know if the new DF systems are now in France?"

"No, this I do not know. I will keep my ears open and see if I hear anything in the office of the *Kriminaldirecktor.*"

After passing this information on Monday morning, *Papillon* leaves the convent early and makes her way to her home. By 8 a.m. the following day, she is at her office of the Criminal Director's accounting desk.

Oberst Buchner Flies to Augsburg, Germany:

The city of Augsburg is highly industrialized and is one of several cities that manufactures aircraft. Two assembly lines are at the Augsburg BMW factory, the manufacturer of engines for the *Bf-409 Messerschmitt* and *Heinkel-He 111*. When Buchner was stationed near the Gablingen airfield, he made close acquaintances with several design engineers at the BMW plant. He would go to Augsburg, visit with his wife and his one remaining son, and pay a formal visit to the BMW plant.

The officials at the plant welcomed Buchner as they would a hero returning from the front lines, fighting the savages of the world. Before leaving Paris, Buchner had telegrammed the BMW plant, stating that he wanted to discuss their ideas on improving the ability to direction finding a radio wave. With the heads up from the telegram, the engineers at the BMW plant would be ready to discuss their ideas.

Oberst Buchner arrived in his transport plane and landed at the Gablingen airfield. That evening, he had dinner with his family and had a restful night at his home in Augsburg. The following morning, as agreed, he met with Hans Weber, the President and chief engineer at the BMW plant. Buchner was dressed in his Gestapo uniform, jackboots, and air medals that plated his left chest. The officials at the BMW plant saw Buchner as a loyal friend of the company. During his flying days, he profusely complimented the engineering staff with their design of the Bf-409. The Colonel claimed that the Bf-409 was second to none. Due to the *Oberst* stamp of approval on the Messerschmitt, the BMW officials had become millionaires. They had much to thank *Oberst* Buchner. The BMW officials treated Buchner like a king, and Buchner liked the idea that he was being catered to. Now, the Colonel wanted the company to assist with radio direction equipment. Hans Weber saw this as another opportunity to advance the company's coffers.

After profusely acknowledging Buchner's flying days and his recognition of becoming a German fighter ace, the conversation got down to business.

Herr Weber asked, "*Oberst*, how can we be of service to our country?"

"*Ya, wir mussen eine moglickeit haben, den standort eines senders schnell zu bestimmen.*" (We must have some way to quickly determine the location of a transmitter.)

"*Jawohl,* when you sent us your telegram, we brainstormed, and we have several methods that could be immediately deployed. We will need communications between the intercepting stations. First, the bearing lines must be transmitted automatically between the intercepting stations;

second, we will need an improved antenna. We have designed a logarithmic antenna that has improved gain and a much narrower beam pattern."

Herr Weber says, "You need a 'log periodic antenna,' which has the antenna elements cut at different sizes. The antenna elements are both in the vertical and horizontal planes. The design of the antenna was by our partners Manfred and Schwarz. As you know, Manfred and Schwarz designed the aviation instruments on the Bf-409."

Oberst Buchner is impressed with the explanation and asks, "May I see a demonstration?"

"Yes, of course, we leave immediately; our vehicles are ready. It is only a thirty-minute drive on the road to *Oberammergau*. We have some vehicles waiting. If you want to go now, I will call and have the vehicles at our front entrance in five minutes."

"Yes, of course, I would like to see the demonstration today. I am afraid that the war effort demands my return to Paris as soon as possible."

"Yes, of course. Let us walk out to the front entrance. The cars should be ready."

A caravan of five cars starts on the road to *Oberammergau*. Oberst Buchner and Herr Weber ride in the bulletproof Mercedes with front and back cars acting as guard shields for the Colonel. Two additional cars have BMW engineers and technicians inside. Herr Weber wants to make sure that the demonstration goes perfectly. He knows a good demonstration will result in a multi-million-mark contract to build DF systems for all German armed forces. The caravan arrives at the test site. Herr Weber explains the test set-up to the Colonel. Two technicians, the chief engineer, Boris Becker, and Weber, squeeze into a communications van.

Becker explains the test. "We have four transmitters throughout our test range and four intercept stations. Our technicians are in communications using encrypted radios. All the intercept operators are scanning the radio frequencies. As soon as one of the intercept operators detects a radio transmission, that frequency is automatically transmitted to the other three stations. The radios are automatically tuned, and lines of bearings are transmitted to all four stations. The result is that a location is plotted on the oscilloscope."

"*Jawohl,* but does it work?"

"We shall see." One of the technicians barks into his microphone and gives one of the transmitters a frequency. The scanning radio detects the frequency and sends a signal to all DF radios in the four DF vans. From that point, everything is automated. In less than one minute, the DF vans have a fix.

Buchner, "Impressive." He then asks, are the antennas omni-directional?"

"No, the antennas need to have a narrow intercept beam. This is how they determine the line of bearing. The intercept vans must have two antennas: the omni-directional and the pointing antenna."

"Can we make an antenna with both Omni and directional properties?"

"No, the requirement is that these systems be transportable; that is impossible."

"How soon can you have four systems delivered to Paris?"

Herr Weber confers with his chief engineer. He then says. "In two weeks, we can have sixteen systems here in Augsburg. We can deliver to the Gablingen airfield, and you can have a transport plane ready. You will need to provide the communications vans in Paris. We can send four trainers with the systems, one for each. Depending on the priority, production units can be rolled off within thirty to sixty days."

"We will need at least fifty systems for France alone."

"As soon as *Herr* Speer from the production ministry gives us the word, we can start our manufacturing process. We will need parts from various sectors of the economy; Speer will have the parts needed to be designated as critical."

Oberst Buchner, "Yes, I understand; I will prepare the required paperwork to have the parts needed as critical."

That afternoon, *Oberst* Buchner drives back to the Gablingen airfield, and he is back in Paris within five hours. He feels confident that Herr Weber, BMW, and Manfred and Schwarz will have the first four DF systems in France in two weeks. He will need to start thinking about where best to use the systems.

The day after Buchner arrives in Paris, he confers with Rauch.

"*Obersleutnant* Rauch, we will have four state-of-the-art DF systems arriving in two weeks. Each system consists of four intercept sites. Where is it best to install the systems?"

"How will the systems arrive?"

"They are being flown from Augsburg."

"I will check with the office of the *Kriminaldirecktor* and see where the resistance is most active."

Rauch is now excited that something is being done. He quickly has a command car take him to the municipal building near the Notre Dame cathedral. He storms into the building and demands to see the Director immediately. He is turned down due to the Director's appointment and will have to wait until the end of the day. However, the Director will be returning from his meeting in the 20th *arrondissement*, which is the furthest away from the city's center. This most likely means he will not return to the office until after 7 p.m. Rauch does not wish to wait that long and demands to talk to someone knowledgeable of the resistance attacks.

The head clerk tells Rauch, "That would be Inspector Dubois. He is sitting over there."

Inspector Dubois was in the French police and now is a member of the Malice. He is what one would call 'a reluctant collaborator'. The Inspector is only required to do the minimum: complete a job, get paid, and put food on the table. He only achieved this effortless job due to his reputation as an excellent inspector. Inspector Dubois has a desk in the open area, within two or three desks from *Papillon.* Rauch walks over to the Inspector and stands rigid above his desk, his nose up in the air.

Lizzette noticed a German officer standing at Inspector Dubois's desk. She calmly turns her head to be able to listen to the conversation.

Rauch, "' Stand at attention when a member of the Gestapo addresses you!"

Dubois quickly stands, clicks his worn-out shoes, and says, "*Heil* Hitler. How can I be of service?"

"Follow me." Rauch starts walking but soon realizes he does not know the office complex.

He turns and says, "Find an office where we can have a private conversation."

224

"Jawohl Herr Oberst."

Rauch looks at Dubois and needs to correct him on his proper title. He then follows Dubois into what looks like a cleaning room. Rauch is fuming, he shouts, "I am an *Oberst* in the Gestapo, is this the best you can do?"

"Yes Sir, I am but a Frenchman in the Malice. We are not allowed in the offices of German Officers."

Lizzette now notices that Inspector Dubois and the German Officer are walking toward the back offices. She sees that there is some confusion. She will later ask Inspector Dubois why the German SS officer visited the Offices of the French Criminal Division.

Rauch cools down and decides that the cleaning room will do. He only needs to know where the resistance is most active.

He asks Dubois, "Inspector, where in France is the resistance most active?"

Without hesitation, Dubois responds, "The resistance is most active around the city of Lyon. Lyon is in Vichy territory. They could send me to Lyon, and I could clean it up in one month."

"Veil Danke, that will not be necessary," but Rauch makes a mental note and thinks *perhaps I can use him later.* Rauch turns to leave and goes out of the wrong door.

Dubois shouts to the Rauch, "Sir, follow me. I will lead you out the front entrance. "Dubois hesitantly gestures Raunch in the right direction and watches him storm off.

Dubois goes back to his desk, muttering to himself, "Fucking idiots, and they want to rule the world?"

While Dubois is in a semi-state of anger, Lizzette asks, "What was all of that about?"

"Fucking idiot, you would think that the Gestapo would know where the northern resistance is most active. Shit, everyone in north France knows that the resistance is most active in the area south of Paris, near the town of Vichy."

Lizzette pretends as if she has no interest in what Inspector Dubois has told her. Lizzette then asks, "So they go to Vichy, then what?

"Seems that the Gestapo has some wonder machine that will locate the transmitter in seconds."

Papillion, "So, why the rush?"

"According to that ass-hole Colonel, the Gestapo is flying the special equipment to Paris next week. The new Colonel is under pressure to produce results ASAP." Dubois then tells Lizzette, "On Thursday the German's are flying a special plane with DF equipment."

Dubois then thinks for a few seconds and says, "I think that I have already told you too much. I best keep my mouth shut."

Dubois relaxes and thinks, *after all, Lizzette is only a woman and probably didn't understand anything I said.*

He convinces himself that there is nothing to worry about, for Lizzette would be the last person who would go running to the resistance.

* * *

Lizzette must get the information to Renard through the butcher shop safe house. She must send a coded message that reads, *"Special DF equipment leaving Augsburg on January 21 (1941) en route to Paris. The aircraft is a German Heinkel-He 111 transport."*

Papillon leaves the encoded message with the butcher, unaware if the message will ever get through. The butcher *Monsieur* LaPlante wraps the message in a newspaper, which is used to wrap a half-pound of bacon. He gives the bacon to his contact and quickly forces himself to forget about the exchange. Three days later, a wireless message is received by SOE. Colonel Susan Phillips is given the message. In-turn, she contacts the GCHQ MI6 and gives them only what they need to know regarding the immediate danger that her covert agents are in. MI6 then contacts the Air Command Headquarters. Included in the Air Command staff meeting is Colonel Harr, the commander of the Polish Fighter Squadron. Colonel Harr has a premonition that the new DF equipment and the recent rescue of his fighter Herman Hutchinson are related.

Colonel Harr asked General Emerson if he could look into this new development; he said, "I think it is related to our recent successful rescue of two of our pilots. We must assist the resistance. We must protect the resistance. They will be needed when we attack mainland Europe."

The General agrees to have Colonel Harr investigate the situation and report back to the command staff before taking any action.

Colonel Harr now meets with Captain Kowalski and Captain Hutchinson. Captain Hutchinson agrees that the Intel could have only come from *Papillon*. We must take some action to prevent the DF equipment from reaching Paris. Colonel Harr working with the Bomber Command, assigns a high-altitude reconnaissance long-range aircraft to the Heinkel aircraft's anticipated date flying from Gablingen airfield to Paris. They know that the stars will need to align just right to intercept the transport plane. Unknown to SOE, MI6 has intercepted comms traffic between Augsburg and Paris with the flight's date and time. The information that is given to the Air Wing is disguised as information coming from an informant. The reconnaissance flight still occurs. Reconnaissance flights are flying too high, and the planes are too fast. The Germans see them as a low reward and high risk and only note that an unknown high-altitude aircraft was in the area, this will cover the shooting down of the transport Heinkel aircraft.

Captain Kowalski volunteers himself for the mission. He is the most experienced and will need to fly by dead reckoning. He knows the Paris area very well from his days with the French Air Force and has the highest probability of mission success. A Spitfire with extra fuel tanks is outfitted for the flight to Paris and back. A round trip to Paris from an airfield in Dover is 460 miles. The Spitfire with two drop tanks extends the range of the Spitfire to 960 miles. Ski will fly his Spitfire south and drop his extra fuel tanks as he nears the Normandy coast. This will allow for a total range of 700 miles, with the ability to loiter in the air above Paris for forty-five minutes. Being an experienced pilot, he knows the likely flight path of the Heinkel transport. If the Germans do spot him at the altitude he is flying, it will appear to be a recon flight (the Germans do not have radar).

Ski flies fifteen minutes east of Paris and spots the Heinkel transport aircraft. He checks the tail number and is in luck. He comes up high with the sun to his back and fires the Spitfire cannons. The German aircraft offers no opposition. It is a transport aircraft with no guns. Ski looks down at the destroyed aircraft as it spirals down to earth. Kowalski circles the Heinkel's crash area and sees a bright red-orange mushroom cloud of black smoke as the aircraft crashes to the ground. The Germans will classify this shooting as a target of opportunity. Ski flies back to Dover and reports that the Heinkel was destroyed. The significance of the German Heinkel's destruction is lost in the statistics of war.

The reaction to the downing of the Heinkel-He 111:

Oberst Buchner has now turned his attention to the next phase of eliminating the resistance, thinking of his infiltration plan. Buchner has assigned *Obersleutnant* Rauch to the details of planning to find the location of the transmitters; as such, Rauch is waiting at the Paris airfield to meet the transport plane. Rauch is eager to get started and is already planning his method of executing the plan to find the location of the transmitters.

The aircraft from the Augsburg Airfield is scheduled to arrive at 4:30 p.m. It is now 4:45, and the aircraft had not arrived. Although the Germans are very punctual, one thing they cannot control is the weather. The weather between Bavaria and north-central France was confirmed to have good weather conditions, so Rauch did not expect the plane from Augsburg to arrive fifteen minutes past the scheduled time. At 5 p.m., the aircraft still has not arrived. *Obersleutnant* Rauch climbs the stairwell to the control tower. He knocks on the door and shows his Gestapo credentials.

"*Feldwebel* (Sergeant), what is the flight status from Augsburg?"

"Yes, sir, could you provide some additional details?"

"It is a Heinkel-He 111, transport aircraft which departed Gablingen airfield at 12 noon today."

"*Jawohl,* the flight was to arrive at 4:32 this afternoon. It has not landed."

"*Feldwebel,* transmit to the aircraft at once and see if you can communicate?"

"*Jawohl Oberst*." The sergeant transmits on his radio but receives no response.

The sergeant then says. "I will contact the control tower in Dijon and see if the aircraft communicated with them."

After one minute, the sergeant turns to Rauch and says. "*Oberst* Rauch, the transport plane flew over the Dijon control tower on schedule. I am afraid that there has been some problem."

Oberst Rauch says with some indignation, "*Feldwebel,* do not just sit there, find out what the hell happened to my aircraft?"

228

"*Jawohl Oberst* Rauch."

The sergeant frantically starts calling all control points, but no one knows the status.

After more than twenty minutes of silence, he tells Rauch, "Sir, no one has heard or seen the aircraft. The plane was probably shot down."

"Could it have landed or crashed due to an aircraft malfunction?"

"Not likely; if it had encountered aircraft problems, the pilots would have had time to transmit a distress call. It appears that the aircraft had a sudden catastrophic failure, which normally indicates that it was shot down."

Rauch has seen this type of aircraft loss; it is a roll of the dice. Being at the wrong place at the right time. Some English pilot likely spotted the transport plane, and then they took the opportunity to shoot down the Heinkel-He 111. Rauch thinks, Goddamn miracle weapons, they have the priority. The DF equipment is the single most important item to find and destroy these traitors. Hopefully, we will receive the equipment in less than two or three months.

Rauch drives back to Paris and tells Buchner the bad news. Buchner did not expect the plane to be shot down, but he accepted that the Brits have a vote in the war outcome. He sees the loss of the DF systems as a minor set back. He will need to expedite the production systems' delivery in what he hopes is less than two months. In the meantime, he and Rauch will start working on the plan to infiltrate the resistance.

Chapter Twenty-Five
Juliette Delivers Transmitters
German Occupied France

MI6 has intercepted a series of communications from Albert Speer, the German Minister of Armaments and War Production. These radio intercepts have indicated that the radio direction-finding system, which the Germans have code-named Freya, is nearing production. The Germans intended to conduct operational testing along the French and Holland coastlines. British aerial intelligence has indicated that the radio intercept antennas are installed twenty kilometers inland from the English Channel coastline. MI6 has requested that SOE task the French resistance for real-time visual intelligence. Colonel Richardson from MI6 has asked that he be given an audience with Colonel Phillips. Colonel Richardson is stationed at the super-secret Bletchley Park buildings; thus, meeting at the SOE headquarters on Baker Street is best. Attending the meeting are Colonel Phillips, Captain Hutchinson, and Colonel Richardson.

Colonel Phillips says, "Colonel Richardson, I want you to meet Captain Hutchinson. The Captain oversees all taskings of our French resistance assets. He has personally been in occupied in France and has direct contact with the leaders of the resistance. He is cleared at the highest levels and may be briefed on the intelligence you have collected."

'Thank you, Colonel; our source for this information is highly classified, but I can assure you that it has a very high degree of confidence. Combining our intelligence with aerial photographs, the Germans are installing a radio intercept station in the *Putanges-Le-Lac* area of northern France. As you can see, it is situated approximately twenty kilometers from the Normandy coast."

Captain Hutchinson views the photograph and says, "I am familiar with the area. I believe it is where I was hidden before my return to England."

Richardson, "The area is heavily wooded, with small mountains and valleys. We believe that the Germans have selected this spot for two reasons: one, it is secluded and away from any Frenchmen who would report the construction to the British, and two, it is the only area with a mountain to install the antenna."

"The fact that it is in a forest and in a secluded location will work best for the resistance. What is it that you need from us?"

"We need intelligence, then we need to know how many guards are also the workers. Is the control station at the antenna building? If not, where is it? Is the station manned 24X7? If not, when do the construction workers stop their work?"

Colonel Phillips, "Do you plan on destroying the facility? If so, how?"

"At this time, we do not know. First, we need visual information. The initial phase should be to observe the facility strictly. You think that your assets in the field could provide this information?"

Captain Hutch, "Yes, we have assets in the area, and I am sure we can complete the first phase."

"How soon can we have the info? This information is critical to maintaining our advantage in the aerial warfare with the Germans."

"We will task our assets in France today. We should have a reply within 48 hours. At that time, we can tell you how soon we can have a team on-site and collect the information."

"Thank you; when you have a team tasked, please give me status and let me know an approximate date of the data being available; based on the initial reconnaissance, we can then decide how best to proceed."

That evening Herman has his radio team send a message to Renard, requesting the reconnaissance mission. In 48 hours, a return message comes back. The resistance will have a team at the location within a week. Renard also has alarming news; the situation has become oppressive and excessively harsh. Heinrich Müller, the Chief of the German Gestapo, has issued draconian laws. Since Operation Barbosa, Germany has conscripted all German men aged eighteen to forty to be in the Wehrmacht. Germany needed able-bodied body men and women to work in German factories to manufacture war materials. Frenchmen and women were being rounded up like cattle and being shipped to labor camps.

The Gestapo Chief in Paris, *Oberst* Buchner, ardently believes in the "Final Solution." He has ordered all Jews, Gypsies, persons with physical ailments or congenital diseases, and all undesirables to be loaded onto cattle wagons and shipped to concentration camps.

Oberst Buchner has a special hatred for members of the resistance and English pilots. Escaped prisoners have reported that the Gestapo used many forms of torture to extract information from his prisoners. These methods include the following: starvation, regular beatings with clubs and whips, sleep deprivation, confinement in dark cells, solitary confinement in heat sheds, chokeholds to deprive the brain of oxygen, forced feeding of urine, salt water, and submersion in cold water. Despite all these atrocities, captured members of the resistance do not break. And the few that do provide information that is either false or unusable. The resistance members have cover names, so their capturers never know their real names. The members are also encouraged not to give up. They say, use all the bullets in your firearm and leave one bullet in your handgun to use on yourself---dead men can't talk.

Renard sends the message and says, "We need the new radio equipment, the advanced German equipment is starting to go operational. According to our source (Papillon), this equipment will find our transmitters and render our communications with the SOE obsolete."

Hutchinson, "OK, go ahead and conduct the surveillance; I will see what we can do to expedite the advanced radio equipment."

Herman now discusses the situation with Colonel Phillips, "Colonel, we need to get the advanced radios to the resistance immediately, they may not be able to communicate with us within weeks."

"What is your recommendation?"

"Really, no choice; we need to parachute two radio systems and send a trainer radio operator. The best solution would be the Americans. They were sent here to conduct radio training; Vargas, Valencia, and Santiago would be able to provide the training."

"I agree; we will talk to them and see if they volunteer."

"OK, I will take the train to Milton Hall tomorrow and discuss the situation with the three."

Following a two-day Train ride, Herman arrives at Milton Hall. Francisco had received a telegram that read, "Captain Hutchinson arriving in two days." Nothing else was stated as the mission to arm the resistance was considered to be classified.

The train from Edinburg arrives at the Milton Hall train station, and Francisco and Andres are waiting for the Lieutenant. As Hutchinson disembarks, Francisco and Andres immediately recognize the Lieutenant. Francisco and Andres walk toward Hutchinson and his bags. Hutchison smiles and with a hearty, "Good to see the both of you. I can't thank you enough for my rescue from the French coast."

Francisco also smiles, "Good to have been of service. And what brings you to Milton Hall?"

"Yes, sorry I could not say much in my telegram. We have been given the go-ahead to arm the French resistance. I am here to discuss with you our immediate plans."

"OK understood, I have arranged for a secure room to begin our discussions," Andres informs the Lieutenant.

They arrive at a Quonset Hut located on the outer perimeters of the base. Already at the secure location is Juliette. Francisco introduces Juliette, and the discussions begin.

Hutchinson begins, Mi6 has detected that a new radar site is being constructed on the French coast. We need a reconnaissance team to lay eyes on the installation and report back to us. We have two problems: who conducts the recon, and how does the information get back to us?"

Andres then gives a solution to the first problem, "We can have the resistance provide the information."

"Yes, I agree, but who?" Hutch then answers his question. "We need to contact Renard, the leader of the Auvergne Forest resistance group."

Hutch continues, "Second, we need comms."

Francisco then offers a solution to the second problem. "The transmitters from MIT arrived last week."

Hutch smiles and says, "Excellent. Who goes, you or Andres?"

"Neither do we send Juliette; she is our best radio operator and has undergone commando training."

Hutch shakes his head and says, "A woman? I don't know if Colonel Philips would approve?"

Juliette has been listening quietly but stands and, with a determined expression, sounds off, "Come on guys, you think because I am a woman that I cannot handle this assignment? Not only do I know the advanced transmitters and have completed commando training, I know the area. I was born in France and speak like a native. My father was a physics professor at the University of Strasburg. My mother is a German Jew. They met when my father was in the U.S. Army during WWI. In 1932, my family moved to Argentina because Argentina allowed unrestricted immigration from Germany. After moving to Argentina, my father started a company building radios. This is where I learned about radios, and I joined the HF amateur club. At eighteen, I moved to New York City and enrolled at the City College. Last year, I joined the U.S. Army as a second lieutenant, and due to my language skills, I was assigned to the logistics command in Ogden, Utah. From there, you know the rest of the story."

Francisco now interrupts and adds to her resume. "Captain Hutchinson, I need to add some additional info. She excelled at the training center in Ogden and was key to the mission when we had to uncover the German network on the U.S. East Coast."

Hutchinson now asks, "I understand that you know the area in Northern France. Is that correct?"

"Yes, I am very familiar with northern France. I have family in France, and often I would stay the summer with my aunt."

"OK, you will be the first of the SOE agents that will infiltrate the German-occupied territory. We will arrange the required documents to identify you as a French woman from northern France.

Within two weeks, the documents will be completed, and her cover name will be Aimee Dupree from Dijon, France. Besides fully knowing her new identity, she needs to know the French nation's current state. She studies the country's two zones, the German and the Vichy zones. In two weeks, she is ready for her mission.

Hutchinson has the SOE radio operator transmit to the French resistance that two advanced transmitters and an operator will arrive via aircraft at 2 a.m. on a selected date. The aircraft is a Westland Lysander: a long-range, quick takeoff and landing machine built to operate in grass fields. They pick a time when there is a full moon and no overcast so the pilot can navigate by dead reckoning and landmarks. Ten minutes before the appointed hour, the resistance members have built fires to indicate the landing strip. The plane will only be on the ground long enough to offload the transmitters and the trainer-operator. The resistance has two British fliers that had been shot down while returning to England. At 2 a.m., the plane is on the ground. In seven minutes, the ground crew turns the aircraft around, retrieves the cargo, and the Lysander only uses one hundred yards to become airborne yet again. Just as quickly as it landed, it disappeared back to England.

The resistance teams of four are busy loading the transmitter crates onto a meatpacking truck. They only realize that the trainer-operator is a woman once they are on the road to their safe location deep in the forest.

As the resistance leader, Renard welcomes Aimee, "Welcome to France."

Aimee, *"Merci beaucoup"*.

"Oui, Merveilleux."

From this point forward, the conversations are in French.

Renard, *"Mademoiselle,* my cover name is *Renard*; we must have one for you. What would you like your cover name to be?"

"Pierrot."

"Excellent, it fits you perfectly; you are like the many sparrows we have in France, flying free as they wish."

Pierrot (Juliette) and Renard arrive at the safe house. The boxes are off-loaded, and the transmitter is set up. Pierrot takes about thirty minutes to punch up her message. She confides in a book with a table of frequencies that may be used. She prepares the preamble and connects the black box to the transmitter, and in less than two minutes, using four different frequencies, a thirty-four-minute message is transmitted.

Renard and the three other resistance members watch in astonishment. She tells them that SOE knows she and the transmitters have arrived safely.

Renard says, "I know you think the Germans have not detected the transmission, but we should move to a second location."

"Agreed. Can we leave a lookout on the hill and see if we have German DF trucks arrive in the next few hours?'

"Yes, that is a good idea."

The team moved to a new location and started planning their surveillance of the *Freya* Site.

Renard, "The DF site is a two or three-day walk from here. We know the area quite well. We should have no problems with the surveillance."

"Yes, I also know about the area. When I was seven or eight, my family would often picnic in the forest on the Normandy coast."

"Under normal conditions, we would take the train, but we will take the mountain trails and travel at night to ensure we complete the mission. There will be three of us, plus yourself. My team will have Marcin, Argos, and I. From your photos, it appears that we should be able to survey the site from the adjacent hill. With binoculars, we should be able to determine the number of workers and guards."

"Do we know if the workers are French, Spanish, or German?"

"They will not be German. Most likely forced labor workers from Russia or Azerbaijan. The supervisors may be Spanish. If they are, these workers can easily be bribed. We will use some of the francs that you brought on your plane, even though we are armed. We will make all attempts not to shoot our guns. We fully understand that this is only a reconnaissance mission."

The next day, the lookout reports that no German DF trucks arrived at the site.

Renard, "That's very encouraging; the Germans did not detect the transmission."

The team has one 30X60 single scope on a tripod and three 10X30 binoculars. All are camouflaged green with nonreflecting lenses. The 30-magnifying single scope has a camera mount to allow for pictures to be taken. During the three-day trip, all are wearing clothes that easily blend into the forest. On the day of the surveillance, they wear face paint, a stocking cap, and their hands are painted: everything black. They carefully remove any object that may reflect in the moonlight. For the men, the most challenging is not smoking.

The photos show an adjacent hill in the next valley; however, the Germans have a guard post. They decide to survey the guard post from the adjoining hill. They determine that there are four guards on duty, each shift is 12 hours. The guards seem to be bored while making their two to three-hour rounds. The team decides that two team members will quietly move to the surveillance hill immediately after a guard completes his round, leaving them two hours of surveillance. The next two-man team will wait until the next guard's round is completed and take their position for another two hours.

The team completes two days of surveillance and then backs off for five kilometers to discuss their findings. The discussion is all from memory, as the photos will need to be developed later in a dark room.

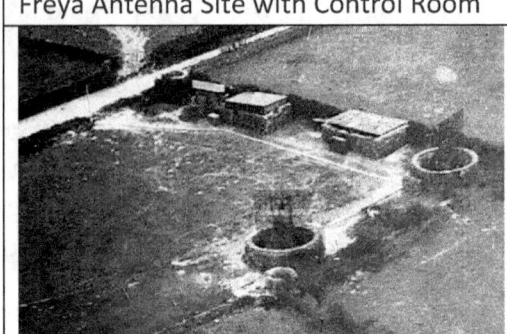

Freya Antenna Site with Control Room

Renard begins, "There are two antennas with what appears one main control center. We need to concentrate our attention on the control room. This is where the data will be stored regarding the design."

Pierrot now gives her opinion. "Yes, the control center is our main objective. This is where the operational data will be stored. Plus, there will likely be design parameters and the system's full capabilities."

"I counted from ten to fifteen workers. They are working eighteen hours a day. From six a.m. to midnight."

Marcin, "There seem to be four to five German technicians. They were wearing working clothes. Probably workers from the Manfred and Schwarz Company, the manufacturer of the DF system."

"Do we know if the workers are French?" asks Pierrot.

Argos, who is from the area, says, "Yes, I think that they are from the nearby towns."

"OK, do we know if we can identify the workers and ask the local resistance cell if any of them could be bought?" asks Marcin.

Renard, "I am the only one that could do that. The local resistance leader knows me. OK, we have two tracks to follow: One, determine where the contractors live, and two, can any of the workers be bought."

Pierrot, "I can venture into the town and see if I can determine where the contractors are living."

"OK, but you need a reason for being in the town," says Argos. "Let me go with you as your escort. This will look normal, and I know several people in the town."

Renard, "Good idea, this will be natural; you are returning to get reacquainted with your friends. While you do that, I will contact the local resistance leader and see if any workers can be bought."

Renard contacts the local resistance leader, who has a small butcher shop on the edge of town. He knows that none of the workers favor the resistance, because they are being paid livable wages and do not want to turn against the German company.

However, Pierrot and Argos have better luck. Argo's friend, Henri, gives them some helpful information. Henri is a truck driver. He tells Argo that a shipment is made to the compound at least once or twice a week and delivers the building material.

Argos, "Henri, are you the only driver?

"No, we have four drivers. It depends on who is available when the shipments arrive."

Henri continues, "The German guards have a couple of Gestapo agents. These agents guard the antenna control room. Only the Gestapo and employees of the construction company are allowed in the control room bunker. I can only assume that there is some very sensitive information in that bunker. Everything that I haul is building material."

Pierrot (aka Aimee, Juliette) asks, "Do the company employees look like members of the German military?"

"No, they are older men. They look like professors at a college."

"Do you ever hear them speak about what they are doing inside the bunker?"

Henri thinks for a few minutes and says, "They do come out when I deliver a load and direct the off loaders to place the materials. When they see the struts for the antenna structure, they say, *'Ja, Ja, Sehr gut, Das ist die antenne.'*"

"Do you ever see them take blueprints or technical papers into the bunker?"

"No, but they always have briefcases. I overheard one of the men asking another if they locked up and double-checked the lock on all of the materials. Apparently, they lock the materials, and the second person must check to see if they have been secured."

"Do you ever see new personnel from the construction company arrive?"

"Oh, yes, new personnel are always arriving."

"Who checks their credentials?"

"Their security is very tight. The guards at the outer perimeter will check all the workers and anyone entering with supplies. When I arrive, they check my Ausweis, and one guard escorts me to the off-loading area. The guard will stay with the materials until all crates are off-loaded."

"Are the crates opened immediately?"

"Only if there is enough sunlight. Any deliveries after 4 p.m. are not open until the following day."

"So, when the crates are not open, where are they stored?"

"There is a makeshift warehouse. It is guarded 24X7."

"How many guards?"

"Two guards are always on duty. I do not know if they walk the perimeter."

"Merci beaucoup."

Pierrot tells Marcin, "I think we have enough information. Is there anything you would like to ask?"

"Oui, how are the materials from Germany shipped to the location?"

Henri, "Not sure, but I believe that the materials all arrive by air transport. The building of the antenna system is a high priority by the hours that are being worked."

"Merci beaucoup."

After all the questions are asked, Marcin thanks Henri. Marcin, Renard, and Pierrot travel on foot back to the safe location.

Renard, Marcin, and Pierrot now debrief each other on their findings.

Renard summarizes, "There are ten to fifteen workers, most are Russians, and the supervisors are Spaniards. Not likely that they will provide information for francs. Employees from the German construction company arrive on a steady basis. Shipments are moved from the airport to the antenna site by truck. The crates are open if they arrive before 4 p.m. If they arrive after 4 p.m., they are stored in a guarded warehouse. There are two security perimeters: an entry to the compound and an entrance to the antenna build-ing. And finally, classified material is stored inside the antenna control bun-ker." Pierrot transmits the information to Captain Hutchinson at SOE.

***

Captain Hutchinson, Lieutenants Vargas, and Valencia read the re-port from Pierrot. Captain Hutchinson, "Excellent report. We need to brief Colonels Philips and Richardson from MI6."

Within two hours, the Colonels are now present in a secure room of the SOE. Captain Hutchinson briefs the group.

Colonel Richardson says, "I will have Major Jason Ewell, a member of the Special Air Service, contact Captain Hutchison and start planning for the next phase. Major Ewell has more than ten years' experience with the SAS and has successfully completed covert missions in India, Afghanistan, and re-cently in German-occupied Norway."

The following day, Major Ewell and Captain Hutchinson meet at the SOE headquarters. Captain Hutchinson briefs the Major on the findings of the surveillance team. Before the Major's meeting, the captain has communi-cated with Juliette and asked for her opinion on how best to obtain the design plans for the *Freya* system. The captain will present her recommendations to the Major.

Captain, "Our covert assets in France recommend that one or two agents enter the compound through the supply trucks. The trucks would ar-rive after 1600, ensuring that the crates would be placed in storage. That evening, the two hidden agents would pick the antenna control bunker's locks and photograph the design plans. Five additional SAS operators, plus mem-bers of the French resistance, will be outside the guarded compound if armed assistance is required. "

Major Ewell, "Do we have someone who knows what we are looking for?"

"Yes, we have one agent in France, and another will accompany your team."

"Are the agents in good condition, and can they help support a fire-fight?"

"Yes, Sir, they are trained SOE agents."

Captain Hutchinson has selected Francisco Vargas and Andrew Valencia, the most technically qualified SOE members. Their code names are *"Chico" and "*Andrés." Both will be given a new identity, Francisco becoming Jose Gonzales and Andrés as Maurice Celanc. Jose is a Spaniard, and Maurice is a Frenchman. Both are working in the industrial plants in the Normandy area. All their identity papers *(Ausweis),* work permits, and passports have been completed by the SOE.

The fake documents are all completed by a professional printer and look authentic. The SAS team will go in 'naked,' meaning no identity papers. They are all English, and it would be impossible to fake them as Frenchmen or Spaniards.

The Attack Plan:

Major Jason Ewell, a member of the SAS working with the SOE, has an outline of the attack plan. It will be discussed with the field agents and adjusted accordingly. The planning meeting is attended by Colonel Phillips, Captain Hutchinson, Lieutenants Vargas and Valencia from SOE, Colonel Richardson from MI6, Major Ewell, and Sergeant Monroe from SAS.

As the officer in charge of the operation, Major Ewell begins, "Next week on Thursday evening, a bombing raid will be returning from Germany. Undercover of returning bombers, we will fly two Lysander long-range planes to deliver six SAS agents, including myself, plus two SOE agents by the code name *Chico* and *Andrés*."

Captain Hutchinson asks, "Do we have the exact time and coordinates for the parachute drops?"

"Yes, these are the coordinates." The major gives the coordinates to the Captain then says, "As you can see, the coordinates are in France's Vichy zone. The Vichy zone is not that heavily populated, and our chances of not being detected are high. The drawback is that we are a three or four-day travel by foot from our objective."

"This should not be a problem. What about the time?"

"We will need to wait until the bombing raid is on its way to Germany; then, we can provide the time."

"OK, I will notify our agent in France to ready the signal light to indicate the location for the parachute drop."

"The following supplies will be parachuted from the plane: One, six transmitters and all associated support equipment; two, Nobel 808 plastic explosives with remote detonator switches; three, a crate of German Sten guns and Lugers with ammunition; four, German handheld radios to allow eavesdropping on the Malice and German communications, and five, two hundred thousand francs."

Francisco, "We will be adding a key lock gun, handheld cameras, dart gun with disability darts, and camouflage clothes for the resistance fighters."

"OK, we must weigh all the items plus the seven men. This should not be a problem since we have two aircraft."

The major continues, "We will decide how best to enter the command antenna bunker once we are there and study our options. The objective is to enter the bunker with one SOE agent and one SAS agent. Search the building between the hours of 0100 and 0500 and exfiltrate without the Germans knowing we have entered."

"What's the escape plan?"

"One of two things. One, we successfully obtain the information without the Germans being aware, or two, we need to shoot our way out. Should the second be needed, all attempts will be made to protect the SOE agent with the camera. My men have been instructed to fight to the death. We will not surrender; all men will have a cyanide pill, and either uses the pill or their handgun to not be taken alive; we will protect the SOE agent at all costs. Should we be detected once we are inside the antenna facility, if a man is wounded, then we cannot leave a man alive; We know what we must do. The escape will be either by air, submarine or through Spain. We will have a transmitter and request how best we can be extracted."

The discussions end on a high note; Captain Hutchinson says, "Our in-country team is the best we have, I believe in their abilities, and we fully expect a successful mission."

"Thank you, Captain. Let's start gathering all gear and have it at the hanger at the 204th Air Wing airfield hanger. I will have the two Lysander aircraft fueled and ready to fly at a moment's notice."

Chapter Twenty-Six
The Attack on the Freya Site
Northern France

The two Lysander planes are fueled and loaded. The team must be ready at a moment's notice. They are all bivouacked inside the hanger of the 204th RAF Air Wing.

At 15:00, Major Jason Elwell re-ceives a call from Colonel Richardson, "There is a bombing raid scheduled for tonight at 23:00. The returning bombers will be flying over the French free zone. You must be at your designated para-chute drop at 02:00. The resistance has

Lysander Aircraft

been notified. They will have the lighted fires between 01:45 and 02:20."

"Roger, we will depart at midnight."

Major Elwell turns to Sergeant Monroe, "Load the planes and have your men ready to depart at 23:30."

Major Elwell now confers with the two pilots and SOE agents, 'Chico and Andrés.'

"Gentlemen, we must depart to be over the drop zone at 02:00." Lieutenant Gooding, one of the Lysander pilots, looks at the drop zone. He confers with the second pilot and then determines their flight path.

Lieutenant Gooding says, "We must depart at 23:30. We need to cir-cumvent several areas of known anti-aircraft guns."

"Thank you, Lieutenant; we will be ready at ten hundred hours."

Sergeant Monroe and the five-man SAS crew have the two planes fully loaded. Chico and Andrés ensure that the six transmitters are correctly packed and the parachutes on the crates are secure. The pilots supervise the loading to ensure the proper weight distribution on their respective planes. At 22:00, the two Lysanders leave the 204th Airfield and fly south 100 km from the French coastline. They enter the French air space just north of the

Pyrenees mountains and fly east. For the next three hours, they do not encounter any problems. Only the droning of engines and the hardened silence
of the men's thoughts fill the plane. At 01:30., they reduce their flight altitude
slowly from 10,000 to 2,000 feet. As they are nearing the drop point, they
encountered heavy anti-aircraft fire. The entire plane starts to vibrate as if
every rivet is going to come loose. Flashes of light following in a linear pattern
start rushing toward the plane. The sounds of anti-aircraft flak guns and
shrapnel bounce off the skin of the planes. Speaking through the airplane radios, Lieutenant Gooding transmits to Major Elwell and Sergeant Monroe on
the second plane.

"Bailout now, we cannot sustain the enemy flak guns much longer;
we need altitude, or we need to abort!"

Major Elwell, "Sergeant Monroe, jump now."

With the command, the equipment crates are shoved off the planes, and SAS
crews, Chico and Andrés, jump off the aircraft. The two Lysanders quickly gain
altitude and escape the blistering flak guns. Fortunately, the SAS, Chico, and
Andrés are experienced paratroopers who control their parachutes to land
near the equipment crates. The infiltration team has landed four kilometers
from the designated drop point. The resistance had heard the drone of the
two planes and saw that they were undergoing heavy flak. The parachutes
were painted black, but the crate parachutes' buckles reflected some moonlight to let the resistance fighters know they were off target by four kilometers. The resistance team quickly boarded their two meatpacking trucks, and
within ten minutes, they were at the drop point.

The concern was that if they had seen the parachutes, the Vichy police
and Milice might have also seen them. They had to assume they had been
detected and work double-time to clear the area. Upon identifying themselves with the proper passwords, the combined teams loaded the two trucks
and were safely located. They drove away, using dirt back roads with the
lights on the trucks painted blue. From the side windows of the trucks, they
could see the lights from the Milice police's vehicles arriving at the drop location. The resistance followed their escape plan; by daylight, they were fifty
miles from the drop zone.

They converse with the resistance fighters only after they are safely in a barn. Francisco and Andrés are now the links between the resistance and the SAS.

Waiting in the barn was Renard, *"Bienvenue, les amis."* (Welcome friends).

"Merci Beaucoup," answers Francisco and Andrés.

All team members are introduced using only first names and the cover names of the resistance fighters. All conversations are now in French, with Francisco providing the translation. Renard explains that they are a four-day journey away from the communications station. Travel will be by a meat wagon, using two horse-drawn wagons, and then on foot. The SAS soldiers, Francisco and Andrés, must dress as peasants. This is a regular occurrence in the French countryside. The radio transmitters are stored in the barn's hidden cellar, and training will occur after the raid has been successfully completed. All attention must be placed on the raid.

Andrés, "Where is Pierrot? Is she safe?"

Renard, *"Oui,* Pierrot and my fighters are near the communications site. She is safe."

"Merci Beaucoup."

Major Elwell, Francisco, Andrés, and the SAS soldiers all dress in French peasants' clothes. The problem will occur at the border between the German and Vichy zones. The plan is to have the SAS members Francisco and Andrés dismount the wagons and use Resistance fighters as guides to cross the border from high in the mountains. Two resistance fighters from the area will cross the border as farmers carrying sacks of potatoes and soybeans. The two fighters have the proper *Ausweis* and are known to the border guards as residents. They have no problem crossing into the German zone. After ten kilometers, the wagons stop at an inn, and the SAS soldiers, Francisco and Andrés, again travel by wagon. For the next three days, they do not encounter any problems. On the fourth day, they kit-up with their regular SAS camouflage uniforms and are fully armed. Two of the resistance fighters carry items needed for the infiltration: one backup transmitter, bolt cutters, wire cutters, shovels, key lock guns, plastic explosives with remote denotator switches, ammunition, flashbangs, grenades, and other items that may be needed. They arrive at a safe location at the end of the fourth day. It is a farm with several large barns and wheat silos. Pierrot and Argos have developed all the pictures and have created a makeshift table using two sawhorses and several bales of hay for chairs. After introductions are complete, Pierrot and Argos give the briefing. Pierrot first explains in English, then in French. She hands out the pictures and briefs the SAS, Francisco, and Andrés on the number of workers and German guards. She describes the security and the trucks that bring supplies from the airport and train station.

After the briefing, Pierrot says, "Gentlemen, we have some additional news. Argos and I have seen increased activity at the communications site. I requested an update from SOE on any new intelligence."

Major Elwell, "Have we received the information from British Intelligence?"

"No, not yet; however, British intelligence has seen a significant increase in chatter regarding the comms site."

"When do we expect the additional data?"

"My best guess is within the next two days. SOE has recommended we wait until the Intel agents at MI6 have better info."

"OK, we can wait two days but no more. Waiting in this safehouse cannot go on indefinitely,"

Renard, "I agree, this is not one of our normal safehouses. The Germans will sooner or later send a patrol in this area."

Pierrot, Francisco, and Andrés all agree. Andrés tells Pierrot to send a message to SOE and let them know that we wait for two days. If we have no further information, we will proceed as initially planned."

Pierrot looks around the barn, and Major Elwell agrees, "Send the message."

"Roger, I will send the message tonight."

A return message is received the following day: *"Dignitaries will visit the site one week from today to witness the initial operation. Two engineers from the manufacturer, Manfred and Schwarz, will be at the site two days before the visit by General Hermann Göring and the Paris Gestapo, Oberst Gunter Buchner".*

Juliette has an idea after hearing that the site will have a visit from two engineers from Manfred and Schwarz's firm.

She first confers with Francisco and Andrés. "Remember our mission against the German Bund?"

"Yes," replied Francisco and Andrés.

"I think we can do the same here."

"OK, what do you have in mind?" Replies Andrés.

"The Chateaudun Airfield, where the two employees of the *Freya* design firm, will be landing fifty-five kilometers from Paris. The employees will then travel by car from the Airfield to the communications site. There will be several locations where we can stop the car. We subdue the two engineers, and you and Francisco can take their place. The same as we did with the company from South America."

Pierrot continues, "I need to message Captain Hutchison to see if they know the two engineers' names. We can have Renard's Resistance prepare two Ausweis and company I.D. cards showing your picture with their names. Using this method, you will gain entry to the communications site control bunker."

Francisco, "OK, go ahead and send the message. We must brief Major Elwell and Renard on our recommended approach."

Andrés, "Yes, we need to brief them, but I see no reason for their objection."

Juliette now asks for a meeting to discuss their idea. Francisco and Andrés will be taking a major risk. They will present their idea to the assault group and explain their successful mission against the German Bund. The success or failure of the mission will depend on their ability to act and speak like native Germans and their technical skills. Both Francisco and Andrés are confident in their German language skills. Both grew up speaking German. They believe Dr. Fry taught them the theory of direction-finding to convince the Germans that they were engineers from Manfred and Schwarz.

Francisco begins with their idea. He explains their experience in successfully passing for Germans and that the SOE has selected them for the mission because of their technical expertise. From the beginning of Francisco's explanation of the approach, Major Elwell would prefer something else. He will not be in control. However, he will allow the SOE agents to complete their plan, and after the entire plan is presented, he will object based on any problems or complications he finds.

The presentation now shifts to Andrés, "Renard, we will need your help. We received a message with the names of the two German engineers. Their names are Albert Schonberg and Joseph Walters. We will need to have new identity cards made up with our pictures. Also, German passports with our pictures. Can you have these done in the next two days?"

"Yes, my Resistance contact in the area can have false Ausweis and passports prepared. Do you have passport-quality pictures?"

"Yes, anticipating that we would need new identity cards printed, we all have brought the needed pictures."

"If I can have the pictures today, I will contact the resistance leader by nightfall and have them prepare the documents."

"*Merci beaucoup.*"

"We need to know where to set up a false checkpoint and apprehend the company representatives."

"*Oui,* I know of several locations where this could be possible."

"Next, we need to know where the German checkpoints will be. The *Ausweis* and passports must be presented at these locations."

Major Elwell now has his opening, "What happens if they do not accept your documents as authentic?"

Pierrot. "We then go with the original plan. We will apprehend the two engineers within two or three kilometers from the entry checkpoint. We will immediately attack the communications center if Francisco and Andrés are not allowed through the entry checkpoint. I will enter the command shelter and search for the documents. We will need to have the diversion attack at the front gate. Renard and his resistance fighters will engage. Francisco and Andrés will be there and take the initial action to subdue the guards and not allow radio traffic. The explosives surrounding the compound need to be in place. Using the remote detonation switch, the C4 plastic will explode, further adding to the confusion. The SAS will provide the firepower to allow me to enter the control shelter and take any information on the D.F. design."

Major Elwell, "What do we do with the two captured engineers?"

Renard, "That will be our problem. Either we will keep them as a trade with the Germans, or we will kill them. I guess that they will be precious to the Germans, and we can use them to release some of our resistance fighters from prison".

After hearing the SOE agents' preparations, Major Elwell agrees but clarifies that it is a SOE plan. If things go south, he doesn't want to take the blame.

He responds, "OK, when are the two German engineers arriving?"

Pierrot replies, "We only know that it will be three or more days from today. We must have everything in place two days from today. If all items are not in place, we abort and have no choice but to execute the backup plan."

Major Elwell, "OK, I will have my men install the remote explosives on the compound's outer perimeter. The explosives will be installed on the evening of the day that our two SOE agents enter the compound. The explosives will be used as diversionary blasts when the two SOE agents enter the compound."

Renard, "I will contact the resistance leader tonight and give him the pictures with the two engineers' names."

Andrés, "Renard, we need some clothes that are being worn in Germany. Do we have any?"

"Yes, these should be easy to find."

Pierrot, "OK, everything is in motion; we meet daily and review the progress. I will contact London and obtain any updated information."

The following day, they agreed on the location of the apprehension. Argos has provided clothes that a typical civilian would wear in Germany. Francisco and Andrés have scouted the kidnap location. Renard has assigned two fighters to be at the airport's exit and report when the two engineers are on the road. This information will be passed using the regular phone service and agree that the word phrase, 'The *Rossignols* (Nightingales) are singing tonight." This will indicate that the two German engineers are driving to the facility.

On the fourth day, the airport lookouts call the number and report that the *"Rossignols* are singing tonight". The plan springs into action. Francisco and Andrés move to the kidnap point. A false checkpoint is ready to be constructed when the vehicle is five minutes from the designated location. One lookout is posted two kilometers from the false checkpoint with an old French radio. The vehicle passes, and the lookout keys his radio, *"Verte,"* (Green).

Two members of the resistance spring to action and quickly erect the checkpoint. In one minute, the vehicle arrives. The resistance fighters are dressed in Wehrmacht uniforms and ask for their papers. They check their papers and tell the driver and the two engineers that they must step out. They will need to inspect the vehicle. One of the engineers becomes indignant and demands to know who ordered the search. The resistance guards remain silent and point to where the two engineers and the driver must stand. Three resistance members quickly apprehend the driver and the two engineers from behind. They place potato sacks over their heads, tie them up, and place them in the meatpacking truck. They will be driven to a safe location.

Francisco, Andrés, and the new driver now head to the communications center. The next step will tell if they continue with Plan A or go to Plan B. They arrive at the communications center's entry gate.

The guard comes out and says in German, *"Ausweis bitte."* (I.D. card please)

"Herr Schonberg, Unternehmen Ausweis bitte." Francisco shows his company I.D., *"Herr Walters, Unternehmen Ausweis bitte."* (Company I.D. please)

"Reisepass Bitte." (Passport please)

Both Schonberg and Walters show the guards their passports. The guard looks at the driver and tells him he cannot enter. Herr Schonberg and Walters must wait at the building next to the guardhouse. The driver must turn around and head back to the airport.

Schonberg and Walters are in. They wait for fifteen minutes, and *Hauptmann* (Captain) Volker enters the guard facility. *"Herzlich Willkommen."*

Andrés replies in German, "Good to be here; we look forward to seeing the system become operational."

"Yes, of course, first, we must give you a pass. This pass will only be good to enter the control center. You cannot go into our military facilities. These are only for members of the German military. I am sure you understand. We must keep our secrets away from the bastard English."

"Ja, Ja, of course. We understand the need for secrecy."

After obtaining the pass badges, *Hauptmann* Volker tells them that they will always have an escort.

Francisco asks, "We have much work to complete before the VIPs arrive. We have been ordered that the system will be operational when they arrive."

Andrés, "Is the scheduled day still next Thursday?"

"No, I guess you didn't hear because of your travels. They will be here next Tuesday,"

Now, Francisco really plays the part, *"O Mein Gott!* Now we know that we must work 24 hours a day!"

Andrés, "Can we get to the control center now?"

"Sehr gut, you can see the *Kommandant* tomorrow. I agree we must have the system operational by next Tuesday. I am in charge of the operation of the system. Not having the system operational next Tuesday will reflect badly on me."

Volker thinks briefly and then says, "Regarding your escort, *Doktor* Valhalla can be your escort tonight."

Hauptmann Volker worries *that should the system not be operational, it will reflect poorly on his performance and reassign him to the eastern front.*

Hauptmann Volker escorts them to the control room. He uses his badge to allow them entry to the control center and says, *"Doktor,* the experts have arrived."

Dr. Wolfgang Valhalla looks at Schonberg and Walters with some skepticism and doubt but decides to say nothing. He has never personally met either of the two engineers, but he had expected them to be older. He waits one day to test them and determine if they are qualified. If they are not qualified, he will expose them as frauds.

Both Schonberg and Walters also detect Dr. Valhalla's apprehension but say nothing. Captain Volker sees the cold shoulder given by Dr. Valhalla but considers this a good sign. Dr. Valhalla was a typical, "know it all intellectual" and that *Hauptmann* Volker was beneath his ability to comprehend such highly technical subjects.

When *Hauptmann* Volker had told Dr. Valhalla that two expert engineers were being sent from Germany, Dr. Valhalla saw this as a demotion. He was concerned that *GruppenFuhrer* (General) Göring would see that he could not implement the design and would suffer the consequences. He was going

to expose Schonberg and Walters as amateurs in the field of radio propagation and communications.

   Hauptmann Volker exited the bunker and told the three, "I expect a lot
of improvement in tomorrow's status report, *Heil* Hitler."

   The three technicians did a partial wave, and all said, "*Heil* Hitler."

   Now they get down to business, Schonberg asks Valhalla, "Doctor, may
we see all of the design papers?"

   "Why, you are here to implement the final antenna elements to improve the radio wave's angle of arrival accuracy. I will only allow you to inspect the design of the antenna."

   Schonberg says, "Dr. Valhalla, the radio waves' accuracy is directly related to the ability to measure the phase relationship between the antenna
elements. The placement of the antenna elements is critical. Also, the instru-
mentation that is being used to measure the phase relationship must be
tuned correctly."

   Schonberg was thankful for his night sessions with Dr. Fry.

   Dr. Valhalla thinks *these two are not idiots; it looks like they know what
they are talking about. It's good to have two minds that are on my level. "Sehr
gut*, I will bring out the blueprints and the design documents so we can study
them together."

Walters notices a sign that reads, *"Nicht Rauchen."* He sees the Doctor has
two packs of Turkish and Lucky Strike cigarettes lying on his workbench.

   He thinks *I will use that later.*

For six hours, the three engage in the details of the *Freya* design. The Dr. is
impressed with the technical knowledge of both Schonberg and Walters. He
thinks, perhaps I was wrong, these young engineers and scientists are the
Reich's future. He had heard of a brilliant young engineer by the name of
Werner Von Braun, and he accepted that the Schonberg and Walters were
from the same crop of the new German scientists.

   It was now 11:30 p.m. when Dr. Valhalla said, "We must close at midnight. We can begin again in the morning."

   Schonberg, *"Hauptmann* Volker gave us permission to work through
the night."

   "Yeah, just like him. He's a real asshole, he never tells me anything. He
goes around simply saying *Heil* Hitler. He will suffer the consequences if we

do not have this system operational by next Thursday. He's the reason we are behind. Always getting in the way---a real bureaucrat."

Dr. Valhalla says, "I will need to get a good night's sleep. I am not as young as I used to be. You will be fine working in the control room. There are a couple of bunks in the storeroom if you need some rest. I will try and be back tomorrow at 9 a.m. *Guten Abend.*"

"Sehr gut, Doktor Valhalla, guten nacht." (Very good Doctor Valhalla. Good night)

After the doctor leaves, Francisco tells Andrés to go outside and have a smoke.

Francisco, "I will start photographing all of the design plans."

Andrés, "Remember to keep talking in German, if we speak any other language outside, our voices will carry, and the guards will detect the different language."

"Ja, nur Deutsch." (Yes, only German)

After working for an hour, Andrés notices *Hauptmann* Volker is on his way to the command bunker. Andrés quickly opens the door and says, "*Hauptmann* Volker is coming up; hide the camera."

"Keep him busy for a few minutes and let me clean up a bit."
Volker climbs the stairs and sees Walters smoking.

He says, "Good to see that you are good German workers, I wish all of my workers were like you----working through the night."

"Hauptmann, would you like a cigarette?"

"Ja, I will take one of those Lucky Strikes."

"So, you like American cigarettes?"

"Ja, much better than the Turkish brand. Did you know that American companies make the best cigarettes?"

"No, I did not know that."

Hauptmann Volker shows off his knowledge of American history and tells Walters, "Tobacco came from the American Indians; thus, the Americans have very good tobacco and the best tobacco plants." He talks nonstop for fifteen minutes about American tobacco. During this time, Schonberg has neatly stacked all the designs.

Walters asks, "Would you like to step inside and get a status review of our progress?"

"Nein, you best keep working."

"By the way, Dr. Valhalla said that the VIP's would be here Thursday?"

"Nein, its Tuesday, you can tell him to get his fat ass to work and get the job done!"

"Jawohl, Hauptmann Volker."

Volker turns and says, *"Heil* Hitler," climbs down the stairs and leaves.

SAS Team and Resistance:

From the time that Francisco and Andrés entered the command bunker, Major Elwell, Renard, and Pierrot have been tracking every move. The question now becomes, do they exfile tonight or tomorrow night. The team will need to know by 3 a.m. they need sufficient time to place the remote explosives with the remote detonators.

At 2:30 a.m., they get the signal from Walters (Andrés), "We exfile tonight".

Quickly, the SAS team covertly moves to the perimeter of the compound. Francisco has taken photos of the complete Freya radar system. The plan is to destroy the antenna system and leave the documents. After photographing the design documents, they are placed back in the fireproof safe. After the bunker is destroyed, the German investigation will find all the documents in the safe. They will conclude that the objective of the raid was to destroy the physical structure. The design will remain a secret to the third Reich.

Andrés and Francisco, with the camera safely in his backpack, move down to the perimeter fence. Sergeant Monroe is waiting at the designated point. He uses his wire cutters to cut a fence hole. Francisco, Andrés, Pierrot, Renard, and Argos quickly move to a safe location. The resistance has arranged for them to be driven to Sister Patricia's convent. They now have a two-hour head start on any Germans who might follow them.

Major Elwell sends a team through the fence and into the command bunker; remote explosives are scattered inside. Major Elwell will wait until 5:50 a.m. and detonate the explosives. Large balls of flame are seen for miles. The *Freya* antenna structure is completely destroyed. The German guards quickly surround the property, one kilometer outside the perimeter fence. At 08:00 a.m., they report to *Hauptmann* Volker that no resistance fighters have been found. The two engineers, Schonberg and Walters, have been kidnapped. The safe container is retrieved after the smoldering command bunker is watered down, and all the design documents are secure. *Hauptmann* Volker silently thanks Schonberg and Walters for having the foresight to have locked the documents in the safe. This will only delay the installation of the *Freya* network for two or three months. The only thing lost is time and two engineers from the company of Manfred and Schwarz.

SOE and SAS Teams:

The SOE team recognizes the value of the captured German engineers. Pierrot sends a message and requests for a Lysander flight to pick up the two Germans. Within days after the attack, a Lysander lands and agent Francisco and the design documents are flown back to London. Additionally, the real Schonberg and Walters are also flown to London. Juliette and Andrés will remain in France to conduct radio training.

Upon landing at the 204th Air Wing airfield, Lieutenant Vargas, Captain Hutchinson, and Colonel Phillips, decide to purposely send a radio message to the American Office of Information, that German scientists have been captured. The message had low-grade encryption, so the Germans will be able to decrypt the message. The game of espionage and counterespionage is always a cat and mouse game. SOE now talks to Colonel Richardson from MI6 to see if the ruse has worked.

One week after transmitting the message of the German scientists' capture, a message was intercepted that had been transmitted by the German Paris Gestapo. The message reads, *The Freya program has not been compromised as no documents were stolen, and the captured scientists only know a small part of the design. The design is heavily compartmented, and no changes are required to proceed with the design and installation. The saboteurs will soon be captured and killed, and no intelligence has been compromised.*

Hauptmann Volker and Dr. Valhalla:

Hauptmann Volker receives a reprimand for having the two scientists kidnapped from under his nose but receives high marks for having the procedures in place that saved the design documents.

Dr. Valhalla completed the design from the information gained when he reviewed the data with the young engineers. The loss of the two engineers is simply two persons lost in the battle with Britain. They are confident that the two engineers will reveal no trade secrets. They are loyal Germans and have been raised to be believers of Hitler and the Reich. They can be recovered once Germany conquers England.

Major Elwell and the SAS team:

Major Elwell and his six additional SAS team members successfully completed their mission. After setting off the explosives, they deliberately moved away from the SOE agents and the design documents. With the invaluable assistance of the French resistance, the team embarked on a challenging journey on foot along France's western coast. It appeared that the entire German Army was on high alert, actively searching for the saboteurs. On the third day, they encountered a small German patrol.

Major Elwell issued orders, "Sergeant Monroe, take two men with you and eliminate the patrol quietly using your knives. We cannot afford to let them radio our position."

"Yes, Sir," replied Monroe.

Monroe and two other SAS members swiftly approached from behind, eliminating three members of the German patrol. However, there was a complication – it turned out to be a five-man patrol. Two of the German patrol members were on lookout duty, smoking cigarettes on a small hill. They heard the commotion and descended with their Sten guns set on automatic fire. A fierce firefight ensued, resulting in the loss of three SAS soldiers, including Sergeant Monroe.

Now, the SAS team numbered two soldiers and two resistance fighters. In a critical battlefield decision, Major Elwell instructed the two resistance fighters to escape under the cover of darkness. He aimed to mislead the Germans into thinking that the entire operation was British, thus preventing reprisals against the French population.

The following day, a major firefight erupted. The two-man SAS team managed to eliminate more than fifteen SS German troops after hours of intense combat. Exhausting their ammunition, plastic explosives, and hand grenades, Major Elwell and Private McCarthy found themselves with no other option. They both placed their .45 caliber revolvers to their heads, pulled the hammers back, and with unwavering military resolve, Major Elwell uttered aloud, "God save the King." The subsequent loud bang marked the end of Major Elwell's life, and a second self-inflicted shot brought Private McCarthy's life to a close. None of the SAS soldiers would be taken alive, as they possessed critical information about the successful raid and the resistance. This mission was just one of many undertaken by the SAS and the SOE, concealed from the world --- a testament to the sacrifices made by British SAS commandos. These unsung heroes served as saboteurs, special operators, spies, counterspies, and, following the Allied landings, as vital assets within the British, Canadian, American, and other Allied armed forces. They remain among the forgotten heroes of World War II.

Chapter Twenty-Seven
Analysis of the *Freya* Data
GCHQ, England

MI5 now had two young German engineers, Albert Schonberg and Joseph Walters, who had important information on the *Freya* system.

The prisoners, as civilians, are treated by the British per the Geneva Convention. However, the possibility existed that one of the two would provide valuable information. Inspector George Harry Woodard of Scotland Yard conducted the interrogations.

Inspector Woodard first interrogates Joseph Walters since he appears to be the younger of the two engineers. Walters was closed-lipped and only gave his name, nationality, and date of birth. Joseph would have none of it after trying to engage in a friendly conversation. He knew his rights, and he more than once made it known that he was a civilian and, as such, was entitled to the articles of the Geneva Convention. Inspector Woodard mentioned more than once that Germany nor Japan had signed the Geneva Convention.

Nevertheless, Walters was a dedicated Nazi and repeatedly said that it would be in his best interest to treat him well because it was only a matter of time before Germany would rule England. At times, Walters would repeat the speeches given by Hitler---word by word. After more than two days of trying, the Inspector decided to move on; perhaps the second prisoner would be more agreeable to providing information.

Inspector Woodard called Colonel Richardson from MI6, "As you requested, I have completed my first round of questions with Walters."

"Excellent, I will be right over in fifteen minutes." The Colonel enters a makeshift office, which MI6 has provided to Inspector Woodard.

Inspector, "I am afraid that I do not have much to report. The Germans have trained him, and he is familiar with the Geneva Convention."

"Horse Feathers!" says the Colonel, "The Germans never signed the Geneva Convention!"

"Yes, I know, but Mr. Walters is not in the military and was not captured on English soil. We cannot treat him as a spy."

"OK, but there must be something we can do to make him talk?"

"Perhaps the only thing we can do is to place him in solitary confinement and feed him the minimum of rations. Perhaps in time, we can trade him comforts for information."

"OK, let's confine him to a single cell and provide only the minimum of rations. Do we have any choice?"

"No, not really, however, I advise you, we are not allowed any type of physical torture; we are not barbarians like the Germans."

The Colonel looks dejected and says, "Perhaps Schonberg will open up and provide us some information about the *Freya*."

"OK, I will begin tomorrow. Have the prisoner brought to the interrogation room at 8 a.m."

The following morning, at 7:50 a.m., Albert Schonberg sits in the interrogation room. At 8:05, Inspector Woodard walks in; he sees the young German engineer and offers him a cigarette. Schonberg takes the cigarette and looks at Woodard, waiting for a light. The Inspector takes out his lighter, flips open the top, and, with his thumb, rolls the more lightweight ball, and the lighter has a tall, flickering flame. He moves the flame toward the cigarette. Schonberg lights his cigarette and inhales, filling his lungs with nicotine.

Schonberg takes several drags from the cigarette and finally says, *"Danke Schon."*

Woodard thinks *that's a start, more than I got from Walters.* The Inspector uses his fifteen years of experience and starts talking about life in general. He will try to develop a rapport with Schonberg. The Inspector senses that Schonberg has an entirely different personality than Walters. Schonberg is more relaxed, carefree, and easily carries on a conversation. Unlike Walter's attitude of superiority, Schonberg shows no signs of the German *Ubermenschen*. Woodard is a professional interrogator; as such, he knows that one method of obtaining information is to have the person being interrogated developed a trust with the interviewer. Inspector Woodard talks about his upbringing on a farm in northern England. This tactic allows Schonberg to speak about his upbringing.

The Inspector asks, "Where did you obtain your education?"

"I was selected to take advanced science and engineering classes from the time I was six years old. I found mathematics to be very intriguing, and my father was a college professor at the Basel Institute of Science."

"Interesting, but isn't Basel in Switzerland?"

"Yes, but before the war, it was common to have students from Germany attend classes in Switzerland. However, with the war, the borders have been closed."

"So, your father was a professor at the Basel Institute of Science? What is he doing now?"

"He was hired as a consultant by the company Manfred and Schwarz. After getting my engineering degree, I was drafted into the Wehrmacht. However, when Albert Speer was looking for a young scientist and engineers to work on the 'Wonder Weapons' program, my name came up as an expert mathematician. Thus, I was released from the Wehrmacht and assigned to the civilian corps of engineers."

"So, your family has other scientists and engineers?"

"Yes, not only on my father's side but also my mother. I have a great uncle from my mother's side who was born in Germany but now lives in the states."

"And who is this uncle of yours."

"My great uncle is Albert Einstein. I was named after him. I have never met him. My mother told me that *Onkel* Albert was on a tour of America in 1933, and he elected to stay in America because of his Jewish ancestry."

"So, if your *Onkel* Albert was Jewish, that would also mean you have Jewish blood."

"Yes, that is correct. I have about 25% Jewish blood. My mother is almost 50% Jewish. However, due to my father being Aryan, the German authorities have chosen to overlook our Jewish connection because of his education."

"So, you are not worried that sometime in the future, Müller will not make some new law that makes all persons with Jewish blood to be enemies of the state?"

"Yes, I am worried about my mother. No harm would come to my parents if I were employed by Manfred and Schwarz and working on the *Freya* project.

Inspector Woodard thinks momentarily and asks, "Herr Schonberg, where do your parents live?"

"They live in the small town of Lorrach, near Basel, Switzerland."

The Inspector looks at a map on the interrogation room wall and says, "Herr Schonberg, I can talk to British Intelligence and see if we could secretly move your parents from Germany to Switzerland."

Schonberg is not stupid, "And what would you want from me?"

"Once we successfully move your parents to Switzerland, we want you to work with us. Just like your *Onkel* Albert is working with the Americans."

"Will you allow me a day to think about your offer?"

"Certainly, we can discuss it tomorrow. This will also allow me to talk to my contacts at British Intelligence, and I can give you some idea of how your parents would be moved to Switzerland."

The following day, Schonberg says he will only agree after believing his parents will be safe. Woodard had expected that Schonberg would first need to know some details of the escape plan. Having anticipated Schonberg's apprehension, Woodard required some details about the parents.

"What are the ages of your parents?"

"My father is forty-eight, and my mother is forty-seven."

"Are they in good health?"

"Yes, they are both in good health. Then Schonberg volunteered some useful information, "Both my parents are hikers. On the weekends, they hike the Alps."

Woodard now has the information he needs; he asks Schonberg, "Do you know which hiking trails they take?"

"No, but when I was young, their favorite path was near the Swiss border where you could see the *Jungfrau* Mountain."

"OK, allow me a couple of days to talk to members of British Intelligence, and we can design a plan."

Woodard returns to Colonel Richardson and tells him that the elder Schonbergs are hikers. This offers the best opportunity to capture them and move them across the Swiss-German border. First, they need to contact Frau and Herr Schonberg. They must be cooperative captives; otherwise, the kidnapping will not work. Colonel Richardson asks Woodard to have the young Albert prepare a letter that only he could have written. A British member of the SAS will cross the border and see that Schonberg receives the letter.

The Germans have not publicly announced the destruction of the *Freya* site, nor have they informed the relatives of either Albert Schonberg or Joseph Walters that the British have captured them. Inspector Woodard explains the plan to Albert.

He says, "Can the British make it look like they were captured against their wills? This way, there will be no arrests on my uncles, aunts, and cousins."

"Of course, that's perfect; the Germans will think that your parents have been captured to make you talk."

Albert is now excited and will now rest peacefully when his parents are "abducted" from Germany.

Woodard reports to Colonel Richardson that Albert has agreed. If we rescue his parents from Germany, he will gladly provide the design details and ideas for defeating the advanced radar. Albert writes the letter, and a British agent delivers the letter to the Schonbergs in Germany. Herr and Frau Schonberg take their regular Sunday hike, and at the designated point, two British SAS operatives dressed as German hikers whisk the couple into the forest's foliage. Items from the Schonbergs are left at the scene, indicating that they were forcibly abducted.

A German patrol is sent to investigate the Schonbergs when they have not arrived at a designated checkpoint. They find evidence that an abduction has taken place. The German patrol reports the disappearance to the local German Kaserne. The following day, the Germans found evidence that a covert team had crossed the border into Switzerland after searching the area. When the elder Schonberg's disappearance was reported to General Goritz, the commanding General in the southwestern portion of Germany, the Germans concluded that they were being used to make the younger Schonberg talk. After Albert's parents were safely in the British consulate in Zurich, Albert was elated and offered his services to the British Intelligence Service.

As the negotiations with Albert took place, Colonel Richardson informed Colonel Phillips of the possibility that Albert would work with British Intelligence. Colonel Philips informed Captain Hutchinson, and he, in turn, informed Lieutenant Francisco Vargas. Francisco was the best person to discuss the *Freya* System since he spoke German, was technical, and had in-depth discussions with Dr. Valhalla. However, Francisco knew that his expertise was different from a scientist or engineer. He requested that Dr. Fry from MIT be flown to England to direct the technical discussions with Albert Schonberg.

Colonel Phillips readily agreed and decided through the U.S. Embassy to have Dr. Fry journey to England and direct the technical discussions with the young Albert Schonberg. Before the arrival of Dr. Fry, there was much that had to be accomplished. Inspector Woodard arranged for a get-acquainted meeting between Albert and Francisco. It had been decided that the raid's details on the *Freya* site would not be discussed with Albert. After Joseph and Albert had been kidnapped, Albert had been told that a team of SAS operatives had successfully raided the *Freya* site and that the design documents were seized. The fact that Francisco had impersonated him was not revealed.

On a cold winter evening, Inspector Woodard, Albert, and Francisco met and engaged in conversations that would have each get to know each other. Francisco talked about him being raised by a Mennonite family in Mexico. Thus, the reason for his ability to speak German. Francisco said his mother immigrated to the United States in the 1920s. Albert was astonished that a Mexican Mennonite was a Lieutenant in the British Army. Albert knew stories like these did not exist in Germany; Francisco would have been branded as an *Untermenschen* (subhuman) and have been killed at an early age, or if he had survived to manhood, he would be in a forced labor camp.

Albert told his story of growing up in fear because he was 25% Jewish. The only reason that his family did not suffer the consequences of being Jews was because his father had served in the German Army in World War I and because his father was a college professor teaching advanced mathematics. Albert had inherited his father's talents, and after graduating from college, he had to join the German Army. Fortunately, his superiors had learned of his engineering skills, and he was transferred to a high-tech company, Manfred and Schwarz. Technically, he was still in the Army, but his superiors thought it best that he be integrated into the Manfred and Schwarz Company as a civilian. He had been told that he could best observe the workers at the plant and report any spies or saboteurs.

That evening, it was apparent to the Inspector that Francisco and Albert had become good friends; they were both young, unmarried, enjoyed a few beers, had a common interest, and both saw their technical jobs as hobbies, not work. After 1 a.m., the two had engaged in technical discussions about automobile engines, computing machines, encrypting codes, the future of flight, and how to end wars. After 3 a.m., they both retired to their respective barracks and agreed to meet the following day at mid-day and begin the *Freya* program discussions.

Francisco asked Albert, "Could you first provide a history of the Freya development?"

"Of course, the first tests were laboratory tests as early as 1937. In 1938, a prototype was tested by the Kriegsmarine. This prototype was more of an Identify Friend or Foe (IFF) system. This initial system was known as the FUG 25a."

"So, what was the purpose of the initial prototype?"

"Yes, the main purpose was to increase the range. With the FUG 25a, a range of 100 km was possible."

"So, was the *Freya* initially developed to support IFF?"

"No, we already had an IFF system; however, the new designs supported an early Identification Friend or Foe (IFF) version. Aircraft were equipped with the newer FUG 25a Erstling "IFF" system. Testing conducted in 1938 indicated that ranges of 100 to 125 km were possible."

"So, how did testing on the IFF lead to the new and improved direction-finding?'

"Like all new developments, the IFF resulted in the newer improved "AN" version, which introduced a switchable phasing line for the antenna."

"Can you explain how phasing improved the accuracy of the direct finding?"

"No, I was not directly involved in the direction-finding computation using the intercepted waveform phases. I only know that the use of the phase of the intercept waveform resulted in a significant improvement."

At this time, Francisco has not told Albert that Dr. Fry was on his way to England. Francisco will wait until Albert has completed his debrief. He also hopes that Albert has information on future developments for the *Freya* system.

Francisco asks, "How does the phase switching help with the direct finding accuracy?"

"Here is what I know. I know this not because I understand the theory but because I was involved in field testing in Germany."

Albert now explains what he knows, "Switching in the phasing line leads to a phase displacement of the antenna's radiation pattern, and with that, a narrow beam pattern is accomplished from either left to right or right to left. The switching is completed in fractions of a second; thus, the antenna beam may be scanned across the antenna elements in fractions of a second. This produces a picture of items being illuminated with the radio beam to allow the precise location of the object being illuminated."

"This new system sounds extremely complicated. Does the operation of the system require advanced training to operate?"

"Yes, not only to operate but the system must be calibrated continuously. This was one of the reasons for Joseph and I being sent to the *Freya* site. We were to perform the Phase One test and calibration."

"And, from a theoretical standpoint, what accuracies were you trying to achieve?"

"Theoretically, the chief design engineers at the Manfred and Schwarz Company had calculated an accuracy with an angular resolution of 0.1 degrees."

"Were you involved in what countermeasures could be used against the *Freya* system?"

"No, predicting what countermeasures the British would take was not in my department. That would have been in the *"Radio Gegenmassnahme Abteilung."* All of the work being completed was strictly compartmented. However, I was told that the British would have no answer to the new radar system. The *Freya* would reverse the outcome of the war between the RAF and the Luftwaffe."

Dr. Fry Arrives:

265

After one week of discussions between Francisco and Albert, Dr. Fry arrives at the Bude airport. Francisco, Herman, and Karina drive to Bude and meet Dr. Fry at the airport. Herman and Karina sit up front, and Francisco and the Doctor are in the back seat of a four-door 1937 Chevy sedan. On the six-hour drive from Bude to GCHQ headquarters, Francisco has a chance to de-brief the Doctor on the situation with Albert.

Francisco, "Dr. Fry, Herr Schonberg is a German Jew who is a brilliant scientist. His great Uncle is Albert Einstein. He says that he was named after his great uncle."

"Interesting. Does he know his uncle?"

"No, he knows of him from his mother. However, since Hitler came to power in the early '30s, they do not discuss any connection to Dr. Einstein."

"I take it that Herr Schonberg has a degree in engineering?"

"Yes, he has a degree from the Basel Institute of Science."

"And does he know the methods for comparing the different RF en-ergy in the intercepted waveforms?"

"No, the *Freya* system does not use the waveform's amplitude or RF energy. They are using phase comparisons."

"Hmmm…. phase comparisons. I suppose that phase comparisons could be done, but you would need some exact antenna placement. Also, the size of the antenna must be very large."

"No, the transmitting antenna frequency is in the 250 MHz range; thus, the reflected waveforms are measured in inches and not tens of me-ters."

"This is going to be very exciting. I have always thought that increas-ing the radar frequency would allow smaller antennas, but today's technology will not allow oscillators in the 250 MHz range. Obviously, the Germans have solved the problem."

Dr. Fry, with all due respect, we …. a, a, you are not here to design a new radar for war use. The British Chain Guard system is working very well. We are asking you to investigate the Phase comparison methods of the *Freya* and come up with countermeasures."

"Well said, young man. If I stray off the objective, just remind me to get back on track."

"Yes, Sir, will do."

Freya Countermeasures:

After Dr. Fry arrives at GCHQ, he is immediately given an isolated laboratory and given all the Freya raid design documents. The Dr. is introduced to the minimum number of personnel. Should countermeasures be found, this will be highly classified and have the same priority as the Bletchley Park team working on code-breaking. Albert is not even told of the American expert working on the design documents. Only Francisco is allowed to work with the Doctor.

After one week of studying the design, Dr. Fry has his first thoughts, "One method of defeating the radar signal is to retransmit false reflections. This would create false readings on the operator's display. For example, a single bomber could carry the "False Transmitter," the Germans would interpret the reflections as 10, 20, or 30 bombers. This would have the German fighters chasing a ghost bomber squad."

"A second method would be to use a noise jammer. This would overwhelm the signals from *Freya*. A single aircraft will fly 50 miles (80 km) off the enemy coast. This would blind the *Freya* radar for 35 to 30 miles along the coastline. For example, a 200-mile (320 km) gap could be knocked into the German's radar coverage using nine aircraft. At the same time, additional jammers could be carried in the bomber groups to counter the inland *Freya* network."[24]

---

[24] Drew, The Defiant One 1996,
267

Chapter Twenty-Eight
Gestapo Reaction to the Freya Destruction
Paris, France

The reaction to the destruction of the Freya site had the Germans in a high state of agitation. *Oberst* Buchner, the Paris Gestapo Chief, was to participate in the dedication of the *Freya* site with *GruppenFuhrer* Hermann Göring. Buchner knows that he will need to answer to Göring. And soon after that, to the *Reichsfuhrer* Heinrich Müller. Immediately following the Freya site's destruction, *Hauptfach* (Major) Wilhelm Weiner, the Gestapo senior officer at the *Freya* site, started tracking the English SAS team. Major Elwell from the British SAS had a six-hour head start, and with the help of the resistance, they were 50 kilometers south of the Freya site. The Germans used spotter planes, and the French Milice had picked up the trail by the third day. Major Elwell and his five commandos could hold off the German SS troopers until the fourth day. After a courageous battle, all six SAS soldiers were killed. Much to the dismay of *Hauptfach* Weiner, the German scientists were not with the English assault team.

Major Weiner then radioed to Buchner, "*Oberst* Buchner, we have engaged in a battle with the English commandos, and they are all dead."

"What the hell are you telling me---- our scientists were not with them?"

"*Jawohl Oberst,* they were not with them."

"So, what the hell are you doing to find them?"

"Sir, our scientists were likely carried off by the second team of English agents or perhaps the resistance."

"Yes, I agree; go back to the radar site and start interrogating all Frenchmen that live in the area."

"*Jawohl, mein Kommandant.*"

Hauptfach Weiner takes his S.S. troops back to the *Freya* site. He is assigned over 100 German soldiers to interrogate all French citizens who live within twenty kilometers of the radar site.   After two days, there has yet to be any information after asking the residents for any information on the two German scientists' disappearance. *Oberst* Buchner is furious with *Hauptfach* Weiner. Buchner decides to order Weiner to come to the Gestapo headquarters in Paris. Buchner has a spacious office on the fifth floor of the Majestic Hotel. His office has a balcony, which offers a view of the Eiffel Tower. Weiner enters the headquarters building and is directed to the office of the *Kommandant*.

He walks toward the elevators when a sergeant of the S.S. tells him, "The elevator is for special use and VIPs; others must use the stairs."

"I am *Hauptfach* Weiner from the fourth arrondissement. I should be considered a VIP."

The sergeant looks down a list of names and says, *"Entschuldigung, ich sehe nicht Namen nicht auf der liste der wichhtigen personen."* (I do not see your name on the important person list).

"There must be some mistake; I demand to see the *Kommandant!*"

"Fifth floor, office of *Oberst* Buchner."

As the Major is climbing the stairs, he understands that he is here to get a royal ass chewing.

He thinks *I need to tell the Colonel that I will take drastic steps to have some Frenchman talk.*

Major Weiner reaches the fifth floor, huffing and puffing. He rests for a full minute before entering the *Kommandant*'s office. Two S.S. guards are stationed in front of the large oak double door. As he approaches the *Kommandant's* office, one of the guard's snaps to attention, clicks his boots, and says, "Heil Hitler."

The second guard. *"Ausweis Bitte."*
Weiner shows the guard his military I.D. and starts walking toward the big oak doors, but the guards block the entrance.

Weiner thinks, *Of course, he has not returned the salute*. He says, "*Heil* Hitler."
Now, the guards allow him to enter the office of the *Kommandant*. The first office is the reception area.

A tall, stern-looking woman in an S.S. uniform looks at Weiner and asks, *"Bist du Hauptfach Weiner?"* (Are you Major Weiner?)

"Ja."

"Du bist spät!" (You are late!)

The aide officer looks at the Major in disgust and mumbles in a low voice, "Germans are always on time. How will we win the war with idiots like this major?"

Weiner hears the aide officer but chooses to say nothing. Finally, he enters Buchner's office. It is heavily decorated with the German flag, a picture of Adolf Hitler, the Colonel with a Messerschmitt in the background, and a picture of his wife and his son Otto.

Buchner looks at Weiner; he purses his lips, shakes his head in a disgruntled motion, and says, "*Du bist spät!* "

"Entschuldigung, Bitte, (Please excuse*) it will not happen again."*

"Fine, major, we are here to discuss your poor and dreadful performance at the Freya site. How the hell did the English team infiltrate our defenses and destroy the site?"

The major tries to answer, but Buchner cuts him off, "You have put me in a terrible position. I was on a fast track to being promoted to General, but your incompetent performance has put a damper on my promotion."

Again, Weiner tries to tell the Colonel about his team tracking the English raiders and killing them.

Buchner cuts him off, "Yes, but what happened to the scientists?"

"Sir, we have been questioning-----a, a, interrogating the Frenchmen in the area, it is only a question of time before we extract some information. I am sure that the English had help from the resistance."

Buchner now shouts, "Goddamn it--- time! That's exactly what we do not have."

"Sir, the news is still good: our armies will soon conquer Russia, and Rommel will soon capture the oil wells in Saudi Arabia."

Buchner says, "Don't believe all that damn propaganda from Goebbels. We have sunk the three British aircraft carriers. If you carefully examine the picture, it is always the *"The Ark Royal*." He says we are the most intelligent people in the world, but he must also think we are the most naïve and gullible.

"Yes, Sir, I see your point."

"Now, let's hear what you have to say about how you are going to find the members of the resistance who worked with the English. Also, we need a heavy form of reprisals. These Frenchmen must pay a heavy price for working with the enemy. They need to understand that they are a conquered people. They are now living in a German country. Anyone working with the resistance is treason; the penalty is death!"

Women and Children Arrested by the S.S.

"Yes, Sir, we are very close to extracting that information. We are interrogating all Frenchmen, including women and children."

"Major, I am giving you one week to find these traitors; if you do not, you will be court-martialed for failing to protect the radar site. I need not tell you the verdict if you are court-martialed."

"Yes sir, death by a firing squad."

"Now. Be on your way, and failure is not an option. By the way, when you come back and tell me how you found the two scientists and that you have eliminated a major cell of the resistance, do not be late!"

"Jawohl mein Kommandant!" Weiner stands, clicks his jackboots' heels, and gives the salute, "*Heil Hitler.*"

Buchner stays seated because of his wooden leg and repeats, *"Heil Hitler."*

On the six-hour ride back to the radar site, Weiner must think of a way to extract information from the French residents. His problem is that the radar site is in the countryside, ruled by the resistance. The farms and villages are populated by young children, women, and older men who survived the winter war of 1939. All men between the ages of fifteen to forty were either killed or captured when the Germans invaded France. The surviving young men and women fled to the dense forest of the French countryside, and most joined the resistance. These young fighters would rather die than be captured by the Germans. Rooting out the resistance is dangerous.

    Hauptfach Weiner will have no choice but to post flyers in all the villages and farms. The flyers are in German and French, and state;

> *"Achtung, wenn niemand den verborgenen Ort der*
> *entführten deutschen Wissenschaftler preisgibt,*
> *werden jeden Sonntag zehn Franzosen auf*
> *dem Stadtplatz aufgehängt."*

> *Attention, si personne ne dévoile l'emplacement*
> *caché des scientifiques allemands enlevés, dix*
> *Français seront pendus chaque dimanche sur l*
> *a place de la ville.*

> (Attention, if no one comes forward with the hidden
> location of the kidnapped German Scientists, ten
> Frenchmen will be hung every Sunday in the town
> square.)

    Hauptfach Weiner allows one week to pass after posting the leaflets in all villages within a twenty-kilometer radius of the radar site. After one week, no Frenchman came forward with information. Weiner selects a village where he believes the escape route was used to abduct the scientists. He drives down the main road, and with much fanfare, he randomly points at a home. Six S.S. stormtroopers kick in the door and bring all persons found in the house out of their rooms. After three families have been selected, they have ten people. They are between the ages of seven and fifty: six women and four men. The ten are then ceremonially marched to the town center. Their hands are tied behind their backs, they are carried up to footstools, and a hangman noose is placed around their necks. The Germans use three trees to swing the ropes around some low-hanging branches.

    Weiner now uses a bullhorn and shouts angrily in German, "Last chance for someone to come forward and save your fellow countrymen and women. After shouting twice, the ten Frenchmen and women start shouting, *"Vie à la France, Vie à la France!"*

The shouting of "Long live France," angers Weiner. The Major then orders his S.S. stormtroopers to kick the footstools from under the French citizens who were chosen for execution. Each man and woman fall in unison, and the hangman's noose slowly strangles the victims. All ten victims hang from the tree branches in the town square for two to three minutes; they resemble puppets attempting to dance.

Hauptfach Weiner orders four S.S. stormtroopers to stand guard on the hanging bodies. The bodies will hang in the courtyard for one week until ten new people are hung. The procedure is repeated the following week in the next village. Still, no one has come forward.

After the second hanging, he receives a message to report to *Oberst* Buchner in Paris. He has nothing to report, and he now fears for his life. He arrives fifteen minutes before his appointed time, climbs the stairs, and waits in the reception area.

At the precise time of his appointment, the Colonel's aide comes out and says, "*Oberst* Buchner will see you now."

Weiner enters Buchner's spacious office. Buchner is now standing and overlooking the Eiffel Tower. Weiner enters, stands in the middle of the office, smartly clicks his jackboots' heels, and extends the *"Heil Hitler"* salute. Buchner slowly shuffles to his desk chair, dragging his wooden leg behind his body. As before, he does not offer the major a chair or give him the at-ease command. Nothing is said for a good minute; Buchner, with his deep blue eyes, continues to stare at Weiner. With his cap under his left arm, Weiner now starts to sweat. The drops that emerge from his forehead drip into his eyes.

Finally, Buchner states with anger in his voice, "*Hauptfach* Weiner, you have failed!"

"Permission to speak, sir."

"Ja, mach weiter, aber mach es kurz!" (Yes but make it short!)

"Sir, I am sure that the French will break. I have now hung twenty Frenchmen, and I am sure that someone will soon come forward."

"No, major, you will never find our scientists. I fear the English and the French resistance has completely outsmarted you!"

273

"No, sir, I am sure that they are still in France."

"No, two days ago, I received a classified message from the Gestapo in southern Germany. The English crossed the Swiss-German border and forcibly kidnapped the parents of one of the scientists. The English will be using one of our scientists' parents to extract information. You see, the English also uses torture tactics to extract information. Our intelligence has indicated that our two scientists are in England."

"Yes, Sir, this will not happen again."

"You are correct, *Hauptfach* Weiner; we cannot allow this to happen again." Buchner now speaks into his inter-comm and orders his aide, "Send in *Feldwebel* Schon."

Sergeant Schon is six foot, four inches, solid muscle, and has two additional S.S. troopers with identical bodies at his side.

Oberst Buchner, "*Hauptfach* Weiner, your trial was held yesterday, and the court agreed that you are guilty of negligence, failure to perform your mission, and failure to protect the Reich's major assets. Your sentence is death by a firing squad. *Feldwebel* Schon will take you to your prison cell, and you will be shot at sunrise tomorrow."

"Permission to speak."

"Denied, *Feldwebel* Schon, you have your orders."

"*Jawohl, Heil Hitler.*"

The following morning, *Hauptfach* Weiner is executed.

Oberst Buchner takes a new approach:

Oberst Buchner has been at his post in Paris for six months. He has a better feel for combatting the resistance. The brute force method of rounding up suspects and using enhanced torture methods does not produce the results to satisfy Berlin. His latest phone and message exchanges with the *Reichsführer*, Heinrich Müller, were not pleasant. The destruction of the radar site has the attention at the highest level. Müller will want to know what Buchner is doing to destroy the resistance. It was evident to Buchner that the killings of the French population would not yield the results desired. Buchner has now concluded that the resistance is organized in cells. One cell does not know what the other is doing. The primary architect of the resistance is the

English SOE. The communications between the resistance and the English must be stopped.

He was programmed to have received the advanced Direction Finders, but they have been delayed. The ability to locate the resistance transmitters would cut the snake's head and destroy the resistance's command-and-control communications. Buchner has continuously queried the D.F. equipment's status but was told a schedule was unavailable. The reason is that Hitler prioritized the advanced rockets built in *Peenemünde* by Werner Von Braun and the German scientists. All other programs, including direction-finding equipment, were being delayed.

Buchner now turns to a second method to destroy the resistance. This method was "counterespionage." He would have the Gestapo office in Paris to identify possible candidates to be trained to infiltrate the resistance. If the Gestapo could place "moles" in the resistance, the mole would provide the resistance to the hierarchy, thus destroying the resistance from within.

Chapter Twenty-Nine
Lizzette Becomes a Double Agent
Paris, France

Oberst Buchner has been at his Paris-assigned post for over six months. Since his arrival, things have not gone as expected. Buchner has unleashed his chief henchman, *Obersleutnant* Siegfried Rauch, to use advanced torture methods to extract information from suspected resistance saboteurs. Thus far, the results have been less than expected. In the next two months, he will have an inspection from Berlin. He currently has a substantial black mark for his performance. The destruction of the *Freya* radar site and the two German scientists' kidnapping occurred in his area of responsibility. He knows that not having the advanced DF systems has hindered his progress. However, shifting the blame from the poor performance to decisions made by Adolf Hitler is a nonstarter; the *Führer* is never wrong. Should he even utter such remarks, it would be professional suicide and perhaps even his life. Buchner will gain some points, having killed the English SAS operatives, and for the execution of Major Weiner, but in the end, the responsibility was his. He needs to achieve results within the next two months.

Buchner now turns to *Obersleutnant* Siegfried Rauch. Rauch is a mean-spirited officer in the SS. Since arriving in Paris, Buchner has given Rauch free rein to root out the resistance. Rauch has executed hundreds of Frenchmen, but the attacks by the resistance continue unabated. Also, all attempts to infiltrate the resistance have been failures.

Buchner, "*Oberst* Rauch, why have you failed to infiltrate the resistance?"

"Herr *Oberst* Buchner, we found two prisoners who said they could penetrate the resistance if we released them from prison."

"*Ja*, and what happened?"

"The first person was found shot through the head, execution-style; the second, we have not heard from?"

"Do you think he has been killed or just run off?"

"If I had to guess, I would say that he has been killed."

Buchner is now angry; he stands and walks with a patented shuffle, dragging his wooden leg.

He stands two inches from Rauch and shouts, "You think? You Think? You are an officer of the *Schutzstaffel;* I do not want wild guesses as to what you think. I want straight answers. I want solutions, not some damn excuse about what you are thinking. It would help if you implemented a solid plan. Do you understand?"

"Jawohl mein Kommandant! Heil Hitler!"

Buchner drags his wooden leg back to his chair behind his desk. He looks straight at Rauch with his penetrating blue eyes and says, "If we do not kill at least one member of one damn cell, one of us is going to be demoted, and it's not going to be me. Do I make myself clear?

"Jawohl mein Kommandant, absolut klar!"

"Gut, dass sie haben drei tage um mir einien Plan!" (You have three days to present me a plan!)

"Jawohl, Ich verstehe, Heil Hitler!"

Obersleutnant Siegfried Rauch's Plan:

Rauch has extensive experience in working with murderers, thieves, and organized crime. Before the war, he was a street thug in Hamburg. Rauch had always come out on top of dealing with gangsters, thieves, murders, and other illegal activities. By the time he was twenty, he had graduated from stealing from homes and stores and broken into pawnshops, and excelled in hostage killings and abductions. On multiple occasions, Rauch had been hired to abduct a family member from a wealthy background and hold them in some hideout until his client would pay him a large sum of money, usually over twenty thousand marks. Siegfried soon learned that abducting someone they loved was the key to making people pay. The more love, the more money he would get. Rich people would pay anything to get their kid, wife, mother, or any loved relative back alive, especially since the Hamburg police wouldn't even investigate gangland-type murders. They believed it was best to let these gangsters simply kill themselves.

After thinking about what he had learned as a common thug in Hamburg's streets, he would apply the same technique to infiltrate the resistance. He needed to find individuals who were French, solid citizens who could be blackmailed to work for the Gestapo. He needed a list of French soldiers who had been captured in the war. He knew the mighty French Army of over 1,500,000 men had surrendered to Germany. Many of these captured Frenchmen had been killed in their march or executed in the prisons. He needed to find the names of French soldiers who were still alive and in German prisons. He would then have some clerks go through the names and find these imprisoned Frenchmen's mothers, sisters, or wives. He could offer special treatment to their loved ones once he knew the relative living in France. On the other hand, if they did not cooperate, then the imprisoned French soldiers would be tortured and, if required, killed.

After careful thought, he concluded that the best candidate would be a prisoner with a young wife and children. He thought with over one million French soldiers in prison, he could indeed find several desperate fitting candidates. Once the candidates were identified, he would have the French Milice conduct a background investigation. Once they passed the background investigation, he would personally conduct a face-to-face interview.

Siegfried first needed the names of all French soldiers from the Paris area who were in German slave camps. To do this, he would need the authority of *Oberst* Buchner. This was the plan that he would present to the Colonel.

On the third day, Rauch makes an appointment to see *Oberst* Buchner, "Sir, I have a plan to present to you."

"Very well, proceed."

Rauch gives him details of the plan. Buchner likes the idea and says, "How do we get started?"

Rauch is not a fool; he needs Buchner to participate in the plan. He wants Buchner to buy in. Rauch poses his problem in the form of a question.

"*Oberst* Buchner, I need to find the husbands of the wives who remain in France. How would *"WE"* go about finding these men?"

Buchner takes the bait, "We can get a list of all Frenchmen from the Paris area in our prisons."

278

"Sir, there are over one million prisoners. How do we find prisoners from the Paris area?"

Buchner now sees Siegfried for what he is: a dumb lowlife with a military specialty in the ability to kill. This man does not have a conscience. He is not aware of the German penchant who is keeping records. Only the *Schutzstaffel*'s dedicated officers are aware of the meticulous records held in the German Army. Finding prisoners from the Paris area will not be difficult to find.

Buchner tells Rauch, "I will send a message to *Reichsfuhrer* Müller to send us a list of all prisoners' names with addresses in the Paris area."

Rauch, "You can also include in your message that *Oberst* Siegfried Rauch is the task leader."

Rauch wanted to remind Buchner that he had the former Paris Gestapo chief removed. He has friends in high places.

"Of course, you owe your rank and position to the *Reichsfuhrer.*"

"Jawohl Oberst Buchner.*"*

Oberst Buchner went through several channels, and within a week, the Reich prison administration sent over one thousand names of capable prisoners who were captured when France surrendered. Of the thousands, roughly half are still alive. Buchner sends the list to Rauch; Rauch then takes two days to methodically go through the list and select only married men with children. The list is now reduced to a mere several hundred. He takes the list to the office of the regional director. The chief of the regional director is a Gestapo *Hauptfach* (Major) named Elias Schottenheimer.

Rauch, "*Hauptfach* Schottenheimer, I have a list of over two hundred French prisoners who are married, have children, and live in the Paris area. You are ordered to provide the information on their families. I need to know where their wives or parents work."

"Jawohl, Oberst Rauch, Ich warden ihre angeforderten informationen in zwei Tagen haben!" (I will have your information in two days).

As requested, the information is provided in two days. Rauch reviews the report and further reduces the list to eight candidates. Rauch now goes to the office of the *KirminellerDirektor* and speaks to Chief *Inspektor* Becker.

"*Inspektor* Becker, you must order these five women to enter your office for interrogation."

"Of course, and what crimes have they committed?"

"We suspect that they have been dealing in the black market."

"*Jawohl Oberst* Rauch, may I have some details of their activities in the black market?"

Rauch is now agitated and shouts, "Inspektor, these women have been accused by their fellow countrymen of dealing in foreign currency. You are to question them while I watch through the one-way window. Do you understand?"

"*Jawohl, Oberst Rauch! Heil* Hitler."

"When you order them to appear, you are to let me know. I will watch your interrogation techniques through the one-way window."

"*Jawohl, Oberst* Rauch.*"

The *Inspektor* has his police unit deliver a summons to the women selected by Rauch. Even though the *Inspektor* is a German official, he is not in the *Schutzstaffel (SS)* and does not believe in advanced interrogation techniques. *Inspektor* Becker is not an idiot; he knows that Rauch is interested in how the women react to the interrogation. The Inspector knows what the Gestapo is capable of. It is best that he asks no questions and do as Rauch has ordered. The Inspector interrogated the three women. All women react identically, afraid and unsure as to why they are suspected of dealing in the black market. Two admit that they traded for small amounts of eggs and cheese for their hungry families. They all start crying and ask for forgiveness. The fourth woman is different. She is strong and defiant in a formal manner. Her name is Lizzette Raymond. Inspektor Becker begins as he has with the other women.

"*Madame* Raymond, you are being accused of dealing in the black market. Do you deny the accusation?"

Lizzette, "*Inspektor* Becker, it is evident you do not know who I am. I work in the office of the *KirminellerDirektor.* The same office that you work in. I report to *Monsieur* Forte, the French official who ensures that the Frenchmen do not engage in black marketing."

Becker has no demonstrable reaction but assumes that *Oberst* Rauch was aware that Madame Raymond was in the office of the *KirminellerDirektor* for unknown reasons. He believes that Rauch wants to see her response to the interrogation. Becker continues with the questions.

Finally, he says, "*Madame* Raymond, I hope you are telling me the truth. We will check that you work for *Monsieur* Forte. If you are lying, you will be charged and brought before the Gestapo to account for your false-hoods."

"*Merci Beaucoup,* you will see that I have not lied."

"Yes, of course, *Madame*, I am simply doing my job."

Rauch has been viewing and listening to all the interrogations. He has found the person to infiltrate the resistance. She is perfect! She wholeheart-edly believes in the German occupation, has an imprisoned husband, is a mother to two small children, and lives with her parents. Now, he needs to recruit Madame Raymond to become an agent of the Gestapo. He must first manipulate her into becoming an agent of the Gestapo. Second, she will need training on how to deceive the resistance. Rauch knows that if he can pull some strings, Madame Raymond will be his best agent to infiltrate the re-sistance. For her sake, she better be a good actress. If not, then her children will become motherless.

Lizzette Raymond (Papillon) reaction

The only thing that Becker concluded correctly about Lizzette is that she is a strong woman, intelligent, and an outstanding actress. When Lizzette received the summons to appear before *Inspektor* Becker, she decided not to tell her boss, *Monsieur* Forte--at least not yet. She would wait and see what game the Gestapo is playing. While she was being falsely accused and inter-rogated, she knew that someone important was behind the one-way window. She knew that she was being analyzed for some other job. However, before taking action, she would need to wait and see if she could please whoever was behind the glass.

Lizzette did not need to wait long. Two days after the Becker "inter-view," *Monsieur* Forte came to Lizzette and told her that she was to meet *Obersleutnant* Rauch. The meeting was to be the next day at 10 a.m.

Lizzette knew that it was not related to her work with the resistance. She was under an intense cover; not even Renard knew her real name. Be-sides, if her cover had been blown, the Gestapo would have arrested her at 3 a.m., days ago. No, it had to be something else. She decided to dress in her best business attire to present herself as professional and well-groomed. She arrived at the office of *Obersleutnant* Rauch fifteen minutes before her appointment and waited in the Majestic Hotel's lobby. She made it a point to greet every officer with a "Heil Hitler" to prove her loyalty to the German cause.

At 9:55 a.m., a sergeant came down and asked, "*Madame* Raymond?"

"Ja, Ich bin Frau Raymond."

"Bitte, folge mir." (Please follow me)

Lizzette walks into the office of the Lt. Colonel, and Rauch stands and says. *"Wilkommen Madame Raymond.* Please have a seat on the sofa."

Rauch pulls up a chair opposite Lizzette and offers her a cigarette, *"Bitte ein cigarette aus Amerika."*

Lizzette does not smoke, but she senses it would be best to accept the cigarette for the conversation.

She says, *"Danke, Amerikaner zigarette sehr gut."*
After some chitchat regarding the weather, France's conditions, and the fact that the war is going well for Germany, Rauch asks about her children. Lizzette was prepared for the Colonel to bring up the children. She can tell from his aggressive body language that if he doesn't get his way, her children would be harmed.

Then Rauch drops a bombshell, "Frau Raymond, for your dedicated support of the Reich, I have taken the opportunity to research your husband's name. I believe his name is Felipe, and he is a Lieutenant in the French Army. Is that correct?"

"Yes, that's correct."

"I am pleased to report that your husband is alive and held in a prisoner-of-war camp near Berlin."

"Oberst Rauch, that's wonderful news; is it possible for me to write to him and send him some much-needed items, such as mittens, and perhaps I can knit him a sweater?

"Madame Raymond, surely you understand how the world works. We do something for you, and you do something for us."

Lizzette remains calm, but her happiness at hearing that Felipe is alive makes it impossible to control her facial expressions.

She regains her composure and asks, "Is there some way you can assure me that Felipe is alive?"

Rauch angrily says, "You have the word of an officer of the *Schutzstaffel!*"

"Oberst Rauch, perhaps you have forgotten that I work in the German office administration. I am well aware of the *Schutzstaffel's* word."

Rauch says no more. Under normal circumstances, he would order the bitch to be shot. Rauch now regains his composure and thinks *I need her, do not lose control.*

Lizzette now addresses *Oberst* Rauch, *"Oberst* Rauch, you have asked me to this interview to perhaps help out with your attempts to reduce the level of violence against the German occupation."

"You are a most perceptive person, yes. I want your assistance in reducing the violence in France. We are a most benevolent occupier. We have given France a new form of government, and we are systematically extracting the undesirables from your country. Germany will rule the world for one thousand years. We are the new Roman Empire. We will bring honor and stability to France and the entire world."

Lizzette knows better, but she needs to laud praises on the Colonel. Like most German officers, he thinks he is smarter than everyone else, especially a woman.

She then asks a direct question, *"Oberst* Rauch, what exactly do you want from me?"

"Frau Raymond, I see that you are most direct. I like your attitude. I see that you have already adopted German customs. Yes, I will tell you what we are asking. We need you to infiltrate the resistance and direct us to their leaders. This is the only way that France can achieve greatness and stability."

"Oberst Rauch, I am but a simple Frenchwoman. I work hard in the office of the *KirminellerDirektor,* and I have been a loyal employee; I know nothing of spying on any person, let alone the resistance."

"Yes, we are quite aware of your background. That is precisely why you will succeed. The resistance will never suspect you."

"Oberst Rauch, I am afraid that I cannot accept your most generous offer."

"Madame, perhaps you do not understand; it is not a friendly request; it is an order. Should you choose not to honor my order, strange things could happen to Felipe, and we would not want any accidents to happen to your adorable children."

Lizzette was prepared for some threat to be directed at her, but she had not imagined that the danger would be to those she loved the most.

She then said with some reservation, "*Oberst* Rauch, it appears I have no choice."

"I am glad that you have chosen wisely."

"As I said, I am a simple woman, I will need some training on how to spy."

"Yes, the secret intelligence service of the Wehrmacht will provide you with a training course. You understand that you cannot discuss your new position with anyone."

"Yes, Sir, I most certainly understand. Should the resistance know of my connection to the German Intelligence, I would see a quick death."

"Yes, that is true. I will prepare your papers for the *KirminellerDirektor* for your transfer to the *Gestapo*."

"Sir, I would like to have a three-day pass to collect my belongings at the *Direktor* and explain to my family my promotion. I will need some time to arrange my affairs for my transfer to the Intelligence Service."

"Yes, of course, I will arrange for you a five-day pass."

"*Veil Danke, mein Kommandant.*"

Rauch thinks *she is even calling me her commander; she is eating out of my hand; perhaps later, I will extract sexual favors; she is most attractive.*

Lizzette contacts the resistance.

Papillon needs to contact Renard. However, before Lizzette would use her standard procedure to send a signal to the resistance, she would need to determine if the Gestapo was monitoring her movements. On the day after she agreed to work for the Gestapo, Lizzette would first test to see if she was being tailed.

Lizzette first reported to her job at the office of the *KirminellerDirektor.* Lizzette followed her usual routine; she used her bicycle to travel the three miles from her home to the *KirminellerDirektor's* office building. Lizzette then went to her boss, *Monsieur* Forte, and informed him of her transfer to the Intelligence Service.

Forte, "Yes, I was informed late yesterday that you were being transferred. Please be careful; I do not know what you will be doing, but working with the secret police cannot be all that safe."

"Yes, I am aware, but I had no choice."

Monsieur Forte knew precisely what she was saying. Lizzette had two small children and a husband, who was likely in a German prison. He knew that she had no choice.

As Lizzette went through her personal belongings, Forte told her, "Should you ever need a friend in the Directorate, please do not hesitate to let me know."

"Merci Beaucoup, Monsieur Forte."

Lizzette places her packed knit purse in the basket on her bicycle's front handlebars and pedals towards her home. She purposely rode through less populated neighborhoods and took the long way home. Within the first ten minutes, she sees two men trying to follow her. They are in a black Mercedes and stick out like two carrots in a basket of onions. Once Lizzette determines she is being followed, she pedals to her home, deposits her belongings, and waits to confront *Oberst* Rauch the following day.

Early the following day, she pedals her bike to the office of the Gestapo. Again, she realizes that a man on a bicycle is following her. Halfway to the Gestapo office, the man following her disappears, and a different man is now pursuing her.

Lizzette thinks *they must think that I am really stupid, that a woman knows nothing of surveillance.*

Lizzette walks into the Gestapo office and politely asks if she can speak to *Oberst* Rauch. "Do you have an appointment?"

"Nein, but if you tell him that *Frau* Raymond would like an audience with him, I am sure he will find time in his busy schedule to speak to me."

The receptionist looks at Lizzette with some disgust and says, "Very well have a seat. I will see if he will see you."

Much to the receptionist's surprise, she returns from *Oberst* Rauch's office and says, *"Oberst* Rauch will see you in ten minutes."

"Danke."

In ten minutes, the receptionist escorts Lizzette into the Colonel's office.

Rauch, "My, my back so soon? Don't tell me that you have already broken into the resistance?"

"No, I have not, and I may never be able to penetrate the resistance. Tell your men to stop monitoring my every move; the resistance is everywhere. They may be the street sweepers, butchers, police officers, candlestick makers, carpenters---anyone. If you keep following me around, the word will surely get back to the resistance that your agents are following me. Heaven only knows I may already be damaged goods. Tell your men to stop immediately!"

"*Frau* Raymond, I like you even more today than yesterday. You passed the first test. You are very observant. You will make an excellent agent for the Gestapo."

"*Oberst* Rauch, do I have your word that you will not place me in the predicament of being found by the resistance? Do not have your men following me!"

"*Ja, du wirst nicht verfolgt.*" (Yes, you will not be followed)

Lizzette knows that having an officer of the Gestapo give his word is worth about as much as a snake, indicating that it will not strike.

For the next two days, Lizzette goes about her regular shopping routine at the market, standing in the queue for rationed items and traveling between cities using trains and buses. After being assured that she is not being followed, she shops at the butcher store and leaves a message. Like before, the butcher *Monsieur* LaPlante wraps the note, along with bacon, in a newspaper, gives the bacon to his contact, and forgets about the exchange. Lizzette will now meet Renard on the third Sunday of the following month.

In three days, she will report to the Intelligence Service and begin training to become a double agent.

Chapter Thirty
The Changing Tides of War
Pacific and Atlantic Theaters

From September of 1939 to mid-1942, the war in Europe and the Pacific was going very well for the Axis Powers. Germany now controlled Europe from the Spanish Pyrenees to Norway, and the German Armies were on the outskirts of Moscow. Rommel and the Afrika Korps were only miles from the Suez Canal and would soon control the oil fields of Saudi Arabia. The areas shown below are the countries conquered and occupied by Germany in the summer and fall of 1942.

German Occupied Territories 1942

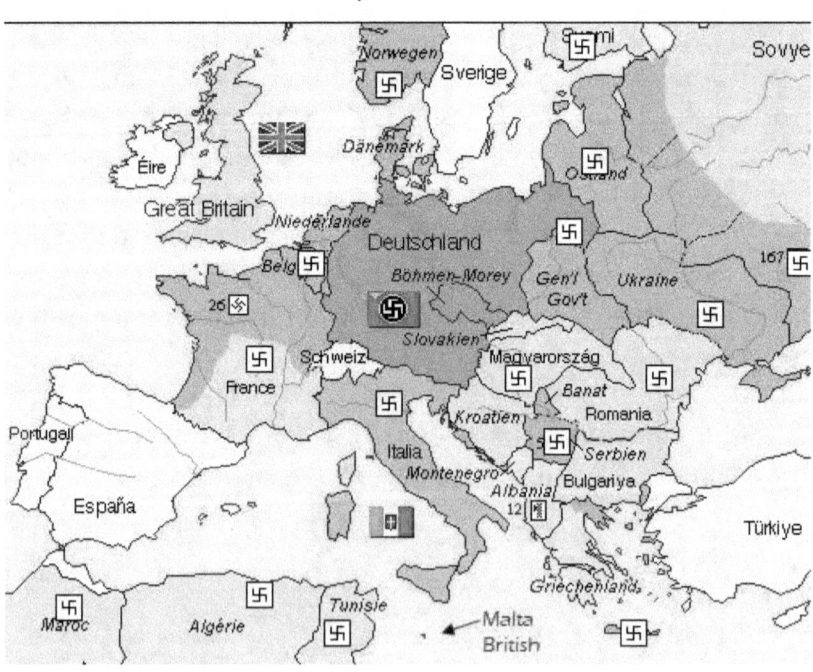

The above map shows the following territories occupied by Germany.

--As far east as the town of Mozdok in the Northern Caucasus in the Soviet Union.

--As far west as the island of Ushant in France.

--As far north as the settlement of Barentsburg in Svalbard, Norway.

--As far south as the island of Gavdos in Greece.

--Morocco, Algiers and Tunisia in Africa

Outside of Europe proper, German forces effectively controlled Egypt, Libya, and Tunisia in Africa. These territories were at times under Italian and Vichy French rule between 1941 and 1943. German military scientists established the Schatzgraber weather station base (1943–1944) as far north as Alexandra Land in north Russia. The Germans also operated weather stations in Greenland at the Edelweiss base (1942-1944). Additionally, German Kriegsmarine (Navy) vessels operated in all of the world's oceans throughout the war.

A major turning point in the war occurred in the winter of 1942-43. In the early 1940's General Erwin Rommel was in charge of the German Afrika Korps. Under Rommel's command were 275,000 harden and experienced German soldiers. Initially, General Rommel had major successes, and the British labeled him the as the "Desert Fox" due to his ability to win all of his battles with the British. However, the Germans relied heavily on oil coming from the Romanian oil fields. As shown in the previous map, the island of Malta was strategically placed between the German forces in Europe and Africa. Malta remained under British control throughout the war and played a pivotal role in the Germans' defeat in WW-II.

In July 1942, Hugh Lloyd was relieved of the RAF command on Malta. Since the war in North Africa, Malta was under siege by the Germans. The Germans were continuously bombing the British base on Malta. Using Beaufort and Spitfire aircraft, the British had successfully fought off all German attempts to destroy the British garrison in Malta. In England, the British High Command felt that a man with past fighter defense operations experience was needed. The British RAF had not placed a commander with more Air

---

[25] Wiki German Occupied Territory 1942

Defense experience due to priority being given to the homeland's defense. Air Vice-Marshal Keith Park replaced Lloyd as Air Wing Commander. Park arrived on July 14, 1942, by flying boat. He landed during a raid, although Lloyd had explicitly requested, that he circle the harbor until the raid had passed. Lloyd met Park and admonished him for taking an unnecessary risk.[26] Park simply answered, "In war, risks need to be taken. I needed to assume command as soon as possible."

Vice Air Marshall Park had faced the German Luftwaffe General Kesselring in 1940, during the Battle of Britain. During that battle, Park had advocated sending small numbers of fighters into battle to meet the enemy. There were three fundamental reasons for this. First, he would maintain some fighters in reserve, only to be used when needed.

Second, small numbers were quicker to position and easier to move around. And finally, the preservation of his force was critical. The fewer fighters he had in the air (he advocated 16 at most), the smaller target the numerically superior enemy would have.

Until this point, the Spitfires had fought defensively. Before Park's arrival, the Spitfires scrambled and headed south to gain height, then turned around to engage the German bombers over the island. Park reversed these tactics because the circumstances were different. With plenty of Spitfires to operate, Park's battle plan was to intercept the enemy and break up his formations before the bombers reached the island.

Now, with improved radar and quicker take-off times (two to three minutes) and improved air-sea rescue, more offensive actions became possible. Using three squadrons, Park asked the first to engage the escorting fighters by 'attacking them' out of the sun. The second would strike at the escort Messerschmitt fighters, or, if unescorted, the bombers themselves. The third was to attack the bombers head-on.[27] The impact of Park's methods was immediate. His *Forward Interception Plan*, issued officially on July 25, 1942, forced the Axis to abandon daylight raids within six days. The Ju 87s bombers were withdrawn from operations over Malta altogether. Kesselring

---

[26] Holland, James (2003). Fortress Malta: An Island Under Siege, 1940-1943.London: Miramax Books. ISBN 1-4013-5186-7.

[27] Ibid

responded by sending in fighter sweeps at even higher altitudes to gain the tactical advantage. Park retaliated by ordering his fighters to climb no higher than 6,100 feet (1,900 m). While this did give away a considerable height advantage, it forced the Bf 109s Messerschmitt's to descend to altitudes more suitable for the Spitfire than the German fighter. The methods brought by Park from the Battle of Britain had a significant effect on removing the German siege on Malta.[28]

The years 1942 and early 1943 was particularly impressive for the Allied forces stationed in Malta. Two-thirds of the Italian merchant fleet was sunk; 25% by British submarines, 37% by Allied aircraft. Axis forces in North Africa were denied around half of their supplies and two-thirds of their oil. [29]

Stationed on Malta was Wing Commander Patrick Gibbs and the 39 RAF Squadron. The squadron was flying the new Spitfires and Beauforts. Gibbs and his pilots were all experienced fighters from the air battles with the German Luftwaffe over the English Channel and bombing runs into German-held territories. The Air Wing now placed maximum pressure on German shipping in route to the Afrika Korps. Rommel's position was now critical. The army in North Africa was starved of supplies while the British reinforced their lines in Egypt, before the Second Battle of El Alamein.

Rommel complained to the German High Command in Berlin that he was severely short of ammunition and fuel for any offensive action. The Germans organized a convoy to relieve the difficulties. The British super-secret program "Ultra," intercepted the German communications, and the Wellingtons of Squadron 69 confirmed that the German operation was real. Gibbs's Spitfires and Beauforts sank two supply ships, and a British submarine sank a third supply ship. Rommel still hoped another tanker, *San Andreas*, would deliver the 3,198 tons of fuel needed for the Battle of Alam el Halfa. Rommel did not wait for it to dock and launched the offensive before its arrival. The ship was sunk by an attack led by Squadron 39.[30] Of the nine German ships sent, five were sunk by Malta's forces. The Spitfires and Beauforts were having a devastating impact on German fuel supplies, which were now nearly

---

[28] Ibid
[29] Ibid
[30] Ibid

used up. On September 1, 1942, Rommel was forced to retreat. General Kesselring ordered that the *Luftwaffe* fuel be provided to Rommel. However, this denied Rommel's round forces air support, thereby increasing the effectiveness of the Allies air superiority over the front line. [31,32]

In August, Malta's strike forces had contributed to the Axis' difficulties in forcing an advance into Egypt. In that month, 33% of supplies and 41% of fuel were lost.[33] In September 1942, Rommel received only 24% of the 50,000 tons of monthly supplies to continue offensive operations. During September, the Allies sank 33,939 tons of shipping at sea. Many of these supplies had to be brought in via Tripoli, many kilometers behind the battlefront. The lack of food and water caused a sickness rate of 10% among German soldiers.[34] The British air-submarine offensive ensured no fuel reached North Africa in the first week of October 1942. Two fuel-carrying ships were sunk, and another lost its cargo despite the crew managing to salvage the ship. As the British offensive at El Alamein began on October 23, 1942, Ultra intelligence gained a clear picture of the desperate Axis fuel situation. On October 25, three tankers and one cargo ship carrying fuel and ammunition were sent under heavy air and sea escort and were likely to be the last ships to reach Rommel while he was at El Alamein. Ultra-intelligence intercepted the planned convoy route and alerted Malta's air units. The three fuel-carrying vessels were sunk by October 28. It cost the British one Beaufighter, two Beauforts, three (out of six) Blenheims, and one Wellington. Rommel lost 44% of his supplies in October, a jump from the 20% lost in September.[35]

[31] Spooner, Tony (1996). *Supreme Gallantry: Malta's Role in the Allied Victory, 1939–1945*. London. ISBN 978-0719557064.

[32] Holland, James (2003). Fortress Malta: An Island Under Siege, 1940-1943.. London: Miramax Books. ISBN 1-4013-5186-7.

[33] Levine, Alan (2008). *The War Against Rommel's Supply Lines, 1942–43*. Stackpole Books. ISBN 978-0-8117-3458-5.

[34] Spooner, Tony (1996). *Supreme Gallantry: Malta's Role in the Allied Victory, 1939–1945*. London. ISBN 978-07119557064

[35] Levine, Alan (2008). *The War Against Rommel's Supply Lines, 1942–43*. Stackpole Books. ISBN 978-0-8117-3458-5.

Siege lifted:

In August 1942, 163 Spitfires were on hand to defend Malta; 120 were serviceable.[36] On August 11 and 17, and October 24, 1942, under the respective actions, Operation Bellows, Operation Baritone, and Operation Train. The aircraft carrier *HMS Furious* brought another 85 Spitfires to Malta. The Spitfires were often asked to undertake flights of five and a half hours; this was achieved using 170-gallon ferry tanks. The ferry tanks, combined with a 29-gallon tank in the rear fuselage, brought the total tank capacity up to 284 gallons.[37]

Despite the British forces' successes on Malta, the German *Luftwaffe* renewed its attacks on Malta in October 1942. Recognizing the critical battle was approaching in North Africa (Second Battle of El Alamein), Kesselring organized *Fliegerkorps II* in Sicily to neutralize the threat once and for all.[38]

To counter the pending German attack, the British were now equipped with the newest Spitfires Mk VBCs. Over 17 days of continuous air combat, the *Luftwaffe* lost 34 Ju 88s and 30 Bf 109s Messerschmitt's. RAF losses amounted to 23 Spitfires and 20 crash-landed. The British lost 12 pilots killed.[39] On October 16, it was clear to Kesselring that the defenders were too strong and called off the offensive. The situation in North Africa required German air support, so the October offensive marked the Luftwaffe's last major effort against Malta.[40]

The losses left the German and Italian air forces in a depleted state. They could not offer the air support needed for the Afrika Korps. However, Malta's situation was still stringent going into November, but Park's victory in

---

[36] Delve, Ken (2007). *The Story of the Spitfire: An Operational and Combat History*. London: Greenhill Books. ISBN 978-1-85367-725

[37] Price, Alfred (1997). *Spitfire Mark V Aces 1941–45*. Oxford: Osprey Aerospace. ISBN 1-85532-635-3.

[38] Price, Alfred (1997). *Spitfire Mark V Aces 1941–45*. Oxford: Osprey Aerospace. ISBN 1-85532-635-3.

[39] Scutts, Jerry B. (1994). *Bf 109 Aces of North Africa and the Mediterranean*. London: Osprey. ISBN 1-85532-448-2..

[40] Hooton, E. R. (1997). *Eagle in Flames: The Fall of the Luftwaffe*. London: W&N. ISBN 978-1-85409-343-1.

the air battle was soon followed by news of major success at the front. At El Alamein in North Africa, the British had broken through on land, and by November 5, they were advancing rapidly westward. News soon reached Malta of Operation Torch, the Allied landing in Vichy French Morocco and French Algeria on November 8. Some 11 days later, news of the Soviet counterattack during the Battle of Stalingrad increased morale even more. The extent to which the success in North Africa benefited Malta was apparent when a convoy (Operation Stoneage) reached Malta from Alexandria, Egypt, on November 20, virtually unscathed. This convoy is seen as the end of the two-year siege of Malta. On December 6, another supply convoy under the code-name Operation arrives in Malta.

On December 9, 1942, a convoy of one dozen supply ships, destroyers, and mine sweepers (Operation Portcullis) reached Malta without suffering any losses. After that, ships sailed to Malta without joining convoys. The capture of North African airfields and the bonus of having air protection all the way to the island enabled the ships to deliver 35,000 tons. In early December, another 55,000 tons arrived. The last air raid over Malta occurred on July 20, 1943. It was the 3,340th alert since June 11, 1940.

Operation Torch

On November 8, 1942, the Allies invaded French North Africa. French colonies in the area were dominated by the Vichy French, formally aligned with Germany but mixed loyalties. Reports indicated that they might support the Allies. The American General Dwight D. Eisenhower, commanding the operation, completed a three-pronged attack on Casablanca (Western), Oran (Center), and Algiers (Eastern), then a rapid move on to Tunis.

The Western Task Force encountered unexpected resistance and bad weather, but Casablanca, the principal French Atlantic naval base, was captured after a short siege. The Center Task Force suffered some damage to its ships when trying to land in shallow water, but the Vichy French ships were sunk or driven off; Oran surrendered after bombardment by British battleships. The Eastern Task Force met less opposition because the French resistance had staged a coup in Algiers, and the Allies were able to push inland and compel surrender on the first day.

The success of Torch caused Admiral Francois Darlan, commander of the Vichy French forces, to order cooperation with the Allies, in return for being retained as High Commissioner, with many other Vichy officials keeping their jobs. Darlan was assassinated soon after, and the Free French gradually came to dominate the government. Operation Torch was a compromise operation that met the British objective of securing victory in North Africa while allowing American armed forces to engage in the fight against Nazi Germany on a limited scale.[41] It was the first mass involvement of US troops in the European-North Africa Theatre and saw the United States' first major airborne assault.

---

[41] Watson, Bruce Allen (2007) [1999]. *Exit Rommel: The Tunisian Campaign, 1942–43*. Stackpole Military History Series. Mechanicsburg, PA: Stackpole Books. ISBN 978-0-8117-3381-6, OCLC 40595324.

Chapter Thirty-One
Buchner becomes the Handler
Gestapo HQs, Paris, France

The defeat of the Afrika Korps was a major blow to the German Army in France. Of particular concern was the performance of the Vichy government in North Africa. The Vichy army, with over 125,000 men, surrendered within one week to the Allies, landing in North Africa. This was a forbearance of the things to come in the south of France. Hitler immediately ordered the German authorities to command the Vichy government in southern France.

After the Germans and Vichy forces' defeat in North Africa, the commanding German General in France, Dietrich von Choltitz, ordered German officers to assume command of the French Vichy. *Oberst* Buchner has now ordered that the Gestapo use all methods to determine the intents of the Allies in southern France. The heightened state of readiness is required to collect intelligence from the French members of the resistance. Buchner calls a staff meeting to discuss all the needed preparations.

Buchner addresses his staff, "We have been ordered to arrest all members of the resistance and extract any information they are receiving from the British."

Sturmbannfuhrer (Major) Wilhelm Weber, "Oberst Buchner, the French resistance is very active in Lyon; I would suggest that Oberst Rauch and I be detailed to Lyon. There, we can work with *Hauptsturmfuhrer* (Lead Captain) Klaus Barbie."

"Yes, that would be an excellent idea; however, *Oberst* Rauch has been assigned to an important investigation in Paris. I will confer with *Oberst* Rauch and assign his duties to someone with equal capabilities."

"Danke mein Kommandant."

Buchner thinks reassigning Rauch to Lyons is a good idea. He never has liked having a fox in his henhouse; however, he must not be too agreeable to lose Rauch. It needs to appear that reassigning Rauch to Lyon is in the best

295

interest of the Reich. He will use the back channels to have the Reichsfuhrer Heinrich Müller order his transfer. Buchner sends an encrypted message to Müller and asks for his recommendation on whom he should send to Lyon to take command of the fight against the resistance. Buchner sends three candidates; two are little-known captains, and the third is Rauch. Buchner receives the expected response in two days: "Assign *Obersleutnant* (Lt Colonel) Rauch to Lyons. Effective immediately, promote Rauch to a full *Oberst*." Buchner is surprised by the promotion. He surmises that Rauch has back-channeled communications with Müller and has taken credit for finding the "perfect person" to act as a mole in the French resistance. Buchner thinks, *if that is what it takes to rid the bastard from my ranks, then so be it*. He is, however, resentful that he has not been promoted to General. Buchner will take personal control of the woman's mole. When she provides the intelligence from the resistance, surely, he will receive the promotion.

After one week of new assignments and working sixteen hours per day to expand the Gestapo to all of France, he receives the news he has been waiting for. Reichsfuhrer Müller will be in Paris in fourteen days to review the plans and preparations that have been made to staff the Gestapo offices in southern France. The message from Müller reads, "After reviewing your plans and preparations and if they are acceptable, I would like to know your progress in the infiltration of the resistance."

Now Buchner knows that the weasel Rauch had direct communications with Müller. He knew that only three people knew of the mole project: the woman, Rauch, and himself. He never told Müller of the plan, and sure as hell, the woman had no means of communicating with Müller. It had to be Rauch. He now wonders, "What else did that little rat tell Müller?"

Buchner must first tell Rauch that Müller issued Rauch's order to be assigned to the Gestapo in Lyons. He must also perform a ceremony to promote Rauch to a full *Oberst*. Buchner thinks Barbie will be assigned to Rauch, with Barbie and Rauch in Lyons, I pity any Frenchmen in the resistance. There will not be any Frenchman between the ages of fifteen and fifty left in Lyons in two months.

Buchner must first get a debrief from Rauch regarding the woman who has been "blackmailed" to work for the Gestapo. Rauch is now untouchable; he will soon be promoted to full Colonel and always have the protection of Müller. Rauch does not comprehend the dire situation with the allies now in North Africa. The German Command does recognize the problem, the French Vichy is a paper tiger. The German reasoning is that the French are weak; they have no backbone and are soft and spoiled by their fine foods, wine, and love of life. They lack the military discipline of the Aryan race. The French Vichy government, the Malice, and their ragtag Army will not assist the German Army. On the contrary, if they follow the African Vichy government's example, the French would quickly turn on the Germans and join the Allies.

Buchner is a graduate of the German military academy and is well educated and recognizes the pending danger. He must be able to control the woman's mole. Hopefully, Rauch has been working with his covert agent, and he has some helpful information. This information will be an absolute requirement when Müller visits in five days. He will first get the debrief from Rauch, and then interrogate the woman agent. Buchner, "*Oberst* Rauch, have you been in contact with our covert agent who will infiltrate the resistance?"

"*Jawohl, Oberst* Buchner.*"

"Tell me the latest information that she has reported."

"She is very meticulous and cautious. She is trying to find someone who may be connected to the traitorous organization. She claims that she is having problems making contact. The problem is that most Frenchmen know she was working with the French Civil Administration Office."

"So, you are telling me we have nothing to report when Müller visits next week?"

"That's correct." Rauch smiles internally---*Buchner is going to get a royal ass-chewing.*

Buchner also thinks *I will tell Müller that we have nothing. It is because Rauch insisted that he be in charge. Rauch knows nothing about Spycraft. His expertise is advanced interrogation techniques.*

"Very well, since you will be leaving for Lyon, I will be her handler until I find someone of equal ability as yourself. Now, how do I contact her?"

"*Jawohl Kommandant.* When she needs to contact me, she writes a letter, which is a postcard addressed to the secret address of the Gestapo. She writes in the postcard, 'My children do not feel well, I need to arrange for a doctor.' This is the code sentence that we must meet."

"Ser gut, and where do you meet?"

"We have a prearranged location. It is the third bench across the Seine River, directly in front of the Louvre Museum. Third bench from the Port du Carrousel bridge toward the museum."

"I will send a sergeant to fetch her."

"That will not work. She will be expecting me. Her instructions are to not meet anyone except myself or *Oberst* Buchner. I gave her your name in case, for some reason, I was not able to attend. Also, the meeting must be held covertly. Should you go, you will need to dress like a French peasant. You certainly cannot meet her in your *Sturmstaffel (SS)* uniform."

Buchner did not like dressing as a French peasant, but he recognized the need to protect his assets. After completing his discussions with Rauch, a postcard was sent to Lizzette to meet on a specific date. The date was twelve days from the day that the postcard was mailed.

Two weeks from the day the postcard was mailed, as scheduled, Müller arrives in Paris. He first meets with the Commanding General Dietrich von Choltitz. Discussions center on the defeat of the German forces in North Africa and the preparations needed to repel any beach landings in northern or southern France. After two days of discussions on the English Channel preparations and the south coast of France, private meetings are held within the Gestapo. Oberst Buchner concentrates on the number of Jews and other undesirables that have been shipped to the concentration camps in Germany. He purposely does not provide any metrics on the war against the resistance. After Buchner completes his presentation, Müller asks, "Have you penetrated the resistance?"

"Nein, Reichsfuhrer Müller, we do have the perfect person to penetrate the resistance. *Oberst* Rauch had been her handler, but with Oberst Rauch being reassigned to Lyon, I will take personal charge of our spy."

Müller says, *"Oberst* Buchner, perhaps you do not remember, I demoted the last person in your position due to his total failures and incompetency. If you did not have such a distinguished career as a fighter pilot, I would replace you and transfer you back to Vice Marshal Göring. Perhaps Göring can find you a job behind a desk in some flight operation on the eastern front."

"Jawohl mein Kommandant, now that I have assumed direct control of the situation, we will have our mole inside the resistance within six months."

"Six months?"

"Nein, you must place your informant inside of the resistance within three months. You are to provide me with written monthly reports of your progress. Is that understood!"

"Jawohl mein Kommandant. Heil Hitler!"

Müller waves his right hand, repeats the Heil Hitler, and then says, *"Misserfolg ist keine option"* (Failure is not an option).

Lizzette received the postcard with the instructions to meet at the predetermined site. Since having been recruited by the Gestapo, she had yet to provide Rauch any information. She simply told him that she needed to wait. She had sent messages through several Frenchmen that she was interested in joining the resistance. Thus far, she had not been contacted by anyone claiming to be a member of the resistance. She would wait as long as possible and not tell the Gestapo any true or false information. However, she knew that she would need to give Rauch some information sooner or later. Soon after being recruited by the Gestapo, she had contacted Renard of the resistance. They both believed this would allow her to obtain valuable information from the Germans. However, Lizzette would need to provide some truthful information to the Germans so as not to raise any suspicions.

Renard and Lizzette concluded that Lizzette would weave a story of the difficulty she was having in contacting the resistance. She would need to convince her handler (Rauch) that the only way she could break into the resistance was to have information that would benefit the resistance. Thus, when Lizzette received the postcard for a meeting, she correctly concluded that the meeting was the quick collapse of the French Vichy in North Africa. This had to have the Germans worried about the Vichy government in southern France. Lizzette would use this to get an advantage.

On the day of the meeting, as directed by Rauch, Oberst Buchner was seated at the appointed bench. Lizzette observed a French peasant sitting at the bench from a secluded area on the opposite side of the river. From across the river Seine, Lizzette recognized that it was not Rauch. Her training as a resistance fighter and the Gestapo's additional training allowed her to recognize the walk and different persons' gait. She was confident that the man on the bench was not Rauch. She crossed the river and walked toward the man on the bench. She walked past 'Buchner,' and determined that it was Buchner using her peripheral vision.

Buchner also recognized Lizzette but said nothing. As Buchner tracked Lizzette with his peripheral vision, he thought this woman is perfect. Her Gestapo training has made her into a world-class spy. Lizzette then sat on the bench next to Buchner. After five minutes, she got up, walked to Buchner's bench, and sat next to him.

She then said, "Do you have a cigarette?

Buchner, "*Oui,* but only Turkish."

Non, merci, (No thank you) I only smoke American Lucky Strikes."

Having successfully passed the prearranged password and response, Lizzette and Buchner got down to business.

Typical of German efficiency, Buchner immediately got down to business, "Rauch has been promoted and reassigned. I am now your handler. You will only answer to me. In time, maybe one or two months, I will assign a new handler."

Lizzette does not respond to the sudden removal of Rauch. This can only mean the Germans are preparing to replace the French Vichy.

Buchner says, "We need information on the French Vichy in North Africa. What were the circumstances of the Vichy government collapsing so suddenly? Were they infested with traitors? The French resistance in the south of France would know this. We need intelligence regarding the resistance. Are there traitors amongst the Vichy government in south France? This is your task----- these are your orders. We must have this information."

"Oui, Oui, mon Kommandant. It has been impossible to crack the French resistance. I am afraid that my prior association with the French Civil Authority has tainted me. I need to convince my fellow countrymen somehow that I have valuable information. If I could have some information of little or no value, I could tell those I think have contacts with resistance, and then perhaps they would contact me. You do realize that the resistance may ask me to prove myself with some rebellious act. Being a woman, they may ask that I provide some information from the directorate. The information would

not compromise any German actions, but it would be seen as valuable to the resistance.

Lizzette and Renard:

Renard and Lizzette meet in the underground tunnels of the convent. Renard tells Lizzette, "You must be very careful. Playing a double agent is very dangerous."

"I really have no choice. I only need to play my role for one or two years. The Allies in North Africa and the defeat of the Germans in Stalingrad are very encouraging. The Germans are worried and nervous. Up to this point in time, there have only been German victories."

"Perhaps, but you know what is said when you corner a bear. The bear is the most dangerous when cornered."

"Yes, that is true, but I already have some valuable information. Although not said, Rauch is being reassigned to Lyon. This is where we have the most activity. Thus, it is only logical that he be assigned to Lyon. We must tell all of our resistance cells to lay low for a few weeks. Rauch and Barbie will be on the prowl."

"How many of the new communications systems do we have?"

Renard, "SOE has now parachuted more than thirty systems. Juliette, Andrés, and Francisco have been working seven days a week, sixteen hours a day. They have done an excellent job training our radio operators. We now have thirty cells with the newest radios. Thus far, the Germans have not been able to locate our transmissions. By the reaction of the German DF units, they are not even aware that we are transmitting. I instructed all cells to transmit short messages on the old transmitters. Transmit, run, and hide. Thus far, the Germans believe that we are only transmitting at five to fifteen minutes increments. This would lead them to believe that they are winning the comms war ----they have us on the run."

Lizzette thinks…. *After Buchner gives me the enticement, this may be some information that I can give them. It will serve to strengthen their belief that they, for all practical purposes, have shut down the radio communications of the resistance.*

Lizzette tells Renard, "You should allow some of the old transmitters to be captured. Perhaps you can transmit with one unit and leave a second unit totally destroyed. Make the Germans believe that they were close to capturing the radio operators. They heard the DF trucks and escaped. It would be natural to destroy the equipment that was left behind. After a half dozen close calls, we can completely discontinue using the old transmitters. This will give the impression that they have completely shut down our ability to communicate with the British."

"Excellent idea; we can slowly do this over 30 to 60 days. This will appear to the Germans that they have solved the problem with our ability to receive messages from the British SOE."

"Yes, it will be very interesting when I have my next meeting with the Colonel."

Buchner and Lizzette:

Three weeks from their previous meeting, Buchner and Lizzette meet again on the bench opposite the Louvre Museum. Unknown to Lizzette, Renard gives an anonymous tip to a small Gestapo regiment near the Louvre Museum, "that a French peasant who is a member of the resistance will be sitting at a bench opposite the Louvre Museum." Rauch had given instructions to Lizzette always to wait at least fifteen minutes after Rauch (in this case, Buchner) had sat down. As Lizzette watched from across the river, two motorcycles with sidecars came from opposite sides of the dirt path. The four SS troopers quickly grabbed Buchner and threw him to the ground. With one large SS trooper placing his knee on Buchner's throat, a second trooper tied Buchner's hands, roughly picked him up, and threw him in a police van that arrived within minutes of the two motorcycles. Throughout the arrest of Buchner, Buchner kept shouting, *"Ich bin Oberst Buchner, Ich bin Oberst Bucher!"* The SS troopers paid no attention---this happens all the time; when they arrest a suspect, the suspect will always say it is a mistake. This one takes the cake; no fucking way that he is the commander of the Paris Gestapo!

The police van arrives at the SS sector regimental headquarters. As they drag Buchner to a cell, the *Hauptmann* (Captain) notices the prisoner dragging a wooden leg. He shouts *Halt! Bringen sie den gefangenen hierher!* (Bring the prisoner here!) The captain orders the prisoner to be untied and roughly sit him at a chair opposite the captain. They bring water to Buchner, and after ten minutes, Buchner has regained his composure. He starts shouting at the captain: you imbeciles, idiots, stupid dummkopfs. Do you know that I am Oberst Buchner, your *Kommandant*!

The captain profusely apologizes, he says, "We have been looking for a member of the resistance that closely matched your description."

"My description, my ass, does your suspect have a wooden leg?"

"No, Sir, but you were sitting down. My men could not tell that you had a wooden leg."

Buchner thinks about his arrest and concludes that the Gestapo troopers were only doing their job. Buchner then tells the captain, "I was on an undercover assignment. Your men only did their duty. Due to the sensitivity of my mission, you will not report this incident. Is that understood?'

"*Jawohl* Heil Hitler."

As the arrest of Buchner is taking place, Lizzette watches with astonishment as the events unfold. She knows that eventually, the arresting SS troops and their commander will conclude that they have arrested the *Kommandant* of the Gestapo in Paris. She only watches until Buchner is thrown on the ground; Lizzette has a sixth sense that it is best to vacant the area. Fortunately, the area around the Louvre is heavily populated, and she loses herself in the crowd. She now has a decision to make, should she wait for Buchner to contact her or should she contact Buchner. She weighs her decision and concludes that the threat from the Gestapo is still very much a possibility. She decides to take the initiative and contact Buchner. She fears that doing nothing will only result in possible repercussions that may impact her husband and family.

One week after the Louvre incident, she dresses as an old woman and visits *Oberst* Buchner. She walks to the guarded Majestic Hotel's gate and is immediately stopped by the German guards. She still has the original letter, which ordered her to see *Oberst* Rauch. Lizzette explains to the guards that she knows *Oberst* Buchner and that they only need to call on their telephone and ask the Colonel if he will see Lizzette Raymond. The guards order the older woman to wait until they receive word from inside to allow her to enter. After more than thirty-five minutes, the guards receive word to let her in. She shuffled her feet to imitate an older woman and enters the main building of the Gestapo headquarters. A sharply dressed lieutenant in an all-black SS uniform is waiting for her. He looks at Lizzette with disgust, and with a commanding voice, he orders her to follow him to a holding cell.

Ten minutes later, *Oberst* Buchner enters the room. He looks at the twenty-three-year-old woman who looks like she is sixty-five and says, "Bravo Madame, excellent disguise."

Lizzette says the disguise is for the resistance. Also, it is best that the fewer people that know of my true identity, the better. Lizzette remains quiet about the incident at the Louvre. She will let Buchner bring it up. As she expected, Buchner asks, "Did you see the incident at the park bench?"

"Jawohl Oberst Buchner."

"Yes, I did think that you did see it. It is good that you were not arrested."

"Danke."

I am glad that you are here. I see that you wish to work with us."

"Ja mein Oberst," says Lizzette. "Since you were coming to our meeting last week, do you have some information I can use to penetrate the resistance."

"Ja, I do, you can tell them that you are aware of the new direction-finding equipment that we have. You can tell them that we are far advanced in the area, and it is best if they do not communicate with English Intelligence."

Lizzette, "But I know nothing of radio communications, much less what you call direction finding,"

Buchner listens carefully and after one minute of silence, he gets up and walking in a goose step fashion with his wooden leg, he again sits down and says, "You are absolutely right. That's the beauty of the direction-finding information. It is simply some information that you overheard. Why did Rauch not think about this months ago?" After thinking for a few minutes, he tells Lizzette, "Yes, you can tell the resistance about our new direction-finding equipment."

"Yes, some technical information I overheard would be most helpful."

Lizzette has always sensed that Buchner and Rauch did not get along. Rauch was always bragging about the fact that he had the ear of Müller and that he had canned the last Gestapo Colonel. Anytime he wished to have

Buchner removed, he could send a message through back channels, and he would be promoted to Colonel. He would then be in command of the SS. Lizzette said, "*Herr Kommandant*, more than once, I suggested to Rauch that I give the resistance some enticement, but he always said, *"Nein, I and only I, will think of what is best."*

"You are correct, we need to give those traitors some enticement, just a nibble, and we take a bite."

"Oui, mon Kommandant."

"After we conclude our discussions, I will have a radio technician give you a thumbnail summary of the capabilities of our new DF equipment. The information will be strictly operational."

After the discussions with Buchner, Lizzette meets with a radio technician, and she now has the "enticement" she needs to make contact with the resistance.

"Ja, Herr Oberst, that is excellent information. I believe I can be grateful for the resistance with this type of information. Once they trust me, I can begin passing you valuable information."

"Excellent, Madame."

"Herr Oberst Buchner, we need a new, safe place to meet,"

"Yes, we do. Perhaps you could recommend a place."

"Yes, Sir, but I would also recommend that you not personally be involved. We can meet in the lobby of the Hotel de Ville. You have my picture; your courier will have the *Le Figaro* folded under his left arm and provide the correct password. No need to change the password and proper exchange---- remember cigarette and American Lucky Strike."

"Yes, yes, of course." As Lizzette gets up to walk away, Buchner says, "Madame, the most important question that needs an answer is where will the Allies attack, northern or southern France. That is the most important question that needs an answer."

"Jawohl Herr Oberst, I will need some time to gain the confidence of the resistance before they entrust me with that type of information."

"Madame, you have proven to be a most resourceful woman; I am sure you can think of some way to obtain that information."

"I will certainly try my best."

"Madame Lizzette, trying will not be enough. Remember your husband and children."

With the threat hanging over her head, Lizzette shuffles out of the room and exits the Majestic Hotel.

Chapter Thirty-Two
Arming the resistance
Auvergne Province, France

1942 and 1943 were extremely active for both the Axis and Allied warring nations. The summer of 1942 was the zenith of the Axis powers and expansion, but by the end of 1943, the momentum was now with the Allied nations.

The year 1943 was the year of the Casablanca Conference. At the conference, the Allied leaders discussed the invasions of Europe and Sicily and the need for "unconditional surrender." The day and nighttime bombing of Berlin commenced. The U.S. successfully executed the bombing of the German naval base Wilhelmshaven. The Russians were victorious in Stalingrad; over one million German soldiers were captured and marched to the prison camps in Siberia. In September 1943, the Allies invaded Sicily.

The outcome of the advances made by the Allies resulted in the Germans inflicting heavy punishments on the conquered people. In September 1943, the Germans assumed full control of the Vichy government. The German Gestapo was now given the authority to use brutal techniques to suppress any actions against the French resistance. The lesson learned in the German North African defeat was that the Vichy government would not fight against the Allies. The Germans now replaced Vichy officials and the Malice with the German Wehrmacht and the Gestapo.

The Germans' brutal actions against the French population also impacted the French population's resolve. From 1940 to 1942, there was some resistance to the German occupation. However, up to the winter of 1942-1943, the resistance was independent cells with no central control. These resistance cells comprised a ragtag mix of Frenchmen and some Spanish. Their weapons were often old WW-I surplus single-action rifles and whatever weapons they could steal from the Germans.

In early 1942, the British developed a strategy to train and arm the resistance. The responsibility to train and arm the French resistance was given to the Special Operations Executive (SOE). In 1941, Colonel Susan Mildred Phillips and Captain Herman Hutchinson had been providing limited support to the French resistance. In 1942, the SOE was given an unlimited budget to arm the French resistance. After the funds and the orders was given to the SOE, Colonel Phillips began immediately with the plans to arm the resistance.

Colonel Phillips, "Captain Hutchinson, what is our current readiness in France?"

"For the past year, we have provided advanced communications systems. Our assets in France report they have trained twenty French operators on the new communications equipment. Since they began operations with the new communications gear, none have been detected by the Germans. However, some of the cells are still using the old transmitters. The Germans are locating these resistance cells using the old radios.

"Do we have some idea of the number of resistance fighters?"

"Yes, our main assets in France, Juliette, Francisco, and Andrés, have been assigned to France's south, north, and eastern portions. The reports by our agents are that some French men and women would join the resistance, but they need more organization, training, and weapons.

"What is the status of our training school for our covert agents."

"We now have over fifty agents ready to be inserted into France and provide the organization and training."

"Do we have the weapons?"

"Yes, German Sten guns, German Moser rifles, Lugers, grenades, and explosives. The Americans have also provided bazookas."

"OK, we need a coordinated plan on how best to arm and train the French resistance."

"Yes, madame, I will begin immediately to ask for information from our assets in the field."

Hutchinson communicates with SOE assets:

Hutchinson sends an encrypted message to Juliette, Francisco, and Andrés. The message read, "SOE will be sending fifty covert agents to assist and train the French resistance. Weapons, clothing, money in francs, marks, and pounds will be included. Request your recommendations on how best to supply this large influx of agents, training, weapons, and funds."

Juliette, Francisco, and Andrés quickly determined that this request must be coordinated with Renard and Marcin. Within ten days, the group meets in the Auvergne Forest. The Auvergne Forest has been used by Renard, Marcin, and his small resistance group since the Germans invaded France.

The Auvergne Forest is mountainous and heavily wooded, with plateaus, valleys, gorges, slopes, and jagged volcanic rock. The forest is generally cold and wet. It is inaccessible by motor vehicles. There are no roads, only dirt paths, hidden logger trails, caves, and steep cliffs. The forest is ideally suited for guerrilla warfare and is known as the Fortress of France. The terrain gives the resistance the ability to hide from the Germans. Each time that the Germans tried to search for Renard and his men, the German patrols had all been killed. The forest belongs to Renard and his men; they know every tree, bush, cave, and escape route. The Germans are at a distinct disadvantage; it would take thousands of troops to flush out Renard and his men.

In the two years of the war, Renard and his men have used a series of caves that act as their staging areas. Renard has approximately one hundred men. He says he could have more but will need weapons, clothing, food, and funding to increase his army size. Included in the fifty men are a dozen who were miners before the war. They use their skills to dig a series of tunnels that connect large rooms to house the men. The tunnel complex has been built to allow for false tunnels, confusing any person needing more detailed knowledge of the cave complex. Additionally, landslides can easily be created to seal any section or sections of the caves and tunnels.

The four men and Juliette meet in one of the cave complexes, acting as a conference room. Candles provide the lighting. Chairs, tables, and beds are also available in the complex. Other than they are in a cave, they could be in a villa in the French countryside. The cave complex has a small opening for concealing the cave complex, plus several well-concealed escape tunnels. The perimeter is guarded 24X7, seven days a week. Thus far, in the two years since the beginning of the war, no German patrol has come within miles of the cave complex.

Juliette begins the discussion, "We have received a message from SOE. They are ready to begin arming the resistance. We need your ideas on how best to proceed."

Renard, "That's excellent news. We need weapons and clothing."

"What weapons would you prefer?"

"All German, Sten guns, Moser rifles, machine guns, Lugers, grenades, plastic explosives with fuse, remote fuses if they have any. Also, we need money, Francs, Marks, and English Pounds. Additionally, canned foods, cheese, bread, canteens, boots, spyglasses, single tube, and binoculars."

"What about training?"

"Yes, we will need training on the bazookas, explosives, remote detonator fuses. Also, we need more trainers on the comm gear. Any agents that are sent will need to speak both French and German. If they know a third language, that would also be good. We have Spaniards, Poles, Greeks, and Italians in our ranks."

"OK, how many resistance fighters can you recruit?"

"Recruiting is not a problem. I can have 10,000 show up in the Auvergne Forest tomorrow. But it's not a good idea. I recommend that we start with four camps. The main camp would be here in the Auvergne Forest. The second is in the north between Calais and the Normandy coast. A third near the Spanish border and finally a camp in the north of Marseilles."

"How many fighters can you train?"

"We have fifty agents ready to send to France. All can speak fluent French. They are British, Canadians, Americans, Poles, Italians, and Spanish."

Renard asks, "Americans, can they speak French and German?"

"Maybe not German, but French, yes. You need to remember America is made up of immigrants from all of the countries in Europe. Some also speak German. We had many German Jews who fled Germany in the 1930s. Similar to Albert Einstein."

Marcin says, "If you have fifty agents ready to be sent to France, I recommend that we keep our groups to one hundred or fewer. Send forty agents, ten agents to train one hundred resistance fighters."

Francisco, "Yes, I agree; we train the additional fighters as soon as we train the initial one hundred. According to SOE, weapons will not be a problem. The problem may be how to deliver the required items and the forty or fifty agents."

"The delivery will be a SOE decision. If we have any recommendations, now is the time to speak up," says Andrés.

"OK, I will communicate our recommendations to SOE and give the location of the four initial sites. I will ask for weapons and the other items to equip one hundred and twenty fighters. This will give us a surplus of much-needed items. I will also ask for two hundred boots. The main sizes will be nine, ten, and eleven. We will also need sizes eight, twelve, and thirteen," says Juliette.

"Also ask for boots in ladies' sizes, many of our fighters are women," says Marcin.

"Good point; how many?"

"Twenty-five percent of all materials to be worn should be for women. We have a lot of women fighters."

Renard asks, "Who is our supply coordinator at SOE?"

"You know him as Armand."

"Armand, he is a good man. I know that we will finally get our weapons. You give us the means, and we will kill many Germans," says Marcin.

"Our mission will be sabotage. We are preparing the battlefield to assist the Allies when they land in the north or the south," says Francisco.

Juliette communicates the resistance's recommendations to Hutchinson. The decision is to move the agents and the materials using aircraft and submarines. The aircraft will be the Lysander's flying from England. The shipments using submarines will be using the Mediterranean Sea. The Lysander's are preferred due to their ability to land and take off on short-grass fields, and they are super quiet. The Lysanders will fly to the northern and southern resistance camps on the next full moon. The Lysander's are painted all black with no markings. The disadvantage of using the Lysander's is that only two agents may fly in the plane, and two crates of materials may be taken. The crates will have the required weapons and materials to staff ten resistance fighters. The two Lysander flights are successful. Now, the southern and northern resistance camps have Francisco and two additional SOE agents, plus the ability to fully arm ten additional fighters. After two other flights, it was determined that the process of manning the sites with the ten agents and the materials for one hundred resistance fighters was slow. Armand discusses the problem with Colonel Phillips. Colonel Phillips discusses the situation with the 5th bomber wing to see if a larger plane could parachute the supplies and men. Major Reed from the 5th Bomber Command has a solution, "We could use a Wellington bomber to parachute the materials to a drop zone."

"What is the risk factor."

"It will depend on the situation on the ground to parachute the men and materials. The aircraft is a long-range bomber capable of safely carrying your covert agents and the material crates. The Wellington was

Wellington Bomber

designed as a long-range bomber and has conducted nighttime bombings in Germany."

Colonel, "The plane will need to fly blind, and the pilot will need to use ground features. No radio contact or waypoints will guide the plane's flight. The only time the pilot will know if it is at the drop zone will be when the resistance fighters turn on their torches or their fires."

"Well, that is a problem; the bomber pilots are not experienced in flying blind. They would likely be lost. Thus, I can provide the planes but not the pilots."

Colonel Phillips, "Thank you very much, Major Reed. I will discuss your recommendation with my men and see if we can find qualified pilots."

The Colonel goes back to the SOE command and discusses the solution the Bomber Command offers. They can provide the planes but not the pilots."

Hutchinson thinks about the problem, and after several minutes, he offers a solution, "Colonel, I know where we can find experienced Wellington pilots that fly using no instruments."

"Excellent, and just where can you find these pilots."

"The ATA fly all types of planes and never use instruments."

"Excellent; I will contact the ATA command and request their best pilots to fly the missions."

Colonel Phillips now discusses the request with the ATA Wing Commander, Colonel Rita Givens. Colonel Givens, "You know, of course, all my pilots are women. Currently, the unwritten policy of the RAF is that women will not fly combat missions."

"Technically, these flights will not be combat flights."

"You are correct; to not violate my standing orders, any pilots from the ATA would need to volunteer for the flights.

Colonel Givens, "I do not see a problem. Should I request volunteers, I will likely have all ATA pilots volunteer since they all believe in the war. Germany must be defeated. I am sure that they will all volunteer for these flights."

"Thank you. When could you announce for volunteers?"

"As soon as tomorrow."

Colonel Givens posted a flyer on the ATA bulletin boards, and as expected, over one hundred ATA pilots volunteered. The day after the posting, Colonel Givens sends the list of all the pilots who have volunteered. After Colonel Phillips receives the list, she notices that Karina Hutchinson has volunteered. She decides that selecting eight flight crews, a total of sixteen pilots, will be based on pilot experience. Captain Hutchinson will not be a member of the selection committee. The selection of the sixteen pilots is completed within days of receiving the complete list from Colonel Givens. Included in the sixteen pilots is Karina Hutchinson.

The evening of the day that Karina volunteers to fly the Wellingtons, Karina tells Herman that she volunteered to fly the covert flights.

Herman, "Yes, it comes as no surprise, when Colonel Philips said that we would be asking for volunteers, I knew that you would volunteer."

"Are you on the selection committee?"

"No, Colonel Phillips thought it best if I was not involved in the selection. However, if the selection was based on merit, I had no doubt that you would be one of the sixteen pilots."

Karina, Kathy, and Karrie, the 3K's are on the list of the sixteen pilots as expected. The team of sixteen ATA pilots is assigned to the SOE, and their training begins immediately. All are experienced Wellington pilots; thus, there is no need for flight training. The training is primarily on the topographical maps of France. A refresher course is provided on the sextant's use of the stars for Earth's locations. Communications with Juliette, Francisco, and Andrés have provided four locations for each of the three sites to be armed using the Wellingtons. The fourth site in southern France will be armed using a submarine.

The eight flight crews meet every day. All ATA pilots use topographical maps and bombing surveillance photos to identify landmarks for their night flights. The plan will be to fly with a full moon. Ideal landmarks are bodies of water, such as lakes and rivers. These bodies of water will reflect the moonlight. The second landmark will be silhouettes from the ridge of mountains. All towns in France have been blacked out; thus, lights from cities or towns will not be available.

Additionally, training is provided in evasion tactics. All pilots are healthy and have been in a continuous physical training program. Should they be shot down and need to parachute into enemy territory, they should be prepared to live off the land for up to one week. The resistance will be notified, and all attempts will be made for rescue.

After their preparations, the initial three flights will be to the southern, northern, and eastern regions. The most difficult and dangerous will be the flight to the Auvergne Forest. The flight time to the drop zone is two hours from the French coastline, and the total flight time from take-off to landing in England will be six hours. The Wellington has been designed for long-range bombing missions and will support eight hours of flight time. The pilots will be Kerrie, Karen, and Karina. Kerrie will fly south, Karen will fly to the northern side, and Karina, the most experienced, will fly to the east, the Auvergne site.

The three pilots and their co-pilots have all completed their flight plans. Flying will be by dead reckoning. The flight path will be by time and compass. The planes will fly in a set direction for the calculated time to observe a body of water. The backup plan will be to use the sextant by using the stars to calculate a position. The entry to the French coastline will be where the Germans have no radar coverage. The Germans have only eight Freya sites operational. Two of the sites have been destroyed by the American and British Air Forces.

314

All operations will be carried out in the dead of night. Karina, who has a longer flight, departs at 10 p.m. Kerrie departs at 11 p.m. and Karen at midnight. Karina has 4,000 pounds of weapons and the required materials packed in eight crates. The Wellington's front, back, and top guns have been removed to allow the maximum payload to be delivered. Ten covert agents are also on board. All crates and the agents will parachute into one of the designated drop zones. The zones have been labeled zones 1 through 4, with zone 1 being the primary drop zone. Karina's plane flies south toward the Bay of Biscayne. After flying past the Bay of Biscayne, the plane zigzags east toward the Auvergne Forest. After two hours of dead reckoning and having the co-pilot check for the position, the plane approaches the drop zone at 12:37 a.m. Karina sees the fires surrounding the drop zone. Karina corkscrews the plane down to 2,000 feet. She expertly levels the plane and turns on the yellow light—one minute to jump time. The green light comes on, and the crates are pushed out, followed by the ten covert agents. The entire operation is completed in two minutes.

On the ground, Juliette, Renard, and Marcin have been waiting for the plane. They hear in the distance the growling rumble of the Wellington's propellers. Renard signals to his men to light the bonfires. Four fires are quickly lit to identify the drop zone. Juliette looks to the sky and sees

Resistance Commanders

the Wellington's silhouette. She speaks to Renard, "That's it, a large bomber plane. Prepare to receive all agents and weapons. and materials."

Renard orders his men, "Prepare to drive the trucks to the landing area."

The plane turns and begins a second run over the drop zone. Juliette, Renard, Marcin, and his men cannot see the canopies or the crates. All items are painted black. However, the covert agents have directional torches (Flashlights). Using the torches, the agents signaled toward the burning fires. Renard's men rushed to the falling crates. They quickly cut the cords of the parachutes. Load the eight crates into four trucks. The ten covert agents are safely transported to the cave resistance complex using additional trucks, vans, and old model cars. All parachutes have been collected in less than ten minutes, crates loaded, and all fires have been extinguished, and the drop zone has been returned to its original state. The following day, all weapons are removed from their crates and issued to the one hundred resistance fighters. Next to the Sten guns and other weapons, the resistance fighters most appreciate the boots. The ten covert agents arrive at the cave complex at 3 a.m. They all get six hours of sleep and are ready to begin their training of the resistance fighters.

Karina's return flight to England:

After the agents and crates are parachuted into the drop zone, the Wellington plane is now 4,000 pounds lighter. With the offloading of the 4,000 pounds, the aircraft may now achieve its maximum 325 mph. The flight back to England will trace the trip to the drop zone in the reverse order. The Wellington turns west, again using dead reckoning, they fly zigzag flights to the Atlantic Ocean. After flying for one hour and thirty-five minutes, Karina is startled by tracer rounds coming from her starboard side. Immediately following the tracer rounds, a German Messerschmitt flies next to her plane, flying in the opposite direction. Karina quickly makes a decision to descend and seek cover in a cloud formation. Within minutes, the Wellington is hidden in the clouds. However, she can only stay in the clouds for a short time. As the Wellington exits the clouds, she sees that the Messerschmitt is still prowling. Karina turns the bomber into a sharp dive and returns to cloud cover. After more than thirty minutes of making racetrack turns in the clouds, she exits the cloud cover, and she and her co-pilot no longer see the Messerschmitt. Karina looks at her fuel gauge, and the co-pilot calculates the amount of flight time they have left. The calculation indicates that they will not be able to make any English landing strip.

Karina now makes the decision to fly south toward Spain. It would be best to bail out over the land if they run out of fuel. Bailing out over the ocean would likely end in death. The waters are too cold, and rescue would likely not occur for hours. Karina and her co-pilot, Mary Shivers, calculate that they will be near the Spanish border when they run out of fuel. To conserve fuel, they take the plane to 30,000 feet, where the atmosphere is thinner, and the engines can work to maximum efficiency. Karina has also learned from her barnstorming days that she needs to test the condition of the plane. The German fighter's tracer bullets had come very close to the Wellington; thus, there may be some damage. She and her co-pilot, Mary, go through a checklist to check if any damage occurred. The last thing they check is the landing gear. It appears that the landing gear is not coming down. Karina tells Mary to go back through the plane, go to both the front and aft gun positions, and visually inspect to see if the landing gear is coming down. Using the plane intercom system, Mary keys the intercom button from the back-gunner position, "I do not see the landing gear coming down."

"Roger, go to the mid-section of the plane and see if you can use the hand crank to lower the landing gear."

"Roger, going to the mid-plane maintenance section."

"Call me when you are there."

"Roger will do."

Mary, "I am at the mid-section. Got bad news, I can see that the landing control cable has been cut when we took fire from the German fighter."

"OK, return to flight cockpit."

"Roger returning now."

Karina, "Here is the plan. We fly inland until we have ten minutes of fuel left. We reduce our altitude to 6,000 feet and bailout. We may be over the Pyrenees. The mountain range closest to the Atlantic has peaks to 5,000 feet. Hopefully, we can make it to the Spanish side. If not, we should be close to Spain, and we use our legs to cross."

Mary, "Can we use our radio to let SOE know where we are?"

"Probably not a good idea, the Germans would intercept the transmission, and they would likely find us before a rescue party would find us. I did a lot of mountain climbing in my younger years in the New Mexico Mountains. Best to take our chances without the Germans knowing where we are."

What about the German pilots? Will they not report our plane?"

Yes, but they do not know that the plane is damaged. The Germans will likely conclude that we are now back in England. Besides, they have a lot more to worry about than one British Wellington surveillance plane."

As planned, Karina brings the plane down to 6,000 feet. She points the aircraft toward the Atlantic, and they bailout. The plane has five minutes of fuel and flies over the French coastline. Both the German guards and the residents of Bayonne's town see the flight of the Wellington descending and crashing into the Atlantic. It is one of many planes that are being shot down by German anti-aircraft guns. The Germans make a note in their logbooks, and the residents of Bayonne only make a mental note of the crashing plane. Within ten minutes of crashing into the Atlantic, the plane sinks, and no traces of the plane can be found.

As Karina and Mary float down to a valley in the Pyrenees, Karina can see what she thinks are the waters of the Bidasoa Bay and River. The river forms the border between France and Spain. However, they will likely be landing in France. She signals to Mary to follow her down to the valley. From her experience in years of mountain climbing, she knows that the river basin will likely provide an unobstructed area to land the parachutes. The good thing is that it is still dark; thus, they will not be observed, but she cannot see the landing terrain. For this very purpose, both she and Mary have a portable altimeter to have an idea when she will hit the ground. Karina lands first and lands in a grass field. Mary is hung in a tree branch but is not injured. Using her knife sheathed to her ankle, she cuts the parachute cords and drops to the ground. Karina climbs the tree and cuts down the parachute. They need to bury the two parachutes; no trace can be left that two persons have parachuted into southern France. The area is controlled by the Germans.

Chapter Thirty-Three
Karina in German Territory
South France

Soon after the Wellington's delivered the agents, weapons, and materials to the northern, southern, and eastern camps, they reported that all items had arrived safely. The reports indicated that all planes had parachuted the agents and crates. The aircraft had safely turned and started their returns to England. Colonel Phillips, Colonel Givens, and Captain Hutchinson all anxiously await the Wellington planes' return. At 2:30 a.m., the northern plane being piloted by Kathy lands safely at the SOE airfield outside South Hampton. At 2:45 a.m., the southern aircraft piloted by Kerrie also lands safely at the SOE airfield. Now they wait for the last flight. They expect the eastern plane to arrive sometime between 3 and 4 a.m. The plane piloted by Karina and Mary has the longest flight; it is expected to be the last flight to land. The aircraft has an extended flight capability; however, it left the ATA airfield at 10 p.m., and it needs to be back by no later than 4 a.m. At 4:30 a.m., it is apparent that the plane will not arrive.

Since the flight is in enemy territory, no rescue flights will be flown. It is possible that the plane ditched in the Atlantic. However, it is too dangerous to launch rescue operations along the coastline. The Germans are heavily armed with anti-aircraft guns, anticipating a beach attack by the allies. Captain Hutchinson says, "I know she is alive. She is a real fighter. If she finds a way to find her way back to England, she will do it."

Colonel Phillips says, "We can contact Francisco in the south of Spain and have the resistance in south Spain start making inquiries to see if she and her co-pilot Mary Shivers parachuted into southern France."

"Yes, I will have a message sent to both the eastern and southern camps to query the local population to see if any Wellington planes have been shot down or crashed or if any pilots have parachuted into the area. Both being women, the local resistance will know if they are in the area."

On the day Karina and Mary should have returned, an all-points en-crypted message is sent to all fifty resistance radio stations in France. Captain Hutchinson says. "It's a good thing we have the fifty transmitter/receivers in the field. Kudos to Juliette, Francisco, and Andrés for having completed the training."

Karina and Mary have now buried their parachutes; Karina checks her compass and pulls out a map of France from her backpack. They have provi-sions for five days; they are at the base of the Pyrenees mountains. Karina confers with her map and decides to avoid all towns where the Germans have small garrisons. As they start their march south, they see that they must cross a mountain range of 4 to 5,000 feet. These are the mountains that she was trying to avoid. Based on the estimated distance to the base of the moun-tains, it is apparent that she mistook the body of water for a different river. Tonight, using their sextant, they will use the stars to determine their loca-tion. Using the map, they slowly and carefully transverse the countryside. They crossed several dirt roads where they heard German voices. They can smell the cigarette smoke and assume that the German patrol has stopped for a break. The Germans are complaining about being stuck in this remote shit hole. They joined the Wehrmacht to kill the enemies of Germany.

First guard tells the second guard, "When I get relieved, I am going to rape every Jew woman I can find. The second guard laughs and says. "Yes, we rape them first, then we drag them to the deportation station. I understand that we have built some crematoriums in Poland. We need to rid the Earth of these scums."

Both Karina and Mary know enough German to understand what is being spoken. They are now thinking *not only about escaping but also about killing the SOBs.*

After half an hour, they hear the half-track vehicle start up and rum-ble away down the dirt path. They cross the dirt path and continue to the base of the mountains. As the sun sets, they see a small cave where they can stop and sleep for the night. Tomorrow, they will start climbing the mountain. The one advantage to being in the country is that the sky is lit with thousands of stars. Finding the north star is not a problem. They use the sextant and now know they are fifty miles from the border. Normally fifty miles in four days would not be a problem, but the mountains and evading German patrols will restrict the miles they can walk in one day. When they do reach the border, that will be another problem.

On the second day, they start up the mountain. At 2 p.m., they hear the sound of several sheep—*baa, baa.* Karina slowly inches up the ridge and sees a young man herding his sheep. After conferring with each other, they decide to approach the young man. If he is a friend, he can help. However, if he is a German collaborator, they will need to kill him with their handgun. Karina slowly approaches the boy. Being a woman, she hopes that the young man does not see her as a threat.

Karina says first in French, *"Bonjour, Je suis un ami."*

Then she says in Spanish, *"Hola, soy una amiga."*

The young shepherd smiles and responds in Spanish, *"Hola, quién eres tu?"* (Who are you?)

From that point, the conversation is half Spanish and half French. Spanish and French are so similar that Karina can be talking in French and the young shepherd in Spanish, and they would understand each other.

Karina then answers his question, "My friend and I parachuted from a supply plane. We were attacked by a German plane."

Karina and Mary introduce themselves using their cover names.

The shepherd tells them, "My name is Emilio."

Emilio continues, "Yes, I see many English and American pilots crossing through here, but they always have a guide to cross them through the mountains. If you do not have a guide, you will not survive."

"Do you know where we could find a guide?"

"Yes, but I cannot leave my sheep. My uncle will kill me if anything happens to the sheep. It is our livelihood. Without sheep, we have no food, no money to buy clothes, nothing, so you see, I cannot leave our sheep."

"Esta bien, can you tell us where to find a guide?"

Yes, but the village is far away, the best thing to do is to wait here with me for two days. Then my uncle will come, and he can help you."

Karina feels safe with the young shepherd, but Mary senses something is wrong. She tells Karina.

Karina then says, "Women's intuition, perhaps you are right. We will keep our guard up and see what happens."

Later that day, the young shepherd moves the herd up the mountain where he has a small cabin, and the sheep are fenced in. Between the three, they share their food and have a good night's sleep. Early the following morning the shepherd has seen that the two women are armed with handguns and knives, but after talking to Karina and Mary, he now sees them as simple women pilots who ferry planes for the English. He has been told that the English are short on pilots, and they teach women how to fly planes. He sees them as no threat to him; after all, they are only women. They probably don't even know how to load the pistols, let alone how to fire them. After inspecting the Cabin, Karina and Mary accept the shepherd's offer to stay in the mountains.

Karina and Mary are still determining if the shepherd is a friend or foe and would turn them over to the Germans. The Germans are paying 10,000 francs for information on Allied pilots. Karina and Mary must remain vigilant. On the third day, when Uncle Flavio is to arrive, Mary, who has the morning watch, notices that a German patrol is approaching the mountain cabin.

Mary quickly tells Karina, "I see what looks like a German patrol approaching from the valley."

Karina and Mary rush to an observation point. They carry their backpacks, which have their binoculars and weapons. Both women lay prone; thus, the Germans cannot see them. They crawl up to the highest point on the ridge. Karina reaches into her backpack and pulls out a pair of binoculars.

She looks through the binoculars and says, "Well, looks like we have our answer; that little shithead has sold us downriver for his ten pieces of silver. He is talking to the Germans and pointing to the mountain cabin."

Mary, "It's a good thing we never really trusted the little shithead."

"Yeah, now we know what we need to do."

"Yes, I know. I will crawl down to the cabin and get more ammo magazines," says Mary.

Karina and Mary are now fully armed. They pull out the Sten Guns and open the folded stock to insert a 40-bullet magazine. They both pull back the slide, and a bullet is inserted into the chamber.

Karina, "Now we wait."

"We have an advantage; the little shithead has told the Germans that we are women and that we were simply flying a supply plane. The Germans will think that we pose no threat," says Mary.

"We will soon know. It will depend on how they approach the mountain cabin. If they simply drive up and bust open the door. That will tell us that they are over-confident. If they stop some distance from the cabin and approach slowly from different sides, then they see us as Allied soldiers," says Karina.

"OK, here they come. The shepherd is riding with them."

"Yes, I see that. I think that he will ask us to come out, and the Germans are going to hide behind the mountain and ambush us when we come out."

"Stand by, we can see the entire field from here. When the shepherd walks up to the cabin and enters, we open in fully automatic and kill the four Germans."

"What about the shepherd?"

"Depends on what he does. We cannot let him escape. We will need time to get distance between us and the Germans."

The German half-track stops a good distance from the mountain cabin. The four German soldiers and the young man dismount. The four German take positions to the left and right of the cabin door. The shepherd enters the cabin.

Karina motions, "You take a right, and I take a left."

The Germans are intently looking at the door. Karina and Mary stand up on the ridge and open fire fully automatically. The Germans never saw what hit them. All four Germans were dead before they hit the ground. When the shepherd heard the automatic gunfire, he knew it had to be the Germans. He could recognize the smooth sound of the Sten Guns, "RA-TAT-TAT, RA-TAT-TAT."

He was confident that he had earned 20,000 francs. When he opened the door and stepped outside, and saw the four German soldiers riddled with bullet holes, he was flabbergasted, astonished, and bewildered. He quickly lost control of his senses and started running down the road.

Karina looked at Mary and said, "He should not have run!"
Both Karina and Mary opened fire and killed the young man.

Karina said, "We had no choice," as tears entered her eyes.

Quickly, the women regained their composure and went back into the cabin and started searching for documents and any hidden compartments. After fifteen minutes of searching, Mary finds a ledger with English and some Spanish names. They were all pilots with 5,000 to 20,000 francs written to the right of the name.

Karina said, "Place the ledger in your backpack."

They threw all the bales of hay into the sheep corral. They also filled the water trough. After that, they carried all the dead bodies into the German half-track. They took rakes and shovels and cleaned up all the blood. After that, they returned to the cabin and straightened all the chairs, tables, and beds. They then jumped in the half-track and started driving up the mountain. Using a map found in the cabin, Karina pointed to the right and told Mary, "Drive up that gorge; looks like it will lead to a mountain pass."

"Okay, what about the bodies?"

"We drive until we can dispose of them in a location where they cannot be found. The map shows a small lake about five miles along this valley. We can weigh them down with rocks. That should keep them underwater for at least a month."

"I didn't like killing the shepherd, but after we found the ledger, it at least makes me feel better."

In two hours, they come to the lake. They drive the half-track to a ridge. They weigh down each body with sacks found in the bed of the half-track. They fill the sacks with rocks, tie them to the bodies, and roll the bodies off the truck and into the lake.

After the task of getting rid of the German guards and the shepherd boy, they travel the forty miles to within two miles of the border. Now, they need to think about how to cross the border.

Karina says, "We will scout the border along this section and determine the best way to cross, but we cannot wait too long for the Germans; they will have no problem tracking us---with tracks made by our half-track. They will find us in two or three days."

Mary says, "We have one day to collect Intel. After that, we will need to make a decision. We either shoot our way to Spain or we find a river crossing?"

Yes, I agree. We need to climb to the ridge and scout the river. You go down river and I go upriver. We scout for six hours and return to this point. After we scout the river, we then determine if we try crossing through these heavy currents for somehow cross over the border bridge."

As planned, Mary and Karina scout the river several miles down and upstream and return to their observation point.

Mary, "I had no luck, the river current is even strong down river. There is a large stream of water flowing into the river and increasing the strength of the current. Hopefully you found some place where we could cross?"

"No, the river gorge increases in depth, thus the water is crashing against the embedded large boulders. We would never make it across the river. I am afraid that our only options are to go back and see if we can find members of the resistance and they could hide us," says Karina.

Mary thinks about the two options and says, "Option two will not work. Remember, we have the German patrol one day behind us. We will likely need to shoot our way through the border river bridge."

"I agree, we have three hours of sunlight. We wait until tonight and shoot our way across after the midnight border guards take their stations. We will need to approach the guard gate in stealth mode. If possible, we use our knives and quietly cross the bridge. If we get that lucky. The next problem will be the Spanish guards."

Karina continues, "Crossing at the bridge will be a very high risk, but we have no choice. We wait until tonight and take our chances. Let's get some sleep. We are going to need all of our energy tonight."

Resistance Camp South France:

A small Resistance group on the outskirts of Bayonne received the message sent by the SOE. The leader of the resistance was Javier del Monte. Javier had been told by an old woman up early and tending the chickens that she had seen a British bomber fly over her farm and headed for the Atlantic.

Javier asked the old lady, "What time did you see the plane cross the sky?"

"It was 4 a.m."

"Are you sure?"

"Oui, my chickens always wake up at 4 a.m. I am sure."

"Meri Beaucoup."

Immediately, Javier sends an encrypted message to SOE and to the southern French resistance main headquarters.

The message reads, *"English bomber was seen at a low altitude flying west toward the Atlantic. Contacts in Bayonne indicate that the plane crashed into the Atlantic. By the description of the plane flight, it is likely that the plane was not manned."*

The resistance main camp of southern France is being assisted by SOE agent Francisco Vargas, aka Jose Gonzales, code name Francisco. Francisco immediately jumps to action. He is sure that the aircraft reported by Javier is the aircraft that Karina and Mary were flying. Francisco organizes two search parties; one will search the base of the Pyrenees at the Cardia Pass, and the second will search the French side of the Bidasoa River. Both parties are equipped with HF radios, which allow them to communicate over the Pyrenees mountains.

Francisco tells the leader of the Cardia Pass to keep his messages short, "We do not want the Germans to intercept our messages."

"Understood, I will keep them short," responds the Cardia Pass team leader.

The two teams have mounted horses to allow for their ability to cover the required land and to arrive at their assigned destinations. The Cardia team arrives at the outskirts of the mountain cabin. Team leader Javier and his team of three Resistance fighters are observing the mountain cabin using their binoculars. Javier tells his radio operator to transmit a message to Francisco,

"Enemy at the pass, no sign of the birds, moving south to *España."*

One minute after the message is sent, the response is received, "R," which means received. Francisco and his team know that Karina and Mary are alive and moving toward Spain. He also knows that the Germans are in hot pursuit. He will need to find Karina and Mary before the Germans find them.

Javier also knows that Francisco will need time so that Francisco can find Karina and Mary. He concludes that he has several advantages: the Germans will move slowly, looking for clues on the whereabouts of the missing soldiers; Javier has the element of surprise, and he and his men know the area. He will take advantage of all three.

Javier and his men mount their horses and ride to a location over-looking the pass. Within one hour, the two teams of eight German soldiers are marching up the pass. From a position high in the mountain, Javier and his men open fire on the Germans. All bullets miss their mark as the location of Javier and his men is out of range of the single-action French rifles. How-ever, the gunfire has the intended result. The Germans are delayed several hours as they take cover and shield themselves in the mountain crevices. Af-ter the delay, they again begin their march up the mountain.

Javier and his men continue this harassment for the entire day. On the third ambush, the German Commander decides to take action. He sends four of his men up the mountain to engage the Résistance fighters. It is mis-take, two of the soldiers are killed, and two are badly injured. When the two injured soldiers limp back to the German group, the Commander berates and scolds them as being incompetent. The two injured soldiers are not able to continue with the search. The Commander orders two of his soldiers to return to the mountain cabin and obtain two cargo burros to carry the injured men back down the mountain. After the third ambush and failed attempt to kill the insurgents, the German search team slowly makes their way up the mountain. Finally, after three days, they reach the banks of the Bidasoa. The Germans have a map indicating the border control points. They march to the nearest bridge, which connects France with Spain. The Commander discusses the situation with the border guards.

"*Feldwebel* (Sergeant) Kaufmann, have you had any English pilots masqueraded as foreign peasants crossing this border station?"

"*Nein, Kommandant.*"

"Is there any point where persons could swim across?

"*Nein,* it is impossible; the river has strong currents with rapids and waterfalls. Plus, the water is icy, as the source of the water is from high in the snow-covered mountain peaks."

"*Danke Feldwebel* Kaufmann, *Heil Hitler!*"

The search team commander is confident that the English pilots have not escaped. He orders his team to continue the search along the banks of the river. After not finding the two women, he orders his team to climb the mountain and search all crevices, gorges, and caves within five kilometers of the river bank. Having two women outsmart him will not go well with his Commander. This will likely end his promotion to senior *Kommandant.*

Karina and Mary Escape to Spain:

Francisco and his team arrived on the banks of the Bidasoa River one day before the German team arrived and two days after Karina and Mary had been scouting the border crossing. Their only option was to cross at the border bridge. The river has violent currents, rapids, and waterfalls, with the water crashing into large boulders.

Francisco concludes that Karina and Mary will first collect Intel on the bridge crossing; at least, that is what he would do. Francisco carefully inspects the area surrounding the bridge crossing. He notices two points in the hills neighboring the border crossing. Francisco and his men use the horses to climb the mountain above the two hills. The team dismounts their horses and carefully walk down to the observation points above where he thinks Karina and Mary may be hiding. He knows that the two women have completed camouflage training, and his men will need to oversee the observation points. He knows that, in time, the ladies will need to take a break. He is in luck after using his binoculars to scan the likely observation points. The two gals are resting at an observation point. Francisco sees Karina sitting on a rock and resting her back.

He says to himself, "That's her, thank God."
Francisco carefully walks down the mountain, and when he is in hearing distance, he speaks in a low but deep voice, "Karina, this is Jose Gonzales, code name Francisco."
Karina hears Francisco's voice and his code name.

It has to be him!

She turns and, with her handgun, says, "Is that you Francisco?"

Francisco gives her the code sentence, "The rain in Spain falls mainly in the plains." I'm coming out don't shoot."

Karina laughs and cries at the same time. "Francisco, wonderful to hear your voice! Now let me see you!"

Francisco comes out from hiding, and the two embrace. Francisco then says, "Now, let's get you out of here."

Karina, "Sure, glad to see you; we were all set to try and shoot our way across the bridge."

Francisco, "We will get you to Spain, but not by crossing the bridge."

"How are we gonna do that?"

"We have a hidden method to get you to Spain."

"How? There are only two ways: the border crossing at the bridge or we fly over."

"It will be the second option."

Karina, Mary, Francisco, and his team walk to the most unlikely location on the banks of the Bidasoa River. Javier has now joined the team. He points up a cable that has been anchored on large oak trees on the Spanish and French borders.

Javier explains, "The cable from France to Spain has a slope of five degrees. He speaks to Karina and Mary. We will have two sling chairs with double wheels attached to the cable. Gravity will "fly" you to Spain."

Karina, "How long has this method been employed?"

"If you mean, will it work? Yes, many times."

"OK., we believe," Mary says.

"Before we "fly" to Spain, I have a list I need to show you. The shepherd at the mountain cabin was a German collaborator. He was turning over pilots to the Germans for rewards."

Karina shows the list to Javier.

Javier then says, "Now we know how we were losing a percentage of the pilots. Did the shepherd mention anyone working with him?"

"Yes, he mentioned his uncle," Mary says.

"Was the name Flavio?"

"Yes. That's the name."

"*Muchas Gracias,* we will take care of the traitor."

Karina and Mary are back in England:

Upon "landing" in Spain, Karina and Mary are placed in a forest ranger truck and driven to the English consulate in Salamanca, Spain. Once they are in the consulate, they are on English soil. From the consulate, a message is transmitted to the British Diplomatic Service in London regarding the two fliers that have been rescued. Karina and Mary are twenty-seven of the French Résistance rescued in the last month.

The British Diplomatic Service now sends written correspondence to the respective services listing the names of the rescued pilots. The names of Karina and Mary arrive at the SOE via a normal diplomatic pouch. The clerk at the SOE opens the sealed envelope. She routinely scans the list to review the formal correspondence between the Diplomatic Service and SOE. She does a double take and quickly gets up from her desk and knocks on the door of Colonel Phillips.

"Colonel Phillips, I have wonderful news! You must see this letter from the Diplomatic Service!"

Colonel Phillips reads the letter, and she starts to tear up. As the Colonel's tears run down her cheeks, the clerk Dorothy starts crying with happiness. Colonel Phillips then takes the letter, exits her office, runs down the hallway. She enters the command post of the SOE.

She sees Captain Hutchinson and says, "Captain I have wonderful news, Karina and Mary are alive and safe in Spain!"

Herman cannot believe it, he simply keeps saying, "Thank the Lord, thank the Lord. She is safe and soon will be home!" He also tears up with happiness.

Typically, rescued pilots are transferred back to England via sea transport. The English ambassador to Spain recognizes the significance of the rescue of Karina and Mary. The ambassador makes arrangements to have Karina and Mary flown to England. Karina and Mary discuss the offer and gracefully decline, Karina simply tells the ambassador, "We appreciate the offer, but we need to be treated like all other rescued pilots."

When word reaches London that Karina and Mary had refused to be flown to London, it was not a surprise to Colonel Phillips or Captain Hutchinson. They would simply be treated like all rescued pilots; she and Mary would ship to England via sea vessel.

Chapter Thirty-Four
Gestapo Plans Major Offensive
Southern France

All four major Résistance camps have been fully armed. Three were armed by parachuting SOE agents and weapons using the Wellington bomber planes. The fourth was successfully armed using a submarine on the Mediterranean Sea. The result is that by late 1943 and early 1944, the resistance had destroyed major German arms depots, bridges, and train tracks and attacked the small garrisons in the countryside.

The German High Command has ordered Müller to take immediate action and eliminate all members of the resistance. Using torture techniques on the general French population has had the opposite effect; it continues to grow more deadly every month. Adding to the German problem is that the British SOE is having significant success in arming the resistance. *Hitler orders Reichsfuhrer* Heinrich Müller to travel to Paris and personally address the problem. Hitler goes into a raging fury; he pounds the table, looks directly at Müller, and shouts, "I want the problem solved, no excuses. Tell Buchner and Rauch that their records mean nothing; if the problem is not solved by early 1944, we will take action to place the entire French Gestapo command on trial as traitors and incompetent fools! Is my command clearly understood?"

"Jawohl mein Kommandant! Heil Hitler!"

"Well, don't just stand there; go fix the problem!"

Müller snaps his jackboots; he again says, "Heil Hitler," turning and leaving the room quickly. He wants to impress the Fuhrer that he is rushing to fix the problem. Müller leaves Hitler's command post enters his Mercedes command vehicle, and orders that he be driven to his headquarters. Once in his command car, Müller tells his aide to phone his headquarters on Albert Strasse. He will depart to Paris first thing tomorrow morning. Inform Vice Marshal Göring that I need a squadron of Messerschmitt's to provide protection.

"Jawohl mein Kommandant, Heil Hitler! "

When Müller lands at Tempelhof airport in Berlin, he is told that Göring cannot have a complete squadron of Messerschmitt's for his protection. Müller enters his headquarters and calls Göring.

"Vice Marshal Göring, I need escort planes tomorrow. The Fuhrer has ordered me to go to Paris immediately; it is a most urgent requirement."

"Göring, as the Luftwaffe's supreme commander, says, "Herr Müller, I also have most urgent orders; I am to protect the Fatherland. All my fighter planes are deployed on the Russian front or protecting the Fatherland against enemy bombing."

Göring then says sarcastically, "Perhaps you haven't heard we are being bombed night and day by the British and the Americans; I can spare no fighters for your protection."

Müller is now angry; he thinks for a few seconds and returns the sarcasm, "Wasn't it you who said that Berlin would never be bombed?"

Müller takes the train and is in Paris after an eight-hour train ride. The day that Hitler ordered Müller to eliminate the resistance in France, Müller had sent an encrypted message to Buchner and Rauch. The message stated that an offensive against the resistance was to start immediately. He was to be in Paris within two days to review and approve the plan.

Buchner senses that this is the moment to disobey all protocols and send a staff car to pick up Lizzette at the Bureau of Public Affairs. When Lizzette was told by her supervisor that a friend was asking for her in the lobby, Lizzette could not imagine who it would be. The Bureau of Public Affairs Chief had noted that Lizzette always favored regulations that would favor the French. She was not overt regarding these favors, and if her actions were taken individually, one could not discern that she preferred the French. It was only when the Chief saw these actions in their accumulative that he surmised that Lizzette was a member of the resistance. He then arranged for the stranger to meet with Lizzette in a private room. The stranger, who was a Nazi collaborator, looks like a member of the resistance. After meeting in the private room for the first minute, Lizzette knew that Buchner sent him. The Nazi collaborator said his name was Anton; Lizzette knew that Anton was a cover name, but after he gave the proper passcode, she had to assume that he, indeed, was a courier for Buchner.

Anton said, "*Oberst* Buchner will meet you at the Hotel de Ville tonight at 10 p.m. He needs to know where the resistance has their main camp. He told you that your children's fate will depend on your answer."

"Oui, Merci Beaucoup," I will be there."

Lizzette and Renard knew that someday it would come to her having to tell Buchner the location of Renard's main camp. Renard and Lizzette had agreed that when the day came, she would say to him that the main base of the resistance was in the Mercantour Forest in the south of France. Renard did indeed have a small force stationed in the Mercantour Forest, but Marcin's Resistance group had a well-concealed plan to escape. The Mercantour Forest was also ideal for setting up an ambush when the Germans attacked.

That evening, Lizzette met with Buchner at the de Ville Hotel's restaurant. Buchner had arranged for a secluded table at the far end of the restaurant. Lizzette arrived early, masquerading as an older woman. She sat in the lobby, reading the German Propaganda newspaper. According to the stories in the newspaper, the war was going well. The British and American bombers never reached the heartland of Germany. The bombers were all shot down by anti-aircraft guns and the mighty German Luftwaffe. The German bombing of England was going well, and the Fuhrer expected England's surrender any day. No stories were printed about the Allied advancements in Sicily or the German Armies' defeat in Russia. If one only reads the Goebbels propaganda newspapers, Germany will rule the world by 1946.

After sitting in the lobby for one hour, Lizzette did not detect anything unusual, nor did she see the trench coats of the Gestapo. A half-hour before she met with Buchner, she went to the woman's room and changed her appearance. Within ten minutes, she was now Madame Lizzette Raymond, a well-dressed and wealthy woman. When Buchner arrived, he hardly recognized her, "My, you certainly look different, from an old woman to a beautiful French Mademoiselle."

"Ja, die Deutsche Spionageschule hat mich gut unterrichtet." (Yes, the German Spy School taught me well).

"Frau Raymond, you never cease to amaze me. Well done. Now, let's hope that you have performed well."

"JA, mein Kommandant, what has such urgency?"

"And also, perceptive and insightful."

Lizzette says nothing; she waits for the request that will come from Buchner. After some small talk, mainly about her husband and children.

Buchner gets to the point, "Give me what I need, or your husband and children are in jeopardy. The French resistance has continued to be a real menace. They are growing in strength, and their raids are becoming more frequent, resulting in my soldiers' deaths. My men have families, wives, mothers, fathers, and children like you. We must find these ruthless savages and bring them to justice!"

Lizzette then says, "Ja, Oberst Buchner, you are correct, but I am but a mere woman. I could never imagine having to kill one member of the resistance, let alone hundreds of my countrymen."

Now, Buchner pretends as if he is the white knight coming to the damsel's rescue in distress.

He speaks. "No, No, I would never ask you to kill anyone. What I need from you is the locations of the enemy camps. Surely, now that you have penetrated the resistance, you would know where they are located."

Lizzette needs to be careful; she cannot just come out and tell him where she thinks the resistance camps are located. She needs to make Buchner believe that with the information that she will feed him, he will conclude that the camp is located in the Mercantour Forest.

Buchner, "Which cell have you penetrated?"

"This, I do not know; I only know it is somewhere between Marseille and Paris."

"Have you come into contact with the leader?"

"No, I doubt that I ever will; I am but a courier, similar to the position that I have with you."

"Do you at least have a name?"

"No, names are not allowed in the resistance."

"Surely, he has a cover name."

"Yes, but it might be a woman. The cover name is Chevalier. They call the leader Cheva. My contact often refers to Joan of Arc when mentioning Cheva. That's why I think that it might be a woman."

"Would the location between Paris and Vichy possibly be the main site?"

"Could be, but I don't think so."

"Why not?"

"Reference is often made to the ocean. There is no large body of water between here and Vichy?"

"What else have you heard?"

Lizzette thinks for a few seconds, rubs her chin, and says, "I heard that they received weapons from a submarine."

Buchner now thinks, "Submarine---Hmmm, it would not be possible to land a small inflatable boat on the Normandy coast."

"Why not? The Normandy coast is close to England; wouldn't it be logical that the Brits would use their submarines along the coast near England."

Buchner thinks, *typical woman, what does she know about diversionary tactics? Nothing.*

He needs more time to explain to Lizzette that the Normandy coast would be where the Brits would not have a landing party. It is too heavily guarded. Buchner now puts on his Intelligence hat and asks Lizzette some pointed questions. He senses that she probably knows more than she is exposing but does not realize its importance.

Buchner begins, "Madame Raymond, you must tell me everything, even if you think it is unimportant. Do you understand?"

"*Ja mein Kommandant.*"

"How many of the resistance have you been in contact with?"

"Only two. These are the ones I gave the information on the radios."

"Did they mention their names? They said it best that I did not know their names, not even their code names."

"Where did you meet them?"

"I met them in the Paris *Bosque.*"

"Hmmm, isn't *Bosque*, forest in Spanish?"

"Yes, that's correct. But it doesn't surprise me that we met in the Paris Forest."

"Why not?"

"They were always talking about how the Gestapo will never find them; they have too many safe locations in France's forests."

"Yes, that makes sense; once you have an Army of more than a dozen, you will need to hide in the forest."

Now, Lizzette gives Buchner a small clue. "After I gave them the info on the radios, I told them I needed something from them to satisfy the Germans. They said they understood, but they would need to talk to Cheva. That is when I learned the name of their leader, that's usually short for Chevalier."

One of the resistance fighters said, "You best keep that to yourself. We probably should not have mentioned Cheva."

The second man said, "No, not a problem, it is only a cover name."

The fighter said, "It would take a week, maybe more. Our Chief is in southern France, and we cannot use the radios."

Buchner, "You have been most helpful. I can now find those traitors and give them the lesson they deserve."

"I hope so, but I don't think I told you much."

"Perhaps you are right. I will allow you to write one more letter to your husband."

"You mean I can now write every month?"

"No, I said one letter; after all, your information was not very good."

"Veil Danke Mein Kommandant, I will try harder and see if I can get you better information."

After two hours of grilling Lizzette, Buchner feels he has the information he needs. The hideout is in a forest in southern France, near the Mediterranean. He will check with the Gestapo in Marseille and see what info they can provide. He will keep the information from Rauch. The hideout is in his area of responsibility, and he was unaware. That may knock him down a notch or two.

Buchner calls the Gestapo chief in Marseille and asks what large forests are north of the city. Buchner explains the reason for the call. The Gestapo Chief in Marseille believes that the hideout he is looking for is in the Mercantour Forest. The Gestapo Chief tells Buchner to be careful. He has lost over a dozen men chasing Resistance fighters in that forest. Now Buchner thinks more than ever that he has the resistance location.

Having been a fighter pilot, Buchner is very well thought of in the Luftwaffe. He calls General von Troupen, the Commanding General of the Luftwaffe in France, and requests that planes survey the Mercantour Forest north of Marseille. Buchner tells the Luftwaffe General that it is a top priority. Heinrich Müller will be in Paris in two days, and he needs the information. General von Troupen understands and will order the reconnaissance flights immediately.

Lizzette meets with Renard:

After meeting with Buchner, Lizzette meets with Renard. Lizzette, "I had to tell Buchner the one of the locations of the resistance. As we had previously discussed, he will figure out that the location is in south France north of Marseilles."

"Très bon, on dirait qu'il va prendre." (Very good looks like he took the bait.

"Yes, but we best be prepared. The Germans are planning a major offensive against our bases. We must make him think that the Mercantour Forest is our main camp."

"I will send a message to Marcin to start the preparations. Also, I will have our main camp in Auvergne send five hundred fighters. When the Germans attack, we need to offer strong resistance."

"Do we have an escape plan?"

"Yes, but I will journey to the camp in the Mercantour Forest and assist with the defense."

Lizzette, "This will be a major offensive by the Germans, you best be very careful. I will try to get some Intel on the order of battle. Also, tell Marcin to have some items in the open; Buchner was an Intel Officer and will probably order a plane to survey the Forests north of Marseille."

"Good thinking, I will send a message today and tell him to look for surveillance planes. I will also make sure that his perimeter is secure. The Germans may be sending some scout parties."

"Yes, but we have some time. If the Germans are planning a major offensive, they must send troops from the surrounding encampment garrisons. We will certainly detect that large of a movement. They will be using transport trucks on the roads. This will give us the opportunity for guerrilla warfare. We will make their lives miserable as they mass their troops."

Germans Meet in Paris:

Reichsfuhrer Müller arrives in Paris via a special train. Upon arriving at the train station, *Oberst* Buchner and Rauch await Müller. The reception is complete with an honor guard and a band. The band plays *"Deutschland Uber Alles."* Müller struts off the train dressed in his SS black uniform and holding a crop. He has the crop with his right hand and slowly hits his gloved left hand with a rhythmically pounding motion. Oberst Buchner quickly steps toward Müller with his simulated goose step, stops and emphatically straightens his right arm at a forty-five-degree angle with the palm downward, and shouts, "Heil Hitler!"

Müller places the crop under his left armpit and returns the salute, "Heil Hitler!"

Müller and Buchner now review the SS honor guard. After slowly walking and inspecting the SS honor guards', Müller turns to Buchner and says, *"Ich bin geschaftlich hier. Horen wir uns jetzt ihren plan an, den widerstand zu besitigen!"* (I am here on business. Now let us hear your plan to wipe out the resistance!)

"*Jawohl* Reichsfuhrer, we are prepared to present two plans. *Oberst* Rauch from Lyon will present his plan, and I will present mine. We will follow your guidance and implement whichever plan you choose, or you may have your own idea.

"Wunderbar, now let us get started! says Müller".

Being Müller's favorite, Rauch is allowed to present his plan first. His plan closely resembles his personality.

"My Gestapo troops in Lyon will capture every French male from fifteen to forty and torture each man until we know the whereabouts of the resistance. It is simply a matter of statistics. Eventually, we will find one who is a traitor. This is the only way: advanced interrogation techniques. All of these interrogations will be conducted according to the laws written by our attorneys and approved by the Fuhrer."

"Well spoken, *Oberst* Rauch. I like the plan; however, let me hear what Oberst Buchner has to offer."

Buchner, "*Mein* Reichsfuhrer, I have been in France for two years. The method of torturing all-male Frenchmen from fifteen to forty does not work. This only drives more and more Frenchmen to the resistance. I would venture to make a prediction: as soon as you start to apprehend the men in

Lyons, they will disappear. You may apprehend two or three Frenchmen and use our advanced interrogation techniques to obtain some low-level information, which will prove useless. It will drive all the non-disabled men of Lyon to the resistance. We have placed a spy in the resistance in the last ten months. Indeed, the program started when *Oberst* Rauch was under my command. The program has proven to be most successful."

"Interesting," says Müller, "Continue."

"*Jawohl mein Kommandant,* my spy, who I have trained personally, has infiltrated the highest command of the resistance. With a very high degree of certainty, the resistance's central command post is in southern France. I believe that it is in the Mercantour Forest."

Müller, *"Oberst* Rauch, is this true. Were you the original mastermind of the placement of our Mole?"

Rauch now says proudly. *"Jawohl* Reichsfuhrer, it was I who found the perfect spy. It was also I who did the initial training. I always knew the person I selected and trained would achieve the desired goal."

"Ser gut, Oberst Rauch, *du hast es gemacht."* (Very good, you have done well). So, have you verified that the intelligence provided by your spy is solid, *Oberst* Buchner?" asks Müller.

"*Mein Kommandant,* as you know, I was in the Luftwaffe as a fighter pilot. After my accident, I was the Intelligence Officer for the Fifth Fighter Wing stationed at Gablingen Kaserne."

"Yes, I am fully aware of your service to our country."

"As a Luftwaffe member, I have requested from General von Troupen, Commanding General of the Luftwaffe in France, to provide aerial surveillance. The aerial surveillance should be completed by tomorrow. After the surveillance is complete, we should have the verification that my intelligence is correct."

Müller walks around the conference table, thinking; he looks at Rauch and asks, "*Oberst*, what do you think? Do we use our torture methods, or do we pursue *Oberst*'s intelligence?"

Mein Kommandant, "I would send a scouting party to the Mercantour region and verify the resistance camp forest. Should the resistance be in the Mercantour forest, I ask that my SS troops in Lyon be ordered to wipe them out."

"Of course, the traitors are in your area of responsibility. Why did you not know that they are under your nose?"

"*Mein Reichsfuhrer.* I have been in Lyon for only a short time. I can assure you that I would have found this camp of traitors. I will not fail you."

"*JA, JA,* of course, begin preparations to assemble an Army of 10,000 to 15,000 troops. Use artillery, tanks, and Stuka aircraft to eliminate all traitors. I want this problem solved finally. Report to me with your plans before your attack. I wish to review the plan to ensure success."

"*Jawohl mein Kommandant.*"

As Rauch suggested and Müller agreed, Rauch sent a small scout party to inspect the resistance Mercantour camp. The outer perimeter guards of the resistance camp observed the German scout party but were instructed only to observe. They are to take no action against them. The German scout party reports to Rauch that there is a Resistance camp in the Mercantour Forest. A message is sent to Müller, who has returned to Berlin. Müller reviews the message and authorizes that the plan proceeds. However, before they attack, he will review the plan and give the orders to attack or stand down. Should the attack be successful, he wishes to give Hitler the message that his orders have been successfully implemented.

Rauch now takes complete control of the attack plan. He has purposely left Buchner out of any planning details. He is fully confident that the plan will be successful. He wants to receive full praise for the successful attack. He does not doubt that after wiping out the resistance, he will likely be promoted to General. He relishes the thought of Buchner being under his command.

Rauch now orders that all SS troops in once controlled Vichy French territory assemble outside of a Lyon training camp. Within thirty days, Rauch now has 12,000 SS troops. Ten Panther tanks and Stuka dive-bombers will support the attacking German army. Also, the infantry will have mortars. The battle plan is simple in its overall strategy; the attack will be from the north, east, and south. The west has 100-foot cliffs, with a river at the bottom of the cliffs. Rauch has ordered that 100 troops with eight gunboats guard the western sector. The attack will commence at 5 a.m. with 4,000 SS troops attacking in a pincer movement. Once the estimated 2,000 Resistance fighters have been cornered, the tanks will be ordered to attack, followed by the infantry to demolish the resistance. The SS troops have been ordered to shoot to kill. No prisoners will be taken. After the resistance fighters have been killed, they are to be loaded on transport trucks and piled at the resistance camp center.

Rauch tells his war staff, "The Reich Minister of Propaganda, Herr Joseph Goebbels, has assigned three camera crews to record the victory over the resistance."

Rauch is salivating and is excited about his pending victory. The films that the film crews will produce will show him as a great Nordic warrior who has defeated the barbaric hordes. He will be a hero in Germany. He envisions himself being awarded the "Iron Cross" by the Fuhrer Adolf Hitler. As he orders the attack to commence, he is in his full battle dress and will follow the attack's progress from his command post transport truck.

Camp Mercantour, Resistance:

The Mercantour Resistance fighters followed the entire German operation. The Germans had taken the bait that the resistance camp was in the Mercantour Forest. Marcin knew that the Germans were planning a big operation; thus, it would take time before the Germans could assemble the required troops to attack the camp. Now available to Marcin and his fighters were the weapons provided by the Wellington bombers. Materials were being flown and parachuted: machine guns, grenades, and plastic explosives with remote detonators. Also included was a new weapon, the American bazooka.

Renard travels from his northern headquarters and assumes the overall command. Marcin will be the field commander. Renard and Marcin are two of the original Resistance fighters. They were both in the French Army when France fought the Germans in 1940. All the resistance fighters highly respect them; if needed, they will follow them to their deaths.

Renard now assembles his command staff in the Mercantour Forest. Five hundred fighters have been moved from the Auvergne camp to the Mercantour camp. Renard directly addresses his command staff; Marcin provides a detailed briefing of the battle plan.

French Resistance Hidden in Forest

"Oui, le Komman-dant, we have established sentries at the outermost perimeter of the camp. We have established courier systems to send word to the main camp once we see the approaching Germans."

"Can you describe the courier systems?"

"Oui, le Kommandant, we will not use radios. We need to maintain radio silence. Therefore, we will send the messages using two systems. We use courier pigeons, and as a backup, we send runners."

"How many sentries are we posting?"

"Four sentries for each section, north, east, south, and west, for sixteen sentry positions. Each sentry position will have four men to allow twenty-four-hour coverage."

"How many fighters do we have?"

"Total of five hundred and twenty-five, plus twenty SOE agents and Juliette. We need the SOE agents to staff the two-person bazooka teams. Our fighters have yet to have any actual experience in battlefield conditions. The bazookas will be needed to counteract any tanks or patrol boats on the river. Juliette will be operating the radio. SOE will be working with British Intelligence. The Signal Intercept Division, MI6, will be monitoring radio traffic in the Mercantour Forest area and provide any Intel that will be intercepted."

"Tres Bien, having Juliette on the radio with SOE will be very good. This will provide real-time intelligence."

"Oui, la riviere, s'il vous plait, provide the preparations for the river escape plan." (Yes, the river, please).

"The escape will be by rappelling down the 100-foot cliffs."

"Five hundred fighters, that's a lot of fighters, can we get that many down in a short period?"

"Good question. yes, we have completed some training and practice sessions. Using ten rappel ropes, we can get twenty fighters down in one minute. Thus, one hundred will be down in five minutes, and the 500 fighters will be down in thirty minutes."

"What about the boats?"

"We have twenty-five boats hidden beneath the cliffs. This will be our escape. Intel has told us that the Germans will have gunboats patrolling the river. We will use the bazookas to take them out."

"What if the Germans have troops upriver ready to man fast gunboats to track our escaping army?"

"Oui, we have thought of that. A double chain will be installed underwater. When the battle commences, and we withdraw our forces, we will raise the chain to be two feet below the water's surface. The German fast gunboats will be traveling at high speed. The boats will be completely destroyed when they hit the under-water chain."

Renard, "Very well done. Do we have eyes and ears on the German build-up?"

"Yes, Sir, the Germans are assembling 12,000 men, tanks, transport trucks, and other support equipment. Assembling an Army of this size cannot be done without our men in the Lyons area not noticing. We are getting daily reports."

Chapter Thirty-Five
The Lyon Gestapo Battle
Mercantour Forest

The Lyon Gestapo has control of the pending attack on the resistance camp in the Mercantour Forest. The Gestapo scouts have reported that an estimated three to four hundred Resistance fighters are camped in the forest. Oberst Rauch has overall responsibility for planning and leading the attack. *Oberst* Buchner has requested that he be involved in the planning for the attack. Rauch has refused the offer; however, Rauch will allow a representative of the Paris Gestapo to be in his command center only as an observer. *Oberst Buchner has appointed Hauptmann* (Captain) Elias Fischer to represent the Paris Gestapo.

Topographical maps and aerial photographs are being inspected in the Lyons command center. *Oberst* Rauch stands before the large table and asks *Hauptmann* Kitschier, "Do you have the advanced troops ready to encircle the resistance fighters?"

"Jawohl mein Kommandant, I have five hundred fighters for each of the four sectors. They are ready to be placed in a position to prevent traitors from escaping. I am ready to order them to proceed on your command."

"Ser gut, are 500 troops on the cliffside sufficient?"

"Ja mein Kommandant, these troops will be five kilometers from the cliffs with two spotter teams. As soon as the main forces attack, 100 of the 500 troops will use the riverboats to position themselves on the river's opposite side. Resistance fighters who attempt to escape will be easy targets as they climb the cliffs."

"How many riverboats will be in position, and what weapons will they carry."

"Ten riverboats will be anchored in the river fifty kilometers from the cliffs. With their top speed of 40 knots, the boats will reach the cliffs in less

344

than one hour. All boats are armed with 50-caliber machine guns. Each boat will have five Waffen SS troops, armed with the Mauser MG 42 machine guns."

"Where will the main forces be stationed, and how do we move them to their attack position?"

"The key to success will be a *blitzkrieg*. We have used our *blitzkrieg* tactic successfully throughout the war. This will be very easy compared to our invasions of Holland, Denmark, France, and Russia. We have a superior army, well-armed, trained, and outstanding, experienced leadership. Thus, I see no flaws in our planning."

Oberst Rauch now stands tall and firm at the planning table's head and says, *"Ja ich sehe keine Mangel."* (Yes, I see no flaws). However, I would like to see the scenario played out on the planning table."

"Jawohl mein Kommandant."

Hauptmann Kitschier orders the Battalion commanders to describe how they will prosecute the attack. As the commanders describe their responsibilities, sergeants holding extended poles move the military pieces around the table. As the simulated Battle is played out on the conference table, Oberst Rauch orders, *"Halt!"* (Stop).

The simulated Battle now has all the resistance fighters surrounded, and the Gestapo Waffen SS troops are ready for the kill. Rauch orders the following steps be taken.

"Radio my mobile command post that we now have the traitors encircled and there is no escape. I will personally lead the final charge. We will offer that they surrender. I wish to capture as many alive to hang them all from the trees. Hundreds of Resistance fighters hanging from the trees will make a wonderful propaganda film for Herr Goebbels."

Rauch points at one of the cameramen assigned to the pending massacre and asks, "What would make the best propaganda film?"

"Sir, catching them alive would make for a better film. When you string them up, we let them suffocate slowly. As they are suffocating, they will go through gyrations; their bodies will be turning and twisting, and they will be like dancing puppets. The more live bodies we capture and hang, the better."

345

Rauch, *"Perfekt, das warden wir tun!"* (Perfect, that's what we will do.) Rauch now knows that this will be his moment of glory. The video will likely be shown to Hitler; he thinks *there is no way that I will not get my General rank."*

After an all-day session at the command post-conference planning table, the Lyon Gestapo is ready to commence Operation *"Ausloschen."* The advance groups of 500 Waffen SS troopers are ordered to move to their positions.

Mercantour Forest:

Renard, Marcin, and the captains of the resistance have been monitoring the movements of the German Waffen SS troops. Also, Juliette has been receiving constant updates from the SOE. A major advantage of the resistance is that the Germans adhere to a strict military chain of command. This strict military discipline also propagates to the order of Battle. Commanders in the field will always carry out the orders as given. The battles are generally controlled by the command post. Thus, as the troops move into position, the commanders will always report their location and permission to proceed.

The weapons crates that have been delivered to the resistance have also included advanced radio intercept equipment. The SOE agents involved with the weapons equipment have been providing the French fighters with training. Francisco and Andrés have been assigned to the Mercantour team to aid the intercept operators. Francisco and Andrés have surveyed the Mercantour forest area and have selected the two highest points in the adjacent mountains to install the radio intercept equipment. These high peaks are usually inaccessible by humans as they are surrounded by granite cliffs that only professional mountain climbers could scale. As is typical, the resistance has men from all walks of life. Included are experienced mountain climbers who had worked for the French forestry department. The two professionals, Rupert and Henri, are in their twenties, athletic and muscular. Rupert and Henri assemble all their mountain gear, and in two days, they have scaled the granite cliffs. Rupert from one mountain and Henri from the second mountain have dropped ropes with climbing knots to allow the radio operators to climb the mountain. Francisco climbs one peak and Andrés the second. Six resistance radio operators now climb the mountains with their backpacks loaded with the equipment. There are three operators per radio intercept location, plus Francisco and Andrés. By the second day, they are ready to monitor the German communications.

The resistance must maintain radio silence, it is a well-known fact that the Germans have advanced intercept and direction-finding equipment.

Francisco, using what he learned from Dr. Fry, has crafted antennas with directional capabilities. The two sites need to know the Lines of Bearing (LOB's) from each mountain site to plot the German transmitters' locations. To achieve the required communications, the two teams will use directional flashlights. The flashlights will use Morse code to flash the dots and dashes. The locations of the Germans will be communicated to the resistance command post using courier pigeons.

Renard knows that the key to their escape will be the ability to overcome the SS troops and riverboats to be used by the Germans to block his men from escaping. The idea to install the steel cables across the river came from Juan Salazar of the Spanish resistance group. Juan is known as the *"El Matador."* He has earned the name *"Matador"* because he is ruthless regarding Germans. The story that circulates in the resistance camps is that he has personally killed more than fifty Germans. His group of fifty fighters has a reputation of offering no mercy. Juan was raised in the Pyrenees mountains. When the Germans occupied his village, they killed all the village members because they had let an Allied fighter cross through their town. The German commander accused the village elders that they had given refuge to the Allied flyer; thus, the Germans lined up his father, mother, two sisters, and twelve other village members and gunned them down. Juan had seen the massacre from high in the mountains. Although Juan was only nineteen when his family was massacred, he quickly became one of the most notorious resistance fighters. At twenty-two, he was one of the most wanted of the resistance fighters. The Germans had placed a bounty of 50,000 francs on his head. Juan carried a folded poster of the most wanted man in France in his backpack as a badge of honor. Before he executed any German, he would make sure that he showed him his badge of honor.

As Juan had grown up in the Pyrenees, his main job was to tend the sheep. To earn side money for the family, he also worked for companies installing cable car systems in the Spanish French mountains. One day, the time would come when the Germans would attack the mountain fortress, and an escape plan had to be designed and implemented.

Marcin had been discussing the need for an escape plan with the resistance leaders. The idea was being discussed to escape down the cliffs. Rappelling down would be fine for the resistance fighters. The average age was twenty-eight, and all were in good health and in good physical condition. The escape would be down the ropes and to use boats to sail down the river. Juan was known with his cover name, *"Mata,"* short for *Matador*.

Mata had been invited to the discussions, but it was not anticipated that he would offer any solutions. After listening to the French resistance fighters, he said, "You need to place underwater cables on both the upstream and downstream portions of the river."

Marcin, "How would that work?"

"We place two three-centimeter diameter cables across the river. Anchor the cables on one side of the river to underwater boulders. The other side of the river uses pulleys to hide the cable up the river embankment. Install the cable on a gear system that offers a mechanical advantage to allow a team of men to crank up the cables at one-half and one meter below the surface. Any German powerboats would be destroyed if they tried sailing through the area."

"Good idea. Has this ever been done before?"

"Yes, my grandfather told me that the Americans used this technique on the Hudson River to keep the British from sailing up the river to American settlements during the American Revolution."[42]

After Marcin heard that the technique had been used before, he asked Mata if he and his men would install the underwater cable (chains). Mata and his men then raided a German warehouse that was lightly guarded. The Germans did not believe that the items in the warehouse were anything of value. Mata and his men knew that the warehouse would have chains used

---

[42]

Letter from Henry Wisner and Filbert Livingston to New-York Committee of Safety: Soundings of Hudson River in the Highlands American Archives Series 5, Volume 3, Page 0812 November 22, 1776

on ships to attach the anchors. The chain systems were installed and operational one year before the Germans started planning their attack.

An additional advantage that the French resistance has is eyes on the enemy. The Germans control the cities and towns. However, the country belongs to the resistance. In late 1943 and beginning in 1944, the winds of war were now blowing in favor of the Allies. The French had few, but they had enough short-wave radios to listen to the BBC. They knew that liberation would soon come. The only question was when. Now, 99% of the population supported the freedom fighters directly or indirectly. Such was the case with Jean-Claude, a ten-year-old farm boy. Jean-Claude was busy completing his chores when he heard the rumble of heavy transport trucks. He knew that it would be German trucks or tanks, he quickly hid and observed that the column had trucks hauling riverboats to the river. After the column passed, Jean-Claude promptly went to his house and told his mom that he had to go see his friend Astin. "It is essential. I will be riding *"Noir."* "(Jean-Claude's favorite stallion).

His mom always knew that Jean-Claude was a courier for the resistance and was proud of her son, but she knew it was dangerous. She simply said, "Don't ride at night; stay over Astin's house if it gets dark."

"Oui maman je resterai avec Astin." (Yes, Mother, I will stay with Astin tonight.)

Jean-Claude rode all night, and the next day at midday, he was stopped by the sentries guarding the resistance camp.

Jean-Claude, "Monsieur, the Germans are driving gunboats upstream from your camp. I think that they will be attacking soon."

Raphael, one of the guards, mounts his horse and says, "Follow me."

"Oui, Monsieur." The two ride their horses to the main camp. Raphael and Jean-Claude quickly fast walk to the command tent of Marcin.

Raphael, *"Le Kommandant,* our young courier, has some important information."

"Tres Bien, what is it you have, Jean-Claude."

"*Le Kommandant*, I counted trucks with ten gunboats driving on the road to the docks upriver from your camp. There were also ten transport trucks with Waffen SS troops and supply trucks. I know the area very well.

They should be there by now and could launch an attack on your camp any-time."

"Jean-Claude, you have done well; we will prepare for the fight im-mediately."

"S'll Vous plait, I would like to stay and help. My father has taught me how to shoot a rifle."

"No, Jean-Claude, you are more valuable with your eyes and ears in the countryside. It is best that you return to your farm."

Not happy, Jean-Claude mounts "Noir," and returns to his farm. Marcin now knows that the attack is imminent. He now confers with Renard in the main command post. The defense lines are set up and ready. Marcin orders that fifty hidden plastic explosives with the remote detonators be placed strategically on the campgrounds. Mata and his Spanish fighters, plus seventy-five French fighters, take their position upstream along the riverbanks. They conceal themselves in the trees and bushes. Using the inter-cepted radio locations from the two mountain teams and Intel being provided to Juliette from SOE, the Battle will be directed by Renard at the central com-mand post and Marcin as the battlefield commander.

The resistance forces prepared for a well-organized retreat as the sentries detected the advancing column of German troops. Pigeons were swiftly released, and within ten minutes, both Marcin and Renard were aware that the Germans had initiated their attack. As the German forces advanced, skilled snipers positioned on the hills methodically took aim, fired, killed, and then withdrew. Employing guerrilla warfare tactics, the snipers systematically eliminated individual German soldiers. Recognizing the threat posed by these snipers, the German field commander ordered two squads to climb the hills and eliminate the sniper threat. The snipers promptly vacated their positions, retreating half a kilometer away to set up for new sniper attacks.

After slow but steady progress, the Germans reached the outer de-fenses of the resistance stronghold. The resistance fighters put up a valiant effort, despite being vastly outnumbered at a ratio of 20 to 1. Following their practiced strategy, they began a strategic withdrawal toward their base camp. The defensive perimeter continued to shrink minute by minute. In re-sponse, the German field commander ordered his tanks to move forward and attack.

The resistance had strategically fortified their fallback defensive perimeter with imposing ten-foot-tall dirt dunes. As the tanks advanced and crested these dunes, their vulnerable underbellies were exposed. Employing swift blitzkrieg tactics, all the tanks launched a coordinated attack simultaneously, leaving their undersides exposed within seconds. Unbeknownst to the Germans, a formidable force of twenty bazooka teams lay in wait. As the tanks maneuvered over the dunes, exposing their weak points, the twenty bazooka teams unleashed their rockets, creating distinctive contrails and a thunderous whooshing sound. The landscape erupted in fiery explosions, enveloped in black smoke and shrapnel. Within a mere thirty seconds of crossing the dunes, fifteen tanks were reduced to smoldering wrecks, while two managed to clear the dunes only to be swiftly targeted by bazookas. Multiple rounds struck their treads, rendering them immobile.

Meanwhile, fifty tenacious resistance fighters relentlessly rained gunfire upon the advancing German troops, effectively impeding their progress. Simultaneously, three hundred more resistance fighters descended via cliff ropes, heading toward their escape boats.

As the resistance fighters began their descent, Mata's group of fighters took the German troops by surprise as they traversed the riverbed. The four hundred Waffen SS soldiers found themselves exposed with limited cover, easy prey for the resistance fighters. In a matter of minutes, only one hundred Waffen SS troops remained, seeking refuge behind large boulders, awaiting the arrival of gunboats and confident that the Battle would soon turn in their favor.

The distant sound of approaching riverboat motors alerted the remaining German troops to the impending reinforcements. Positioned within effective firing range, the gunboats unleashed their fifty-caliber machine guns with a relentless RAT-TAT-TAT. The surviving German troops believed victory was imminent.

However, as the gunboats sped toward the cliff-descending resistance fighters, the two leading vessels struck submerged cables, causing them to tip and capsize. German gunners were thrown into the water as the boats exploded into a fiery inferno of debris. Following closely behind, additional support boats raced forward at speeds of 45 knots but were unable to halt their momentum in time to avoid the chaos and destruction caused by the explosions. The first support boat collided with debris and floating bodies, igniting the high-grade alcohol fuel and resulting in further destruction. The remaining boats attempted U-turns but were met with zero visibility due to the smoke and debris, ultimately crashing into each other and meeting a similar fiery fate.

In a well-coordinated pincer movement, the resistance fighters who had rappelled from the cliffs and Mata's fighters entrapped the remaining German troops. Over one hundred Germans perished, while some attempted to surrender. Regrettably, Mata's fighters showed no mercy, swiftly eliminating the surrendering soldiers at point-blank range.

Before the Battle, Rauch had ordered Stuka dive bombers from the Luftwaffe to be on standby. When the Battle reached a critical juncture, Rauch transmitted a radio message to the Paris airport, requesting that the Stuka dive bombers be ready for deployment within two hours. The plan was to have the Stukas poised for action when needed. This radio communication occurred through the long-range HF network, which encrypted all transmissions using enigma machines.

MI6 in London intercepted this communication, and as previously arranged with Juliette, P-51 Mustang fighters were dispatched from Malta. The Stuka dive bombers had been on standby for twenty minutes, awaiting the ground-to-air signal from the Gestapo command post to commence their attack. However, before receiving their orders, a squadron of P-51 Mustangs descended from above. The outcome was decidedly one-sided, with four Stuka dive bombers destroyed during the initial wave of the attack. The remaining three Stukas attempted to evade the P-51 fighters, but the new P-51s swiftly caught up, ultimately shooting them down.

The Battle at the resistance main camp reached its climactic conclusion, with thousands of German Waffen SS troops encircling Renard, Marcin, Juliette, and the resistance fighters. As planned, the resistance fighters began their rappel descent down the cliffs. When the SS troops reached the midpoint of the camp, Marcin issued the command to detonate twenty-five concealed explosives. These plastic explosives detonated in a meticulously timed sequence from the camp's outer perimeter to its center, resulting in the deaths of thousands of German troops and the injury of thousands more. Amidst the ensuing chaos and pandemonium, all resistance fighters, including

Marcin, Renard, and Juliette, successfully rappelled down the cliffs to reunite with Mata and his group of fighters.

Francisco, Andrés, and the radio operators, positioned on their vantage points, witnessed the fierce Battle unfolding. Upon the remote explosives' detonation, all the radio operators began their descent from the mountain peaks, joining Mata's fighters. As the combined groups of resistance fighters executed their escape, Marcin ordered the detonation of the remaining twenty-five concealed explosives. The fifty boats carrying the resistance fighters escaped downriver from the camp.

The Aftermath of the Battle:
The results are the resounding defeat of the German Gestapo. Ten gunboats and fifteen tanks are destroyed, and two are deemed unusable. Seven Stuka dive bombers were destroyed. Over 1,500 German troops are dead and over 2,000 injured. There is, however, a silver lining: the Mercantour camp has been overrun and destroyed. Rauch orders that the Goebbels film crew record the destroyed resistance camp. Rauch orders that all dead resistance fighters be brought to the center of the devastated area. After searching through the destroyed buildings, none are found. Rauch is delirious with anger.

He shouts, "Look again, there have to be dead bodies of the resistance!"

Again, none are found. He correctly concludes that the resistance carried away any dead resistance fighters. The Goebbels cameraman gives Rauch an idea.

He tells Rauch, "There are resistance clothes in building number five; dress some of your dead warriors in the clothes of the resistance. No one will ever know the difference. We have been lying since 1938, one more lie; no one will know that you were so soundly defeated."

Rauch screams at the cameraman, "Defeated! No, look at the destroyed camp. You call that a defeat?"

"*Ja, Ja Mein Kommandant,* a resounding victory. The video we send to Goebbels will show your glorious defeat of the resistance."

Rauch orders that twenty dead Germans be dressed in the clothing of the resistance and strung up. The twenty "fake" resistance fighters will not be convulsing, quivering in suffocation, or dancing like puppets, but they will undoubtedly be hanging from the tree branches. The propaganda video is completed, and Rauch is ready to send it once he drives back to the Lyons' headquarters.

As Rauch is back at his headquarters, Hauptmann Elias Fischer, the Oberst Bucher representative, knocks on his office door.

Rauch says, "Enter, what can I do for you? Seems you disappeared when the bullets started firing!"

"*Nein, Oberst* Rauch, I did not disappear. As you ordered, I was there as an observer and was not to engage in any combat. I have sent my report to *Oberst* Buchner, here is a copy of the report."

Rauch scans through the report, and as he is reading the report, the veins in his neck start to inflate, and his face starts to turn from pink to red to pale.

He shouts, "Why was I not given a copy of this report before you sent it to *Oberst* Buchner?"

"Sir, I do not answer to you. My command structure is with the Paris Gestapo."

"Has the report been sent to *Oberst* Bucher?"

"*Jawohl,* the report arrived in Paris last night via the transport plane."

"Your actions are treasonous. I will report you to Müller himself."

"May I remind you that should you report me to Müller an independent team will investigate, and you may suffer the consequences."

Rauch looks at Fischer with disgust and shouts, *"Verschwinde aus meinem Buro!"* (Get the fuck out of my office)

Fischer leaves Lyon that afternoon. Rauch destroys the video propaganda film made by the Goebbels camera crew. He orders that the camera crew be shot as traitors.

Rauch writes a letter to Müller and Goebbels, *"The resistance camp was destroyed. We suffered less than 10% casualties and minimal damage to our resources. The camera crew members were all killed when the resistance exploded a concealed explosive while they were filming. They all died as heroes for the Fatherland. Long live the Third Reich, Heil Hitler!"*

Chapter Thirty-Six
Felipe Joins the Resistance
Northern France

Felipe Raymond, Lizzette's husband, was in the French Army Reserve in 1939 when the Germans invaded Poland. France had a treaty with Poland, an invasion of Poland was an invasion of France. Thus the France declared war on Germany. However, the French were content that Germany would not attack France. The French had invested heavily in the Maginot Line. The Maginot Line consisted of a reinforced concrete wall along the entire French-German border. The general consensus amongst the French population was that the barrier was not penetrable. The French thought that they were safe behind their fortress. In addition, the French had the largest and best-equipped army in Europe. It was the opinion of the French High Command that the Maginot Line was impassable and impenetrable. The French were all living a superficial life full of wine and dance. They were confident in their leaders that the military would protect them from the Huns.

In May of 1940, this imaginary protective cocoon was shattered when the Germans invaded Holland and Belgium and marched south toward France. The French quickly called up their reserves to bolster the northern frontier. Felipe was a lieutenant in the French Army reserves and only had one week to say his farewell to Lizzette and their two young children. Felipe was assigned to an intelligence company, as he knew two foreign languages, German and Spanish.

As an intelligence officer, Felipe was assigned to the Signals Intercept Company. Felipe was using his knowledge of the German language to interpret German communications. The army elements of the regular French Army were all on the eastern front along the Maginot line. At the time of the German invasion, the French had a *laissez-faire* attitude. No one in either the Government or the military would take command and direct that the country's full resources be marshaled to counter the German blitzkrieg, which was attacking from the north. Within a short three months, the German Wehr-macht had conquered Norway, Belgium, and Holland. In the next month, the Germans had the northern French forces completely surrounded. Felipe's intelligence company had no choice but to surrender.

When France surrendered to Germany, more than 1.83 million French soldiers were marched to Germany. Most French prisoners of war were not held in camps; instead, over 93 percent of French prisoners of war lived and worked on *Kommandos* or work details.[43] Under the terms of the Geneva Convention, NCOs were exempted from work during captivity like officers. However, with Hitler's ever-expanding appetite for more conquered land, all German men from eighteen to fifty were drafted into the German military services. With victory after victory in 1939, 1940, and 1941, the German military had no problems finding recruits. This German Army and Navy expansion left the German homeland void of working labor. To address this problem, the Germans, contrary to the Geneva Convention, would take prisoners from France and force them to work in factories, mines, shipyards, or agriculture fields. Workers were fed and technically earned wages; however, virtually their entire wages were paid directly to the German army, and prisoners were only allowed to retain 70 pfennigs per day.[44]

From 1940 to the middle of 1943, Felipe was assigned to work in Dusseldorf in a ball bearings factory. In the three years that he worked in the factory, he was guarded by German guards, but he was well fed and lived in a prison camp for officers. The prisoners slept in bunk beds and policed themselves to maintain high hygiene. However, beginning in mid-1943, conditions started to change. The ball bearings factory was destroyed by Allied bombing, and Felipe was transferred to agriculture work. The Allied bombing brought stiff repercussions from the Germans. Often, after a major Allied bombing, the German guards would take it out on the prisoners. Once, after the British bombed a nearby town and killed several civilians, the German guards singled

---

[43] Fishman, Sarah (April 1991). "Grand Delusions: The Unintended Consequences of Vichy France's Prisoner of War Propaganda"

[44] 28 D'Hoop, Jean-Marie (July 1987). "Les prisonniers français et la communauté rurale allemande (1940–1945)". *Guerres mondiales et conflits contemporains* (147): 31–47 ISBN 0984-2292-JSTOR 25730420.

out a British pilot and clubbed him to death. Felipe tried to keep out of trouble, and he planned to survive until the war's end.

After the factory bombing, Felipe was transferred to the agriculture fields in Bavaria. He felt fortunate that he had been transferred where conditions were better and were protected from Allied bombing raids in rural areas of the Bavarian countryside. French and English prisoners replaced locals who were being conscripted into the German army.[45] Late in the war, guarding the prisoners came to be regarded by the Germans as an unnecessary waste of the workforce - it was thought unlikely that a prisoner would attempt to escape in a country where he did not know the language. This meant prisoners were allowed a broad measure of freedom compared to the stalags. The French, English, Canadians, and other Allied soldiers could work in factories and agricultural fields. However, they were always kept under armed guard.

Initially, the German population accepted the French and British prisoners with curiosity. However, as the war turned in favor of the Allies, the civilian population began to see the captured prisoners with anger and animosity. When the prisoners worked in the field, older men, women, and children would often throw stones at them and launch into a verbal tirade of cuss words and demeaning phrases.

Late one afternoon, a British bombing raid was targeting the railroad station near the agriculture field. A rogue bomb fell close to the work crew, and the blast killed the detail of three German guards. The guards would always come to the agriculture field in transport trucks. These trucks would be used to pick up the prisoners and move them to and from the agricultural fields. After the attack cleared, Felipe noticed that the guards were dead and the truck was damaged. Felipe and his fellow prisoner, an English man named Johnny Edwards, were still alive. They quickly investigated the truck's cab and found some German uniforms and a compass.

Felipe spoke native German, and after three years of working in the factory and the agriculture fields, he would easily pass for a German citizen. Johnny had learned some German but would never pass as a native German.

Quickly, Felipe developed a plan, "We would move south toward the Swiss border."

---

[45] Ibid

Felipe knows that he is between Stuttgart and Friedberg. He is only 80 kilometers from the border if they can get to Friedberg.

He then tells Johnny, "We walk ten kilometers to the train station in Oberammergau. From there, we can ride the train to the outskirts of Freiberg."

"Will the military Ausweis of the guards get us to Freiberg?"

"Yes, I believe they will. I heard the German guards once say that their military Ausweis would get them as far as Oberammergau. Oberammergau is a little out of the way, but it will get us to Freiburg. Once we are on the train, with our uniforms, we should be good to Friedberg."

Felipe, "Check the truck glove compartment and see if we can find anything else of use. I will check the dead Germans and see if they have any Marks on their bodies."

Johnny checks the glove compartment of the truck and finds detailed maps, binoculars, and fifty marks. Felipe checks the three dead guards and finds another sixty-two marks.

Felipe, "OK, get their Lugers and their Mauser rifles. We need to look like two German soldiers on leave."

Johnny, "What do we do with the dead Germans?"

"We need to drag them into the copse of trees and hide them in the bushes. All we need is a one-day head start. After we hide the bodies, we need to get going. We have three hours of sunlight. Let's take advantage of the daylight."

After hiding the bodies, Felipe and Johnny walk down a dirt road to Oberammergau. After walking for one hour, a farm truck comes up behind Felipe and Johnny. The farmer stops and asks if they need a ride.

Felipe says, *"Ja, Bitte, wir wurden uns freuen aus Oberammergau."* (Yes, we would appreciate a ride to Oberammergau.)

"Yes, I can give you a ride to Oberammergau, but you must ride in back of the truck with the turnips and potatoes. You will need to place the tarp over your body. We have English and American planes seeking targets of opportunities. If they see two German soldiers riding in my farm truck, they will likely shoot the truck, *verstehen?* "

"Yes, we understand and *Danke Schon*."

In two hours and one hour of daylight left, Felipe and Johnny arrive in Oberammergau. They quickly walk to the train station. The last train to Freiburg leaves in thirty minutes. They purchase their tickets and easily pass through the checkpoint. One of the guards detects his accent and snaps to attention, believing he is an officer from the Berlin area. Once arriving in Freiburg, they can only travel closer to the Swiss border with proper documents. The rest of the journey will need to be on foot. Felipe and Johnny use the marks taken from the dead German guards and buy Alpine hiking clothes. Should they be stopped by German patrols, they will need a cover story and special Ausweis papers that show that they live in the area. They have no passports, no Ausweis, and no documents that will indicate that they are residents of the region. This will be the most dangerous part of the journey; any German patrols must not stop them. They must travel through the most rugged and densely forested areas to increase their safe passage chances. Felipe estimates that the journey will be three to four days. They use the three dead German guards' ration cards to buy four days' worth of foodstuff. Felipe uses the map found in the guard truck, and they begin the journey to the Swiss border.

One advantage of the location is that it lies at the base of the Swiss Alps, characterized by rugged mountains, making it challenging for the Germans to patrol effectively. However, the drawback is the challenging terrain of the mountains. Despite this, Felipe and Johnny have no alternative but to attempt to cross these formidable peaks.

The initial two days of their journey pass without incident as they follow mountain trails previously cut by loggers. On the morning of the third day, they find themselves just twenty kilometers away from the base of the mountains. Consulting their map, they identify three possible mountain passes: one at 950 meters (3,000 ft.), another at 1,500 meters (4,900 ft.), and the highest one at 2,286 meters (7,500 ft.). The first two passes are easier to traverse but likely to be heavily patrolled by the Germans. While less guarded, the third poses the challenge of navigating snow-covered terrain.

Johnny makes a decision: "Let's take the highest pass. All English pilots undergo survival training, and I can fashion snowshoes from branches and twigs we find at the mountain's base."

Felipe raises a concern, "What about the cold weather?"

Johnny reassures him, "If we double up on our clothing and complete the snow pass in a day, we'll stay warm from our body heat. If we do need to stop for the night, we'll avoid making a fire as it would attract the Germans."

"Alright, we travel through the night. Let's begin our ascent to the high pass."

After five hours of cautious climbing towards the high pass, they spot a German guard detail. Felipe and Johnny lie low on a ridge, observing the guards with a pair of binoculars they acquired from a guard's truck glove compartment. They count six guards in a shelter with a continuously smoking chimney, suggesting 24 by 7 guard duty. The Germans have strategically stationed their border post at the narrow pass's entrance, making it impossible to pass unnoticed.

Upon careful inspection, Johnny suggests an alternative, "We can climb to what appears to be a small cave on the right side of the pass. The climb seems steep but manageable. Once we reach the cave area, we can descend to the gorge's base and bypass the guard path."

Felipe agrees, taking the binoculars, "Let's go for it."

The climb to the small cave entrance goes smoothly, taking two hours to reach the point where they carefully descend. Successfully circumventing the guards, they continue their journey towards the Spanish border. However, a small stone dislodges while descending and triggers a minor avalanche. The noise alerts the German guards, leading to a tense encounter.

One guard spots Felipe and shouts, "*Halten Sie!*" while preparing to shoot. Johnny, reacting quickly, fires his Mouser rifle, hitting the guard accurately. The guard tumbles down the mountain. Chaos ensues as the remaining guards open fire indiscriminately. Felipe and Johnny find cover behind large boulders and gradually ascend the mountain pass, nearing the tree line.

Johnny plans ahead, "We need to collect branches and twigs of the right size to make our snowshoes for tomorrow."

After an hour of searching, they find the necessary materials. The following morning, dark clouds gather, and snow flurries start. They hurriedly eat breakfast, aiming to cross the pass before a snowstorm traps them. As they ascend, they hear the distinct sound of tracked vehicles, spotting German snowcats behind them. The snowcats have bulletproofed cabins, rendering their rifles useless. They must create as much distance as possible and hope to reach the Swiss border before the snowcats catch up.

Adding to their challenge, the snowfall intensifies, making it difficult to outrun the Germans. They reach a level plateau in the pass, and the snowfall intensifies. The Germans, operating the snowcats, can clearly see Felipe and Johnny in their brown and green hiking attire. The snowcats are equipped with loudspeakers.

Felipe hatches a plan, removing one of his snowshoes and wrapping his stocking cap around its toe. He instructs Johnny, "Put your Sten gun on full auto and position it over the boulder. Fire toward the snowcat."

Johnny complies, firing the Sten gun in automatic mode without looking over the boulder. Felipe raises the snowshoe with the stocking cap, waves the stocking cap and Johnny continues firing the Sten gun---rata, tat, tat, tat. As predicted, the snowcat's 50-caliber machine gun returns fire, but its large bullets strike the boulder, tearing the stocking cap off the snowshoe and causing shells to spray above the boulder. The impact produces a cloud of snow and ice shards, causing the ground to tremble.

Blinded by the snow cloud, the German gunner loses sight of Felipe and Johnny. Felipe urges Johnny, "We need to run to higher ground quickly!"

As they make their escape, the ground starts to shake, and fissures appear in the snow. Within moments, an avalanche begins with a rumble, gaining momentum and thundering down the mountain pass. The two snowcats vanish beneath the wall of snow.

Two hours later, Felipe and Johnny safely cross the Swiss border. Swiss border guards arrest them but soon realize they are French and English. They are taken to the English consulate in Basel, where they are admitted to the English hospital to recuperate and enjoy hearty meals. The British Embassy and the Free French in London are informed of the successful crossing of the German border by the French soldier and English pilot.

Felipe Flies to France:

Felipe and Johnny are flown to Malta. There, they wait two weeks for a convoy to sail to England. The convoy has twelve ships plus three escort destroyers. The Mediterranean Sea has been cleared of German submarines, but the Atlantic is still very dangerous. German submarine wolf packs prowl the ocean, especially surrounding Great Britain. There are several submarine sightings during the voyage, but the destroyers sink the submarines or sail off without engagement.

After landing in South Hampton, Felipe is driven to the Free French Headquarters of Charles De Gaulle. The French have been notified that Lieutenant Felipe Pierre Raymond escaped the Germans. The British Ambassador had written a detailed letter outlining the heroic escape of Felipe and Johnny. The French Government in exile wanted to promote Felipe's heroism to inspire the nation of France.

However, the admiration of the nation of France would need to wait until after the Allies invaded France. The less that the Germans knew regarding the escape of Felipe, the better. When Felipe arrived at the Free French headquarters on Carlton Gardens Street, St James's, London, he was quickly swished from the car to a private meeting with General Charles DeGaulle. Felipe was treated like a conquering hero; Charles DeGaulle himself greeted him with open arms. A French honor guard with full colors was present as Felipe was walked to a special room at the Free French headquarters. As Felipe entered the small reception room, the band played La Marseillaise. Felipe was awarded the Croix de Guerre. The medal was awarded for distinguished acts of heroism involving combat with the German forces. He was promoted to Captain. His escape from Germany was directly responsible for killing twelve enemy soldiers, and he was credited with the destruction of several enemy transports. He was also credited for assisting in the escape of a British RAF pilot.

When Felipe was asked to say a few words to General De Gaulle's staff, Felipe began by saying, "My fellow countrymen, I am truly honored to accept this medal. However, this medal symbolizes the many Frenchmen who have never lost faith in our ultimate victory. I especially wish to thank General de Gaulle. He alone was the voice of the Free French Against all odds. He fought the Nazi and he would not surrender, and with our comrades in arms we will be victorious. I now wish to quote from *La Marseillaise,*"

"Arise, children of the Fatherland.

Our day of glory has arrived.

Against us, the bloody flag of tyranny is raised.

Do you hear, in the countryside, the roar of those ferocious soldiers?

Our day of total victory is near.

I have never lost faith in the ultimate victory of France."

***

Felipe completes his short speech with the "V' for victory and says, "Vive la France!"

After the impromptu ceremony, Felipe met with Colonel Rene Laform Lopes. Colonel Lopes oversaw the French resistance fighters.

Colonel Lopes, "Captain Raymond, you have a most impressive resume. We are currently massing hundreds of thousands of troops, 5,000 aircraft, and 1,000 ships to invade Nazi Europe. The day of the invasion has not been set. When we do invade, the resistance will need to play a vital and important role."

Captain Raymond, "Tell me my assignment, and I will do my part in the defeat of the Germans."

"Oui, Capitaine, I am sure that you will. We have developed a close working relationship with the British SOE in the last two years. It is this office that coordinates the activities of our French resistance fighters. The SOE has supplied weapons, money, foodstuff, and agents to assist our compatriots. We will assign you to assist our resistance fighters in our country."

"Oui, Monsieur, will I be working with the SOE?"

"Oui, I will contact my counterpart, Colonel Susan Phillips at the SOE. She will have her staff brief you on the conditions in France today."

"Oui, Coronel."

The following day, Captain Raymond meets with Colonel Phillips and Captain Hutchinson. After the introductions, Colonel Phillips provides an overview of the support the SOE has given the French resistance. She stresses the importance that the resistance will play in the coming invasion. After some top levels of strategic planning, Colonel Philips turns over the briefing to Captain Hutchinson.

"Messieurs, allow me to now have Captain Hutchinson provide some details of how we believe that Captain Raymond can greatly assist our battle with the Germans."

Captain Hutchinson says, "Captain Raymond, your command of the German language and your expert knowledge of the German command structure can greatly assist the war effort. The prime objective of the resistance in the next year will be to prepare to sabotage German roads, bridges, and ammunition depots. We need as much information as possible on the concentration of troops, supplies, and reserve forces before our invasion. We believe that your knowledge of the German state of mind and the activities in Germany will allow you to penetrate the German command structure and obtain valuable information."

Captain Raymond, "I will certainly do my best. How will I be inserted into France?"

"Yes, we have been successful in one of three methods: one, by a Lysander plane, which lands in a remote grass field. Two, you parachute in and three by submarine. Parachuting is not advised. You would need some time to train and prepare; by submarine would take some degree of planning with the Royal Navy; thus, the best method is by plane."

"How soon do I leave?"

"There is some training and planning that needs completing. We need to give you a cover name and prepare documents. Also, we will brief you on what we know regarding the German command structure, which you will be trying to penetrate."

"OK. When do we get started?" asks Felipe.

"We start immediately. We have prepared for you to stay in our accommodations. You have a private room in building 1534. There, you will find documents, which we have obtained from our resistance fighters, which provide the names, ranks, and responsibilities of German officers in northern France. You will need to commit all of this information to memory."

"Excellent, I will begin tonight."

Captain Hutchinson, "Captain Raymond, may I call you Felipe?"

"*Oui, Felipe c'est tres bien*, (Yes Felipe is OK) and what is your first name?"

"Yes, of course, you can call me Herman or Armand if you prefer."

When Felipe and Armand reach Felipe's private quarters, Armand suggests they both be seated at a table. They both take a seat. Felipe senses that this English Captain with an American accent wants to tell him something off the record.

Armand begins, "Early in the war, I was flying Spitfires in defense of Great Britain." Armand then tells Felipe of his plane being shot down and his rescue by a French fisherman and a young French woman named Lizzette. Armand states, "I believe that the young woman was your wife."

With the mention of Lizzette, Felipe starts to tear up. He takes a small towel and wipes his eyes.

"Oui, I am sure that it was my wife. Can you tell me the details of how she assisted you?"

"Yes, of course, but you realize she is likely working with the resistance. When the resistance rescued me, I was in France for over three months. I came into contact with the leaders of the resistance. This is the reason that I do not fly any missions over France. Should I be shot down and captured by the Germans, I could be tortured and be forced to reveal some of the members of the resistance."

Felipe is now even prouder of his wife.

He asks, "Do you know if she is well?"

"Yes, she is well and living with your two children and her parents outside of Paris. I shouldn't tell you any more than I have already told you."

"Yes, of course. Thank you very much for the wonderful news. Now I am ready to fly to my home country and assist with the Germans' defeat."

In two weeks, Felipe completes his preparatory studies. His cover names (French and German) with all documents are complete, and he is ready for his assignment. On the next full moon, a Lysander plane flies to France, lands in a small grass field, and returns without incident. The name of the pilot was Karina Hutchinson.

Chapter Thirty-Seven
Felipe and Lizzette Reunite
Northern France

In the spring of 1944, Renard, Juliette, and Marcin are waiting in an open field along the French countryside on a moonlit night. At 1:33 a.m., they hear the distinct slow buzzing sound of a Lysander plane engine. Marcin ordered that powerful torch (flashlights) received from the SOE be turned on and aimed at the sky. The Lysander plane slowly flew over the lit airfield and banks to its starboard side. Juliette uses her torch to flash the dots and dashes of Morse code to indicate that it is safe to land. Upon seeing the all-safe signal, the pilot circled the grass airfield and descended toward the landing strip. The pilot was an expert with the landing. She had successfully performed identical landings throughout France for the last year.

As the plane came to a standstill, resistance members ran to the plane. The engines remained running to allow a quick turnaround and take off. Three passengers dismounted, and three crates of supplies were offloaded. Juliette, Marcin, and the resistance members waved to the pilot. Once the passengers and the supplies were offloaded, the ground crew turned the plane in the direction it had landed, and the Lysander rumbled down the grass airfield to quickly gain altitude. Karina looked down at the resistance members and waved goodbye. The ground crew looked up at the sky and waved to indicate that all had gone well.

The three passengers were quickly placed in a farm truck with a tarp. The supplies were placed on burros, and the airfield raked to hide the fact that an aircraft had landed. From plane sighting to leaving the landing site, the entire operation was completed in less than fifteen minutes. The English pilots and the resistance ground crew had been doing the maneuver for over two and one-half years and officially became experts. All crew members knew their responsibilities where the landing and offloading of passengers and supplies from the SOE had become routine.

Captain Hutchinson from the SOE had communicated with Juliette and the resistance that the three passengers were special. They were to direct the activities of the resistance in preparation for the Allied invasion of Europe. As such, Renard, the ranking member of the resistance, had journeyed from northern France to meet with the three English special agents. The three English agents were safely driven to the resistance camp in the Auvergne mountains. Once they were safe in the camp, the three English commandos and the resistance leaders met to discuss the details of the preparations.

Renard, *"Beinvenue en France."*

Felipe, *"Merci Beaucoup."* In perfect French, Felipe introduces himself and the other team members using their cover names, Kiros, Rodney, and Tommy. It is apparent to Renard that Kiros is French and Rodney and Tommy are English.

Renard, "Do you wish to speak in English?"

"No, that will not be necessary. As you can tell, I and Rodney and Tommy speak French."

"Très bon, Alors francais ce sera." (From this point forward, all discussions are in French.)

Felipe (aka Kiros) now provides the details of who they are and what they will be directing, "We are here to plan and direct a series of clandestine actions to be carried out by your resistance fighters to facilitate the conduct of military operations for the Allied invasion."

Renard, "I have over 1,000 fighters here in the Auvergne Forest, and others are well hidden throughout France. Since the Germans took control of France, we have had no problem finding resistance fighters. If the SOE provides the weapons, we will do our part."

"The Allied command plan is to parachute hundreds of commandos from the British Special Air Services (SAS). These commandos will be embedded into your resistance fighters. We will sabotage the bridges, ammunition dumps, and communication sites, small concentration of German troops, attack convoys, and any other activities to disturb the Germans as the invasion begins."

"Do we know when the date of the invasion will be?"

"No, it is still months from now. Our job is to identify the attack points and be ready when we are signaled to begin our operations."

Tommy, an expert in communications, says, "Communications between us and the SOE is a key point for our resistance activities. Messages to and from London will use the transmitters provided over the last two years. Also, the BBC will be broadcasting "personal messages"."

Renard interjects, "Allow me to introduce Juliette; she was one of the English SOE agents' forerunners. She is our expert in communications."

Juliette says, "When we receive the hidden messages from the SOE, we must tell the general public that the invasion has begun. When that happens, all Frenchmen will rise against the Germans."

Marcin, "We lack weapons to arm the thousands of resistance fighters. We need modern recoilless rifles, anti-tank bazookas, heavy machine guns, explosives, grenades, grenade launchers, flame throwers, mines, and training for the thousands of Frenchmen who will join us."

Kiros says, "After identifying our targets, we plan to have hundreds of special agents from the SAS who will work in small teams of three or four soldiers. All of the SAS agents speak French, German, or Spanish. The idea is to have a multi-lingual team who are experts in communications, demolition, and the long rifle. However, they specialize in killing. Their motto is "Surprise, Kill, Vanish". These agents are nicknamed "Jedburghs"."[46]

Kiros continues, "The plan is to have all actions behind enemy lines throughout France to slow the progress of German reinforcements. We will avoid systematically sabotaging the infrastructure to preserve what may be useful to the Allied Armies. For this purpose, precise instructions will be transmitted to us when the invasion begins. We need to provide information to the SOE on the condition of the beaches from Normandy to Calais, as well as information on troop strength, placement of guns, airfields, ammo dumps, panzer divisions, supply storages, oil tanks, railroad yards, factories, and anything else that will hinder their ability to make war.

---

[46] '1944, an Allied Team with the French Résistance." A memoir by OSS Jedburgh Robert R. Kehoe.

After a long day of briefings and discussions on how best to obtain the information to assist on the day of the invasion, Kiros (Felipe) asks Renard, *"Puis-je te voir en prive?"* (May I see you in private?)

"Oui, bien sur." (Yes of course)

Monsieur Renard, "During my discussions with Captain Hutchinson of the SOE, he informed me that he was shot down in the English Channel. A fisherman rescued him and was then assisted by a young lady and a Sister in a convent."

"Oui, bien sur, I was aware of Captain Hutchinson. After he recuperated in the convent, my Marquis aided in his escape via a submarine.

Kiros, "I think it is important that you know my real French name. However, this cannot go any further than the two of us. Do you agree?"

Renard thinks for a few minutes and says, "It is best that I do not know your real name. Why is it so important?"

"Allow me to explain, I was a lieutenant in the French Army in 1940 and was captured by the Germans. Three months ago, I was a prisoner in a German work detail. I escaped from Germany by crossing the Swiss Alps. When I was a prisoner in Germany, I received a package from my wife every month. I wrote to my wife, and due to the assistance of The Red Cross, she received my letters."

Renard is thinking----*why is he telling me this?* If he escaped from prison, then his wife would be very happy. Renard, after a few moments of silence, then says, "Your wife must be pleased. Does she live in England?"

"No, she knows I am no longer a prisoner. This is my dilemma. You see that young lady that helped Captain Hutchinson is my wife----Lizzette?"

Renard now understands the problem. He says, "So why is that a problem? You know that she is also a member of the Marquis."

"Renard, you know more than what you tell me. Is that so?"

Renard says nothing, and Felipe explains, "I had been a prisoner in Germany for three years before I heard from my wife. In the last year, my packages through the Red Cross arrived without the Germans holding them hostage and requiring anything from me. Since the packages started arriving with such a high frequency, it had to be that the Germans were allowing the packages to come through. In my last year in Germany, I thought she was now a collaborator and worked with the Germans. I was starting to doubt her faithfulness to me. However, when Captain Hutchinson told me that she had assisted in his escape, I became puzzled. Kiros asked Captain Hutchinson, "If he knew that Lizzette was a member of the Marquis?"

"What did Captain Hutchinson tell you?"

"He said it would be best if I waited until I was in France. As you know, Captain Hutchinson thinks very highly of you. He said that I should ask you, because you would know how best to answer the questions regarding my wife."

"Yes, I now see the problem. She has not received any letters from you, and Lizzette will think that the Germans have killed you."

Renard says, "Give me a few minutes to think through all the options and I will tell you which is best." It was as if time had slowed immensely for the next two minutes. Then, Renard says, "Let me give you the complete story."

"That would be best."

Renard begins to tell Felipe the story of the web that the Germans laid on Lizzette. He tells Felipe of *Oberst* Rauch and Buchner. "However, Lizzette is not only very beautiful but also very smart. She becomes a "Double Agent." I am sure you were getting favorable treatment in Germany because Lizzette is feeding *Oberst* Buchner information on the Marquis. However, all the information she is giving the German Gestapo has been coordinated with me. Last year, she told Buchner that our main camp was in the Mercantour Mountains. It wasn't, but we did move 500 resistance fighters to the mountain, where we defeated a much superior German Army."

Felipe is very thankful for the information and then says, "You must tell her that I am well and have joined the Marquis. The problem is that there is no telling what the Germans will tell her about my escape. To save face, I guess that she will be told that I was killed trying to escape and the Germans will now turn to our children for leverage."

Renard, "Yes, you are correct. But we need to go one more step. We need to get Lizzette and your family out of Paris. Being a double agent will only work for a short time; it is time to get her out of the claws of the Germans."

The Plan to Rescue Lizzette:

Felipe and Renard now meet to discuss the best way to rescue Lizzette from the German Gestapo claws. Felipe says, "Any rescue of Lizzette will also need to have my children and Lizzette's parents moved from our home."

"I agree," says Renard.

"Since the Gestapo believes that she is a German mole, would it be possible to have Lizzette and the family simply disappear as a result of a Marquis retaliation?"

"Hmmm...that is a good idea. We need to think like the Germans. What is Intel most important to them?

"How about some bogus landing site for the Allies? Perhaps a date of the landing?"

"No, the Germans would not likely believe her. The Allied High Command would keep that information private from the resistance. It needs to be more believable."

"We could have Lizzette report the bogus information regarding some activities that your resistance is planning," says Felipe.

"Yes, that may work. I can have Marcin plan a raid on a small factory producing casings for their machine guns when Lizzette informs Buchner of the pending attack. The Germans would likely have hundreds of SS troops ready to spring a surprise ambush. Marcin will send an advance scout team and discover that the Germans are waiting for our raid. We leave some evidence that a resistance scout team had discovered the pending ambush."

"Yes, that should work. Buchner will conclude that his mole, Lizzette, has been compromised. Buchner then goes through the normal procedures to meet with Lizzette. Lizzette does not confirm the request for the meeting. After that, he will have no choice but to send an undercover agent to my home. Of course, Lizzette, my children, and her parents will not be there."

Renard, "I can have Marcin and his men "apprehend" Lizzette and the children and move them to a safe location."

"Where would they be moved to?

"The convent is ideal. The children and Lizzette's parents can be hidden in the underground tunnels. It is where Captain Hutchinson and dozens of Allied fighters have been hidden throughout the war. I will need to meet with Lizzette and complete the details. After Lizzette, your children, and her parents are safe, you will meet with her at the convent. She shouldn't know that you have joined the Marquis. While she is still under some Germans' control, she shouldn't know of your whereabouts."

Renard meets with Lizzette:

As is normal, Renard meets with Lizzette on the second Sunday of the month. Lizzette has been attending church every Sunday since she was four years old. Should she not attend church, it would be seen as out of the ordinary. Nevertheless, she still does not trust Buchner. Since the time that Rauch had her movements monitored, she remained vigilant that Gestapo agents are not tailing her. After using her spy craft by doubling back and using the reflections from shop windows, she is satisfied that she is not being watched. After attending the regular church service, Lizzette enters the confession booth. Within ten seconds, Sister Patricia opens the booth's back door. Very quietly, they walk down a hallway together. A hidden and well-concealed hatch door is opened, and Lizzette walks down a set of stairs to the tunnels below the church and convent.

After several turns and the hidden doors opening, Lizzette comes to the meeting room with Renard. Renard begins, *"Bon a voir,* you look well."

"Merci Beaucoup."

"Lizzette, we have much to discuss. The war will soon be concluding. I do not doubt that we will be victorious. However, I am very concerned for your safety. You are in great danger as a double agent. We need to have you and your family escape from the Germans."

"Yes, I have also been concerned. With the Allies defeating the Nazis in Africa and moving up the Italian boot, the Nazis are becoming even more murderous. Every day, ordinary Frenchmen are being accused of being part of the Marquis and executed."

"Yes, I have a plan to rescue you."

Renard then tells her of the plan. She is to have one more meeting with Buchner. She tells him of a planned attack by the resistance at a small factory in Paris's fifth arrondissement.

Lizzette agrees with the plan and provides one additional item, "When you have Marcin and his resistance fighters come to my house, tell them to search the house thoroughly. Make it look like you are trying to find any additional materials that I may have on the plans of the resistance. Also, when Marcin's men apprehend me, have them treat me harshly. Several neighbors have never taken to me working for the French Civil authorities. This will add to the story of my family and I being uncovered by the resistance."

"*Oui,* I will tell Marcin to have him and his men act the part."

Lizzette meets with *Oberst* Buchner:

Buchner and Lizzette meet at their scheduled meeting at the Hotel De Ville. Lizzette is dressed in regular clothes that a twenty-something-year-old young woman would wear as an office clerk. Buchner is dressed in a suit with a trench coat and a fedora hat. As Buchner is taking his seat, Lizzette says, "You stick out like a sore thumb. Even my children would know that you are a member of the secret police."

Buchner is in no mood for banter. He says in the stern voice of a General addressing a private, "Madame Raymond, a need some actionable intelligence. Something I can use immediately to kill or apprehend members of the resistance. Ever since our enemies' defeated Rommel in the African desert and their landing in Italy, the resistance has been attacking bridges, railroads, and troop convoys. I need some intelligence to wipe out at least one cell."

"*Oberst* Buchner, I have some very good intelligence that you could use to ambush a pending attack on a factory in the fifth arrondissement."

"*Sehr gut, Wunderbar!* Do you know the date?

"Yes, one week from this coming Monday."

"Very good, I will see that your letters to your husband get to him immediately."

Oberst Buchner, "I have not heard from him in over three months. Is there something wrong?"

"No, it is all this bombing by the British and the Americans. No doubt, the mail has been interrupted. I am sure that all is good. Do not worry."

Lizzette leaves the hotel restaurant and ensures that the receptionist and the hotel workers have seen her with the German secret police.

Lizzette leaves a message under a park bench. The message is for Renard. One of Renard's men picks up the letter. The letter reads, "The camping trip is as agreed, *Bonne Chance*." (Good Luck)

The plan works to perfection; Buchner has assigned one hundred SS troops to wait in ten trucks two kilometers from the factory. Two of Marcin's fighters carefully crawl up to the ten transport trucks. The resistance transmits in the clear to one fighter next to the factory. The transmission says, "Abort! Abort! It is a trap." After a moment, the radio goes silent.

As expected, the Germans intercept the transmission and report to Buchner that the attack was well planned. But the resistance foiled the attack when the ten transport trucks were found. Buchner gives credit to Lizzette. Her Intel was good.

Buchner waits one week and breaks all agreed protocols by sending an undercover agent to Lizzette's home. The undercover agent reports that no one appears to be home. Buchner now sends a Gestapo team to investigate. The team reports that the house is in shambles. It is apparent that someone was in the house. They were searching for information. The team leader reports that a neighbor said that on Tuesday, a team of Frenchmen entered the house and that Madame Raymond, her children, and parents were pushed into a truck with a tarp cover.

The apprehension of Lizzette is of little concern to Buchner. He thinks *she was not that smart after all. The resistance would see that she and the family disappear--He has more things to worry about.*

Lizzette meets her Husband:

At 3 a.m., a team of shabbily dressed Frenchmen kicked open the Raymond house's back door. After spending around fifteen minutes in the house, Lizzette, her two children, and her parents were roughly escorted into a truck covered by a tarp. Lizzette had told Renard to have his men come between 3 and 4 a.m. Lizzette knew that Madame Baguette would hear the noise, and she would be viewing the "fake" arrest from her second-floor window. Madame Baguette was the ever-present nosy neighbor, the neighborhood gossip woman. She was known for always telling the neighbors Lizzette was a German collaborator. After all, she worked as a French civil servant.

Anyone who had a job in the government had to be at least a German sympathizer. She was sure that someone had turned her in.

After a four-hour-long bumpy ride, Lizzette assured her children and parents that everything would be all right. Finally, the truck arrived at the convent. The truck entered the courtyard of the convent where Sister Patricia was waiting. The Raymond family then was hurriedly taken two levels down into the cave complex. They were shown what was to be their home for the next four months. The children, Mom, Dad, and Lizzette, settled into the convent. Their rooms were deep underground, well hidden from any inspections by the Germans. The family was instructed to remain in the rooms which would act as their residence until the end of the war. Should sister Patricia deem that it was safe, they would be allowed to have one-half hour in the enclosed courtyard on any given day.

After breakfast, Sister Patricia told Lizzette that Renard and some of his men were scheduled to arrive within the next three or four days. They were traveling through the backwoods; thus, their schedule was dictated by German patrols. Lizzette was not concerned, as Renard had undoubtedly traveled through the backwoods hundreds of times in the last three years.

Lizzette asked Sister Patricia, "What is the latest from the Allies?"

"The Americans and British are advancing up the Italian peninsula. There is word that the Allies have amassed hundreds of thousands of soldiers on the British Isles. No doubt the Allies must have thousands of ships and aircraft ready to invade the continent."

"Do you still have the hidden radio?"

"Yes, perhaps after your family goes to bed, I can bring the radio out of hiding, and we can listen to the BBC."

Lizzette and Sister Patricia take a private stairwell to the attic that evening. Sister Patricia has an old Bakelite English short-wave radio powered by Sister Beatrice on a bicycle-pedaled generator. As Sister Beatrice pedals the bicycle to produce electrical power, the BBC French-language broadcast starts promptly at 10 p.m. and goes until midnight. The announcer first came on and gave fifteen minutes of the latest news. The broadcaster mentioned the war was going very well for the Allies. General Patton's Army was rapidly advancing up the Italian peninsula. The Russians were regaining the lost territory in Ukraine and had recently over-ran the Germans in Crimea. The most exciting part of the evening was the news that General Eisenhower was now the Supreme Allied Commander in England. The apparent reason was that the Allies were nearing the point of the attack on the Germans in north-central Europe.

Lizzette says, "The Germans respect General Eisenhower but are deathly afraid of Patton. Buchner and the Gestapo think of Patton as one of their own; he is ruthless, intelligent, and his men would all take a bullet for him."

"Do the Germans think he will lead the main spearhead into France?"

"Yes, I often heard the German officers talk about their fear and respect of Patton."

After the fifteen minutes of war news, the announcer goes through the encrypted messages for the resistance. The messages are "Elroy, your aunt Maple is due to have a baby on June 15," or "Mantilla will be on a steamship to York".

Sister Patricia says, "Perhaps hidden in these messages is a signal to Renard to prepare for the invasion. We will need to wait and see."

"I am glad that I was able to listen to the news from the BBC. When you listen to German propaganda, it is one victorious battle after another. They keep repeating that the German Third Reich will last 1,000 years. The German propaganda machine repeats their lie after lie. Even some of our own French people start believing these lies."

Lizzette asks, "Does Renard come by the convent often?"

"No, we keep his visits to the minimum. It has become very dangerous to travel long distances through German-controlled territory. He always travels through the countryside and avoids cities and large populations."

"So, his primary purpose is to have discussions with me?"

"Yes, he is likely interested in your thoughts on Buchner and the Paris Gestapo."

"Oui, Très bon."

Lizzette thinks for a few seconds and asks, "Are we still in contact with the American flyer I transported covertly to the convent in 1940?"

"Oui, I think you are talking about Captain Hutchinson. He did return to England after convalescing here at the convent for several weeks. Renard's men moved him down to the Bay of Biscayne, and he boarded a submarine.

According to Renard, he is now a Captain and has been assigned as the coordinator for all flights, providing weapons and materials to the resistance. Renard always has news from Captain Hutchinson when he arrives."

"That will be very good; all the news I have is from the German side. I hope to have long and detailed discussions with him. Having "worked" for the Gestapo, I know some critical fortifications."

Renard and Felipe:

Renard and Felipe have been living in the Auvergne Forest. Since Felipe arrived from London, all attention has been placed on possible targets once the Allied invasion begins. Felipe has been kept posted on the rescue of Lizzette, his two children, and Lizzette's parents. Initially, Felipe wanted to be part of the rescue team; however, it was deemed to be too risky. It was best that the rescue team come from Marcin's resistance fighters. After Felipe has been in France for several weeks, Renard tells Felipe that an encrypted radio message was received that Lizzette and the family are now safely at the convent.

Renard and Felipe now plan to travel to the convent in northern France. Renard displays a map on the conference table and shows Felipe the travel route, "Felipe, we will first head north along this canyon. There will not be any German patrols along these hills. It is not to assessable by vehicles. We will be safe along the route. Next, we travel east and then south. We should reach the convent in four or five days."

"Do we take any weapons?"

"*Oui,* we each will have a Sten gun, Luger, and knife."

"We will have provisions for four days. If need be, we do have some safe houses along the way. However, it is best to avoid visiting any of the safe houses. We never know who German collaborators are. Now that the Germans are offering bounties, French citizens have been turning in any Frenchman providing assistance to the Marquis."

On the evening of the fourth night, Renard and Felipe are on a hill overlooking the convent. Felipe, "Can I assume that Lizzette still does not know I am accompanying you?"

"*Oui,* there was no reason to let her know. It was best that we keep it a secret. Since we received word that your family was now safe in the convent, it was best not to respond to the radio transmission. So, we will first contact Sister Patricia when we are in the convent. She also does not know that you are with me. We can discuss your reunion with your family when we meet her. Remember that the fewer people that know that you escaped from Germany and know that you are with the resistance, the better."

"*Oui,* I see your point. But I am excited, nervous, and happy that I will soon be with my family again."

"How old were your two kids when you left for the war in northern France?"

"David was almost two, and Yvonne was five."

"So now they are six and nine."

"*Oui,* David will not know who I am, and Yvonne may remember me. I am sure that they have been through a lot. Thank God that they had Lizzette to give them strong support."

"*Oui,* you are lucky to have a wife like Lizzette; she is not only beautiful and intelligent but also has a strong moral compass," says Renard.

After additional discussions about Felipe, Lizzette, the children, and Lizzette's parents, Renard says, "Tonight we will enter the convent. I will scale the northwest corner of the building using the drain spout. From the roof, we will enter through the roof entrance to the attic. This has been our normal entrance for the past four years. Once I reach the roof, I will throw down a rope for you to climb up. Can you climb the rope?"

"That should not be a problem; we trained on the technique in the Army."

"*Très bon,* we start moving down to the northwest corner at 2 a.m."

As discussed, Renard and Felipe are dressed in black pants, shirts, knit caps, gloves, and black face paint. They slowly and carefully move down to the northwest corner of the convent. Renard uses the agreed signal with Sister Patricia; Renard makes the distinct sound of a Nightingale--- "chirp, chirp, chirp......peat, peat, peat." Renard waits for a minute and repeats the sound of the Nightingale. This time, Renard hears the return cooing of a dove. Renard again repeats the sound of the Nightingale, and immediately, the dove responds. Renard quickly scales the wall. Sister Patricia is waiting on the roof with a rope. Renard throws the rope down. Within twenty seconds, Felipe is on the roof. Without a word spoken, the three quickly go down a flight of stairs and enter a Spartan but comfortable living room.

Sister Patricia, "Renard, it is good to see you. I trust that you had no problems traveling from your camp location?"

"Oui, we encountered the usual German patrols but easily evaded them."

"I am sure you are tired and would like some rest before meeting with Lizzette?"

Renard looks at Felipe, then at Sister Patricia. "Sister Patricia, let me introduce my companion, Felipe Raymond."

Sister Patricia looks puzzled and pleasantly surprised before she can say a word. Felipe crosses the room and greets Sister Patricia with two kisses on her cheeks. Felipe says. *"Oui,* Sister, I am Lizzette's husband."

Sister Patricia, "Oh my God, it is you. Thank the Lord! He has answered my prayers." She reaches out to Felipe, "Is it you? You look as handsome as ever. Lizzette has always prayed for your return. I will go tell Lizzette that Renard has brought with him a most honored guest. I will not tell her who the honored guest is......I am sure she will have tears of happiness when she sees her Husband. I will go wake up, Lizzette. I will only tell her that Renard has some news that cannot wait-----she must see Renard now."

Sister Patricia hurriedly walks to the rooms where the Raymond family has set up residence. Sister Patricia softly knocks on the door; Lizzette comes to the door in her nightgown and sleepy eyes. Sister Patricia immediately tells Lizzette, "Do not worry, nothing is wrong. You must get dressed. Renard is here and has some important news that cannot wait until tomorrow."

Lizzette knows that in this war, some things cannot wait. She dresses quickly, comb her hair, and straightens her skirt and blouse. As she walks with Sister Patricia, she notices that Sister Patricia is walking faster than usual and thinks, *The Allies are attacking tomorrow! What else could be this important*?

Lizzette and Sister Patricia enter the room, they find only Renard. Renard says, "Lizzette, I have someone that I would like you to meet."

Felipe then comes out from behind a standup clothes closet. He is dressed in his French military uniform, that he wore when he left for the war in 1940. Lizzette could not believe her eyes. She starts crying with happiness, runs to Felipe, and throws herself into his arms. Lizzette's legs are turned at the knees and Felipe twirl's her in the air. They kiss like only the French know how to kiss. Lizzette continues to sob. Now, Sister Patricia is crying and both Renard and Felipe have teary eyes. After a few minutes of reuniting, Lizzette finally says, "I must go get our children. Yvonne remembers you and David is always asking when his Papa is coming home."

Felipe replies, "Perhaps it would be best if I go with you and I can also meet with your parents."

"Oui, let's do that." says Lizzette.

Lizzette and Felipe walk down the hallway to the Raymond rooms. Lizzette tells Felipe, "You wait here. I will go get Yvonne and David." Yvonne enters the room, rubbing her eyes----she looks at her Papa, runs to him, and jumps into his lap, "Papa! Papa!"

David, with a teddy bear in his left hand and who does not remember his Papa, reacts to his sister's emotions, runs to Felipe, and yells, "Papa! Papa!"

While Lizzette and Felipe visit with their children, Sister Patricia has arranged a separate bedroom for the Raymonds. The children are so excited they do not wish to leave their Papa's side. For the remainder of the night, Yvonne sleeps on her father's left side and David on his right. Both have their arms surrounding Felipe's waist.

Chapter Thirty-Eight
Preparations for the Invasion
Normandy, France

In May of 1944, the Allies had amassed over 2 million men, 5,000 planes, 1,000 boats, and weapons from small arm guns, artillery pieces, tanks, and additional weapons of war. Both the Allies and the Germans know that an invasion is pending. The only question is when and where. Before the Allies can begin the invasion, hard intelligence must be obtained. The Allies learned from the failed invasion of Dieppe that proper planning and execution were essential. The Dieppe raid was poorly planned, resulting in a disaster for the English and Canadian forces. The Allied High Command, headed now by General Dwight David Eisenhower, had carefully planned, prepared, and practiced all aspects of the invasion of Europe.

The French resistance is to play a minor but significant role in Operation Overlord. The role they had been assigned was to initially provide intelligence on the German forces before the beginning of the invasion; the resistance would provide detailed descriptions of the terrain and German gun emplacements and the placement and strength of the German troops from Cherbourg to Calais.

On the day of the invasion, the resistance was tasked to destroy bridges, cut down trees to stop or delay the movement of German reinforcements and use guerilla tactics to attack German troop concentrations. The Allied Command wanted the resistance to conduct operations throughout France to require the Germans to use troops and counter these resistance attacks. The use of German troops in France's interior would result in fewer troops being available to counter the Allied invasion. In May 1944, the resistance had over 10,000 fighters scattered throughout France.

The key to the success of the resistance attacks will be through coordination. Should the attacks occur simultaneously throughout France, the Germans would need to assign many troops against the resistance. The ability to communicate amongst the resistance cells will play a vital role. Over 100 HF transmitters have been supplied by the SOE. Renard and other resistance leaders have distributed the radios to the numerous resistance cells in France. Juliette remains with the main headquarters of the Renard group in the Auvergne Forest. Francisco and Andrés have been deployed along the Atlantic coast, near Cherbourg and Andrés near Calais. Additional resistance cells will provide information on the location of aerial targets once the invasion begins.

Felipe and Lizette are now assigned to the Renard group, where they and hundreds of resistance fighters will be listening to intercepted German radio and telephone communications and analyzing the intercepted unencrypted traffic.

Francisco has been assigned two French resistance fighters and three Jedburgh English SAS commandos. Their assignment is to report on a five-mile stretch of land along the Normandy coast. They are to covertly stay in place and provide intelligence to Captain Hutchinson at the SOE.

Once the invasion begins, they will disrupt the German lines of communications and destroy any bridges to prevent the re-enforcement of troops to the Normandy beaches. The Francisco group of six fighters set up camp roughly twenty kilometers from the coastline. They rotate two fighters every eight hours. The two-man teams will deploy covertly to hidden locations along the coast where they are expertly camouflaged. Their faces are painted black, and they are wearing knit caps; the gloves have the fingers cut off, and they will be using 20x1 binoculars. All members of the team are armed with Sten guns, Lugers, and sheathed knives. Weapons will only be used in life-or-death situations. All attempts will be made to remain undetected.

From the first day to the third day of the surveillance, Francisco, the resistance fighters, and the Jedburgh SAS commandos use their binoculars, and they report.

"Reporting from latitude X and longitude Y. Sandy beaches, ten yards with the tide in, 40 yards with the tide out. The beaches all have I-Beams, approximately six feet by one foot, welded in an X-cross and dug into the beach. Crosses are approximately six yards from each other. They are installed in a random pattern. These crosses are being used as tank or water landing barriers. At the beach's edge, there are approximately ten yards of barbed wire. Approximately ten to thirty yards from the edge of the beach are concrete pillboxes with machine gun placements. Pillboxes are placed at approximately one hundred yards. Allied soldiers who make it to the barbed wire will be sitting ducks for the machine guns. These machine gun placements will need to be eliminated before Allied troops can advance. Machine gun nests are occupied by a team of eight German SS troops. The meal trucks arrive every day to feed the troops in the bunker. The outhouse has been dug approximately thirty yards from the pillbox."

On the fifth day, as they are surveying the coastline, Sergeant Harris Mayberry from the Jedburghs recognizes the 352nd German infantry division's arrival. The 352nd division is seasoned by long months of fighting on the Russian front. Sergeant Mayberry, with deep concern, says, "This information must be transmitted to London. This will be valuable information on the strength of the Germans."

Francisco responds, "Yes. We will certainly include this information in our report."

Francisco and his surveillance team of six commandos move every three days to a section of the coast with different terrains. They come to the La Pointe du Hoc cliffs on the tenth day. Once more, Francisco and his six-man team survey the German fortifications. The report is as follows.

"Reporting from latitude X and longitude Y. The Cliffs at La Pointe du Hoc are approximately 100 feet in height. They overlook the English Channel on the northwestern coast of Normandy in the Calvados section of France. The German Wehrmacht has fortified the area with concrete casemates and gun pits. The fortifications have six captured French First World War vintage GPF 155mm K418 guns in open concrete gun pits. The battery is operated by the 2nd Battery of Wehrmacht Coastal Artillery 1260 2H KAA, to defend the attack from the Allied attacks. Included in defense of the cliffs are elements of the 352 Infantry Division."

The report continues, "There is construction activity which indicates that newer German guns are replacing the older 155mm guns. It appears that only two of the six guns are operational. The two functional guns overlook the beaches and will threaten any beach landings. Should all six guns be completed, the guns would result in heavy casualties to the Allied landing forces. Four of the gun casemates have what appear to be telephone poles as the construction continues. The fortifications include an H636 observation bunker and L409a mounts for thirty 20mm anti-aircraft guns. Two of the older 155 French guns also seem to be moving. The guns are being moved from Pointe du Hoc to a battery point near Maisy's town."

Andrés commands, "Two members of the resistance and three Jedburgh SAS commandos will survey the area surrounding the port of Calais." After the survey, the Andrés team reports:

"The German 15th Army is currently deployed in Calais. They are preparing to defend against the anticipated attack by the Allies. The Germans have built strong fortifications along the entire coastline from fifty kilometers below to 50 kilometers above Calais' port. The Germans expect the Allies to attack at this point. There are two elite Panzer tank divisions with the new Tiger tanks stationed at the port of Calais."

After surveying the port of Calais, Andrés receives a message that his team needs to survey the coastline near the village of Merville. Aerial photographs indicate that there are heavy guns, and the Allies must know if the guns are operational.

Andrés and his team report, "The Merville Battery comprises six 155 mm guns, several anti-aircraft flak guns, and six machine gun nests. The encampment is surrounded by coiled barbed wire and anti-tank concrete barriers."

The British consider the Merville Battery guns a prime obstacle to the Allied landing's success. A message is sent to the resistance to question French prostitutes who work the bars in the area. The French prostitute reports to the resistance that the Germans are not anticipating any attacks soon.

Note, True Story: LTC Terence Otway, Commander 9th Parachute Battalion 15th Parachute Division, had been assigned to take out the Merville Battery Guns. He is worried that his men would have loose lips and would spill the beans ahead of the June 6, 1944, invasion. Having been given this top-secret mission to attack the Merville Battery on D-Day, LTC Terence Otway had to ensure the mission would not be compromised. The Colonel arranged for the **Air Transport Auxiliary** (ATA) women to send thirty of the prettiest members, dressed in civilian clothes, into village pubs near where his soldiers were training. The women were asked to do all they could to discover the men's mission. None of LTC Otway's men gave anything away.[47]

Felipe's and Lizzette's Teams Intercept Phone Communications:

On instructions from London, Renard has hundreds of five and six men-teams to assist the English SAS commandos collecting valuable information for the pending invasion. The Germans, fearing that the Allies would intercept their R.F. radio communications, protected their communications by using landlines. These landlines have been strung across telephone poles and underground tunnels. Lizzette, having worked in the French Civil Offices, and Felipe, from living as a captive in Germany, had a good idea of where and how these communications systems were built. The Germans believe that installing the phone lines underground will prove to be bomb-proof. The underground cables were protected from bombing but were accessible to "wire-tapping."

Lizzette knows that the designs for these communications tunnels are kept in the Office of the French Telecommunications. The plan is to have Felipe use his fake I.D. and German uniforms (brought from London) and request (demand) the French authorities to review the plans. Lizzette knows all of the officials and the codewords for the request of the documents. Felipe and Lizette are now in the Signals Intercept Division of the Renard Resistance group. They and hundreds of resistance fighters who understand German will listen to intercepted German telephone communications. The intercepts are all in the clear and not encrypted. Felipe now uses the disguises prepared by MI6. He is now Hauptmann Wolfgang Werner from the Abwehr, the German Military Intelligence.

Lizzette says, "Disguising as an Abwehr officer is perfect. The Abwehr and the Gestapo hate each other."

"*Oui,* I also saw the animosity in Germany. The *Abwehr* comprises former German police officers and does not play with a heavy hand. They receive their direction from the military chain of command," says Felipe.

---

[47] The Imperial War Museum, BBC iWonder, BBC D-Day.

Renard reminds Felipe, "When you enter the office of Telecommuni-cations, your guard detail is from the Jedburgh SAS commandos. The only problem that you must guard against is that they do not kill any Frenchmen at the Telecommunications office."

Hauptmann Werner (aka Felipe) tells Renard, "They are professionals and will not use deadly force unless necessary. Killing officials at the Telecom-munications Center will only give us a setback. They know and understand the plan."

The next day, *Hauptmann* Werner and his German guards drive to Vichy, where there is a Telecommunications Office. They go to the Vichy Of-fice and do not encounter any problems. *Hauptmann's* papers are in order. When the guards recognize his Berlin German accent, they quickly snap to attention and give the *Heil* Hitler salute. Felipe plays his part to perfection. If he sees anything out of place, such as a helmet not on tightly or a belt buckle not centered, he orders the guard to correct his appearance, "You are a pro-fessional German soldier; be proud to be an Aryan who will soon rule the world!"

The guards always snap to attention and say, *"Jawohl mein Komman-dant!"* The command car with the open transport truck carrying six German guards stops in front of the French Telecommunications Office. *Hauptman* Werner enters the lobby of the Telecommunications Office and demands to see the Officer in charge.

The clerk hesitates, and Felipe tells him in French with a German ac-cent, "You have five minutes to fetch the supervisor, or I order my men to arrest you for not responding to an order given by a German Officer!"

"Oui, Capitaine."

In two minutes, the Telecommunications Office Chief Engineer says, *"Oui Capitaine,* how may I be of service?"

In broken French, Felipe says, "I would like to see the plans for the tunnels with the telecommunications lines."

"Capitaine, this I cannot do. By order of the Gestapo."

"*Monsieur,* I am sure you know the difficulties we have between the Gestapo and the Abwehr. I can assure you that the Gestapo will never know. However, if you do not cooperate with the Military Abwehr, you will be arrested and charged with obstruction of an investigation. Do I make myself clear?"

"Oui Capitaine, do I have your word that the Gestapo will never know?"

"Jawohl Monsieur, I am an Officer in the Abwehr. Unlike the Gestapo, you have my word."

With the understanding that the Gestapo will never know that the Abwehr inspected the communications tunnels' plans, Felipe and two members of his guard detail inspect the communications plans. They purposely do not remove any of the plans. *Hauptmann* Werner assured the French supervisor that this inspection never took place. Felipe and his guard detail leave and head back to the Auvergne Forest.

Monsieur Pierre Lafond thinks the German *Capitaine* visit was bizarre, but he should keep his mouth shut. He knows that all of his employees will do the same. If they do talk, it will be to members of the resistance.

Felipe and the SAS commandos are back at the Auvergne Forest. They enter the cave complex and quickly place their memories on paper. There are dozens of major arteries throughout France. The main areas to wiretap are Paris, Vichy, Lyon, and Marseilles. Felipe and Lizzette are assigned wiretapping and analyzing the intercepted data. They carefully select tunnel locations that are accessible by entering through the large drainage systems that have existed for years in most French cities. Teams of four SAS Jedburgh commandos and two French resistance fighters are assigned to each team.

The Signals Intercept (SIGINT) teams were all equipped with an advanced aluminum disc inserted into a recording machine developed by the Amusement Equipment Company Ltd of Wembley, England. The recording machines allowed the SIGINT teams to record all messages and be played back for analysis. These intercepted phone communications provide valuable information to the Allies. It was discovered that Germany had 50 divisions in France and the Low Countries, with another 18 stationed in Denmark and Norway. Fifteen divisions were in the process of formation in Germany, but there was no strategic reserve. The Calais region was defended by the 15th

Army under *Generaloberst* Hans von Salmuth and in Normandy by the 7th Army Commanded by *Generaloberst* Friedrich Dollmann. [48]

The resistance reported that the Wehrmacht was manned mainly with conscripted men from conquered countries. Morale was low; thus, it was believed that they would give up within the first hour of fighting. Through the intercepts, it was learned that the Germans had unreliable captured equipment and needed more motorized transports. Formations such as the 12th SS Panzer Division and the Hitlerjugend were boys as young as thirteen.

It was also reported that personnel and materiel transfers to the Eastern Front had significantly weakened the coastal military installations. During the Soviet Dnieper-Carpathian Offensive in April of 1944, the German High Command was forced to transfer the entire 2nd SS Panzer Divisions Corps from France, consisting of the 9th and 10th SS Panzer Divisions, as well as the 349th Division, 507th Heavy Panzer Battalion, and the 311th and 322nd Assault Gun Brigades. Due to the transfer of German forces stationed in France, the defense of the Normandy coast was deprived of 45,827 troops, 363 tanks, assault guns, and self-propelled anti-tank guns.[49]

Intercepted communication also indicated that transfers were being made to the Italian front: *GeneralOberst* von Rundstedt complained that many of his best units had been sent on a "fool's errand" to Italy, saying it was "madness that frightful boot of a country should have been evacuated ... we can defend the homeland by using the Alpine mountains with only a few divisions."[50]

---

[48] Reynolds, M: *Steel Inferno*, p. 163. Dell Publishing, 1997

[49] Ibid

[50] Ibid

Chapter Thirty-Nine
Allied Invasion
Normandy, France

From June 1 to June 3, 1944, the opening verse of Verlaine's poem *"Chanson d'auttomne"* and 160 other "personal messages" are broadcast by BBC. These coded messages mean that the resistance must be ready to carry out their sabotage actions. The Renard Resistance cell has been assigned to conduct sabotage operations throughout France.

The BBC broadcast of the Verlaine poem indicates that the start of D-Day operations will be within the next two weeks. On June 5, 1944, at 21:15, the following messages were broadcasted: "... wound my heart with a monotonous languor", meaning the resistance now had 48 hours to carry out their assigned sabotage. Later the same day, the BBC broadcasts in code,[51] "Begin the destruction of the French rail lines." The resistance now knows the invasion will occur in the next 48 hours.[52]

All of the French resistance groups had been coordinated using their HF radios, and various groups throughout the country increased their sabotage. The resistance proceeded to cut communications lines, which were installed on poles and underground. Trains, roads, water towers, and ammunition depots were destroyed, and German garrisons were attacked. In the three days before and during the Allies landing on Normandy Beach, the resistance successfully conducted over 1,000 acts of sabotage. Valuable to the Allies was information regarding German defensive positions on the beaches of Normandy. The knowledge of German deployments and their troops' strength was transmitted to the Allies using the SOE radios.

---

[51] *Bowden, Mark; Ambrose, Stephen E. (2002). Our Finest Day, D-Day June 6, 1944. Chronicle. p. 8. ISBN 978-0-8118-3050-8.*
[52] *Lightbody, Bradley (June 4, 2004). The Second War, Ambitions to Nemesis. Routledge. p. 214. ISBN 0-415-22405-5 Retrieved 20*

The Germans became highly agitated during the two months following the Allied invasion of Normandy. Before the invasion, the Germans treated the French with some standoffish respect. It was ordered by the German Wehrmacht not to steal items from the French. Germans who ate at restaurants on the Champs Elysée paid for their meals and were given preferential treatment. They behaved in somewhat of a civilized matter. After the arrival of the American, English, Canadian, and soldiers from over thirty countries, the German's attitude toward the French dramatically changed when Heinrich Müller, the Chief of the Gestapo, issued orders that all persons, French, or otherwise suspected of helping with the Allied invasion, were to be labeled as "traitors." Anyone who is accused of being a traitor was to be shot on the spot. This gruesome "new law" suddenly jeopardized ordinary French citizens. Minor offenses of painting the victory "V" or distributing the many leaflets dropped from Allied planes were met by the Germans summarily executing the perpetrators.

Examples of the actions that the Gestapo was taking are. (1) The Caen Executions: During the night of April 30 to May 1, 1944, the resistance in the Normandy area of France derailed a locomotive, causing rail chaos around Caen for days. The Germans are furious and in-

Civilians Arrested for Minor Infractions

tent on finding the perpetrators to make an example of them.

The secret police, Gestapo, assigned one of their local French agents Serge Fortier to investigate. Serge Fortier is a member of the *'la bande à Hervé'*, a sinister group of collaborators. Serge recruited a bitter team of cronies from the packed neighborhood of Vaucelles for whom justice is less important than money and occasional revenge. They enthusiastically compile a list of suspects of people they have known since childhood.

On May 15, 1944, using this information, the Gestapo launched an anti-communist hunt across Vaucelles. It will become notorious as the 'Vaucelles round-up'. They surround a railway worker's café just a few yards from the station and find many people named on their list. The arrests continue all day and into the night; Achilles Boutrois is arrested at his home; his brother Michel is also arrested.

During the night of June 5 and 6, the Allies began the bombardments of Caen. In Caen's full *'Maison d' Arrêt'*, prisoners prayed for a bomb to break down the walls and release them. They did not know that in St-Lô, the prison was hit, and 42 resistance prisoners were buried under the ruins. The Germans quickly became convinced that Caen could be surrounded by the evening of D-Day. A decision had to be made about the political prisoners' fate, the communists, and the resistance who had networks across the region and threatened German control. During the evening of June 5, 1944, the captives in the Gestapo Caen prisoners could hear bombs and small arms fire. They prayed and hoped that the Allies would soon rescue them. However, the Caen Gestapo had other plans. They had received orders from their headquarters that all prisoners were to be executed, and all evidence was destroyed.

On the morning of June 6, 1944, after 2 a.m., the Allied stopped their bombing. During the null, the prisoners were taken out to a small courtyard and shot. Russians, Rumanians, and other conscripts from the Eastern Front carried out the execution. After the executions, the bodies were loaded on trucks taken to an undisclosed location and buried. That evening, more than one hundred individuals were murdered; these individuals included young boys as young as fifteen, women, older men, and some members of the resistance.

A second (2) example of German atrocities occurred in the Vercors plateau in southern France. When the BBC's call to arms was issued, a newly reinforced Marquis group was destroying bridges, factories, railroads, and German garrisons, causing havoc in France's Lyons areas. General Karl Pflaum was ordered to suppress the rebels. Initial attempts by the Germans to defeat the southern rebels proved fruitless. General Pflaum organized an Army of over 10,000 troops to defeat a rebel Army of less than 4,000 resistance fighters. The resistance fought bravely, but they were simply outgunned and outmanned. The Marquis group was defeated with 840 casualties, comprising

639 fighters and 201 civilians.[53] The remaining members of the resistance escaped in the Alpine and heavily wooded areas of southern France and lived to fight another day.

Although the Germans' southern resistance group was defeated, an uprising such as the Vercors Group played an essential role in the successful invasion of the Allies. General Eisenhower, who was the Supreme Allied Commander, ordered that the resistance sabotage German facilities and troops throughout France. The "pinning down" of German forces in France's interior would only lessen the likelihood that the Germans could concentrate their troops at the point of the invasion.

The Renard Resistance Group:

The Renard Resistance Group had received Verlaine's poem, just like every other resistance group in France. The time for action had finally arrived, a day they had long hoped for and diligently prepared for. The group had meticulously planned, rehearsed, and readied themselves for their sabotage operations, and now, they were ready to set their plan in motion.

Leading the First Group was Marcin, charged with the critical mission of destroying the railroad lines connecting France's interior to the invasion area. Their target: heavily fortified railroad bridges guarded by German troops. Marcin would lead a team of fifty resilient resistance fighters, including Andrés, whose fluency in German made him a Spanish-sounding addition to the group. They were joined by twelve seasoned Jedburgh SAS soldiers, demolition experts. Armed with eight bazookas, each loaded with ten rounds, hand grenades, and Garand M1 rifles equipped with grenade launchers, they were well-prepared for their task. The SOE had airdropped essential equipment, including Brent and Sten machine guns, radios, binoculars, and compasses.

The Second Group, under the leadership of Luciano, consisted of knowledgeable resistance members from the Normandy coast. They possessed intimate knowledge of the local terrain, farms, villages, roads,

---

[53], Ashdown Paddy (2014). *The Cruel Victory*. London: William Collins. p. 277. ISBN 9780007520817.

mountain passes, and German troop movements. Their mission was to provide vital intelligence to the Allies, a dangerous job as they would likely encounter German patrols. To minimize suspicion, this group was predominantly comprised of older individuals, both men and women, as the Germans often underestimated them. A handful of Jedburgh forces were also included, ready to lend their experience and credibility when needed.

Gael Barrel led the Third Group, a fearless warrior with a history of successful raids against German patrols and garrisons. This formidable team consisted of Andrés, twenty Jedburgh warriors, and one hundred French resistance fighters. They were armed to the teeth with Bren machine guns, Lee-Enfield sniper rifles, and heavy 50-caliber machine guns. Equipped with the latest M7 grenade launchers attached to their M1 Garand rifles, they planned to employ guerrilla hit-and-run tactics. Major Ronald Montgomery had carefully selected the toughest and most dedicated among the resistance, starting with 200 and narrowing it down to the best 100 within a month. These fighters were not only physically fit but also driven by an intense hatred for the Germans, having witnessed horrific Gestapo atrocities and brutality.

The Fourth Group, under the leadership of Felipe, had the crucial task of disrupting communication lines. Allied High Command in London had ordered the resistance to sever all landlines, forcing the Germans to rely on radios. This strategic move would enable the Allies to intercept and decipher their messages using Enigma encryption. The Germans' strict adherence to the command structure and detailed orders became their vulnerability, as the Allies could now read their every move, from troop numbers and unit details to attack and retreat schedules and weapon specifics.

The Fifth Group, led by Lizzette and Juliette, remained stationed at the Auvergne Forest base camp. Their mission was to handle communications for all Renard's resistance fighters, maintaining contact with Captain Hutchinson at the SOE.

Lastly, the Sixth Group, commanded by Renard and Francisco, positioned themselves close to the front lines. Their role was to counter any German movements as the invasion began, particularly the transfer of troops and tanks from Calais to the Normandy coast. Armed with an array of weaponry, including Lee-Enfield sniper rifles, M1 Garands with M7 grenade launchers,

Bren machine guns, Sten guns, and essential equipment like radios, binoculars, compasses, and canned food, they were poised to take on any challenge that came their way.

The First Group Destroys Railroad Lines:

Marcin and his team had strategically positioned themselves outside Abbeville, a crucial location between Cherbourg and Calais. In preparation for the impending invasion, the Abbeville railroad junction was the focal point for all trains transporting war materials to the French coast. From their concealed position within a forest approximately thirty kilometers away from the Abbeville rail yards, Marcin had dispatched Andrés on a reconnaissance mission to assess the guard's presence at the station.

Andrés, disguised as a factory worker, confidently approached the guard stationed at the train station. He spoke in a German-Spanish accent, saying, "*Guten Abend der Feldwebel.*"

The sergeant regarded the Spanish-looking individual with disdain and responded, "*Wir erlauben ausländischen nicht die Züge.*" (We do not allow foreigners on the trains.)

Andrés inquired further, "*Warum nicht?*" (Why not?)

"We are on high alert. The railways are exclusively for the Wehrmacht," the sergeant explained.

"When do you think I might catch a train south toward Spain?" Andrés pressed.

"I am just a sergeant; you must speak with the railroad authorities. I don't control train access; I merely follow orders," the sergeant replied.

Andrés offered a polite "*Danke Schon*" and retreated, continuing along the station's rail fence. His observations revealed a heightened level of activity, with German officers from the Gestapo overseeing the operation. Trains were arriving, transporting troops, and concealed heavy equipment, some hinting at the presence of tanks and anti-aircraft guns.

As he walked, he encountered a member of the French police, who admonished him, "You there, get away from the train station."

"*Desole*, I am trying to buy a ticket to Spain," Andrés responded.

"*Idiota, nous sommes en guerre!*" (Idiot, we are at war), the policeman retorted.

Andrés wisely distanced himself from the train station, having gleaned enough information. He eventually went to the countryside, seeking refuge in the safety of the group's barn-based safe house. After mounting his horse, he rode for four hours and eventually reached Marcin's staging area.

Andrés began his report, "The main station in Abbeville is heavily guarded, with an outer perimeter featuring machine-gun nests. We can unlikely breach the outer and inner perimeters without incurring significant casualties."

In the presence of Major Montgomery, Marcin acknowledged Andrés' findings, saying, "*Tres Bien.* We shall proceed to our secondary target: the bridge between Abbeville and Amiens."

Major Montgomery sought additional information, asking, "What do we know about the bridge?"

Marcin offered details, "It's a bridge spanning a mountainous region, approximately one hundred and twenty meters long, supported by four foundation piles. The connection between these support piles comprises boxed girders. The French railway authority constructed it in the 1920s. Two men in our group worked on the bridge during its construction in 1928."

Pleased with the knowledge, Major Montgomery requested, "Excellent, could we speak with these two gentlemen?"

Marcin promptly arranged for Ramon and Filbert, both in their thirties, to join the conversation. They explained their background as construction workers specializing in bridge construction. They had worked on various projects, including the Amiens Bridge in 1928.

Major Montgomery outlined their mission: "As you are aware, we plan to sabotage the bridge to impede the German troops' movement from the interior to the English Channel beaches."

"*Oui,* we understand," they replied.

Major Montgomery inquired further, "What do you recommend? What are the bridge's vulnerabilities?"

The experts responded, "Sir, this bridge was one of the pioneers in using the archway design to span the gorge over fifty meters deep. The weak points are where the base of the archway anchor piles are embedded in the cliff's rock face. We've been fighting for our country since the German invasion in 1940. It is to our advantage when the anchor points are beneath the bridge platform. The bridge will collapse with sufficient explosives placed at the anchor points on either side. When it's time to place the explosives, Filbert and I would like to volunteer."

Major Montgomery agreed, "Yes, you and Filbert will be valuable team members. You can guide our mountain climbers to the base of the cliff, where they can scale it."

Following Andrés' return from Abbeville, the Montgomery assault team received the critical message on June 5, 1944: "The sun rises in the east." This was their signal to disrupt the rail lines leading to the English coast. Their assault on the Abbeville to Amiens Bridge would become one of the 1,000 acts of sabotage carried out by the resistance.

The team, consisting of Major Montgomery, Andrés, two SAS explosives experts, Ramon, Filbert, and two Alpine climbers, commenced their operation in a canyon approximately five miles from the bridge. Equipped with dark clothing, painted faces, and rubber-soled shoes, they were all seasoned night fighters, adhering to their motto, "The Night Belongs to Us." Stealthily, they moved along the cliff's edge to avoid detection. The bridge was guarded by two machine-gun nests on each side, along with two anti-aircraft Flak 38, 20 mm guns.

Upon reaching the bridge's base, Ramon signaled to Esteban, an Alpine climber, indicating the best route for climbing to the anchor piles' base. Their mission was to climb the cliff's surface and lower two ropes, each with knots tied every three feet, to allow the explosives experts to reach the bridge's anchor piles. Esteban, a Spanish Alpine climber from the Pyrenees, successfully reached the anchor piles' base. In contrast, Salvador, the second Alpine climber, used the ropes to transport ninety pounds of explosives and delayed fuses. Ian and James, the SAS explosive experts, also scaled the cliff using the ropes.

Once Esteban and Salvador descended, joining Major Montgomery, Ramon, and Filbert, they pulled out their M1 Garand rifles and readied the grenade launchers in case of need. Ian and James strategically placed nine-pound packs of plastic explosives at ten locations under the bridge, all connected by electrical wires. Detonators were inserted into each pack, with a one-hour delayed timing fuse set. The team had to distance themselves from the bridge bottom before the timer ran out.

As they descended, dislodged rocks began tumbling down the cliff, inadvertently causing a minor avalanche. The guards on the bridge detected the sound and sight of the two SAS explosive experts descending. Before they could react, Major Montgomery's team opened fire with their long-range M1 rifles, swiftly eliminating both guards.

Pandemonium ensued as the German forces, situated at a higher vantage point, returned fire. Realizing that their equipment, including Sten guns, grenades, and launchers, was useless in this situation, the team abandoned it, retaining only their M1 rifles. With a total of forty-five minutes elapsed since Ian lit the fuse, Major Montgomery observed two German soldiers descending toward the bridge anchors. He ordered the team to hold position and maintain surveillance of the bridge.

Without saying a word, eight M1 Grand rifles are loaded with a magazine with eight bullets per mag. The barrage of over sixty bullets kills the two German soldiers going down to the bridge anchor. The Montgomery team has prevented the disarming of the fuses, but they have paid a heavy price ---the Germans now know their position. Knowing that they have been compromised, the team of eight Allied saboteurs begin to run away from the bridge. Within twenty seconds, the German anti-aircraft gun, which has an extended range, starts firing its four guns, a barrage of four loud "Bangs" goes off. The canyon floor erupts, with the rocks being blasted to pieces. Within minutes, all eight of Major Montgomery's attack teams are blown to bits. Included in the group was Andrés.

As the dust settles and the Germans are about to shout in celebration, the ninety pounds of plastic explosions all detonate. Ten blasts occur within two seconds. The bridge's eastern edge disintegrates and pulls the entire bridge structure into the canyon. The German Sergeant in charge of defending the bridge will be strongly reprimanded for failure to defend the bridge. The Sergeant unshoulders his Luger, walks to the edge of the cliff, and shoots himself in the head. His body goes tumbling down the cliff and onto the burning bridge. Of the ten remaining German soldiers, eight are conscripts from the eastern front. They would soon wait for the Allies and surrender. They take their Mauser rifles and kill the two remaining SS soldiers. The dead SS soldiers are then thrown into the smoldering canyon.

Second Group Assists the Allies with Intel:

Luciano Laberge led the Second Group, a team of local members from the Normandy area. Luciano, a twenty-four-year-old farmer with roots in Normandy, had been assisting his father in selling farm products at open markets since he was eight. The Laberge family was well-known and used the telephone system to receive orders from locals. Luciano and his younger sister, Yvette, handled deliveries on Fridays and Saturdays. Initially, they used a horse-drawn wagon. However, when Luciano turned fourteen, the family acquired an old Fiat with a crank start, expanding their delivery range to thirty kilometers from their farm.

In 1940, when the Germans invaded France, Luciano, then nineteen, joined the French Army and became proficient in basic war tactics and marksmanship. Eventually, he was assigned to a sniper squad. Upon learning of the French surrender, Luciano decided to desert from the Army and join the resistance, specifically the Renard group. By 1944, he had become one of Renard's key lieutenants.

When the BBC broadcasted the "Call to Arms" on June 5, 1944, Luciano assisted the Allies in the Normandy coast invasion. All French members of his team hailed from Normandy, possessing an intimate knowledge of the region's geography, including farms, villages, roads, mountain passes, and German troop locations. On the morning of June 5, 1944, the Luciano group began gathering critical intelligence for the Allies.

Meanwhile, Yvette, now eighteen, served as a "runner" during the German occupation, delivering mail to farm communities using her old bicycle. Disguised as the mail carrier, she acted innocently and used simple German words, often incorrectly and with a stutter. The Germans called her the *"Dummkopf Fraulein,"* Her daily rides provided valuable information about German positions, weapons, and troops to the resistance from 1942 until June 1944.

The challenge now was getting this vital information to the Allies while navigating through dangerous German and Allied lines. On June 6, 1944, as the Allies initiated their invasion, the Luciano group prepared for surveillance activities in an underground cave complex concealed behind one of the barn's horse stalls. They would wait until the next day to share their intelligence with the Allies.

On the morning of June 7, 1944, their lookout in the barn's hayloft spotted a German patrol approaching the farmhouse. The patrol included a command car and troop-carrying truck. The Germans requisitioned the Vadney's farmhouse, prompting Monsieur Vadney and his wife to move to the barn. Luciano realized the Germans would use the farmhouse as a command post, as the Allies refrained from bombing civilian targets.

After the Vadney's move, Luciano, and Captain Walker from the Jedburghs devised a plan to attack and eliminate the invading Germans. They would strike at 3 a.m., targeting the guards outside, unlocking the door with Monsieur Vadney's key, and swiftly dispatching the sleeping, Germans. Yvette would shoot any attempting to flee.

At 2:30 a.m., the team was ready. Captain Walker and Sergeant Elliot silently neutralized the guards outside. Inside, the commandos used their Sten guns to eliminate all the Germans, resulting in twelve casualties, including Hauptmann Snyder and the two guards outside. The gunshots were discreet and went unnoticed amid the ongoing small-arms fire between the Allies and Germans.

To contact the Allies, Yvette, and Sergeant Elliott, the eldest of the Jedburghs, would cross the German lines, while Luciano, Captain Walker, and the three resistance fighters would remain behind to safeguard the farmhouse until the Allies arrived from the coast.

Yvette was intimately acquainted with the rural landscape of Normandy, and her reputation among the Germans was that of the hapless mail carrier. In case of a confrontation with German forces, the plan was for Sergeant Elliot to assume the identity of her cousin, Emilie Patel. Neither Yvette nor Sergeant Elliot carried any weapons; discovery of firearms would likely result in their capture or being shot on the spot.

In the early hours of June 7, 1944, Yvette and Elliot embarked on their journey towards the coast. Yvette led the way, skillfully utilizing hedgerows for concealment. Surprisingly, they encountered no resistance from the Germans. The most formidable challenge lay ahead ---- contacting the Allies without getting shot. Sergeant Elliot possessed a cricket clicker issued to all SAS commandos dropped into France, intended for signaling that they were Allies. The dilemma was whether the Allies would recognize the distinct chirping sound.

Yvette successfully guided Sergeant Elliot and herself to within fifty yards of the Allied front lines. There, Sergeant Elliot clicked the cricket twice, followed by three more clicks, signaling "SOS." A squad of US Rangers recognized the distinctive chirps and the SOS signal but remained cautious, suspecting a possible trap. After a few minutes of tense observation, Yvette and Sergeant Elliot crawled towards the Allied lines.

The U.S. Ranger sergeant, through binoculars, saw the two figures approaching their foxhole. He ordered his squad to keep their rifles ready but refrain from firing. After an additional couple of minutes, Yvette and Sergeant Elliot reached the Allied line. The Ranger sergeant checked them for weapons, finding none. Captain Eddie Johnson from the First Ranger Division questioned them, demanding identification, and an explanation of their passage through the German lines.

Now speaking with his distinct English accent, Sergeant Elliot identified himself as a Jedburgh and provided details about his SAS unit and command. Captain Johnson remained skeptical and asked how they had managed to navigate the German lines.

Yvette, who appeared much younger than her actual age, spoke with her French accent, "Sir, Capitaine, my name is Yvette. I am part of the resistance and was born and raised in Normandy. I know this region's trees, branches, valleys, and hidden passages. I guided Sergeant Elliot and myself through the German lines."

After deliberation among the Rangers and persuasive arguments from Sergeant Elliot, they decided to trust the "fifteen-year-old" French farm girl to lead them through the German lines. If Yvette could deliver on her claims, it would be a significant breakthrough in the Rangers' sector.

On the evening of June 7, 1944, Sergeant Elliot, Captain Johnson, and twenty Rangers followed Yvette through the French countryside. Her intimate knowledge of the terrain allowed them to navigate hidden paths, hedgerows, ravines, farmhouses, and tree lines for cover. At 2 a.m. on June 8, 1944, the Rangers reached the Vadney's farmhouse. Retaking the farmhouse provided critical intelligence on German positions in their sector. With this intel, the Rangers, assisted by fifteen English SAS commandos, launched a surprise attack on the Germans from the rear. This daring move created a small but significant breach in the German line, contributing to the Allies' successful establishment of a beachhead in Normandy, thanks to the heroic actions of individuals like Yvette, a forgotten hero of WW II.

Third Group, Attack German Forces:

Gael Barrel led the third group, a fearless warrior known for conducting successful raids on German patrols and garrisons. This group consisted of twenty Jedburgh warriors and one hundred French resistance fighters, making it the most heavily armed among all the groups. Their primary objective was to divert German forces away from the coast of France, preventing them from reinforcing the beach defenses. When the call to arms came, the resistance's extensive actions caught the Germans off guard, resulting in over 1,000 acts of sabotage from June 5 to June 10, 1944.

Gael and his counterpart, Jedburgh Captain Richards, meticulously studied maps and received intelligence reports from the field. They identified several German garrisons near the city of Arras, strategically positioned near the Belgian border. These troops could be swiftly deployed to Calais or Normandy. The resistance planned to attack these garrisons' using mortars and then withdraw. Anticipating the typical German response after a garrison attack, they aimed to lead the Germans into a trap. When the mortars struck the garrison, a small team would dash to a waiting truck and speed down the highway. As the Germans pursued with motorcycles and transport trucks, the primary group of resistance fighters would lie in ambush.

At 8 p.m. on June 5, 1944, the Gael team launched ten mortar rounds into a small garrison near the town of Arras. As expected, the Germans swiftly pursued the resistance fighters. Just three minutes beyond the garrison, the rebels felled a tree, blocking the road. The German pursuit team, comprising four motorcycles with sidecars and a transport truck, all came to a halt. They were like sitting ducks. A group of twenty resistance fighters emerged from the forest and, armed with American-supplied Thompson submachine guns, eliminated all the German soldiers. News of the entire pursuit team's demise reached the garrison commander, who promptly organized two hundred elite SS troops to hunt down and eliminate the saboteurs. This was precisely the outcome Gael and Captain Richards had aimed for. The small German force of two hundred elite SS troops pursued the rebels throughout the night, suffering thirty-two casualties from sniper fire. At 6 a.m., the pursuit team's

Captain received a radio message: "Return to the garrison. The Allies have initiated their invasion."

As the pursuit team returned to the garrison, they encountered fallen trees obstructing the road. Spotting the obstacles, the Germans quickly scattered and were ordered to continue on foot in pursuit of the rebels with orders to kill them all. However, they found no trace of the resistance fighters when they entered the forest. Approaching the garrison, the rebels unleashed mortar fire into it. The German Captain muttered to himself, realizing that this marked the beginning of the end. If they couldn't repel the sea invasion, they wouldn't stand a chance against the combined forces of the Americans, British, and Canadians. He also understood that the rebels would exact a heavy toll for the atrocities committed by the Gestapo and SS over the past four years.

Fourth Group Attack Communication Lines:

Felipe led the fourth group tasked with a specific mission: to destroy the landlines as ordered by General Eisenhower. Felipe's assumption was that the Allies intended for the Germans to rely on their radios for communication, making it easier for the Allies to pinpoint the location of German command posts through traffic analysis. Unbeknownst to Felipe, the Allies had already cracked the German encryption codes and were intercepting all radio traffic.

Felipe, along with Lizzette and Captain Palmer from the Jedburghs, meticulously examined the communication landlines in major cities such as Paris, Cherbourg, Calais, Amiens, Arras, Caen, Abbeville, and others in Northern France. Their primary targets were the coastal landlines and the main headquarters in Paris. Felipe and Captain Palmer organized one hundred teams, each consisting of four individuals, to cut telephone wires and destroy the significant tunnels housing the telephone lines. These tunnels were strategically located in Cherbourg, Caen, Calais, Amiens, and Paris. Three adjacent poles would be simultaneously detonated to eliminate the telephone poles and landlines.

The communication landlines within tunnels had been prepared three months before the invasion with skilled miners from southern France, known as the "rats." Their expertise in tunnel construction was invaluable. Felipe had assigned four-person teams to dig tunnels from the sewer system to the communication tunnels. These tunnels were wide enough for one person to dig and use a square basket to remove dirt or rocks. The rain would wash away the soil when the rains came. The rope used to pull the dirt basket served as a means for extracting the digger. On May 31, 1944, the tunnels in the major cities of northern France were completed. Notably, the tunnel leading to the Paris communications center was only thirty meters from the Gestapo headquarters at the Majestic Hotel, per Lizzette's request.

On June 6, 1944, the call to arms was received, prompting the rat teams to descend into the sewer tunnels of Cherbourg, Caen, Arras, Abbeville, Amiens, Calais, Vichy, and Paris. Working alongside Jedburgh demolition experts, they determined that ten pounds of plastic explosives would suffice for enclosed tunnels, except for Paris, which required twenty pounds in the hope of destroying the Gestapo headquarters. In the early hours of June 6, 1944, the rat miners extracted the Jedburgh demolition experts from their underground work. The fuses were timed to detonate at 6 a.m., coinciding with the invasion's commencement. Over the course of an hour, more than 100 explosions resonated throughout northern France. Three hundred telephone poles came crashing down, and eight explosions rocked the communication tunnels beneath France's northern cities.

Re-Action from the Germans:

On the morning of June 6, 1944, Oberst Buchner was jolted awake by a massive explosion. The sound and the shaking of his quarters led him to believe it was an Allied bomb, even though they had refrained from targeting the city center to protect French monuments. He quickly dressed, and his command car awaited him. He asked his driver, "*Was Zur Holle ist Passiert*?" (What the hell happened?).

"Sir, it appears that the sewer tunnel exploded."

"Damn, the French can't even clean up their shit."

"*Jawohl mein Kommandant, Heil Hitler!*" (Yes, Sir Commander)

"*Schnell Dummkopf.*" (Hurry up, stupid)

The driver remained silent, aware that the Colonel was in a foul mood. Approaching the Gestapo Headquarters, Buchner noticed the building was partially damaged but still standing. A firefighting brigade was on the scene, battling the blaze. Buchner proceeded to enter the building, but a firefighter blocked his path. Buchner pushed him aside and asserted his authority, "I am the Gestapo Chief, and I can damn well enter when I wish."

The firefighter stepped aside, saying nothing but thinking, "F***ing Ass Hole."

Inside the foyer, a wall collapsed on Buchner. Firefighters, along with two others, managed to rescue him from the rubble. Though conscious, Buchner was disoriented. His aide arrived and informed him, "Oberst Buchner, the Allies have initiated their invasion!"

Buchner's demeanor turned despondent, realizing that the end of German rule was imminent. If the Allies prevailed, he would face criminal charges and the gallows. If, by some miracle, the Germans repelled the invasion, he would be seen as a failure by the Gestapo in Berlin, likely leading to suicide or execution by piano wire. His best hope was to follow orders to return to Germany, reunite with his wife and son, and secretly escape to Argentina. Privately, several German Gestapo officers were hoarding gold, which they believed would secure their entry into Argentina.

The German High Command was unconcerned about the destruction of their landline communications, confident in their radio-based communication systems, heavily protected against sabotage and airstrikes. They had successfully repelled Allied attempts to destroy radio antennas along the coast from Cherbourg to Calais, shooting down over 100 Allied aircraft in the process. Since the destruction of the Freya site, no communications site has been compromised.

Unbeknownst to them, Bletchley Park outside London was decrypting all German communications. The sensitive nature of the German Enigma machine decryption meant that only a select few, including Winston Churchill, General Eisenhower, and a handful of generals, knew that the end product reports originated from Bletchley Park.

Fifth Group Provide Communications:

The Fifth Group, under the leadership of Lizzette and Juliette, remained stationed at the Auvergne Forest base camp. Their primary mission was to handle communications for all of Renard's Resistance fighters, ensuring constant contact with Captain Hutchinson at the SOE. The resistance had established a relay system to guarantee that the Allies received critical intelligence regarding the strength and whereabouts of the German forces along the French coast. This system aimed to maximize the likelihood that the Allies would receive up-to-date information on the German forces' locations.

The resistance needed to be made aware of the precise point where the Allied landing force would exert the most pressure. However, Resistance members knew that the Germans had deployed their elite SS troops, heavy Panzer Tiger tanks, and substantial artillery in the Port of Calais. As a result, Renard deployed a dedicated group of resistance fighters to monitor any movements of German personnel or equipment along the coastline. When Operation Overlord commenced, it quickly became evident that intense combat was taking place along the Normandy coastline.

Pierre, the leader of the Recon group, ordered Louis, his best surveillance operator, to infiltrate the Port of Calais and determine what activity, if any, was occurring. Louis successfully infiltrated the outer perimeter of the town and reported, "The Germans are in a high state of activity. They are fueling their truck and tanks. Hitching the artillery to the transport trucks. All troops are in a high state of alert and stationed in mustering stations."

"Are any of the transports moving?"

"No, they seem to be waiting for orders."

"Did you have an opportunity to lay eyes on the coastal artillery positions?

"No, getting close to these at positions is not possible. But I was able to talk to a French dock worker."

"And what did he tell you?"

"From what he has overheard, the Germans fully expect the main attack to occur at the Port of Calais."

"Hmmm, I did hear that General George Patton has two Corps of over 100,000 men and thousands of pieces of heavy equipment and thousands of transport boats near the cliffs of Dover."

"Makes sense; the Germans are waiting for the attack to occur at the Port of Calais."

Pierre now turns to Claude, his radio operator, "Send a message to our command post in the Auvergne Forest that no movement has been detected in the Port of Calais."

Lizzette and Juliette received the message and forwarded the information utilizing their higher wattage HF transmitters to Captain Hutchinson at the SOE. The SOE then communicated this vital information to the Allied Overlord Command Center, "Our assets in France indicate that the German Forces in the Port of Calais have no movement. They are in a high state of alert awaiting orders."

Sixth Group Provide Intel on German Positions:

Lastly, the Sixth Group, under the command of Renard and Francisco, positioned themselves within fifty miles from the coastline. Upon receiving a radio broadcast from the BBC, Renard, Francisco, and more than a hundred resistance and Jedburgh personnel swiftly took up positions closer to the French coastline. However, prior to positioning themselves at their final positions, they would wait for the completion of the expected bombardment by the Allies.

As anticipated, on the evening of June 5, Allied gunboats unleashed a barrage of heavy fire along the Normandy coastline. Following the naval bombardment, British and American bombers dropped thousands of bombs along the French coastline, signaling the commencement of the invasion. By the morning of June 6, a vast armada of Allied ships were positioned along the French coastline.

Once the bombardment subsided, Renard's fighters promptly positioned themselves on high ground overlooking the German entrenchments. Confirming that the Allies were launching their attack on the Normandy coast, Renard issued orders to cover the major roads leading from German supply centers to the coastline. The resistance teams quickly moved to their predetermined ambush locations. Renard and his team were prepared to engage the Germans on the second day of the operation. To their surprise, the Germans showed no signs of moving additional troops, tanks, artillery, or other military equipment. Unbeknownst to them, Hitler believed that the Normandy attack was a diversion, with the actual assault set to occur at the Port of Calais. The delay in deploying reserve troops and relocating forces from reserve depots and Calais would prove costly.

Renard now instructed his fighters in teams of six to ten personnel, "Advance to your predetermined positions and prepare to commence your guerilla warfare."

After several days of inactivity, the Germans finally began moving their troops to support the Normandy invasion. At this point, the Renard group sprang into action, initiating their missions to counter the German movements. Armed with an arsenal that included Lee-Enfield sniper rifles, M1 Garands with M7 grenade launchers, Bren machine guns, Sten guns, and the newly introduced American bazooka, along with radios, binoculars, compasses, and canned food, the resistance swiftly established their positions and launched guerrilla warfare against the Germans.

The teams knew what was required. They were to engage the advancing Germans and delay their arrival at the Normandy beaches. Francisco and his bazooka team waited with anticipation. They had positioned themselves on the main road between Paris and the coastline. On the third day, June 9, Francisco was positioned on a hill overlooking the road to Paris. Before he could see the enemy approaching, he first heard the rumble of the Tiger tanks. Then, he could feel the Earth shaking. Francisco lifted his binoculars and instructed Claude and Reuben, "Arm your bazooka and aim at the bend in the road."

"Claude answered, "Understood, ready to fire upon command."

Francisco waited until the lead tank was within the range of the bazooka. At two hundred yards, Francisco gave the command, "Fire."

The bazooka exploded with a loud bang, the armed projectile left the tube, and a swishing sound was heard. A well-defined contrail was seen from the bazooka tube to the approaching tank. The contrail ended at the base of the tank, and again, a much louder bang was heard.

Francisco immediately gave the command, "Quickly retreat behind the large boulders!" Within seconds after the lead tank was destroyed, the second and third tanks opened fire on the location of the bazooka team. Francisco, Claude, and the team of six fighters escaped harm by only seconds. Now, the team would be engaged in a continuous hit-and-run tactic. The relentless harassment by the resistance fighters against the advancing columns of German troops proved to be a decisive factor. These additional two or three days of delays gave the Allies the crucial time needed to establish their beachhead and begin the process of defeating Nazi Germany.

Chapter Forty
Victory in France
August 1944

The invasion, named Operation Overlord, continued from early June to the end of July 1944. The Allied forces were bogged down in a war of attrition with the Germans. The Allies had established a significant beachhead in Normandy. The invasion force had grown from the initial 150 thousand to over one million men and women. A total of over thirty nations now formed the Allied army. During the two months since the beginning of the invasion, the Allies had yet to have a major breakthrough in the German lines. On the night of July 27, the U.S. Army 30th Infantry Division suffered over one hundred casualties due to Allied high-altitude bombing of nearby German positions. Some of the bombs fell on some of the troops of the 30th Infantry; however, the bombing devastated the German Forces and busted the German defensive line wide open. After the bombing, more than 100,000 Allied combat troops poured south through a gap five miles wide. The Allied troops soon turned toward the German left flank and captured key bridges near Avranches, France, the gateway from Normandy to Brittany. At noon on August 1, 1944, the U.S. Third Army was committed to the fight under Lt. Gen. George S. Patton. The stalemate anxieties of mid-July would soon vanish as the pursuit of the beaten Germans turned into a rout.

On August 19, 1944, the Allies reached the outskirts of Paris. By August 25, the Allies had retaken the city. The citizens of Paris were ecstatic; spontaneous celebrations occurred throughout the city. On August 26, 1944, the Germans formally surrendered to the Free French Army headed by Charles de Gaulle. The German Wehrmacht laid down their arms. The war for the German Army in Paris was over. On August 25, Paris's citizens lined the sidewalks on the Champs Elysée and waved at the conquering Allied Army. The women of Paris threw kisses and

409

jumped on the Allied tanks and hugged the Allied soldiers. Charles de Gaulle and the Free French army led the victory parade.

On August 25, 1944, the Allies entered Paris, France.

However, members of the German Gestapo had other ideas. They knew that they had committed war crimes and would likely end up on the gallows. This was the case with both *Oberst* Buchner and Rauch. When the Allies broke through from Normandy to Brittany, the die was cast. Buchner rationalized that it would be best to destroy all files or carry the incriminating evidence back to Germany. He ordered that all files be burned or to be transported to Berlin. He also had his most trusted officers separately take stolen gold bars and store them in ammunition boxes. Each ammunition box contained gold bars worth millions in German Marks. All containers were loaded on a heavy-duty transport truck, where orders were written that the gold shipment would be delivered to the Gestapo Police Chief Heinrich Müller in Berlin.

There was, however, an exception: several ammunition boxes were loaded in the trunk of Buchner's command vehicle. On August 19, 1944, when the Allies were in the outskirts of Paris, Buchner and his driver left Paris in his Mercedes. Buchner ordered his driver to take the back roads. This would be safer since the Allies controlled the skies, and vehicles identified as German were subject to strafing by the Allied planes. After one day outside Paris, the vehicle had only covered seventy-five kilometers. When Allied planes were spotted, Buchner's command vehicle would seek refuge under trees and wait until the planes were no longer visible. It became apparent to Buchner that the chances of his vehicle being hit with Allied bullets or rockets was very high. He decided to find a French farm and steal a tractor with a farm trailer. On the evening of the second day, he found a farm and used the superior attitude of a German officer. He knocked on the door and demanded that the farmer provide him the keys to the tractor. The farmer, *Monsieur* Belmonte, was not going to give the keys to the German. He knew that once he surrendered the keys, his family would be shot. When Buchner approached the farmhouse in his command vehicle, Belmonte's son, Mathieu, who was a member of the resistance, exited the back door and followed Buchner into the house. As his father was retrieving the keys, Mathieu came up from behind Buchner's back, grabbed him by the neck, and inserted the barrel of an American Colt 45 into his ribs. After Mathieu had the Colt 45 in Buchner's ribs, *Monsieur* Belmonte came out with a shotgun; Buchner was pushed on a chair and securely tied. As Buchner was being bounded, Mathieu noticed that the German had a wooden leg. He knew immediately that his captive was *Oberst* Buchner, the head of the Paris Gestapo.

Mathieu told his father that the German was responsible for killing hundreds of Frenchmen and Allied pilots. *Monsieur* Belmonte said, "We need to tell the local resistance who we have as a captive. They will know what to do."

Monsieur Belmonte took the keys and his shotgun out to his tractor. Before he started the tractor, he walked over to the command car and told the driver to step out. The driver wore the uniform of an S.S. sergeant and had a Luger as a side arm. As the driver was stepping out of the vehicle, he was unbuckling the flap on the gun holster and began to draw his Luger. *Monsieur* Belmonte quickly raised his shotgun and unloaded both barrels into the sergeant's gut. The S.S. sergeant had been responsible for killing hundreds of Jewish farm workers in the area surrounding his farm. This was the least he could do to avenge their murders. After killing the driver, he removed a potential threat to his son and wife; Belmonte started the tractor and drove to the village. At the village, the members of the resistance resembled a beehive. The entire village population was a buzz with word that the Allies were only days from liberating Paris. Upon arriving at the village, Belmonte went to the home of a friend and asked where Henri, the local resistance leader, could be found. His friend told him that Henri could be found on the outskirts of the village at a farm owned by Pierre Lundy. As fast as the tractor could travel, Belmonte drove to the outskirts of town and found Henri. Belmonte explained to Henri that the Chief of the Paris Gestapo was being held as a prisoner at his farm.

Within two hours, the local leader of the resistance, Henri, was at the Belmonte farmhouse. Henri told Mathieu, "I have sent word to our command post in the Auvergne Forest that we have *Oberst* Buchner as a prisoner."

The following day, Renard and Felipe enter the farmhouse; Buchner is being held in the farmhouse's cellar. Renard tells Mathieu to remove Buchner's gag and says, "Herr Buchner, I am the leader of the resistance in northern France."

Buchner then demands that he be freed, "I am an Officer of the German Army, and I should be treated in accordance with the Geneva Convention."

Felipe shakes his head and says, "Herr Buchner, you are not an officer in the Wehrmacht, you are an officer in the Gestapo. Germany never signed the Geneva Convention. You are being accused of war crimes against the citizens of France."

"And just who the hell are you? Some French peasant who knows nothing of treaties or agreements between countries?"

"Allow me to introduce myself. I am Felipe Raymond, a Captain in the French Army. I believe that you know my wife, Lizzette?"

Buchner's eyes grow to the size of two saucers. He starts sweating, and beads of sweat start running down his cheeks. He says nothing.

Renard continues, "Tomorrow, I will have two resistance members whom you personally whipped with your iron chains. They will testify to the killings of hundreds of French citizens who were murdered based on your orders."

"Lies, lies, all lies! You have no proof that I ordered these deaths."

Felipe looks at Buchner with a stern face and says, "*Oberst* Buchner, our French Freedom fighters intercepted a German transport truck carrying over thirty boxes of Paris Gestapo documents.

Then, Felipe opens a box that contains the records of French prisoners that the Gestapo murdered. Felipe holds up a list of over fifty French citizens who were condemned to death. The order was signed by *Oberst* Buchner.

Renard, with a command voice, then says, "Tomorrow, you will be taken to my headquarters in the Auvergne Forest and given a trial."

Buchner still believes he is dealing with "*Untermenschen,*" (sub humans). He says, "You cannot give me a trial. I demand that I be turned over to the Americans or the English!"

Renard pays no attention to the rants and pleas by Buchner.

Within two days, the resistance members held a trial for Buchner.

Buchner is found guilty, and he has no remorse for the thousands of murders committed by the Gestapo; Buchner asks, "I wish to die with a soldier's honor by a firing squad."

Renard looks at Buchner with disgust and says, "You don't deserve to die honorably. You are not only a murderer but the scum of the earth."

The following day, on August 25, 1944, the day of the Paris liberation, Buchner is escorted into the Auvergne Forest. He has his hands tied behind his back. Belmonte drives up in his tractor, pulling a flatbed trailer. Buchner is escorted onto the trailer, and a hangman's noose is secured around his neck. The rope is thrown over a tree branch and secured to the trunk of a large oak tree. As Buchner stands on the trailer acting as the gallows, the crowd, which has grown to over one hundred resistance fighters, starts shouting, *"Longue vie à la France, Longue vie à la France."* Renard gives the order to drive the gallows platform from under Buchner's feet. The removal of the trailer platform acts as the trap door of the gallows; Buchner's body falls three feet, and his neck is snapped. After thirty minutes, the body is cut down from the tree branch and is buried in a non-descript grave. The war against the Germans is finally over for the victorious French resistance.

Epilogue

The war in Paris ended in the summer of 1944. However, the war elsewhere in France and other parts of Europe continued for six more months, until the spring of 1945. After the liberation of Paris, the French Army played a significant role in the drive to Berlin. The French Army assisted the U.S. Army with the liberation of Marseilles and Toulon. The resistance provided valuable information. The report was that the Germans were in disarray and suffered poor morale. The resulting battles resulted in victories that were completed in record time. The only problem that the Allies had is that victories were achieved so rapidly that the supply lines could not keep up with the invading force.

Moving north, the French First Army liberated Lyon on 2 September 1944 and moved into the southern Vosges Mountains capturing the Belfort Gap at the close of November 1944. Following the capture of the Belfort Gap, French operations in the area of Burnhaupt destroyed the German IV Luftwaffe Korps. In February 1945, with the assistance of the U.S. XXI Corps, the German First Army collapsed and cleared the west bank of the Rhine River in the area south of Strasbourg.

The End

Characters:
The resistance Fighters:

Colonel Antonio Vega: The story of Francisco (Chico) Vargas is based on the life of Antonio (Tony) Vega. Tony is a first cousin of the author. From the age of ten to twenty Tony lived with my grandmother and my mother on Glenwood Drive in El Paso, Texas. Tony went to Cooley Elementary and El Paso High School. In high school he was a star football and basketball player. He is listed in the El Paso High School Athletics Hall of Fame.

Tony enlisted in the U.S. Army in 1940 and was assigned to the Quartermasters Command in Ogden Utah. In 1941 he was transferred to England and assigned to the OSS. From 1942 to 1945 he was responsible for providing arms to the French resistance. His personnel records indicate that he was in France during the time period of 1943-1945. In 1943 he was promoted to Lieutenant and in 1945 he was promoted to Captain.

After WW-II, Tony always returned to visit with his grandmother and his aunt (my mother). In 1945, Tony returned to the U.S. and was assigned to Army Intelligence. In 1946, he married his high school sweetheart. While assigned to US Army Intelligence, Tony attended Japanese language schools. In the Korean War, Tony was in charge of providing minesweepers to the Japanese Navy. The Japanese supported the United Nations in the war against North Korea. Tony went on to serve in Korea, Germany, Vietnam, and Panama. Tony retired in 1978 as a full Colonel and lived his final years in El Paso, Texas. Tony died in 1987 and is buried at the Fort Bliss National cemetery.

Service Medals, Citations, and Awards: American Campaign Medal, America and Defensive Service Medal, WWII Victory Medal, European African-Middle Eastern Campaign Medal with Bronze Stars, Army of Occupation Germany, Army of Occupation Japan, Korean War Service Medal, United Nations Service Medal, National Defense Service Medal with OLC, Armed Forces Reserve Service Medal, Vietnam Service Medal with 3 Stars, Republic of Vietnam Campaign Medal, Joint Service Commendation Medal w 5 O/S Bars, Legion of Merit w/1 O. LC, Republic of Vietnam Cross of Gallantry w/Pals, Panama Canal Zone Medal.

Fictional Characters:

Juliette Santiago, returned to England in 1945. There she married an English soldier whom she had met while fighting in France.

Andrew (Andrés), Valencia, was killed in June 1944 while sabotaging a railroad bridge. His remains were never found. He was posthumously promoted to Captain.

Herman (Armand) and Karina Solemn Hutchinson returned to the United States. Hutch was promoted to Major, and Karina was promoted to Captain. Both resigned after seven years in the Canadian RAF. Hutch and Karina moved back to New Mexico. By 1948 they had two children, a boy, and a girl. Herman took over his father's ranch and grew pecans. They both continued flying. Their friendship with Mr. Goodwin grew even stronger. Hutch and Karina also took up rocketry as a hobby.

Sister Patricia continued with the convent and added a school for young boys and girls.

Felipe and Lizzette Raymond, Felipe resigned from the French Army as a Captain. He was recognized by France with the highest award given to him by Charles De Gaulle. Both Lizzette and Felipe opened a restaurant on the Champs Elysée. Lizzette was recognized by the members of the resistance and given the highest civilian decoration by the French Government as having significantly contributed to the defeat of the German occupying forces.

Renard and Marcin are two of thousands of resistance fighters who never were awarded the recognition they deserved. Both Winston Churchill and General Eisenhower stated that the resistance had likely shortened the war by six months. The shortened war saved thousands of lives, both civilian and Allied soldiers. Throughout France, there are thousands of memorials honoring their sacrifice.

All of the above represent the many that fought and died for the preservation of our democracy. All are the Forgotten Heroes of WW-II.